Also available from HarperCollins

*The Weekend Man*
*The Age of Longing*

# IN THE
# MIDDLE
## OF A
# LIFE

# In The
# Middle
## Of A
# Life

*a novel*

# RICHARD B. WRIGHT

A Phyllis Bruce Book

**HarperPerennial**

HarperCollins*PublishersLtd*

*The author would like to thank the Canada Council for*
*timely assistance during the writing of this book.*

IN THE MIDDLE OF A LIFE. Copyright © 1973 by Richard B. Wright.
All rights reserved. No part of this book may be used or reproduced in
any manner whatsoever without prior written permission except in the
case of brief quotations embodied in reviews. For information address
HarperCollins Publishers Ltd, Suite 2900, Hazelton Lanes, 55 Avenue
Road, Toronto, Canada M5R 3L2.

http://www.harpercollins.com/canada

First published in paperback by The Macmillan Company of
 Canada Limited: 1973
First HarperPerennial edition: 1997

---

Canadian Cataloguing in Publication Data

Wright, Richard B., 1937–
    In the middle of a life

1st HarperPerennial ed.
"A Phyllis Bruce book".
ISBN 0-00-648074-8

I. Title.

PS8595.R6I5  1997      C813'.54      C97-930252-8
PR9199.3.W74I5  1997

---

97 98 99 ❖ HC 10 9 8 7 6 5 4 3 2 1

Printed and bound in the United States

*To P ——*
*With love and gratitude*

*Praise to our faring hearts.*

Dylan Thomas

*ONE*

One morning in late March, a Friday, Freddy Landon awakened from a dream about his daughter. It was a weird dream in which he watched helplessly while his daughter and a young man named Ralph Chamberlain set fire to his apartment building. They were both naked as babes and they laughed wildly as he roasted in the flames. On awakening, Landon reached up to touch his throat. It felt bruised and raw. Had someone been choking him too? Then he remembered the drinks he had swallowed during the Late Show. He was just badly dehydrated.

Outside his bedroom window it was still mostly dark, with only a trace of daylight in the sky. Too early to see any weather there. Like many an idle man, Landon had become a watcher of the weather, as observant of the sky and winds as a schooner captain. Not easy to do any more either in a large Eastern city, where the sky is usually hazed over with arrant particles and the four winds bear fumes of sulphur and brimstone. Landon fingered his throat and summoned forth the dream, unreeling it before his mind's eye like a strip of film. His daughter and the young man and the building in flames; his own pajama bottoms ablaze as he flees to the street, hopping about and smoking like a cartoon villain. If he told her, it would probably amuse Ginny, even perhaps draw a thin smile from the young man who had sat in Landon's living room the day before cataloguing the crimes of Western civilization. Landon only half-listened to this dreary stuff. He was worried more about his seventeen-year-old daughter. She had called him from a pay telephone at the airport. This was bad enough, for she was supposed to be in school in New York 350 miles away. The sound of the great jets roared in Landon's ears like a wind tunnel. He had difficulty hearing and complained loudly, more worried than anything else. "Ginny? I can hardly hear you. What are you doing in town? Where's your mother?" He had come from the bath and was standing in his dark hallway, a towel wrapped around his sizable waist. He was dripping water on the floor. "Daddy, I've split," his daughter was saying. "I couldn't take that scene any longer." Landon's heart beat thickly. Split where? What scene? Something was wrong. Where the hell was her mother anyway? Ginny seemed terrifically excited. Was she stoned on something or other? The phone trembled in his hands. Still, she appeared to be in the midst of some adventure. Perfectly natural to be a little overwrought on such occasions. Another jet whistled in his ear. "I wasn't learning anything much anyway," Ginny shouted at him. "Anyhow . . . what good is a degree these days? Everybody has one. A couple of kids I know are selling theirs." Landon couldn't be sure he had heard properly. "What's that? What did you say, Ginny? I'm worried about you. What the hell's going on?"

"Daddy . . . We'd like to come to see you. I have a couple of friends with me."

"Friends?" asked Landon. "Boy friends?"

Ginny laughed. "Well, yes. One of them. His name is Ralph. He met me at the airport and brought along a friend of his. His name is Quarts . . ."

"Yes? Well?" Landon felt suddenly exasperated with everything under the sun. A tiny runnel of water inched its way along a crack in the floor. Landon watched it with mounting irritation. "Ralph . . . Quarts . . . Why didn't you call your own father? I could have met you."

"Daddy, I tried your office and then I remembered you don't work there any more. Have you found another job yet?"

"No . . . But I have some good prospects." He was annoyed with himself for lying like this. "What are you doing in Toronto anyway?" he asked. "It isn't spring vacation, is it?"

"Daddy, I'll explain everything later, okay? I just want to know if we can come over for a visit . . . The three of us, I mean."

"Well of course you can," said Landon. "Why couldn't you, for goodness' sakes? I want to see you. You should know that. What a question!" He paused. "You'll be staying here with me?"

"Well no, Daddy," she said. "Actually I'm staying at Aunt Blanche's." Landon rolled his eyes heavenward.

"Not there I hope, Ginny. That's not wise. What does your mother say?"

"Well, Mother thinks it's fine."

"I don't like it. You're welcome here, you know. I could put you up."

"I know, Daddy, but I've already phoned Aunt Blanche. She's expecting me later. But we'll be seeing you in an hour or so, okay? You're not mad or anything, are you?"

"Well no," said Landon, "but I'm puzzled, Ginny. Baffled, you know. You've caught me off balance here. I'd like to know what's going on."

"Fine, Daddy . . . You still in the same place?"

"Yes."

"Poor Daddy."

"Eh!"

"Bye now."

Landon stared down at his broad feet, lifting one of them slowly to discover the pale imprint of his toes on the boards. Mrs. Kuhl would scold him for that. She would go on about it. The hardwood floors in these old buildings, Mr. Landon. They'll shine like a jewel, but it takes much work . . . much work. And these new waxes they give you? They are not made for floors such as these, you understand. They leave a yellow scum. I have to scrub and scrub.

Well, we all have our problems, Mrs. Kuhl. He could say that to her, but he wouldn't. Besides, good cleaning ladies were hard to come by these days. And she charged what he could afford. What if she did nip now and then from his bottle of Old Troll? No one was perfect. You had to make allowances for people's weaknesses. Live and let live. That was his motto. Sometimes. But now his daughter worried him more than Mrs. Kuhl. She always had for that matter.

In the bathroom he carefully dried his armpits and stepped into clean underwear. Ginny was not a bad girl, but she had a nose for trouble. She appeared to have spent a good part of her life in narrow escapes from harm. Of course he recognized his own bungling nature there and perhaps he exaggerated, but he seriously doubted his daughter's ability to make it on her own.

In many ways she was intelligent enough, but a fatally abstracted air surrounded her. This bemused innocence! It reminded Landon of his own poor mother, whose pots had often boiled to overflowing while she read a novel or stared out the window at a strange bird. And Ginny had had some close calls. As a child she had often ignored warnings and accepted rides in strangers' cars. On holidays at her grandfather's in Bay City she wandered many times across the old wooden trestle at the edge of town, meeting the fast freight halfway over and running for her very life. In the playground she clung with one hand to the uppermost pipe of the monkey bars, absently eating an apple and ignoring the twelve-foot drop to the concrete. Once she came close to poisoning an entire cooking class, serving up some lobster concoction which she had left unrefrigerated overnight. Such people needed protection and characteristically they often insisted on playing it alone. In September Ginny had enrolled at Columbia. She wanted to study the anthropology of primitive peoples and share a walk-up apartment with a girl friend. There was a terrible row over that, but thank God her mother had not knuckled under. Vera was tough about such things and Landon was grateful. After a brief argument *he* would have surrendered. But Manhattan was really no place for this Candide of his! Sooner or later she was going to get it. Last Christmas she had shown him around the big town, gripping him by the elbow and rushing him into taxis like a guide in some Arab city. She took him to strange new haunts in the Village; queer little unlighted places below street level and timbered lofts where the air lay fat and rank with incense. To cover up the smell of burning cannabis, Ginny told him. She knew people in these places and introduced her father to them. Landon tried to catch the names above the freakish Oriental jazz. The faces, some pale, some black, stared back at him and his business suit with sullen mockery in the eyes. He was a curiosity to them, a visitor from another planet. To please his daughter he smoked a little grass, but it only produced a fit of coughing and left him feeling vaguely dizzy. Like my first cigarette, he thought. Smoked in my father's garage the year Hitler shook hands with Signor Mussolini. Yes—Ginny seemed worldly and knowledgeable, but for all of that Landon was bothered by her casual acceptance of the city's seediness and hostility. The dark seething animus of the place seemed to have no effect on her. However, she did not have to live among the resentful majority. Her mother's money took care of that. In his daughter's handbag were credit cards for Carte Blanche, Diners' Club, and American Express. And she could always flee trouble in a taxi.

Landon dusted his toes with Desinex, frowning at the splayed water-wrinkled flesh of his feet. He put on slacks and an old but clean white shirt, open at the throat with the French cuffs folded back over his forearms. His leftover wardrobe! Many of the items were now museum pieces. With slippers on his fragrant feet, he walked to the kitchen and poured some Old Troll into a tumbler, adding a little tapwater. From the old pipes the odor of chlorine rose to his nostrils. He doubted the wisdom of drinking this early in the day, and the doubt cast a shadow over his mind. This drinking! It could get out of hand, and lately he had been tippling more at the bottle. But at least he had no appointments today. Earlier, Butcher had phoned about a job selling real estate, and an appointment had been made for the next day at ten o'clock. He was to see someone called Ozzie K. Smith at Hearthstone Realty on Eglinton

Avenue. He had seen their advertisements in the newspapers and they sounded a bit shady to him. But anyway, it was a prospect. He frankly couldn't afford to be particular any more. Standing by the living-room window, he looked down to the street and sipped his watered whiskey. He didn't like the idea of his daughter staying with his former sister-in-law, but perhaps he was being unkind to Blanche. There was a side to that lunatic woman that deeply affected him, released feelings which arose from some need to set things right for her. However, he had his doubts that this could be done.

During the old dinner parties in the Tudor-style house on Russell Hill Road, Blanche had performed with a kind of eccentric gaiety that was never far from madness. Or so thought Landon. In the early hours of those evenings you always had to contend with this disarming brainlessness, this excited cordiality which never quite concealed hysteria. Blanche freely laid hands on you, offered pistachio nuts and Virginia Ovals, replenished your Scotch with tonic water, and tucked you beneath the chin. Everyone was a perfect darling. All the time, of course, she was taking in enough Beefeater to sink the stoutest-legged sailor. Weirdly tricked out, her weak eyes fitted with enormous false lashes, her cheeks rouged and powdered like some bordello keeper in old New Orleans, the saffron hair piled high atop a small bony head, she flitted from guest to guest, spilling wine on laps and leaving cigarettes smoldering behind the cushions of sofas and chairs. She might appear in robes of brilliant, flowing scarlet, looking like some wacky California cultist, or in a little-girl middy blouse with microskirt and net stockings. All of which only exposed her poor chest and stork-like legs. A pathetic sight! A cracked Auntie Mame!

The specious elegance of those affairs, and of course you never knew what to expect. The only certainty was a scene toward midnight as Blanche grew more watchful of her husband, hovering near the edge of his conversations with lady guests. Until a certain hour when the pressure blew the lid off things and she was seized by rage. Accusing, pointing with long silvered fingernails, the sour saliva spraying everyone in sight, she would hurl forth evil obscenities at every woman in the room, including her own sister. With this madness upon her, she would rend her garments and tear loose her lacquered bouffant until the sad orange hair fell around her shoulders. She looked like a witch of the moors. At such times Landon could only fetch a groan for poor suffering humanity and look at his wife, who usually closed her eyes and appeared to be praying. For what? A bolt from the gods as likely as not, guessed Landon. Something as clean and final as a laser beam. To extinguish Blanche on the spot without a trace. This didn't happen. Order resides within these walls. Who bid no trump? It was painful to recall, but what could you do; the trouble being that Blanche was dangerous. She had taken the Mexican silver carving knife to her third husband, Harvey Hubbard, and tried to remove his member. Landon thought he had read about this sort of thing happening in the Orient, where jealous geisha girls occasionally took a blade to the loins of unfaithful lovers, pickling the severed parts in sake jars. Were such things possible? Well, anything could happen, and Harvey Hubbard was still around to offer evidence on the kinkiness of human behavior.

He and Landon had sat in a booth at the New Cinema Restaurant, surrounded by giant posters of film stars. Harvey drank a glass of buttermilk while he talked about the dread event. A strongly tanned, handsome man with a large bald head, he was a Spadina Avenue Jew, the son of an immigrant rag-picker, or so he claimed. He had changed his name, adopted the ways of the new world, and was now a prosperous stockbroker. He kept in shape with trips to one of Vic Tanny's Health Spas, and his good color came from winter holidays in Bermuda and Westinghouse sunlamps in the fall. A fast talker, a hustler, but essentially kindhearted, he was always giving Landon market tips. However, Landon could never summon forth that particular energy necessary to wheel and deal at the Exchange. Harvey had sat in the booth, pressing fingers to his high firm stomach and frowning as he talked about Blanche's assault. The incident had left him with a stomach ailment, a lesion in his duodenal wall. Now and then he rummaged in a leather briefcase for Gelusil tablets and yeast biscuits. His large brown hands were marvelously expressive, and he used them frequently to tell a tale, especially one as horrifyingly medieval as this. Landon's own testicles tightened and shrank with the telling. Harvey was still full of swaggering street-corner slang from the forties, and he leaned forward in the booth. "Jesus, Freddy. That nutty dame! I'm sleeping in my own bed. All right, I sleep in the nude, a lifetime habit. Besides, it's healthy, the pores get a chance to breathe. And okay, I'm a healthy human male. Not young, but at forty-seven above the national average in condition. You can ask my doctor. He'll testify. I take good care of myself with the workouts and everything. Well, I don't know what I'm dreaming or if I'm dreaming at all, for Christ's sake, but it's up. I can't help it if it's up in my own bed. Maybe I'm dreaming of a hundred beautiful babes giving me the business. Maybe Raquel Welch is creaming for me. Who knows?—

I don't. But it's standing up! There it is, as big as your fist and not to brag. In the steam room at Tanny's I see others. So in she comes, loaded of course and completely out of it. She throws back the covers and sees my thing standing there. And what does she do? Listen, while I tell you what she does. She grabs hold of it. Like this, you see . . ." Harvey squeezed a large tanned fist before Landon's nose. "I wake up and she's got hold of it with one hand. And in the other? What do you think, for God's sake? The fucking carving knife . . . what I carve the weekend roast with. So I grab her wrist . . ."

He held up a hand to measure off a perilous inch with thumb and forefinger. "That close, Freddy, believe me . . ."

"Harvey, don't . . ."

"I'm here to tell you. And what a wrestling match that broad gave me. She may be skinny but she's no weakling."

He was now rotating a forefinger near his right ear. "It'll take a fucking army of doctors to iron that dame out."

Landon had waved to the waitress, ordering another drink. "Are you sure you can't join me, Harvey?"

"No . . . yes . . . no . . . I'd better not," Harvey said, staring glumly at a twelve-foot picture of Sophia Loren, who was standing by a roadside, looking down at him with her skirts hiked up nicely around her crotch.

Yes—Blanche was loony all right. It was true, though, that she had had a rough time of it. Not a tragic case, but an unlucky woman all the same. As she had never wearied of telling Landon during those fall afternoons when he had listened to her troubles. "You see, Freddy dear boy," Blanche had said, sitting straight-backed beside him and spreading fingers across his knee, "after the accident, the damned old money was divided equally enough, but my dear sister, your dear wife, everyone's dear Vera, was also left the looks and the brains. Desperately unfair, don't you think?"

Landon remembered those September Saturdays of twelve years ago. Both he and Blanche were in the thick of marital trouble, both being sued for divorce. Had he visited the woman to comfort or be comforted? Hard to say, but Blanche did all the talking. She was then married to her second husband, Hughes Ritchie. But she was spending her evenings in the arms of Harvey Hubbard, my handsome virile Jewish friend, as she called him in those pre-carving–knife days. Hughes Ritchie was an Upper Canada College old boy and Trinity grad. He ran a family insurance business. Landon liked him well enough, though after a while he wore you down with his bluff English huntsman's manner. As far as Landon could tell, Hughes had been in England only for a few weeks during the Second World War. But he fell in love with the place and returned to Canada, calling everyone an old boy or a good chap. He appeared before you as the veriest fox-hunting squire in merrie olde England. He never entered a room without rubbing his palms together and seeking out a fireplace, even a cold empty one; there to stand with his backside against this dark hole in the wall and ask about drinks. "Look here, old boy, what say to a little Scotch and soda?" A small cheerful soul with strawberry cheeks and a flaring regimental mustache which he regularly waxed. Hughes spent a great deal of time at his club, reading *Punch* and *Country Life*. Blanche complained that he neglected her sexually.

On those afternoons Hughes was always away. He was watching a cricket match at Upper Canada College or riding a horse on a friend's farm north of the city. Vera was away too, working at the advertising agency or visiting her lawyer. Landon and Blanche would sit side by side on the damask sofa in the long rose-colored living room. Outside the leaded windows, the great oaks and maples dropped their bounty to the earth. If you could ignore your personal troubles, it was pleasant enough. An iced pewter jug of vodka and Rose's lime juice stood on the handsome sideboard. Half-dreaming and snug as a priest in his confessional, Landon would watch the leaf shadows play across the walls, elusive light invading the room as the sun traveled across the heavens. Blanche's hoarse gin-soaked voice droned through those lazy hours. Sometimes Landon was smitten by a vague lust: the rapturous slumbering afternoon, the deserted house, the forbidden fruits, they all advanced lewd thoughts. As a boy he had felt these same pangs, these empty-house blues. In those days they were always a prelude to naughty deeds behind the bathroom door. And in the big Tudor-style house on Russell Hill Road, he had more than once considered giving Blanche a bang. As they used to say when he was growing up. He guessed that she was waiting to be asked. She would see it as a fine little joke on Vera. But in the middle of some gloomy chapter in her life history she would cross a meagre leg and Landon would find himself staring at her kneecap; a whitened knobby bone that looked for all the world like the bleached skull of some small forsaken desert animal. Ultimately you had always to reckon with the truth. And the truth was that Blanche was an unattractive woman. What had Hughes seen in her? What did Harvey see in her? The money, Landon supposed. Further investment capital or a hedge against poor times; a rag-picker's poke safely socked away in convertible bonds and blue-chip stuff. Anyway, Harvey got plenty. He was immensely attractive to women, a busy fornicator.

On a few of those afternoons Blanche's son Howard would appear with one of his boy friends. Howard was the unhappy leavings from Blanche's first union with a naval officer during the war. At the time of Landon's visits he was just sixteen, a spoiled effeminate youth who behaved extravagantly. He and his friend would carry on like schoolgirls, giggling shyly as they helped themselves to the pewter jug, disappearing into rooms with shrieks of delighted laughter. Landon always imagined they were goosing one another in some mad gavotte. Blanche thought Howard was a genius with artistic leanings. Landon saw his future in hairdressing and was proved not too far wrong, for most of Howard's friends were now in the business. He spent most of his time with them in their salons and apartments. Like his mother, Howard was an alcoholic and subject also to fits of hysterical rage which left him limp and weeping in some private hospital. Blanche's chronicle of woe! He should have sent her a bill for those sessions. God knows, she paid enough to psychiatrists! If Vera and Ginny felt Blanche was better, Landon was still not convinced. He had not seen her since one snowy day last January. Moving slowly along Bloor Street on his way to another appointment at Power Personnel. For some reason (to postpone talking with vile Ted Butcher?) he had stopped to look through the window of a boutique. To his astonishment, not ten feet from his eyes, was Blanche. She was trying on a fright wig, violet in color. She was stooping before a large oval mirror and fluffing at this wig with her fingers. Howard was there too. In an advisory role, it seemed. He was bending and swooping around his mother like a morris dancer, cocking his head to one side and standing amazed to tap a fore-finger against his jaw. He was vamping it, and the salesgirl was smiling behind her hand. Blanche and Howard were in fits. Risible hysteria! Landon had flipped up the collar of his Burberry coat and hurried on, not wishing to be seen. Now Vera proposed that Ginny dwell under the same roof with those two!

He postponed getting another drink and stood instead by the window. When they finally arrived, he stepped away from the window, keeping well back against the wall, like a sniper, with only two fingers parting the lace curtains. Ginny opened the door of the cab and stepped out in a coffee-colored maxi. There was a tiny green tam on her head, and her tablet glasses glinted in the weak sunlight. Snow had fallen during the day, and the traffic hissed past her on the wet street. She glanced upward without seeing him and bolted for the lobby. She was followed from the taxi by a pale slight mustached youth dressed in Levi's and bush jacket. His dark shoulder-length hair was knotted behind in a ponytail, and a burnt-orange headband circled his temples. Another young man, tall and bony and bearded like a Mormon, got out of the cab. Together they worked Ginny's suitcases from the trunk. The tall fellow was outfitted like a rodeo rider in his flaring striped pants and sheep-lined cowpuncher jacket. Well, this March weather was raw and damp right enough, but still—wasn't there something downright goofy about the costumes of these two birds? The big fellow lacked eye patches and a Stetson but could he not pass for the Lone Ranger? And was the little fellow with his burnt-orange headband reining up as the Tonto of the new times? Difficult to say, but Landon had noticed during his solitary afternoon walks around the town that the young had taken to the dress of the poor and the disaffected. He lived near the university and he watched the students walking to their classes in javexed dungarees with stitched-on patches over the knees and arse, army-surplus canteens and knapsacks slung across their shoulders; the boys with denim brakemen's caps such as his father had worn, and the girls in Mexican ponchos of coarse wool. Sandals on their feet, and their long hair tressed out with ribbons like peasant maids in Maytime. Quaintly enough, some even rolled their own smokes like Depression farmhands.

He stood listening as the cables worked their way through the pulleys of the old iron-cage elevator. The groan and grate of these steel sinews came through his door. He waited, heard the jolting stop and the footsteps in the hall. When he opened the door, Ginny was in his arms, flung there like a missile. He pressed his mouth to her hair. She reared back on her heels and regarded him with eyes astonished and vivid, glowing green lamps. Fired by chemical fuels? wondered Landon. Oh, for the simple days when you could smell mischief on a person's breath! Ginny held him at arm's length and appraised him like an old aunt.

"Daddy! You've put on weight!"

"A little, I'm afraid, yes!"

She shook her head and laughed and turned away, casting about the room with her lively eyes.

"Look at me! Talking about weight!" She dropped the thick blanket coat onto a chair. She *was* a big girl and would have a weight problem one day soon. Already her ass was too big, poor child. Unluckily she's built like me, thought Landon. Heavy in the shoulders and with a ridge of dorsal fat lying behind the rib cage. Fine large breasts but without shape or definition. Beneath the knitted sweater she wore no brassiere; a cosmetic error. She would have to be careful about eats someday. That body was a caloric storehouse. Bad enough for him but worse news for a woman. However, she had an attractive open face. If she watched it, she could emerge a handsome woman at thirty or so. Right now, with her long blond hair twisted into braids and the Ben Franklin glasses, she looked like a student from Amsterdam.

"When are you going to move out of this dreary old place, anyway?" she asked.

"Dreary?" Landon smiled. "I don't find it dreary at all. It's home to me. But they're tearing things down over there." He waved toward the window. "Daily demolition. You can hear them. I'll have to move one of these days. The building's already been sold. The university has bought the neighborhood."

But Ginny was paying him no heed and had moved across the room. "The boys will be up in a minute, Daddy, and you might as well know the story. Ralph's been up here for over a year now. To avoid the draft. So is Quarts. He's from Oklahoma. His father has a ranch out there. He's given up a lot to come to Canada and not fight in their lousy war. He could have been a rich man someday." She said this accusingly.

"Well, I admire principles too, Ginny," said Landon.

"Yeah. But he gets the rap from a lot of people your age, Daddy. So does Ralph—I'm just used to hearing it, I guess— Sorry!"

Landon observed his daughter. The wind was up for sure. Ginny was moving around his apartment arranging things, punching cushions into shape and edging books back into shelves, manifesting a quirky nervous haste. Why, she's quarreled with her mother again, he thought with relief. That's what this is all about.

"Are you okay, Ginny? I mean, really."

"Sure, I'm fine." She had moved back to the window and was again looking down to the street, touching the fabric of the curtain like a shoplifter. "The old city is changing."

"Yes," replied Landon, sitting on the arm of the sofa and watching her.

"I still think it beats New York though," Ginny said, placing a cheek against the glass. "That place is becoming a pigpen." She was suddenly irritable. "Even Mother's had it, and you know how she loves her New York."

"Yes, I do," said Landon.

"Did you know our apartment has been broken into twice since Christmas? They come through the windows, the doors, the skylight. I think the pigs are in on it too. They don't want to catch anybody. It's a war of nerves. Mother's really fed up and that's why she's coming back here."

"Here?" asked Landon, startled. "To Toronto?"

"Yes. Didn't you know? I thought she might have been in touch."

"With me?" Landon laughed. "I haven't talked to your mother since the holidays." Ginny frowned.

"No? . . . Well, anyway. She's quit her job. No . . . that's not quite right. The agency has okayed her transfer back to the Toronto office. They didn't like the idea much, but she told them she'd had it with New York and was moving back to Toronto. Well, you know how Mother can be when her mind's made up. Anyway, she's arriving tomorrow night." Ginny was on the move again, with her back to Landon. He was sure he could hear the sound of popping knuckles. "I thought maybe Aunt Blanche might have called you too. Since we're going to be staying with her until we find a place of our own." Landon passed a hand across his jaw.

"So she's loose again, then! I thought she was still locked up."

Ginny turned and made a sour face. "Daddy . . . That's not like you. Aunt Blanche has not been well, but that's no reason to be cruel."

"No, I suppose not, but I'm far from happy about you staying under the same roof with her. She's insanely jealous of any woman under seventy-five. You know that. She still has these terrific fits. Harvey Hubbard's told me about them."

"Oh, that gross person. What does he know, anyway? Besides, Aunt Blanche is all right now. Really. She's been well for months."

"Well?" Landon tried to conceal his irritation. "Yes. Maybe. But how well is well when you're talking about your Aunt Blanche? Vera should know better than this. You could easily stay at a small hotel until you get settled." A small hotel! The old Rodgers and Hart song. *There's a small hotel with a wishing well.* He and Vera had once leaned against each other to that old tune, played on reedy saxophones, as they swayed across the floor of some supper club before this child of his was conceived. Landon's head sometimes filled up with these old useless memories. And now Vera was hotfooting it back to Toronto, a place she had more than once called a one-horse town. She needed at least six horses. And a carriage. And they were going to stay at her sister's?

"Daddy," Ginny was saying, "did you know that Aunt Blanche stayed with us for two full weeks and was perfectly all right? She's a changed person now, really. And her doctor has given her these terrific new pills. Just in case anything goes wrong."

"In case anything goes wrong," muttered Landon, shaking his head, amused but vexed too by his daughter's untroubled faith in the healing power of pharmaceuticals. Oh, these young, thought Landon, screwing shut an eye against a fluent of sunlight which now streamed through the window into the room. They have taken to cursing science with violent tongues for the havoc it has wrought and the creeds it had doomed. Still, in a pinch, they worship at her shrine. After all, if the worst comes to the worst and threats are actually forthcoming, there are always magic powders for comfort and succor. Had he not talked to a ragged young man in the park about this very thing only a week before? That gaunt Christ-like figure with the haunted eyes had prophesied of the day when the sanitation departments of the world's great cities would discharge massive doses of tranquillizers into the drinking water. "It's the only way, man," he said, picking at the strands of loose skin on his fingers. He seemed to be shedding his skin like a snake. Probably some vitamin deficiency, thought Landon. But the young man wasn't worried about vitamins. He leaned back against the park bench, elbows flared out and long legs crossed at the ankles. "The way I see it, man, is this. We've got to cut down the hostility, get rid of the bad vibrations. Cool everybody down. Why, we're pecking one another to death," he added, alluding to the overcrowded conditions in the poultry industry, a business about which he seemed to know a good deal. Was his father perhaps a rich chicken farmer? Landon wondered about this, watching him drift away to inspect the contents of a trash basket. Well, whatever, Landon wasn't sure that the ragged young man with his dream of perfect tapwater had the answer.

Ginny's cheek was pressed against the glass again and she was looking down to the street, museful and silent as a hospital patient who watches the everyday business of life pass below. After a moment she asked, "What's keeping the boys?"

"The elevator may be stuck," said Landon. "It happens every so often. Perhaps I should have a look." But then he heard the ancient motor hum into life and the creaking cables. It was hauling again. At the window Ginny stood with one hand hanging loose, gnawing away at a knuckle on the other. Landon opened his mouth to speak, then shut it when his daughter uttered a small cry, "Oh, look at that poor little man!" Landon could now hear the quick bright ringing of the knife–grinder's bell. "Who, Rudolpho?" he asked. "That little man down there," cried Ginny, "sharpening knives for a living, the poor old guy." Landon smiled. "Rudolpho's not so badly off. He enjoys what he's doing . . ." But he checked himself. Better not. Ginny was seeing Rudolpho as a quietly despairing soul trapped in meaningless toil. Landon knew better. He had often talked to the grinder man as he passed along the streets of Landon's neighborhood each Thursday. Rudolpho had been around; had fought the Fascists in Spain and the Communists in Greece, had hidden like a bandit in the hills of Albania, had broken bread with wild men of the mountains. He knew a little something about a lived life. Wheeling a stone along the streets of Toronto was all right with him; a peripatetic refuge after a lifetime of strife. Landon was about to say something on Rudolpho when he looked across to the open doorway and beheld the dark-haired young man standing on the threshold like a bridegroom, still clutching Ginny's great white cases.

"Come in, please," said Landon. "And put the baggage down. You look worn out."

"Thanks," said the young man.

"Oh Daddy, this is Ralph!" cried Ginny, loping across the room to link arms with the youth. "Ralph's going to make a movie."

"Is that so?" said Landon. "What's it to be about?"

Ralph Chamberlain frowned with embarrassment. "Well, we haven't got anything together yet. It's about American war resisters in Canada. But we've got to get the bread for it. The corporations tie up the bread, you see . . ." Landon was now looking beyond Ralph to the bearded man who stood by the doorway. Ralph flushed deeply. He wasn't being taken seriously.

"In here, Quarts," said Ginny. "Gee, I don't even know your last name." She turned to her father. "We only just met at the airport."

The big fellow entered the room, bashfully grinning. "Quarts Logan. How do, Mr. Landon?" He stuck out a large paw, which Landon shook.

"Sit down, please," said Landon. "Ginny . . . Ralph. Over there, I guess. Quarts . . . Now, that's an unusual name. I suppose there's a story behind it." Logan laughed, showing large irregular teeth. "Oh yes . . . My real Christian name is Whittaker. After my granddaddy Whittaker. But as a kid I got Quarts. I used to like this frozen orange juice. This Birdseye frozen orange juice! Man, I was wild for that stuff. They couldn't fill me with it. I drank it by the quart . . ." He shrugged and grinned. It was a poor story but the best he could do. Landon found himself liking Quarts Logan.

"And now I suppose you can't stand orange juice," said Landon, fishing like a salesman for conversation.

"Hey now, that is correct," said Logan. "How did you guess that now?"

"Oh, it's usually the way with these stories, isn't it?"

"Why yes, it is."

Landon offered drinks, mindful that nowadays some of the young scorned spirits. He apologized for not having beer. "Can I offer you a little sherry?"

"Sherry's just fine," said Quarts, sitting now with his big candy-striped legs stuck out of the chair like barbers' poles. Ginny hardly heard her father, was already asking Ralph about the movie plans.

In the kitchen Landon took down four glasses and poured from Margaret's bottle of sherry, silently blessing his lady friend for keeping her bottle in his cupboard. For himself he squeezed shut one eye and measured off a generous inch of Old Troll. From the living room he heard Quarts whisper to Ginny, "Do you suppose your father would mind if we rolled ourselves a smoke here?"

"I don't know, Quarts," said Ginny. "I don't think you'd better."

Landon returned, balancing the glasses on an old tin tray which bore a picture of Niagara Falls at night. It came with the apartment. "Here we are now." He raised his glass. "What about a little toast? How about peace, for a start?" From the sofa Ralph snorted, but he raised his glass and everybody sipped. Quarts smacked his lips. "I wish I could see my daddy's face now."

"Why is that?" asked Landon. "Would he not approve of that sentiment?" He lowered himself into the sling chair.

"Hoo, man," said Quarts, trying not very hard to keep the mirth out of his voice. "We come from a long line of warring people, Mr. Landon. My daddy is a colonel in the militia. He's got himself a Winchester thirty-ought-six with a hand-carved butt—listen, it's a beautiful gun—he's got this strapped into the cab of his Chevy pickup. Why, I had two uncles win Purple Hearts at the battle of Guadalcanal. Another one died at Iwo Jima after blowin' up an acre or so of Japs."

"And your father is disappointed in you? . . ."

"Hoo . . . disappointed just ain't the word. He'd gut and sizzle me if he caught hold of me."

"But he's your father. Just a man like anyone else. Flesh and blood . . ."

Quarts shook his head. "You just don't understand, Mr. Landon. I've shamed his name, don't you see? And the whole county knows it . . . Daddy can't look folks in the eye any more on account of me . . ."

"Well, what can you expect, anyway?" said Ralph, sitting straight up. "I mean, our parents are living in another age, man. My father's the same . . . what will people think . . . that's his line . . ."

The deadly earnest tone. Landon detected in this sallow young man with the mournful Fu Manchu mustache a grim missionary type. As Ralph talked, Landon listened, hunkered down and half-hidden in the sling chair, peering across his forty-two-year-old kneecap at the three of them. Ralph was canted sideways like a jack-in-the-box, searching the carpet with a frown as he talked. Logan sat with long fingers laced together across his stomach. Now and then he nodded his head in agreement. Ginny was bobbed forward in her chair, elbow to knee and fist sunk under chin, a captive to this intelligent and indignant man. Landon felt a grieving air settle over him like a miasma. She was hooked. He had hoped to have a private word with her and had asked her before to come into the kitchen with him, but she had stopped him cold with a shake of the braids; a not-now-Daddy-please-can't-you-see-I'm-busy shake of the braids. Then, turning away, had popped fist to chin again. And Landon, being Landon, had not insisted, had not pursued the subject. He would not push himself. It was his besetting sin, the leitmotif in this sad comedy that was his life. Cramner used to tell him that he was a good salesman but he couldn't close. How fond Cramner was of those old merchandising expressions! Seated before a steaming mug of coffee on some grim Monday morning in Winnipeg, Cramner would remind him once again of his shortcomings. Outside the cafeteria the north wind itself buffeted people to and fro. On Portage Avenue the shop signs creaked like old bones, and beneath the gray sky the electric wires sang in the wind. The waitress told them the chill factor was forty-five below zero. That weather—it was an insult to the human heart! Landon watched the counterman wring out the J Cloth and take slow lazy swipes at the glass case where the bran muffins and Danish pastry were on display. How he envied him the simplicity of his job! And Cramner never shut up. "Now listen, Freddy my boy. I don't mean to criticize. It's only a suggestion from a man with thirty-five years in the business. Now, the customers like a nice fellow right enough. But they also like a little authority in the pitch too. Especially the gals. It's that little push at the end that gets you the extra five hundred. And the thing you came for! The buyer's signature. The authorization to move those goods out of the warehouse."

How in the name of God had he ever imagined he could be a salesman? And why had he spent so many years of his life at it? He should have got out of that racket years ago. It was not his line at all. Even Butcher could see that. But at first the business had not seemed to demand the talkative pushy type. After all, it wasn't door-to-door stuff: squeezing the juice out of people in their own living rooms, pushing a contract under their noses which would keep the cookware and encyclopedias coming for the rest of their days. And he sometimes felt that he hadn't been any worse or better than other fellows in the trade. He had checked the customers' inventories, written up the orders, introduced the new designs every spring and fall. Still, he supposed he could have worked harder at it, spent more time hustling for new customers, new angles. And there had been too many funny faces and dialect jokes (his specialty). Another salesman once told him that he had this reputation for not being serious about his work. But who paid any attention to that guy? He was a drunk. Landon was buried so deep in these thoughts that he failed to notice the young people on their feet. They were preparing to leave. Landon sprang from the chair, a sleeping man awakened by a hotfoot. "Here . . . you're not going already?"

"We have to, Daddy. It's getting late." Ginny was already enwrapped in the blanket coat and was winding a long colorful scarf about her throat. Quarts Logan stood near the door, snapping on the metal buttons of his jacket.

"Where's everyone going in such a rush?" asked Landon. "Ginny?"

"We're going to Aunt Blanche's now, Daddy. We'll catch a cab from the street. We'll have better luck down there. You can't get them on the phone at this time of the day . . ."

"Why don't you stay and have supper with me? I'll get you over to Blanche's later . . ."

"Oh I'd love to, really, but Aunt Blanche is expecting us. I called her from the airport."

"Well then . . ."

At the door Quarts Logan leaned into the jamb and regarded Landon with a friendly eye. "I think I am on to your style, Mr. Landon," he said. Chamberlain had escaped down the hall, lugging the great cases. "Yessir," said Logan. "My guess is that you're one of those detached and ironic observers of the passing scene . . . A silent man but a watcher and a listener. Am I right, sir?"

Landon plucked at his trouser seat, which had come stuck to his bottom in the sling chair. "No," he said, "I'm just an unemployed greeting-card salesman."

Quarts Logan snorted in delight and sashayed off down the hallway toward Chamberlain, who now sat on one of the cases in front of the iron cage like Little Beaver at the train depot. At the door Landon touched his daughter's arm. "Ginny? When are we going to have a talk about all this?"

She reached up and pecked him on the nose. "You're sweet, Daddy. And Mother and I know all about your fun and games."

Landon groaned. "What fun? What games?"

"Oh, your girl friend, silly," whispered Ginny, laughing and lowering the tablets. Her naked green eyes shone brilliantly. "The o-t-h-e-r woman. She lives right in the building, doesn't she? Conveenyent! Oh, we know all about you. We've been told."

"You have? Who told you?"

"Ho ho . . . I'll never tell." Why, she was playing the very devil with him!

"Mother's madly jealous, and you know what I think?"

"No, what?"

"I think she's still in love with you. Now, isn't that funny?"

"No."

Ginny reached up and nipped his cheek again. Miss Seventeen once more, a North American Daddy's delight, off to the malt shop with Archie, Jughead, and the whole gang.

"Phone me at Aunt Blanche's . . . and Daddy?"

"Yes? What?"

"Don't worry, huh!"

But worry Landon did and it was not until they were well gone that he remembered something else too. He could not phone her at Blanche's. That number was now unlisted. Harvey Hubbard had told him about it. Harvey still got the latest news through the attorneys, who were putting the finishing touches to the divorce. Apparently Blanche was now interested in playing the good citizen. She was bent on performing useful social acts. It was all a part of the therapy. Her psychiatrist had told her to seek out her fellow man, for he's a brother. And so she had joined a church club which was interested in helping single men who were down on their luck. Or had no luck at all. Each Wednesday afternoon Blanche visited the Good News Mission House on lower Jarvis Street. There she stood behind a counter, wearing a gray smock, handing out work pants and old suit coats. Of course Blanche had to overdo it. When didn't she? And so to the ones with the pleading eyes or the sorriest tale she slipped the odd twenty. The result of which was a flood of telephone calls from characters named Frenchy and Mutt and

Cherry Pie. These calls! They came through at all hours of the day and night: slurred entreaties for money to visit a dying mother in Vancouver, drunken invitations to wine and cheese parties in No. 7 shed on the Bay Street pier abaft the railway tracks. And lewd suggestions aplenty. Some shocked even Blanche. Well, who could blame them for trying? The whole thing was a horrible misunderstanding. And now Blanche's phone number was no longer public information. To see his daughter again, Landon supposed he must visit the house on Russell Hill Road.

The house on Russell Hill Road! He had hoped to have seen the last of that place. Stirring uneasily beneath the blankets, Landon turned his thoughts to the day which now lay before him. In the pale sky behind the Research Library, Venus flamed, luminous and plenary, a last flagrant brilliance before sunrise.

Normally Landon would have welcomed Friday. For a man with no job, Fridays are the end of a week of guilty feelings, feelings which surface while he is walking the streets or reading a magazine in the public library. Or taking a noon-hour snooze in front of the TV. On Friday afternoons, however, the jobless man can relax. He is reunited once more with the community, indistinguishable from his useful neighbors who are taking their weekly break from office and factory. Today, however, Landon could not relax. At ten o'clock he must talk to this Ozzie K. Smith at Hearthstone Realty. Another of Butcher's clients. The hopelessness of these interviews! How many had he endured? It was past reckoning, and the results were always the same. The voices became one voice: "We're delighted you dropped by to see us, Mr. Landon. As I'm sure you can appreciate, we have several applicants seeking this position. After we've had an opportunity to analyze each application, we'll make our decision. If you're successful, we'll be in touch. I hope you've put your phone number down here . . ." Others were more honest and Landon was grateful though his ears burned as though aflame. "Look, Fred, I'll lay it on the line for you. You may be the best salesman in the world." Landon returning this modish young man's smile, capped tooth for capped tooth. Why was he smiling? ". . . But we just can't use you. I don't want to raise your hopes." The young man tapping a fingernail against Landon's application form. ". . . You're what? Forty-four?"

"Two . . . Forty-two."

"Okay, Fred, forty-two. In eight years you'll be fifty, right?" Landon hardly listening, hearing only the numerals clicking in his head like tumblers in some mysterious lock. But my God, the man is right! Fifty years old! Impossible!

"Well honestly, Fred . . . Where does that leave us? Management, I mean. Our pension benefits now begin at sixty, and we're taking into serious consideration the possibility of introducing an optional retirement plan at fifty-two."

"Fifty-two? Retirement?" Landon croaking from a parched throat.

"Correct. And the other factor which we have to take into consideration is the fact that we are a youth-oriented company. Our major market is in the under-thirties age bracket. Now, don't get me wrong. There are exceptions. But a man's peak performing years sales–wise are between twenty-five and forty-five. We have statistics to corroborate this . . ."

And the times were not good. The economists were gloomy. God, what if I had a family to support, thought Landon, and shuddered in his bed. The welfare rolls for sure. As it happened, he wasn't badly fixed. As of this Friday morning he still had his savings, seven thousand and forty-three dollars plus change. But he was dipping into it, and with sinking heart he watched the figure decline each week. The teller in the bank, a pretty girl, looked sympathetic. Still, I'm okay for a while, he murmured to the ceiling. But he was not convinced. And Vera arrived from New York today! What did she have up her sleeve, anyway? He must get in touch with Ginny. Take her somewhere for coffee and talk about these new plans.

He got out of bed and walked to the window, a heavyset man, six feet tall, with a great shock of reddish-blond hair riding his skull. This hair, stirred now to disorder by sleep and restless fingers, was his most striking physical feature. It dominated an otherwise ordinary head, making him appear in fact more handsome than he really was. It lay, abundant and rich, *en évidence* in the sunlight, a gift from his mother and her Swedish ancestors. Sometimes it made him more conspicuous than he wished to be, but when all was said and done, it was a great head of hair, a real lion's mane, and he was proud, even vain, about it. He doubted that he would ever be bald. It was not one of his worries.

Standing by the window in loose green pajamas, he looked down to the street. It was cold for late March and a powdering of fresh snow lay on the ground. In front of Kneibel's delicatessen the sewer smoked into the yellow air beneath the street lamp, and the dark brick houses beyond were lighted here and there by early risers. The neighborhood was waking up. Down Spadina Avenue Landon could see brake lights blazing into life as buses stopped to pick up the Italian laborers on their way to another day of digging the city's subway channels. Could I do that? wondered Landon and decided not. He could never keep up with those tough dark little men. Across the street Kneibel had turned on the lights and was preparing for the day's trade, hefting his crocks of eggs and pickles, setting out his sausage and salamis with a heavy German deliberateness. Between the cracks of the store's shutters Landon caught glimpses of Kneibel's great bald head already gleaming with high color. Kneibel suffered from hypertension and enjoyed talking to strangers about his anxieties. He blamed his troubles on four years in the Wehrmacht when he knew he was fighting for the wrong ideals but was powerless to do anything about it. So he had continued to shoot Russians and Poles on the banks of the River Bug.

Beyond Kneibel's and the old brick houses, the Research Library rose, dark and sheer against the sky. This new Research Library was the latest addition to the City University complex. For the past couple of years the hammering and riveting had given Landon headaches, and though he was not against progress, he disliked this bulky gray pile of cement and glass which pressed itself so powerfully against the sky. The neighborhood bully, awing all other buildings with a show of strength. However, it was to be expected. The university was tearing down the neighborhood, getting rid of the old leaning houses with their cement stoops and the small brick apartment buildings with their birth dates carved into the stone over entrances. Landon's own building had been around since 1912, and sometimes, standing like this at the window, he amused himself by imagining the streets below in those long gone times when this building was spanking new. He guessed it was chiefly a matter of scale. In those days everything must have been smaller. Thus reflecting, he would sight through a circle made by thumb and forefinger, holding it before one eye like a photographer. And there, sure enough, were the high box-shaped automobiles on their narrow tires and the open trolleys, red wood and toy-like, rattling along the tracks with their bells and blue-vested conductors. The people were smaller too. Had he not read somewhere that the average North American had grown a full inch and gained twenty pounds over the last fifty years? I've gained more than my share, he thought gloomily as he walked to the dresser mirror for a look. Drawing on a pair of old trousers, he sucked in his middle to fasten the top button, but it proved too uncomfortable. He sighed and released the button, allowing his wide soft stomach to find its own gravity. These trousers were part of an old summer suit and had seen better days. He wore them now when painting in oils, a pastime he had undertaken on the advice of Margaret. She said it would help to take his mind off his troubles. The trousers were wrinkled and spattered with vivid colors, hanging over his broad hips like harem pants. Once he had been more particular about his clothes. In those days he had been a traveling salesman for a greeting card firm with a closetful of smart suits and nifty jackets. When he came down for breakfast to the dining rooms of the old hotels in Halifax and Montreal, his flaring pebbled Florsheim brogues had given off a rich luster along the carpets of those solemn old rooms with their dark wood paneling. To the waitresses he had been an elegant gent, sitting there with his morning paper folded and squared, propped against the water goblet, sipping his orange juice, and waiting for his poached eggs. But that was all behind him now. He hadn't worked in seven months.

In his tiny kitchen Landon toasted bread and listened to his teakettle. Overhead the solid tramp of feet about their business. Those feet! They belonged to his lady friend Margaret Beauchamp, who was now hurrying about her apartment, already late for the seven o'clock Mass at the Church of St. Basil the Martyr. It being the Lenten season, his devout Margaret received the sacrament of Holy Communion each day. After Mass she would walk along to the old red-brick collegiate on Harcourt Street where she taught English literature to the children of Ukrainian and Italian immigrants. Landon had listened to these footsteps every morning and evening for months, never dreaming that one day they would find their way to his own bed. He had listened to them, knowing only that they belonged to a solidly built, dark-haired woman who had moved in with her mother last Labor Day. Now and then she had smiled at him when they met at the front door or in the iron cage. Usually the weather was cold and she was wrapped up in a heavy cloth coat with her hair hidden beneath a plain hat. But in milder weather he had seen her too, in skirt and cardigan sweater, with rubber-soled health shoes on her feet. Often she was carrying fragrant parcels from Kneibel's; a good-sized woman with strong heavy bones—Slav bones, solid of leg as a ward nurse. To Landon she looked sturdy enough to last a hundred years. A sad shy look to her wide face, a faded rose, a melancholy soul. She was often cradling textbooks in her arms too. Also a worn leather briefcase, an old-fashioned article, cracked and weatherbeaten with numerous buckles and straps holding it together. Years before Landon had seen immigrants with long leather coats carrying such bags. An old maid, he decided, though not so old in years, and foreign, living with her invalid mother, who never appeared to venture out except to dark St. Basil's on Sunday mornings. An early riser, even on weekends, Landon had often seen the daughter pushing the old woman's wheelchair along the street at dawn. That freezing cheerless street in the dim light and this woman pushing the shawled figure in the wheelchair. A Russian scene—the picture of elemental sacrifice and duty. What burdens must some people shoulder! His first impulse had been sympathy. A luckless creature, alone with her books and her sick old lady and her Church. An untilled field. But then the old woman abruptly died in the late autumn, and Landon's life changed too. A queer business this life, and full of quirky happenings, chance events, random decisions that altered your luck for good. Or bad. The salesman pursed his lips to cool the instant Sanka.

He remembered a conversation he had once had with a friend of his, a buyer who lived in another city. That poor fellow was still baffled by the whimsical nature of life's major events. It seems that he had lived side by side with his best friend all his life. They had grown up as pals, played hockey and sandlot ball together, double-dated at the movies. When they married they bought houses next to one another in a new suburb, helped each other sow grass seed, and shared the cost on weed spray. They planned fishing trips together, watched their families grow up and generally prosper. Their wives exchanged recipes. One New Year's Eve the four of them went to a house party. "We all had plenty to drink," the buyer told Landon, "but for some reason my friend drank too much and passed out early. Before ten o'clock. Then, what do you think happened? My wife became so ill that we had to rush her to the hospital, my friend's wife and I. The doctors took one look, poked around her sides, listened to the moans, and rushed her into surgery. Appendix. In an hour they had it out and she was resting comfortably. We went back to the party where my friend was sleeping on a pile of coats in an upstairs bedroom, got him into the car, and took him home to bed. He was out like a light and snoring before we left his room. Downstairs my wife's friend suggested a nightcap. After the ordeal of the evening I thought—what harm? I'd known the woman for years. The clock struck twelve as we raised our glasses. A New Year! "Happy New Year, George," my friend's wife said to me and kissed me lightly on the cheek. And then I don't know. I can't honestly say what came over us. Perhaps it was the simple fact that for the first time we were really alone. The kids were away. My best friend was dead to the world upstairs. My wife was resting comfortably in the recovery room. Anyway, in a twinkling of an eye we were on the sofa with our clothes off! Imagine!" Landon had clucked sympathetically. "We fell madly in love," said the buyer. "I mean the real thing. To be together we told lies. We met one another at laundromats and supermarkets, went to drive-in theaters. Had intercourse in the back seat of my car. Of course we were found out. You can only hide a thing like that for so long. It almost ruined my marriage and my friend's too. I had to move to another town, get a new job!" He swallowed his drink and shook his head, a sadder yet wiser man. "But think of it! I lived beside that woman for twenty years and didn't so much as give her a second thought. Didn't once make a pass at her. Would you believe it?" Landon believed it. Why not? The same thing had happened to him. Anything was possible, including a neighbor's embrace. How can you tell what is going on inside people until you enter their lives? And how do you enter people's lives? Well, if you're not invited, reflected Landon, spreading a piece of toast with low-calorie marmalade, it's largely a matter of chance, is it not? And the owner of the footsteps overhead? If he had not stopped one day to buy a hat, something he rarely did, they might have continued to nod and smile at one another in hallways and entrances. The hat he had bought in a small shop on Yonge Street. Toward the end of a dreary afternoon in early December when the stores were turning on their window lights against the gloom. The hat did not suit him, but he bought it anyway. To cheer himself up or change his luck. He had spent most of the morning filling out application forms and trying tricky quizzes in a life-insurance company. In the afternoon he had sat for two hours in the sales office of a wholesale food distributor. Walking home, he felt the need for diversion, some relief from the tedium of these fruitless interviews. He debated whether to have a drink or two in a bar, eat dinner out, and see a movie. Or buy something new. In any case, an extravagance for a man with no job. Then in the window of the haberdashery he spotted the hat, a sober black homburg, a bald-headed banker's chapeau, exactly wrong for his bright bushy head. Nevertheless, he approved of its severe respectability. Its indomitable presence caught his fancy. The proprietor, a small hectic man, disagreed. "It's not you," he said sternly. "Listen to me. I know hats. Thirty years in the same location. If you want it, I'm selling. Who turns down a sale? But it's not you. For you, my friend, this . . . same low price!" He held up a jaunty little Alpine fedora, a pale checked green with a bright feather scissored into the band.

"Too frivolous," said Landon, for once in his life adamant.

"Frivolous schmivolous, it's exactly you," said the owner.

"Better wrap up the homburg," said Landon grimly. "On second thought," he added, "I'll wear it."

In the subway, shouldering his way among the evening travelers, Landon watched and waited for someone to glance up and discover the homburg with a mocking eye. In the dark glass of the door he himself appraised it, and it did look vaguely screwy, perched bolt upright atop his head like a rabbi's hat. The man was right, thought Landon. I've swindled myself out of $19.95. He should have gone to the movies! When he turned the corner into his own street, he noticed the small crowd in front of his building. An accident! The roof light of an ambulance slowly turned in the freezing air, casting long fingers of dark red light across the pavement and against the side of Kneibel's store. Kneibel himself was standing on the edge of the crowd, a large humped figure in white apron, hands plunged into pockets and fat neck stretched out for a look. Landon hurried on. Kneibel briefly glanced toward him as he approached. "What happened, Mr. Kneibel?" asked Landon, out of breath. Kneibel gave the homburg a searching look. What was this? A large dark bird squatting on a man's head? Landon was not a steady customer and the grocer did not have to be polite. He turned to the crowd.

"The old lady. A thrombosis or something," he muttered.

"Which old lady is that?" asked Landon, looking himself now.

"Up there," said Kneibel. "Mrs. Beauchamp." He did not wish to be bothered. The crowd was parted by a young policeman, and the ambulance attendants carried a stretcher down the cement steps. Under the street lamp Landon saw the slight figure beneath the blanket; an old woman's gray face, the serpent eyes closed. She already looked like a corpse. The attendants quickly slid her through the rear door of the ambulance and hopped in after her on white shoes. The young cop hustled the spectators along, and the ambulance departed with siren howling. Kneibel sighed. "A good customer too."

On the steps the old woman's daughter, a kerchief on her head, stood alone, hugging her bare arms and looking down, utterly bereft, with the eyes of the crowd now upon her. How people love to gawk, thought Landon. Take secret delight in another's misfortune. A good accident makes their day. And I'm no different either. This woman's grief is larger, more spectacular. It's crowding out my own troubles, pushing them into the background. A sad fact of life! The crowd was breaking up, and he ascended the steps, tipping his foolish hat.

"Excuse me. Is there anything I can do? Fred Landon, I'm right below you. Two-one-six."

"Yes, I know." She smiled weakly. The large sorrowing eyes were damp and shining.

"Your mother," began Landon, "is she . . . ?"

"No. But she's very low. When I came home she was on the floor. I suppose she tried to reach the telephone. I don't know how long she was lying there." A tremor ran through her voice.

"They've taken her to the hospital then?" asked Landon.

"Yes."

Landon lightly touched her arm. "Perhaps we should go inside. It's getting very cold." She was abstracted, looking over his shoulder at the traffic. "Yes. But I must get over to the hospital."

"Don't worry about it," said Landon. "I'll see that you get there. But you look half-frozen now. You need a warm drink."

Taking her by the elbow, he steered her into the building. Sometimes he surprised himself, taking command of things like this; a regular Red Cross worker.

In his apartment he mixed two large brandies with water and dialed the taxi companies. Why hadn't the police taken her? The inconsiderate bastards. Outside, the wind was up and a driving sleet began to drum against the glass. Landon parted the curtains. "A bad night," he said to no one in particular. "And the lines are all busy. I guess they're not taking house calls at this hour. Too much street business. Unfortunately I have no car. Sold it several weeks ago. An economy move," he added and abruptly laughed. What did she care about his economy moves with her mother dying?

"I have a car," she said. She was sitting uneasily on the edge of his sofa with her knees together, and fine big handsome knees they were too. Love-starved, Landon looked away. The woman was suffering, near to losing her mother for once and all, and he was ogling her legs. He rose and walked to the kitchen to pour himself another brandy, tipping in an extra measure, an enormous drink. After a moment he heard her say, "I don't drive very often. It's too busy for me." She might have been addressing herself.

"Don't blame you," said Landon from the kitchen. "I myself am nervous behind the wheel. Driving today . . . Well . . . you take your life in your hands every time . . ." He stopped. Why was he always putting forth his side of things like this? Why not settle for heroic silence once in a while? The woman obviously wanted him to drive her to the hospital but was too proud to ask. He sipped his big drink. "Is your car an automatic? The gears, I mean?" he asked, returning to the living room.

"Yes." She had removed her kerchief and to Landon's surprise the dark hair fell to her shoulders, thick but lacking luster, coarse and spiky as pubic hair. Still no beauty, but with a sad heavy sensuality surrounding her. Up close and bare-armed and with this dense mantle of hair, she inspired wonder and bespoke carnal intelligence. And all this hidden beneath cloth coats and plain hats. I was wrong, thought Landon. This is no untilled field. "I only learned how to drive late in life," he continued, watching her. "That is to say, by late—I mean thirty. I had my lessons on an automatic shift. Couldn't manipulate those gears. All that footwork and coordination . . . Beyond me . . . That's why I asked." She was hardly listening, attendant only on the pellets of sleet which now struck the window.

After a moment Landon said, "We'll take your car, I'll drive."

"Oh no . . . I couldn't trouble you with that." She turned her stricken eyes upon him.

"No trouble at all," said Landon, downing the brandy and feeling the warm flush spread through his stomach and chest. "You better go upstairs and get a coat. Dress warmly. I'll meet you in the lobby in five minutes."

"This is really very kind of you, Mr. Landon."

"Call me Fred," said a tipsy Landon.

"All right." She was examining his face with the liveliest curiosity. She gave him her warm moist hand. "Margaret Beauchamp."

"We'd better get going, Margaret," he said.

After she left, he nervously reached up to run a hand through his own rich hair. Instead, his fingers found the brim of the homburg, still perched atop his buzzing head. He wore it out into the wild night.

The first winter storm of the year, and on the street they bent into the ravening wind. With one hand on his hat, Landon used the other to pluck at the stray bits of newspaper flung against his trouser leg. Icy water ran down his cheeks and neck. Beside him Margaret looked anxious. She was putting him to too much trouble. "It's not far now," she shouted as they rounded a corner. She was clutching the knot of her kerchief at the throat like some peasant woman in an old painting, "The Storm." The car, she told him, was kept in a garage behind the hand laundry. She rented the space from the Chinaman. When they finally turned into the alley behind the laundry, a sobered Landon paused to wipe his streaming eyes with both hands. But the alleyway created a draft and the wicked wind sucked the hat off his head. He felt it lift and sail away. Margaret screamed. "Your hat!"

"Never mind," yelled Landon. "It's all right."

"Oh, but it's a beautiful hat," she cried, looking back. "There it is. We can still get it. Look . . ." The hat was lying on the road not thirty feet away. Landon looked and hesitated. It could still be captured. That was his $19.95 lying there on the road. But he wasn't about to make a damn fool of himself by running down the street after it. This fatal hesitation, and soon a gust of wind caught the homburg and sent it spinning along on its brim like a wheel. A comical exit. Margaret gripped his arm. "I'm so sorry. It's my fault. I feel terrible about all this. I'll pay for your hat."

"Not at all," he said. "Don't worry about it."

She was gazing up at his locks, flowing freely now in the wind. "I'm afraid you'll catch your death of cold."

"We better move," said Landon. They hurried on into the alley, where they found some shelter against the row of old wooden garages. In front of one of these she handed him a ring of keys.

"Which key?" asked Landon. Margaret looked ready to weep.

"I'm sorry. I don't know. I've only used the car twice."

"Okay," said Landon, wondering how he got into this adventure. "It's a Yale lock. I'll find it."

With freezing fingers he searched the key ring. What sort of person was she, anyway? He couldn't resist asking, "Excuse me, Margaret, but if you've only used the car twice, why bother looking after it? Renting this space and everything? It must be an awful expense! Why not sell?"

"The car belonged to a friend," she said, "who died a few months ago. It was left to me in the will." She sounded apologetic about it.

"I see," said Landon. Passing on an automobile! An unusual bequest from a friend. What was it anyway—some prize antique? Would he roll up to the hospital at the wheel of a Dusenburg? But she said the transmission was automatic? Still, weren't some of those old luxury wagons equipped with such things? A key finally turned the lock and he pulled open the doors. Luckily Margaret had brought along a pencil flashlight, and now he directed its narrow beam into the gloom. It was stale and hoary, smelling of damp earth and old motor oil. Against the back wall were nailed licence plates from the years 1932 through 1940. Some soul's testimony to ownership of an automobile during the Great Depression. The place reeked of days abandoned and forgotten. In the middle stood the hulk of Margaret's car. It was no Dusenburg but a massive DeSoto, at least fifteen years old, a deep ruby in color; a baroque beauty from the middle fifties! A doctor's car! They opened the stiff doors and climbed in. Inside, Landon pressed his fingers into the soft nap of the seat and sniffed the cold faint aroma of pipe smoke and Evergreen Air Freshener. A bachelor's smell! It had been a male friend then! Beside him Margaret sat stiffly, looking dead ahead with a rigid neck. Did the DeSoto evoke painful memories for her? Lovers' lane monkeyshines in the wide back seat? Her face offered no clues.

After fiddling with the key ring, Landon inserted the ignition key and turned hard to the right. Instead of catching, however, the key merely clicked, metal against metal. He tried several more turns, hearing each time only this ominous click. "What's wrong with, it? Why won't it go?" he asked.

"I don't know," she said. "It happened to me the last time too. You just have to keep trying. After a while it will go. He was going to have it fixed . . ." The dead clicking persisted. "Well . . . I've never seen anything like this before," said Landon peevishly. He had never struck a bargain with the mechanical world. There was bad faith between them. He was forever scorching his fingers on frayed ironing cords or loose sockets. Vending machines gobbled up his coins and then stood silent, refusing to deliver the goods. Landon continued to flick the key back and forth several times. "Well come on now, you bastard," he said, flushing with anger. Margaret began to weep. "I went to the garageman about it," she sobbed. "He said there's something worn. The cold weather affects it. He had no time to fix it . . . I was going to take it back . . ."

Sheepishly Landon placed a hand on her arm. The poor dame! What was he shouting for? She had her problems. "Okay now. We're just having a little bad luck here." He laughed grimly and pulled his Prussian officer's accent out of a hat. "Ze gods are not smiling on us tonight, ja!" He instantly remembered and could have yanked the tongue out of his head. This was no time for foolishness. Still, she wiped her eyes and offered another dim smile. "I'm putting you to so much bother." Landon turned the key once more and was rewarded with a slow guttural growl. "It's going to go," Margaret cried.

"I think so," said Landon, oddly elated. He had been on the verge of surrender. After several more attempts, the balky ignition caught and fired. Landon tapped the accelerator and heard the powerful motor throb into life. His patience had triumphed. "We're in business," he said excitedly, bending forward to examine the dashboard. Choking engine exhaust drifted through the open windows. Landon released the hand brake and nervously eased the DeSoto into the night, its headlights flooding a wooden fence with light, illuminating the heartless message of some spiteful neighborhood tattletale—MARION S. SUCKS. The brutality of these community broadcasting networks, he thought. It's always there. The vicious gossip. He remembered his own childhood, with his mother listening, impatient and angry, but listening all the same to old Mrs. Feeny.

On the street his nervousness eased. The DeSoto was bulky, an immense piece of machinery, but sound through and through, and it handled well even on the slippery pavement. Margaret told him they had taken her mother to St. Michael's, and he turned east to travel crosstown. At the corner of Hoskin Avenue and St. George Street, Landon braked to a stop before a red light. Outside, the sleet had turned to wet heavy snow, and the wind blew it in waves against the glass. Driving crosstown, Landon marveled at the coziness of the big car.

They were heading into the eye of the hurricane in this bubble of chromium and steel. If only the circumstances were more favorable! If only they were venturing forth on a real journey! Despite the foul weather, Landon felt he could drive all night. Straight across the country and away from this damn city of sales managers and marketing men. The rear seat piled high with bacon and egg sandwiches, thermoses of sweetened coffee, and Hershey bars. Some of Kneibel's sugared pastry would be nice too. A trunkful of traveler's checks. Landon smiled at this childishness. Later they might tune in some disc jockey on the old respectable-looking dash radio. He might spin a few old dance tunes for them. Some Jimmy Lunceford or Tommy Dorsey.

> *Grab your hat and grab your coat,*
> *Leave your worries on the doorstep.*

Across the dominion with his neighbor. Over the northland with the tips of fir trees lashing in the wind. And beyond them, the frozen tundra reaching out to the rim of the planet and the distant northern sea. Through that exploded pre-Cambrian rock, now buried deep under snow, and past the forests to prairie country. Yahoo! Past towns and way stations he had glimpsed through sleepy eyes from the windows of trains. And somewhere out there a blinding snowstorm, fueled by seventy-mile-an-hour winds, roaring across one thousand miles of tableland. But still no match for this big landship. Climbing the Rockies with the fat tires gripping each treacherous curve. He'd have those tires checked before tackling Roger's Pass. And climbing, ever climbing, until at last they began their descent to the sea. The Pacific Ocean! Gateway to the Orient!

They had turned southward on the circular drive of Queen's Park Crescent and were about to enter University Avenue when Landon, his mind's eye still focusing on the gateway to the Orient, felt the car lurch and yaw. The rear end seemed to be drawing itself up for a separate charge down the street. Beside him Margaret gasped, "Watch out!" Yes—the car was assuredly moving sideways. Moreover, it appeared to be gathering speed as it went its peculiar way. Don't touch the brakes, he said to himself. He remembered the traffic tip from Spot the Safety Dog. If you watched enough of those television cartoons they could save your life. When deep in the forest, remember the proverbs of Smokey the Bear. Landon fought the wheel, not quite certain what he was up to, resisting somehow the impulse to mash the brakes, terrified by the slow vehicular sway of the big car. He was conscious of Margaret's fingers in the flesh of his arm, yet thankful too that she was there. Mercifully, there was little southbound traffic at this time of the night. Ahead of them only a few cars struggled north from the traffic lights at College Street. With Landon at the helm, the DeSoto sashayed down the wide avenue for a hundred yards or so before coming to an abrupt halt against the curb, twenty feet from the statue of Sir Somebody Prior, who gazed down at them with a mantle of snow over his cold bronze head. With the blood roaring in his ears, Landon settled his own head against the steering wheel and waited for the coronary, the explosion in the chest. After a moment he looked up to see snowflakes dancing like white moths in the beam of the headlights. In the rear-view mirror he also sighted the police motorcycle. He groaned aloud.

"What is it?" Margaret asked in a small dry voice.

"Jesus, I'm dead! He'll throw the book at me." Landon's mind raced onward to bleaker prospects. Police stations. Magistrate's Court. Lawyers' fees. Guilty, Your Eminence! The cop climbed off his machine and walked toward them, enormous in his leather jacket and fur cap with gauntlets on his sleeves and buskins around his calves. Landon rolled down the window, and the cop leaned in on his elbows, a handsome fellow in his thirties with a neat little mustache. Without a word Landon handed over his driver's license, listening to his own heartbeat and Margaret's quick shallow breathing. He couldn't bear to look at her. Through the open window snow poured onto his knees, and the motorcycle radio crackled and squawked of traffic accidents and suspicious persons in doorways. The cop removed a gauntlet and with a fist dabbed at the corners of his mustache while he studied Landon's license.

"Now, Fred," he said, without looking up, "how fast would you say you were going back there? I mean, when you took the curve and got into trouble?"

Landon took a deep breath. "Thirty . . . Maybe thirty-five, Constable . . . but I can explain."

"Seems to me like it was closer to maybe . . . forty-five . . ."

"Oh no . . . no . . ."

"Now, what's the hurry? It's a rough night . . ."

"Yes. It is. Well, you see . . ."

"I picked you up back there. Just as you merged in off Hoskin, and you looked like a man in a hurry . . ." The cop's dark eyes were bridged by wide high brows which arched now as he turned the license over, looking for violations.

"Constable . . . I should tell you that I'm driving this lady to the hospital." Landon spoke quickly, trying to manage a note of urgency in his voice. "Her mother's very seriously ill. She's just been rushed to St. Michael's in an ambulance. I lost control back there, that's true, but you see I'm not used to the car. It belongs to the lady, a neighbor of mine." A credible story. Any reasonable man would believe it.

"Is that so? . . . Well . . ." The cop wasn't sure. He looked across to Margaret and then again at Landon's damp hatless head. "Have you had a drink or two tonight, Fred? You smell a little ripe." Landon's heart froze in his chest.

"Only one, Constable. To settle my nerves. The excitement. When I got home, this lady . . ." He was conscious of the pleading tone in his voice. He was always obsequious, even craven, before authority. But the bastard wasn't going to persecute him for a couple of drinks, was he? They could make it hot for you if they felt like it. The cop returned the license.

"I'm going to check this out. What's the name, lady?"

"Beauchamp," said Margaret, a croak from a dark corner. The cop walked back to his machine and they waited in silence.

Through the falling snow Landon watched a couple walking arm in arm toward the shelter of trees near the Faculty of Medicine. They were moving slowly against the night, warming one another and embracing. Romantic adventure lay ahead. Will I see any of that again? wondered Landon, or is it just for the young? If so, life is a cheat, because I'm still not too old for that stuff. He felt suddenly irritated with the woman beside him. A weepy type and plain too. Another sparrow in this forest of bright plumage. And because of her he was in this pickle. But he also was angry with himself. If he had only gone for a drink instead of wasting money on that ridiculous homburg. He might have met someone tonight; a lonely widow toying with the stem of her sherry glass on a barstool. No— not a widow. A divorcee. Someone who had been hard used and wished to erase the past, not gather in memories and talk about old Bill. He didn't want an evening of memories, damn it. He wanted some action, his share of the good things going on. And here he was, halfway to jail But he knew he was exaggerating his lot. Besides, he had sat in hundreds of bars and he knew that tonight would have been no different. He was no Frankenstein, but he seldom had luck with stray women. In his travels he had met some and listened to their sad tales and tried to cheer them up. A few times he had gone to the well and drank. But the truth was, he hadn't the heart for casual seduction.

After a few minutes the cop returned to wave them on. But not before he placed a warning hand on the door. "You go ahead now, Fred, but take it easy or you'll end up in the hospital too. Or put somebody else there." The motor was still cooking away, and Landon put the car into gear and departed with elaborate caution. He might have been taking his driver's test. As they descended into the gray vaulting canyon of University Avenue, Landon stayed behind a maintenance truck which was spewing salt onto the road, its blue cyclopoid beacon turning weirdly in the snowy air. The cop remained behind them until Queen Street, when he veered to the right and charged ahead, weaving in and out of the thickening traffic until he disappeared.

Gratefully Landon turned eastward, and Margaret spoke at last. "I thought you handled that very well."

"Who me?" Landon snorted rudely. "Hell no. Cops rattle me. I'm no good at all with them. Always feel I've done something wrong. Can't think straight for five seconds." He knew he sounded petulant. Somehow the woman tapped a vein of malice within him. She reached across to touch his arm.

"I'm really sorry to have put you to all this trouble. If I'd only known . . . And your beautiful hat . . ."

"Oh Christ, that hat . . ." He laughed wickedly. "I mean, let's face it. That hat looked pretty stupid on me. Silly really . . ."

". . . Oh no . . ."

"Well, it certainly did, damn it," he said sharply. She withdrew her hand, and inwardly Landon cursed himself again. "I mean . . . relax . . . let's just forget about the hat, eh! What's done is done, and anyway we're almost there." After a moment he added, "I hope your mother's okay."

"I hope she's dead," Margaret said dully. She had turned her face to the side window and was watching the Christmas shoppers hustle through the slush under the neon signs to the warm stores. Had he heard right? Did she say she hoped her mother was dead? What kind of a thing was that to say? He drove on in wondering silence.

At the hospital the emergency waiting room was thick with people. They were standing in bunches by doorways or seated on the long benches against the walls. Some had overflowed into the corridor where Landon now stood waiting. At first he thought there had been some neighborhood disaster, a local apartment-house fire or an exploding gas main. But what did he know about downtown hospital emergency wards? This was just another early evening's business: frostbitten drunks; stroke and coronary cases; bleeding losers of fights; kids who had been injured in playground accidents; people whose fingers had interfered with mill saws and bread knives; the inevitable traffic victims. He stepped back as they wheeled a stretcher down

the corridor. On it, a young woman, moaning, her face blood-
ied and scraped horribly, pockmarked by gravel and stones.
Margaret stood waiting her turn by the high counter. In front of
her a man who had been called away in a hurry. Landon could
see that there had been some hasty attempt to dress up, to put
a respectable face on tragedy. The loose-fitting sportcoat from
the fifties only partly concealed the stained work pants. But the
poor fellow had forgotten his shoes, and on his bare white feet
were bedroom slippers, the backs crushed down by the weight
of his heels over the years. The man looked tired, defeated.
What calamity had hit *him* between the eyes in the middle of his
supper? Now his thin gray face was all fatigue and submission.
On top of everything else—this! How do you quit honorably?
Behind the counter the old nun scratched in her ledger, recording the grim facts. The face enclosed and framed by the stiff
folds of her cowl was yellowing like old parchment, hidden
away from the sunlight by years of indoor toil. The square-cut
spectacles refracted light and protected eyes which could no
longer be startled by sad tidings. They had seen it all, registered
everything with the patience God expects from his servants on
earth. In the fullness of time . . . But Landon felt surrounded by
the awfulness of life, the brute facts of living, the terrible day-
to-day griefs which must be borne. The sickly odor of disinfectant and blood mingled with the smell of unwashed bodies and
clung to the walls. To the starched uniforms of the nurses and
orderlies. It streamed through the air like a fallout and seeped
through Landon's skin to infect his soul. He felt heartsick. A
few paces away a frail man of sixty or so was explaining things
to a policeman. Around his head was an enormous bandage
swaddled like a turban and still leaking blood. One sleeve of his

dirty windbreaker dangled loose and empty, hiding a busted wing. The old fellow had been quickly sobered by his troubles and was trying to strike a reasonable tone with the cop. Next to them stood an Indian woman in her early thirties. She wore a cheap print dress and a short imitation-leopard-skin coat. Once perhaps she had been pretty, but her face was now used up, ravished and alcohol-washed, badly bruised, with one eye swollen and discolored. Her skinny brown legs were covered only by ankle socks, and on her feet a pair of scuffed black ballet slippers. She spoke through bad teeth, corroborating the old man's story, still drunk enough to be bold but shrewdly measuring the cop's patience too.

When Landon looked across the room, Margaret had reached the counter and was speaking to the nun. In a moment he heard the old girl's surprisingly firm voice paging Dr. Dunn on the intercom. From the ceiling speakers the doctor's name boomed and echoed down the corridor. Margaret walked back and joined him, standing dry-eyed and remote. They stood by a wall, enclosed in their own thoughts and with the disinterested ease of a couple long married and accustomed to standing in lines together.

After a moment a nurse touched Margaret lightly on the arm. "Miss Beauchamp?"

"Yes."

"Sister Annette said you were looking for Dr. Dunn. That's him coming down the hall now."

They turned to see a short chubby man making his way around people, his British-cut tweed suit open to a paunchy vest. He was blowing his nose vigorously as he marched along, cleaning out the airholes and dusting off the end with a bunched-up handkerchief, which he then stuffed into a rear pocket. A no-nonsense, busy little fellow, thought Landon. All nerve wires and kinetic energy. Probably quick and smart with the knife. Margaret advanced to meet him, a slow melancholy figure in dark cloth. The little doctor was using his hands to demonstrate something or other. What was it? A blocked valve? A passage that clotted? The frayed wall of an artery that had finally given way under pressure? We did all we could. The doctor shook Margaret's hand and walked away. She returned to Landon at her slow deliberate pace.

"Well, she's gone," Margaret said.

"I'm very sorry."

"It's so strange and sudden." Margaret almost smiled as she reflected on the queerness of these daily facts. Isn't life really the dickens though! Landon could detect no remorse, only stunned awareness.

"You leave in the morning and she tells you to put on your rubbers because the radio said snow." Margaret stopped. "My mother treated me like a child . . . You come back in the evening and she's gone . . ."

Here today, gone tomorrow. That old saying passed through Landon's mind. But flippant or not, it was true, wasn't it? All those old saws were true. You could write the story of life in clichés and you would bear true witness. Margaret shook her head, still disbelieving, still harpooned by the great fact.

"I must get in touch with Father Duffy. And I have to sign some papers and phone the funeral home. There's so much to do . . . Will you wait?"

"Of course. Don't even ask."

"I've put you to so much trouble."

"Please . . ." He pressed her hand and she gave him such a look of gratitude that he felt truly grateful to be there and helping. Was his own lonely heart wandering out to the wars again?

"I won't be long."

"I've got all night."

When she left for the business office somewhere in the bowels of the building, Landon stepped out onto the platform where the ambulances were unloaded. After these claustrophobic smells he needed air. The place was temporarily deserted and he could stand unheeded by the door. The wind had dropped and now a teeming soundless snowfall was covering the city. It fell relentlessly and thick and fast as if the sky itself were eager to be emptied of its burden. And now his melancholy neighbor was relieved of her burden too! There'd be no more wheeling that chair through the streets to seven o'clock Mass. This strange neighbor of his, this dark lady. She appeared to be an honest soul, and perhaps she had spoken the truth in hoping her mother was dead. The old lady could have been a tyrant. Often invalids are quarrelsome and hard to live with. Sometimes there was much to endure, and the best heart in the world could shrivel and harden with time. He recalled a line or two of poetry. "Too long a sacrifice/ Can make a stone of the heart." That was Yeats, wasn't it? Oh, his bygone poetry days! When he had read aloud to Vera during the courting ceremonies. Both of them were often tipsy from too much wine, but he did read well; it was the actor in him, and Vera was impressed. Actually she thought he knew more than he really did about books and ideas. He never told her otherwise. But they weren't bad times while they lasted. Landon was sure that Ginny had been conceived during one of those soirées. That swanky apartment at Benvenuto Place, and Vera always prepared a fine supper, which was eaten late in the evening. On mild spring nights they opened the French doors and looked down to Avenue Road and the streaming lights of traffic. People going nowhere while they sipped their coffee and Grand Marnier, and a leaner Landon warbled from *A Treasury of Romantic Verse*. On the phonograph Vera's heartburning piano music. The woman was crazy for those nineteenth-century Russian exhibitionists who killed you with their sobbing cadenzas. Tchaikovsky. Rachmaninoff. Rubinstein. Moscowski. They tried to wring you dry with their trills and flourishes. For Vera those evenings were cultural events, seminars with the Great Books. And Landon couldn't wait to get her into the sack. But what was it the Indians said? That was all many moons ago.

But what of that sad little adventure on the snowy evening last December? Well—it had changed things for him, brought another person into his life. But really it was a bad script; the lonely schoolteacher meets the middle-aged salesman. It came off the same cob of corn that was served up on TV dramas billed as specials on Christmas Eve. Ninety minutes of poop sponsored by some giant corporation that manufactures electronic eyes and bugging devices. Yes, a bad script, though that comically absurd business about the hat was a nice touch. Could he have written a better one? This was doubtful, for when it came to bad TV scripts, Landon was no slouch. He had a closetful of them, yellowing and musty, tied in bundles and secured by grocery string. Sentimental comedies about old folks living with their children, problem plays about the black family moving into your neighborhood or the schoolteacher putting thirty years' service on the line in defense of a new biology text. Well, at least his heart had been in the right place, though as a matter of fact message dramas were in during the fifties. After the madness of the McCarthy years, the big American networks were pumping forth liberal sentiments every night. Why ignore trends? And so he had tried his hand at everything, even adaptations. In a singular moment of madness he had written to somebody representing Ibsen's estate and asked for permission to rewrite *A Doll's House* for the box. He must have been in a kind of fever during those years. And all that hope and travail? It all came back in large manila envelopes with his own handwritten address across the front and the printed notes from Philco Playhouse, U.S. Steel Hour, General Motors Presents, Studio One, Playhouse 90. Goodbye to his dream of becoming another Rod Serling. Another Reg Rose.

He knew now that his trouble began when he scored early with his first play, sixty minutes of guff which he sold to the short-lived Première Playhouse. It was his brief moment in the sun, and there followed three years of sunstroke and fainting spells during which he actually believed he was a writer. Still, during those brief weeks in the winter of 1954 when they were preparing "A Window on the Heart" for production, he was living it up, basking in the fierce light of flattery from strangers. And Vera Hall was there too. With her blue-black straight hair severely scissored across the brow in bangs, and her sharp nose and the cobalt eyes; a queenly presence in skirts and cashmere sweaters and black stockings. With a snooty English accent picked up after one year at Oxford. She was trying to gain a toehold in show biz by working as some sort of girl Friday at the CBC studios. Landon saw her each day as he went to script conferences with that conceited English queer Basil Johnson. To satisfy his own artistic yearnings, Basil insisted on changing a word here, a phrase there. However, Landon himself was not without vanity. When he marched into the studios with his burnished mane ablaze under the klieg lights (he wore his hair long even during those brush-cut fifties), he knew they were looking. His mother always said he reminded her of the old matinee idol Sonny Tufts. And one March night he took Vera Hall to his three poor rooms on Cecil Street and they watched his play on an old square brown seventeen-inch Philco. It was a live production, and by a miracle no one muffed a line. In fact, the acting was better than the script. It concealed several weak spots. Afterward there was a party at Blanche Ritchie's, and Squire Hughes, standing in the center of the living room with one hand on his paisley waistcoat, proposed a toast in champagne. Those old Toronto bluebloods! They thought they'd bagged a genius, an artistic type, someone to enrich their watered juices. The next day the television columnists called "Window" (as it became known) "A warm and loving look at boyhood life," "A rich and sympathetic portrayal of that difficult time during which worlds collide." Only one bad-tempered man saw the truth and labeled it, among other things, "A soggy biscuit which might be taken with warm milk before bedtime for those viewers who suffer from insomnia." But that fellow liked nothing anyway and was forever making wisecracks. Those hectic days with Vera taking Landon to parties and introducing him to her friends, squeezing his biceps and whispering into his ear when she knew others were looking. For a few weeks there was wild talk of a Broadway production. Well, it had happened to others, hadn't it? One day some character named Nat phoned from Hollywood and asked Landon if he had any scripts hanging around? Did he have scripts? The madness set in.

To begin with, he and Vera were married. At an intimate evening ceremony at St. Jude on the Hill, where they stood before a frowning Canon Wilkins, who disapproved of Landon. The good man had known Vera since childhood, felt responsible for her spiritual life after the death of her parents, and knew that she carried Landon's seed within her. His perfectly spherical bald head glowed like a nimbus beneath the votive candles, and Landon, in blue serge, avoided the severe accusing eyes. But the weather smiled and they stepped from the old vaulted church into a leafy May twilight. Out to the west on St. Clair Avenue they could see a flushed and dusty sky. In Vera's Thunderbird they drove alone to a wedding supper, pursued down the street by Blanche, running on her spiky legs, stopping finally in the middle of the road to blow frantic kisses.

They moved into a new apartment building on St. George Street, overlooking several large dark-brick Victorian homes, college fraternity houses with their Greek-lettered brass plates near the doorway. There were elegant Sunday breakfasts, with Vera dishing up the melon and the eggs Benedict, serving him in a saffron dressing gown which sometimes parted nicely to reveal a rich inner thigh the color of honey. Landon frankly could not believe his good fortune. In the evenings, of course, there was poetry and the rhapsodic Russians. Sometimes a few of Vera's friends from the CBC would visit, mostly pale young women in black accompanied by effeminate men who drank Dubonnet and talked contemptuously of Toronto. There were drives in the countryside with Blanche and Hughes. Winging through the

Albion hills with Hughes at the wheel of his Humber, driving with his hands protected by leather gloves, English-style. They often stopped at a rustic inn for tea and buttered muffins. In the sack Landon and Vera slept naked, and as the summer wore away, he often stroked her mildly swelling belly, marveling at the mystery of life itself. For her part, Vera discovered that she too had a flair for words and won a transfer from the production department into advertising. A few weeks later she accepted a job with Cohen, Crawford, and Aisley. She was soon handling a large lingerie account for them. Landon could now read his wife's prose on streetcar posters and in family magazines. But he was making a poor fist of his own writing. During the autumn he sat at the table and brooded over a silent typewriter, absently watching the leaves fall to the street, where they were stirred and sent flying by passing automobiles. He prayed for rain, a pathetic fallacy, but cheerful weather persisted for weeks and the sky remained irredeemably blue, a giant overturned translucent bowl which poured light through the windows onto his belea-guered head. Outside on the leaf-strewn lawns of the fraternity houses, the college boys shagged footballs back and forth, big well-fed fellows, crew-cutted and wearing Bermuda shorts and white bucks. The music from their Friday night dances drifted across the street and into the apartment.

When the snow fell, he walked the streets, musing like a scien-tist, trying to come up with tricky plots and new angles but often lapsing into dangerous reverie too, glamorous daydreams of riches and fame honestly won. Meanwhile, the manila envelopes came through the mail chute with monotonous regularity.

One Sunday in January, at six o'clock in the evening, his daughter was born and he rejoiced. The obstetrician, another old family connection, was a big horsy fellow who laughed with a mouthful of gold fillings. He was a kidder and a toucher, and he felt the bones in Landon's back as they walked into the hospital cafeteria after the delivery. He gripped his coffee mug in thick heavy-knuckled hands, and Landon sat, transfixed by those great paws which had so recently been intimate with his wife's parts. It was, to say the least, amazing. According to the doctor, it had been an easy birth, and he flashed his gold grinders at Landon. "She's a breeder, my boy. Not like that sister of hers. I had to open her up to get that Howard into the world. Don't know now if it was worth it, if you get what I mean. But little Vera. Just like my first wife, God rest her soul. Fine elasticity in the pelvic region. Oh my yes," the doctor said, chuckling into his coffee mug. "That little girl was built to breed. She could have a dozen with no trouble at all."

Landon dutifully feathered the nest for mother and child; laying in a store of baby food, assembling an elaborate crib (a big job for him), and buying some extravagant musical toys which he felt his daughter might one day enjoy. He was a proud father and on fine afternoons strolled about the neighborhood pushing Virginia Ann, who rode in state in a large wicker perambulator with high wire wheels. Hughes Ritchie had imported it from Harrod's in London. But the apartment proved too small for the three of them, and Vera grew restless with motherhood and with Landon. He wasn't producing the goods. At parties people stopped inquiring about "Window" and one or two malicious types asked him if he had sold anything recently. Vera complained about the cost of things and the confining nature of her life and the early summer heat and the odor from his armpits. The baby was colicky and cross, and at nights Landon walked the floors with the crying infant draped across his shoulder. The neighbors phoned the superintendent and they were asked to leave.

At incredible expense they moved to a house on Dunvegan Road and hired Mrs. Boxley, a gray-haired English grandmother, as housekeeper and nanny. Vera returned to her underwear ads at Cohen, Crawford, and Aisley, and Landon took to the attic, a large bare retreat where he studied the beams and rafters of the old house or sat and wrote implausible dialogue, hunched over an empty and abandoned sea chest, which he used as a desk. Below him Mrs. Boxley ran the vacuum cleaner and sang the wartime favorites of Gracie Fields and Vera Lynn. Sometimes, unbeknown to her, Landon (who enjoyed bygone things too) joined in quietly for a chorus of "White Cliffs of Dover" or "A Nightingale Sang in Berkeley Square."

In the evenings he watched the work of other playwrights being produced on the tube or read books borrowed from the public library. *Ten Steps to Successful TV Writing. The Television Writer's Handbook with a Guide to Markets. How to Sell Your Play on TV!* In a small empty room off the kitchen Vera exercised in black leotards and turtleneck sweater to the music of Swan Lake. She was trying to restore her shape after the baby and had resuscitated some childhood ballet lessons. With her arms akimbo, she performed fierce knee bends or twirled about the little room on a light fantastic toe, frowning at a print of Degas's "Fin d'Arabesque" as she chewed a lip in concentration. With her hair tightly drawn against the scalp into a dark bun and that creepy costume, Landon thought she looked angry enough to eat him alive. He knew she was releasing steam too. That fancy jig was also a war dance.

Meanwhile, his work continued to go badly. In desperation he stopped writing plays and began a novel. It was the childhood business again, but a beginning, and it seemed to work. Suddenly he felt himself in the grasp of something mysterious and remarkable. His flagging spirits began to soar as page after page rolled off his machine. Each day he awoke exalted, his vision enlarged by the richness of this experience. He surrendered to its eloquence and felt an immense and holy gratitude toward some secret inner force. They were right, and damn it, you couldn't fool history. It was a tough and demanding life, but the artists were the lucky ones. He wrote with furious haste, confident that he had found the mother lode, the deep source of all creative acts. Beneath his clacking typewriter the old captain's chest seemed to tremble as it yielded its treasure of nouns and verbs, adjectives and adverbs. Vera noticed his reviving spirits too, and it blunted her growing sarcasm. When he told her he was writing a novel, she remained oddly silent. And thus he wrote like a fiend for two weeks, prodigally burning his candle of inspiration at both ends, until the poor stick sputtered and flamed out and died, casting his attic retreat into gloom.

One Friday, when he sat down expecting another good day's work, he suddenly ran into difficulties. Things no longer seemed to fit as neatly as before. In places the writing looked a bit flat and some of the characters uttered improbable remarks. As he read over his work, he recognized several boyhood acquaintances only thinly disguised. And he had drawn a wicked and distorted portrait of one of them, a man named Jack Spaulding whom he had always disliked. If this novel were ever published, Spaulding might sue; perhaps even come from Bay City to Toronto and flatten Landon with one punch. He was now a high-school gym instructor. But there were other things wrong too, terrible things. These words of his were iron pyrite, fool's gold, not the real stuff at all. Deep within, Landon felt ill, truly nauseated. As he read the pages of manuscript, his own words struck like blows to the solar plexus. He felt himself sinking, and like a dying man he deeply craved a new beginning, a fresh start, another chance. But also like a dying man he knew he lacked both the will and the strength. At ten o'clock he fled from the house and, like a fugitive, hid all day in the darkness of a theater, where he sat through several reels of *The Caine Mutiny*, watching, fascinated, as Humphrey Bogart, in the role of that queer duck Queeg, fingered his ball bearings in the witness chair.

On the weekend he tried hard not to think about the novel. He hungered after diversion, anything to keep his mind from wandering back to the sea chest, that Pandora's box. Vera was ill, suffering from a bad cold, and with abiding guilt in his heart Landon slipped from the house on Saturday and saw three more movies. For the rest of the weekend he slumped in front of the TV set, lost in a maze of football and hockey players, singing puppets and trapeze artists, Elmer Fudd and the Balloon Man. In an upstairs bedroom, Vera lay beneath blankets and quilts reading a novel called *Not As a Stranger*. She was peevish and complaining, a poor patient. Landon's marathon television goggling vexed her, and now and then she would call down about the noise. When he brought her aspirins and orange juice, she was ready to fight. "Well, and how's the weekend going, Mr. Intellectual? Have you worked your way through the Mouseketeers yet?" Landon felt sorry for her. She lay abed, perspiring and pale, her sharp little nose reddened and swollen from frequent swipes with Kleenex, her usual vivid eyes mere dead stones. She knew she looked terrible and she resented the fact. It wounded her vanity, made her more vulnerable. After Mrs. Boxley left for the weekend, Landon wisely marked off his territory and mostly kept his distance. To quiet his infant daughter, he played games on the floor, pulling crazy faces and imitating Donald Duck and Mortimer Snerd. In the old high-ceilinged kitchen he opened jars of mashed carrots and veal, and warmed milk on the gas range, always fearing an explosion as his match touched the hissing vapor and burst into a ring of blue flame. But he was glad to be distracted by these simple chores. With his shirt sleeves rolled up past his elbows, he changed sopping diapers, often plunging pins into the flesh of his thumbs, but not doing badly either and learning much. Somehow he kept the peace, and an uneasy calm lay over the house.

On Monday Mrs. Boxley returned, and Landon climbed the stairs to his attic with a heavy heart. With shaking hands he began again to leaf through the manuscript of his novel. Alas, for Friday's judgment was confirmed in spades. Nothing less than a complete rewrite could redeem this stuff. Was it not time to call a halt to this writing business and join the rest of the world in its ordinary pursuits? He had failed, but so what? Many people fail. Better make that most people. Nothing to be particularly ashamed of, and anyway, if you cared to listen, failure could teach you important lessons. Humility, patience, fortitude, and several other high-minded things. But oh—goddamnit and son-of-a-sweet-bitch—it was a painful lesson. Now he must wear this failure before the world like a harlequin suit. He would be in the public stocks with his head through the humbling hole.

Looking down to the street from his high dormer window, Landon cursed his own ineptness. However, he would have to find a job and write at nights and on weekends. This junk would have to go, and he would look for other work, perhaps in advertising or television. But not just yet. It was early December, and now that he had resolved to alter course, there must be time set aside for adjustment. With his devotion to fresh starts, he decided he would look for a job on the first Monday of the New Year. Somehow it seemed symbolically appropriate. Meanwhile, for the rest of the month he could loaf without guilt and ponder these great changes wrought upon his life. He'd tell Vera on New Year's Eve, and he knew she'd be glad to hear it. She had lost faith in whatever talent she had once imagined him to possess, and she was right. Enough was enough. He felt curiously exhilarated. Someone had lifted the world from his shoulders.

Thus began a week in which he did no more than go through the motions of writing. Each morning he smuggled travel books and Ellery Queen mysteries to his retreat. Also potato chips, Nutty Brunch chocolate bars, and fruit. He suddenly acquired a passion for oranges, and after surgically quartering them with a pocket knife would suck them dry, holding them against his teeth like a boxer's mouthpiece. Winter threatened, and the weather was weird and inchoate, with massive dark clouds rolling across the sky, sending forth showers of hail which drummed on the rooftop over Landon's head. The hail would briefly salt the lawns below and then as quickly disappear before a sudden shaft of sunlight. Chewing his orange pieces, Landon read about elephant hunts in Kenya or stared out the window at the congested sky. Vera was slowly recovering but remained shaky and petulant. To maintain a respectable front,

Landon banged away at the typewriter now and again, hammering out lines of comic-strip profanity; asterisks, dollar signs, and percentage marks. Sometimes he composed goofy sentences. *If life is just a bowl of cherries, who picks up the pits?* Or, *I have seen better days but unfortunately have not partaken of them.* In the late afternoon he gathered together these foolish speckled sheets and burned them in the wastepaper basket; the bitter sneaky ritual of an impostor.

On Wednesday morning of that sad week, after tapping out yet another incoherent message to himself, Landon leaned forward to observe Mrs. Boxley leaving the house to shop for groceries. A few minutes later he heard his daughter. Landon cocked an ear. At first it was only the hesitant cry of a child feeling out the atmosphere, waiting for the footsteps that would bring attention. But slowly it gathered force and rose in pitch and intensity to a shrill ear-blasting wail. It filled the air like the siren for all calamities and pierced the plaster and timber to Landon's retreat. It lasted for a minute or so and then stopped. There followed a second of unearthly silence and then the full alert was sounded, the entire city's warning system; the wrenching gasping scream of panic. Landon guessed that Vera must have slapped the child to provoke this tantrum. Those cries were fearful, the real thing, hysteria. He took the stairs two at a time, his mind affrighted by visions of horror. The woman's temper was black and violent. Had she thrown his daughter against a wall? In a moment of rage anything was possible.

Vera was standing in the middle of the living room, holding the screaming child. Covered by a terry-cloth kimono, with powder-blue pompon slippers on her feet. She looked wild, her cheeks flushed and her dark hair damp and matted. The thought flashed through Landon's mind, she's flipped. It runs in the family. But he realized too that this was a moment of terrible humiliating defeat for her. When she spoke, her voice was low, almost a whisper, and charged with such menace and loathing that Landon shuddered, felt her hatred as a palpable shock wave against his heart.

"Will you do something, for God's sakes? Can't you see I'm sick? How can I be expected to cope with this?"

Her eyes were brimming with tears. Landon took the child and held her close against his chest, walking quickly about the room, crooning softly into the small ear and patting her bottom. But she had spent herself and was now slowing down, lapsing into choked sobs. Her face was hot and wet, and through his shirt front Landon felt the tiny rapid heartbeat. He turned angrily toward Vera.

"What did you do to her, for crying out loud? Throw her against the wall? That's Cabbagetown stuff, Vera. It's not supposed to happen up here in this part of town. You people are supposed to be the civilized ones . . . the leaders of the community . . ."

"Oh, you son-of-a-bitch . . . you rotten bastard." She was standing her ground, and the kimono fell open to a bare boob. A tavern wench from the Middle Ages, thought Landon.

"Well, what did you do, then?" he shouted. "The child was hysterical." He was still walking nervously to and fro. How he hated these scenes! They wore him down. He was no good at this wrangling.

"I slapped the child . . . all right?" Vera cried. "I didn't kill her. I gave the child a slap. I'm her mother. She was crying for nothing."

"Oh yes . . . your slaps," said Landon, foolishly persistent, "I know your slaps."

"Oh, fuck off, Fred . . . That's all . . . Just fuck off . . ." She ran from the room, her pompon slippers slapping the floor, a ludicrous sound. A wretched Landon continued his sentry duty back and forth, with the child now gurgling across his shoulder. He knew he had been too hard on her. She was ill and he should have come down to help when he saw Boxley leave. And what had he been doing? Had he been composing a fine sentence, rounding out a crucial chapter? No—amid Nutty Brunch wrappers and orange peel he had been fucking the dog. He vowed he would repent and be more considerate. Look for a job too, and tomorrow, not next year. In the hallway he zipped the child into a snowsuit and placed her in the high-wheeled buggy. A walk in the fresh air would clear his head. Also cool things out.

On the gray and windy street the shriven sinner, wearing his old college jacket with Arts 51 across the back, pushed his daughter past the homes of the wealthy. One blue-haired old gal smiled down at them from her turret window, cocking her head to one side and twiddling her fingers, a delicate addled gesture. Someone had told Landon that she was the wife of a prominent stockbroker. Apparently she was badly cracked, a prisoner in her own castle and stoned most of the day on Bristol Cream sherry. Nevertheless, Landon saluted her. Even greetings from the mad were welcome on such a dismal day. The baby, snugly cocooned and lulled by motion and the keen air, went to sleep. Landon bought papers at a newsstand on St. Clair Avenue and returned home just in time to see Mrs. Boxley coming down the verandah steps, hanging on to the railing and moving sideways. After the fashion of old folks she was being careful; on guard for ice patches which could send you zip on your arse and break bones. Landon was puzzled to see her leaving at this hour.

"Hello, Mrs. Boxley," he said. "Forget something at the store? I can go if you like. Don't mind a bit."

"No thanks, Mr. Landon; no thanks. Mrs. Landon's given me the afternoon off. Says she's feeling much better, though she still looks a little peaked to me. She should take better care of herself, poor dear. And how's our little darling?" Mrs. Boxley bent over the sleeping child and inspected Landon's handiwork. "There's a pet. Now she's got such a lovely color, hasn't she? It's the fresh air what does it. Oh my, yes." She straightened up and adjusted her hat, a knitted orange and brown tam which she wore at a sharp angle along the side of her head like a Highlander.

"Well now . . . I'll be seeing you tomorrow, Mr. Landon. Ta ta . . ."

"Yes, ta ta, Mrs. Boxley. And thanks for everything."

Mrs. Boxley fluttered a hand in farewell and moved off down the street in her watchful shuffling way. A good old brick, thought Landon, and with faith too. A survivor from the blitz. And she'd lost a son in the war. Well, God bless her! Perhaps they were taking advantage of her. Not paying her enough. When he got a job, he'd raise her salary. A few extra bucks slipped into her envelope on Friday night wouldn't hurt. Her husband was a janitor somewhere. He felt refreshed, invigorated by his walk. Perhaps Vera had recovered herself too. She was often penitent and meek after these outbursts. He'd heat some soup, make sandwiches, and apologize. That was a rotten crack about Cabbagetown. Why not open a bottle of wine too? Who knows? Perhaps she might feel in the mood for a little love. It had been a while now and sometimes this worried him. Even before her illness Vera had fallen into the habit of turning her back to his advances. Or outlasting him by reading long novels by the bedroom lamp until he felt too sleepy to wait for the intimacy of darkness. Wasn't it a little early in their marriage for that sort of thing? These sexual doubts. There was always something.

Inside, the house was quiet, a cool dark tomb with only the hall clock ticking away. Landon walked on stockinged feet to the nursery, undressed the sleeping child, and placed her in the crib. In the kitchen and living room he looked for signs of life. There was a stillness in the air. It was charged with an expectancy that excited the imagination and enlivened hopes. Was his wife upstairs, naked and waiting, forgiving all and eager for the sweetmeats of union? In the hallway, the grandfather clock, a grave old machine, slowly marked the passage of time, announcing the quarters, halves, and hours with bongs and chimes. Between these melodious sounds, it ticked and talked. Each second is precious and not to be wasted, said the stately old timepiece to Landon. Below decks, the oil furnace, a converted coal burner, rumbled into business, summoned to life by the thermostats on the walls. This new noise startled Landon and reminded him too of household chores that required attention. That furnace, for instance; it badly needed cleaning and repairs, seemed on the verge of apoplexy when called for duty. It was an intimidating piece of equipment, which Landon had discovered a few weeks after moving in. A fat gray tubular thing which squatted in the middle of the basement, still sooty from its coal-bearing days and with a bewildering series of pipes and nozzles sprouting from its top and sides. It was covered by some wartime fabric that reminded Landon of institution toilet paper. He doubted that it would last the winter and kept his distance. But he knew he should call the oil company before something nasty happened. Of course, when he rented the house, he hadn't bothered to ask about such things, and the real-estate agent had emphasized the large front rooms and fireplaces, volunteering no information on the plumbing and heating. Besides, Vera knew his cousin or somebody. He came from a good family, had impeccable connections. Unfortunately he was crooked. But the furnace could wait for now.

The granddaddy clock tolled the half hour, and Landon climbed the stairs to look for his wife. He searched the bedrooms. Her own bed was freshly made, the sheets tucked smooth and hidden beneath the varicolored patchwork quilt, a Hall family treasure; a wedding gift from some ancient aunt in Boston. The room itself had been tidied up; the invalid's tray of soiled dishes removed and the books neatly stacked on a bedside table. Someone had opened a window, and the curtains billowing before the breeze were then sucked back to cling against the glass. Had she left him then, deserted the ship at last, scooted out the back door while Boxley was making her laborious sidle down the verandah steps? Above his head he heard a long painful creak; the groan of old floorboards suffering the pressure of human weight. Why, she was in the attic—his retreat—and oh Lord, have mercy for the slack and sinning below! He now remembered that he had hurried away, leaving a sheet of paper in the machine.

When he opened the door, she was waiting for him, standing by the window in wavering shadows cast by the bare branches of trees which yielded to the wind. Behind her, this dark and shifting lacework in the white sky. Vera looked triumphant, even masterful, with her arms folded across her chest. She was wearing a long-sleeved violet blouse and tweed skirt with black stockings and high-heeled pumps. She had used cosmetics too, but sparingly; a little blue shadow around the eyes and a thin strip of scarlet on her mouth. The blue-black hair was freshly scissored across the brow. The illness had left her slightly gaunt, ascetic, a pale fierce little inquisitor from the days of the Early Church. In her hand was the evidence, a sheet of his bird tracks. The attic itself looked seedy enough with its orange rind and candy wrappers, the unsmoked cigars obscenely chewed at their ends and the smudged pages of books on Arctic exploration and Australian bushmen. In the air the acrid smell of burned paper and Landon's own stale wind; unhappy human fallout, absently released and lingering now, a silent reminder of his moral ruin. It was poor ground to defend. Vera seemed to be waiting for the right moment, storing up hostile energies, laying out her strategy, mindful of the proper emphasis and thrust. There was so much to say. How to attack? Yes—inside she was seething, but Landon knew that she might blow the whole thing. Appearances aside, there was no room in the Hall temperament for controlled anger. But he realized now that this was why she had sent Boxley home. The servants must not hear family quarrels. Sometimes you had to hand it to these people. Vera finally laid the page of absurd typescript on the sea chest. "And just what the hell is all this, please? Part of the great Canadian novel, I suppose?" Her voice carried its own low venomous pitch, but it was rising. "And how long has this been going on?" She paused and dramatically turned her back to him, looking out the window and shaking her head. "Oh boy . . . am I the laughing stock of some people . . . Not that I can't say I wasn't warned." She turned toward him again, fiercely pale.

"You know, Freddy . . . I thought once that you had some talent. A reasonable assumption. I really did . . . I thought you were serious about this writing business. And I was willing to give you your chance too . . . I thought that you were at least willing to try. I thought . . ."

"Now, hold it. Just a minute, Vera . . ."

"No . . . You just wait a fucking minute, mister. Where do you get off spending weeks up here in this . . . this—" She dismissed his smelly quarters with a brittle snap of her fingers. "—this pig pen . . . Writing this shit!" She grabbed the typescript and dropped it to the floor, where it sailed away slowly like a dead leaf beneath a chair. "Writing? . . . well, let's be honest, for God's sake. Just this once . . . Scribbling nonsense . . . Meanwhile, eating my food."

"Oh, low, Vera. A palpable hit, as they say, but low." He felt his face begin to redden with anger. Oh, the injustice of this was monstrous!

"Well, it's true, isn't it?" She was standing now, arms akimbo, with white little fists bunched against the hipbones. A carefully aimed blow against the jawline could send her sprawling in spectacular fashion. It was tempting, but was he capable of such things?

". . . Well, answer me, goddamnit. All these months, and what have you been doing for Christ's sake?"

"Where did you pick up this language, Vera?" asked Landon. "At boarding school? . . . Trinity College?" She flamed anew.

"Never mind my goddamn language . . . Bums who live off their wives have no business talking about language. That's bloody typical of you, Freddy. Introduce an irrelevant remark. Bloody typical . . . And I'll tell you something else, Mister Writer. Bums who haven't got the guts to be honest about what they're doing have no business passing judgment . . . telling me I'm some kind of Cabbagetown mother . . ." The tears were starting now, the eyes filling up and glistening. Here it comes again, thought Landon. "What do you know about it, anyway?" she cried. "What do you know about anything? Living in some backwoods town most of your life . . . I never had a mother . . . My sister and I . . ."

"All right . . . all right, Vera. Now listen for a minute. There's been a mistake." She struck at a tear with a hard little fist.

"You're damn right there's been a mistake. This bloody marriage has been a mistake."

"Well, you may have something there," said Landon softly. His anger was subsiding as suddenly as it had risen, retreating to its depths, sleepy beast, where it could seldom be roused to fight. But she was forever bringing up this orphan business. We were just two little rich girls pitched into the cruel world. All right, he felt sorry for her. She'd had her difficult times and had probably managed better than most. Certainly better than her sister. She was made of sterner stuff. Now Vera had turned to the window again and seemed calmer too.

"Now please don't argue about any of this, Freddy, because it's all settled. I've phoned Blanche, and Hughes is coming over at two to help me move out. I'm taking Ginny, of course, and I hope you won't be foolish about any of that. You know you don't stand a chance." She turned again toward him.

"We need some time apart. You can see that for yourself. If, and when, you get a decent job, we can see what happens.

Until then . . . well . . . you can stay in this place and do your work . . ." She swept past him and out the door. Landon stood for a moment before he realized that his hands were shaking. The beast was not yet in its lair. He shouted down the stairs after her.

"Irony was never exactly one of your strong points, was it, Vera?" Always too late with the smart retort, the clever comeback. "I don't even know what your strong points are," he muttered, jamming one of the dead cigars into his mouth. "What a fucking mess this place really is!"

At two o'clock Hughes arrived in his Humber, clearly embarrassed by all this fuss. It wasn't good form, this squabbling, and he moved swiftly about in his small patent-leather shoes, carrying luggage to the cars and smiling weakly, avoiding Landon's eyes. He was the innocent bystander, caught witnessing the accident and forced to take sides, an uneasy position for an equivocal man. Besides, he liked Landon. Landon himself insisted on being a nuisance and sat on a suitcase in the middle of things, smoking a cigar and in a mild queasy fog, having quickly downed the remains of a liqueur bottle: some damn French syrup that clung to the roof of his mouth and coated his throat like cough medicine. It was the only alcohol he could find in the house, and he now regretted his discovery. He felt he could easily retch on the Turkish carpet.

Hughes, deferential and wary, moved around him, employing a series of polite addresses and requests: "Excuse me, Freddy, dear boy," and "I'm sorry, old man, but could I have that piece of luggage you're sitting on?"

"Of course, Hughes," Landon said, removing the cigar from his mouth and looking for another seat. He sympathized with the little man. Vera was magnificent, aloof and haughty, striding about with the day's work sheet.

"Yes . . . that too, Hughes. Please!" She always comes on like the head nurse, thought Landon, watching her through the cigar smoke as she carefully wrapped Ginny in a new pink snowsuit. The child was still sleeping, doubtless exhausted by her tantrum. She offered only a tiny moan as she was lifted and carried to the Thunderbird.

Alone in the house, Landon heard the car doors slam and the motors start up, Vera goosing the accelerator as she always did before takeoff. The bitch has always had a heavy foot, said Landon to himself. Strictly an academic opinion, of course, since he himself did not drive. The sound of the engine noises revving up and then fading finally into space and silence. He sat alone in the deep quiet of aftermath until startled suddenly by the mournful bonging of the old clock, whose solemn notes traveled unerringly toward his nerve ends. He softly swore an oath, vowed he would steal the leaded brass weight and dismantle the chain, render that gussied-up old cuckoo clock *hors de combat* before he left the house.

For three months he lived alone, a writer writing in a world unto himself. The old house ticked and creaked and sometimes seemed to lean with the wind on stormy days. In his attic retreat he chewed cold apples and wrote bad plays. The world passed him by, and he returned the favor. Vera had taken a leave of absence from her job and with Ginny had gone to Nassau to spend the winter with an old aunt. In the spring she returned to a pale and hungry Landon. He had lost twenty pounds and was ready to go to work. They moved into a new apartment and Vera got him a job. In a small advertising agency which handled accounts that no one else seemed to care much about. "Well, you've got to start somewhere, Freddy!" That was her line at the time. He did all right too. For several months he helped to edit *The Urn*, a magazine for funeral furnishers and undertakers. He wrote the copy and laid out the columns of advertising for silk-lined caskets, embalming fluids, and Packard hearses. Landon, smiling in his kitchen, remembered one enterprising fellow from Los Angeles. A tailor named Hagerman! Hagerman wrote his own copy and submitted it each month along with his check. It was always the same, an off-the-rack special on attendants' apparel. He must have bought a warehouse full of the stuff. Probably hot goods. *Name the Size of Your Guys and Economize. One Morning Coat. One Pair Striped Trousers. One Pair Gray Suede Gloves. Act* NOW *and get* ABSOLUTELY FREE. *An LP of Your Organ Favorites.* ALL THE GREAT MASTERS. *Bach. Handel. Victor Herbert. Don't Delay.* SPECIAL LIMITED OFFER.

In those days he arose early to work on new plays. He was brimming with ideas, confident that he could break through again. Another winter descended upon them. And those skies at dawn, with the light struggling to elbow out the darkness, while Landon's reading lamp burned through the breakfast hour. But this early morning routine so fatigued him that by the afternoon he was nodding over his coffin ads and his boss laid down hints. He tried the evenings, sitting at the kitchen table in their new large apartment. But Ginny was young and playful, too full of beans to ignore. After she was in bed, Landon couldn't concentrate. Behind him he heard only the dry thin rustle of *The New Yorker* being quickly leafed through by someone bored. The noise of the typewriter gave Vera headaches and awoke the child. What was he trying to do? Take the best years of her life from her? After these outbursts Vera often took Ginny and spent the night at Blanche's, while Landon hugged cold pillows. Those grim times! For three more years they gnawed at each other's bones, until Vera moved out for good. And one day Landon opened his mail and found a letter from a lawyer. At the agency he was given a new account, Caledonia Stationery, a small greeting-card firm that could no longer afford to hire its own verse writers. He worked in a tiny office overlooking King Street. On boiling July days he sipped Orange Crush through a straw and sent out Christmas greetings to a languid perspiring hemisphere. On stormy December afternoons he watched the pigeons seeking shelter from the wind beneath the cornices and gargoyles of the old buildings. Or looked down on the crowds of Christmas shoppers below and typed out quatrains on Easter bunnies. He and Hattie Wilson! Good old Hattie! Fifteen years older than Landon and stout, built like the farm girl she once was. Years before she had fled her father's acres and run away to Toronto with a soldier who then jilted her. She stayed on to write valentines. Hattie consoled Landon, who was suffering. On Friday nights after work they drank beer at the Towne Tavern, and one evening Hattie took Landon home and gave him a valentine, surprising him with high jinks from a sex manual. Was it not called *Adventures in Love*? But Landon's heart was not in it, and on Monday morning they decided to be just friends in the card business.

They worked at desks in the same office. There were verses for Mom and Dad, marriages, anniversaries, get-well greetings, birth announcements. There were also notes of sympathy, messages of condolence for the bereaved. These were Landon's favorites and he worked over them with care. His experience on *The Urn* came in handy. And these messages were in tune with his suffering spirit. He felt weighed down by heavy griefs. His marriage was in ruins and his little daughter was now living under another roof. The tone of these sympathy notes suited his temper and situation. Smoking a meditative pipe, he combed the Scriptures, stealing from the prophets and other seriousminded men. *My harp also is turned to mourning and my organ into the voice of them that weep.* He was good at it, and the people at Caledonia were pleased. Their busy little sales manager, Earle Cramner, thought Landon had a great future in the stationery business. He was after him to quit writing poetry and do a real man's job. Get out on the road and sell. Somebody named Ed Finegan was retiring and they needed a new man. That Cramner! Landon could see him hustling primitive washing machines or cream separators to prairie farmers in the twenties. Cramner came in for the copy each Friday afternoon, stuffing the pages into his briefcase and snapping shut the buckle. Sometimes he stayed to talk, sitting on the edge of Landon's desk, swinging a leg of gartered silk hose back and forth.

"When the hell are you going to stop writing these hymns, lad?" Cramner would say. "Listen. Take it from Earle Cramner. I've seen a lot of men come and go in this business, believe you me. Well . . . Twenty-five years! You can't ignore the experience. And I'm telling you, you can't miss. Ninety percent of the stationery buyers are women. A big good-looking fellow like you! Why, you'll knock them cold. Only, don't knock them up! It's bad for business. But you'll get plenty of that, laddie, and no fear. Some of the gals out in those prairie towns. They just live for our visits. It's the high point of their year. Why, you're wasting your time here, the best years of your life. Get out and see the country." It was tempting. A change. Another fresh start. The idea of travel greatly appealed to him. Get away. His life had grown stale. He recognized here a family trait, a weakness: the old Lindstrom compulsion to flee when things got too hot. He thought of his own mother, now living in California, having abandoned her small-town Ontario life and started anew. Lord—how many years ago was that? And what hell had been raised! His father never really did recover. That lonely embittered man. He wouldn't even allow her name to be mentioned now. But she couldn't take any more. Landon could see that now, and long ago he had forgiven her. This tendency to take a powder. It was probably in the blood. But Vera had done some running of her own. In the spring of 1961, Vera, freshly divorced, went to New York with Ginny, having had no trouble getting a transfer to the parent office of her agency. And her underwear ads were sensational. Sales were rocketing. While Landon gravely pondered his epitaphs. And Cramner kept after him.

One noon hour Cramner took him to the Caledonia Building a few blocks away. It was early summer and the streets were crowded with shirt-sleeved businessmen and office girls walking arm in arm. Love was in the air, and Landon hungered after life. The sunlight streamed down between the buildings, and vendors sold flowers from pushcarts. Cramner bought a carnation for his buttonhole and offered one to Landon, but he couldn't bring himself to wear a flower, though his heart was brimming like a floodtide. Cramner darted through the crowd like a Baghdad thief, a pushy cosmopolitan haste surrounding his every move. Landon had to hurry to keep up, and he felt foolish and clumsy rushing after the little man.

The Caledonia offices were located down a side street in an old building blackened by a century of the city's smoke and grime. The first two floors were filled with the racketing sound of printing presses. It was straight from the pages of Dickens's novels, and Landon stood to one side, with his hands behind his back, watching doubtfully as elderly ladies tapped away at great black Underwoods, carrying their work in wire baskets to a composing machine at the end of the room. This ancient device hummed and throbbed, attended by a small spry man who jumped about, managing somehow to keep his sleeves out of the maw of the machine with the aid of rubber armbands. Seated at the machine's keyboard was a washed-out looking fellow (was he thirty or fifty? wondered Landon). He wore a denim apron smudged by years of grease and oil. The June sunshine struggled through the tall blackened windows, casting only bars of weak light across the man's sparse gray hair. And here/Only Winter Light/ Through the turning/ Of the Seasons, mused the tombstone poet, feeling sorry for the fellow. But Cramner hurried him through. "Freddy, I want you to see the executive and sales offices. They're upstairs, and that's where you'll be hanging your hat if and when you decide to join us. Which I sincerely hope you will do, believe you me." Why had he listened to that bustling little fraud? But he did listen and he moved into the Essex Arms too, dragging these old scripts with him, though why he did so eluded him. They were only moldering in the closet. Yet they probably did no harm, and in a way they symbolized old ambitions. Sometimes he fetched forth the shooting script of "A Window on the Heart" and looked at his own words, scratched out and changed by Basil Johnson's fountain pen; the ink browning now and the cursive small and lady-like. But some of those plays weren't bad, and perhaps if he had fought a little harder . . . Wheedled, cajoled, bullied, pounded desks, stamped his feet, and wept. He had seen others do this. A pushier man might have had his way and climbed a rung or two. Certainly Basil Johnson could have been leaned on a little harder in those days. Landon still followed his career in the entertainment pages of the newspapers. Basil was now directing celebrities in Hollywood TV specials. It was big business and he was making big money, living in Sherman Oaks with other CBC refugees, swimming before breakfast in his pool. While Landon sat in his nutshell kitchen in Toronto, worrying about his shrinking bank account, sipping cold Sanka.

The creaking and groaning of the elevator awakened him from his reverie, and he arose and walked to the window in his living room. Another daily ritual! Margaret came out the front door and went down the steps of the building. As she passed beneath him, she looked up and smiled, and at his post by the window Landon blew her a kiss from an outstretched palm. This affair of the heart was still a secret to the neighborhood, though he guessed that one or two in the building suspected something fishy. Margaret insisted upon discretion, couldn't bear to have the neighbors thinking anything was amiss. Landon couldn't see that it mattered much. She knew no one and he was acquainted with only one or two, and anyway people now kept to themselves and left you to your own fate. Hard on lonely souls but probably correct behavior for downtown living. If you wanted chumminess, you could always move to the suburbs. Still, she was a teacher of English in a high school and wagging tongues could mean trouble. One had to be careful, she insisted, and so, although she frequently visited him, she was nervous and tense for the first hour, fearful that she had been seen entering forbidden premises.

It had always been like this, everything shrouded in mystery. Since the day of the old woman's funeral when Landon had stood with a handful of mourners, mostly Margaret's teacher friends, watching the priest sprinkle holy water onto the casket. The deep serenity of those burial grounds under the leafless trees. It was calming to the spirit. A snowy day with large light flakes falling soundlessly, covering the shoulders of dark overcoats. They softly fell upon Landon's coppery hair too, and he brushed them away with a bare hand, feeling the dampness soaking his scalp. Beyond the trees and headstones he heard the traffic noises: the streetcars rumbling and swaying in the grooves of their tracks, the blare of automobile horns, the hearkening cries of motion and life. People about their tasks and amusements heedless of this finality. And why shouldn't they be, he thought, squinting up at the swollen slate-colored sky. Life is for the living, and this old woman's journey was now ended. The priest nodded to a young attendant who was standing on the carpet of kelly-green artificial grass. The attendant's back was ramrod stiff and his gray-gloved hands were crossed behind his back. Was he wearing a pair of Hagerman's pants? wondered Landon, looking down at his wet brogues and trying not to smile as he thought about that crafty customer. Hagerman! A man of his times certainly. An opportunist. On the prowl for new ways to make a buck. Forever turning sows' ears into silk purses. He was no doubt a desperate character, probably in the rackets. However, his checks had never bounced. But Harvey Hubbard had once told Landon that the mafiosi were the most honorable gents when it came to legitimate business deals. They craved respectability, wouldn't dream of cheating you. The attendant's shoe discreetly pressed a button, gears engaged, and the casket descended slowly, a gentle gravitation, the last ride of all. One or two could not help leaning forward to watch it go.

Afterward the mourners stood around, talking in low voices and pressing Margaret's hand before moving off to their cars, which soon were rounding the circular drive, their headlights turned on and their tail pipes smoking into the air. Left alone, Landon walked over to Margaret, who introduced him to the priest, a small severe-looking man in his late forties who glared out at the world from behind rimless glasses. Today he even appeared angry with his Maker and several times looked sharply up beyond the trees as if remonstrating with Him for the weather. Meanwhile, he wiped at his high streaming brow with a handkerchief before clamping a flat dark hat upon his head. This was her friend Duffy, though he didn't look too friendly to Landon. He looked cranky and unsparing, a tough little Irish Jesuit who carried about him that chill grudging air of enforced celibacy. He was probably murder in the confession box. Margaret had obviously told him about Landon and his kindness, but the priest was still suspicious and sternly regarded the salesman from behind his schoolmaster's specs. Probably senses an intruder, thought Landon, a Protestant violator. These ones never let you forget the Reformation. Still, he invited this cold little man of God back to his apartment for a glass of wine, though he was frankly relieved when the priest said he couldn't make it. He had another mass to say within the hour, and as if to underline the urgency of his calling, he flipped back the sleeve of his coat and glanced at his watch, strapped to his thin wrist by a band of wide black leather, the unarguably masculine bracelet of a truck driver or a seaman.

Outside the cemetery gates on St. Clair Avenue, Landon hailed a cab. It was driven by a young bearded maniac who manned the wheel with smoldering fury in his heart. Was everyone mad at the general situation today? wondered Landon, clinging with one hand to the wall strap and bracing the palm of the other hand against the seat, hanging on for dear life as they rocketed through the late-afternoon traffic. St. Clair Avenue was clogged with trucks and streetcars, and the impatient driver swung right and plunged southward on Lansdowne Avenue. A sullen fellow, thought Landon, and with no time to curse other drivers either; the anger translated immediately into action. When he climbed into the car, Landon had noticed some paperbacks on the driver's seat. Sorel's *Reflections on Violence, The Greening of America*. Excellent reading for young paranoiacs. Was the fellow an angry revolutionary? No, probably just a university student boning up for a test between fares. But the world was truly a dangerous place and this guy could kill you. They were in the Italian district, sweeping past the rows of rooming houses and the small tobacco and grocery shops. On street stands by the shop entrances the baskets of chestnuts and melons were filling up with snow. At a crosswalk they narrowly missed an old woman making her way across the street. However, Landon was too timid to object and instead sat back, studying Margaret out of the corner of his eye, conscious of their knees touching as they swayed and bumped against each other. Margaret, lost in her thoughts, stared out at the bleak winter street. All in black, of course, mysterious as a woman of the East behind her veil, the handsome legs encased in dark stockings. This blackness! The color of mourning, but also how venereal! How else to account for the sexual enticements of black undergarments? Merchants had always done a brisk trade in Merry Widow corsets, black garter belts, and brassieres the color of night. The old sex business. It was always stirring. But she fascinated him. There had been no relatives at the funeral and he found this curious. He asked about it, hoping she wouldn't think him too nosy. There were aunts and uncles and cousins, she told him. In Montreal. During these last few years, however, her mother had withdrawn into herself, overcome by rancor and pain. After a difficult life she was confined to a wheelchair with crippling arthritis. It embittered her, turned her against everyone. She wished only to die, though this was a sin and she regularly confessed it to the priests, who warned her of the perils of self-indulgence. At first, relatives had been sympathetic, but she insulted them outrageously. She must have hated their vitality, Margaret said. She revived old grudges, resurrected family disputes of long ago. There were quarrels and ugly name-calling. She and her mother moved to Toronto to start a new life. "We are Poles," said Margaret quietly, gazing out at the snow, "and Poles do not forget. They will hate her even in the grave, spit on her memory. You see, they are all my father's people and they always felt that he married beneath him. They think she tricked him into marrying her. There was some talk about a false pregnancy. I don't know the details. My father and my grandfather ran a jewelry business in Cracow before the war. We were well-off, quite prosperous really. My mother came to work in his shop. As one of his clerks. Of course, my father fell in love with her. She was a very beautiful woman once. And my father . . . I don't know, perhaps he was flattered by her attentions. He was very plain, poor man, almost ugly. And this beautiful woman . . . Well . . . Still, to my uncles and aunts Mother was always just a clerk . . . a milliner's daughter. I don't know. Perhaps if they had left her alone. But she had a great capacity for resentment too, and she was proud. For a while we had to live off their charity. It was not very pleasant . . ." Landon watched her closely and listened, fascinated by all this. When they reached Essex Street, he paid off the driver, tipping him too generously after his reckless antics. He helped Margaret from the taxi, and they stood for a moment on the sidewalk.

"I hope you'll come up to my place for some supper!" said Landon. 'Or at least a glass of wine. A little brandy. This has been a rough day for you."

"Thank you, Frederick. Perhaps I will. Can I get something at Kneibel's? Some cheese or cold cuts? I'm not very hungry."

"Don't worry about the food, please. I have plenty. Well . . . Look at me! Do I look underfed?" She smiled as he splayed his fingers against the front of his coat. "There's always food. Come along now." He took her arm, feeling the firmness of the flesh beneath his fingertips as he guided her up the stone steps. He paused before opening the door. Is it my imagination, he asked himself, or am I falling in love?

In his kitchen he stood at the counter in an old cardigan, chopping onions, mushrooms, and green peppers; sprinkling them into an egg mixture in the large black skillet. While the omelette was cooking, he opened a bottle of red wine and sliced some rye bread. He felt expansive, even gay, and worried a little about the appropriateness of this humor. He knew that she was not greatly mourning the loss of her mother, but after all, it was the day of a funeral and no time to be humming old show tunes, as he caught himself doing a few times. Yet it had been months since he had entertained a lady and he could not help this swelling in his heart. While he cooked, Margaret wandered about the apartment, stopping by his small bookcase to inspect the titles, coming often to stand by the kitchen doorway.

"Can I not do something? I feel so waited upon."

"Exactly how you should feel too. You're my guest. I want you to relax and enjoy your wine. Prepare your appetite for one of Landon's great masterpieces. An old recipe, preserved through the ages and given to me in confidence by a friend in Paris . . . a famous chef."

"Is this true?" She raised her dark eyebrows.

He couldn't bear to kid her. "No . . . not really . . . a joke, Margaret. I've never been to Paris."

"Ah . . ." She smiled.

"You like to joke, don't you, Frederick?"

"Well." He stopped. "Yes . . . I suppose I do. A lifetime habit, really. In school I was a fat child. And cowardly too, I'm afraid. I used to get out of scrapes by pulling funny faces. Another kid and me. When they had us backed against the wall, we broke them up with a story or a joke . . . Still, I hope you don't think I'm being callous about your mother. I don't mean . . ."

". . . No, no . . . please. This is exactly what I need." He set up a card table in the living room and covered it with an old but clean tablecloth. "Now, will you look at this tablecloth, for God's sake!" He poked two fingers through a hole. "Well, a plate should cover that. I'm behind in my mending, Margaret, though I shouldn't be. I'm out of work these days."

"Oh, I'm so sorry," she said. "That is sad. A man should have work to do. You are a salesman, I understand? Someone told me that . . . Mr. Kneibel, I believe . . ."

"Yes. Greeting cards. You know the stuff. Roses are red, violets are blue. As a matter of fact—" He laid the plates and cutlery on the table, wondering how much to tell. "—I used to write that junk."

"Oh . . . a poet too." She seemed delighted.

"Ha . . . well, hardly a poet, Margaret, but hold on . . . my omelette."

He seated her and served the food with a flourish. He knew he was being corny, but this exaggerated courtliness and mild clowning did no harm and seemed to please her. She ate his savory omelette almost greedily, and afterward they sat on his sofa like old friends. Landon poured brandy into the coffee. Am I comforting this woman or planning a seduction? he wondered. She had obviously enjoyed the meal, and the wine had left her flushed, a little more spirited. Landon asked permission, then lighted a cigar, admiring her bosom as she leaned forward to sip her doctored coffee.

"You were born in Poland then?" he asked fishing for her story, eager for details of her past.

"Oh yes." She sat back crossing her legs and stroking the hair away from her face. "That was a long time ago."

"And how did you find your way to Canada?" asked Landon. "That is, if you don't mind me asking."

"Oh, it's an old story, Frederick, and a familiar one. The old war business. It happened to so many."

"Yes. Perhaps. But not to me. I've lived such an ordinary life."

"Oh, I don't believe you."

"It's true," he said. "But you have been in Canada many years now?"

"Oh yes." She paused. "I think I will have a cigarette."

"Of course. I didn't know you smoked."

"Only sometimes."

She reached down to her handbag and brought out a small silver cigarette case. Landon held the match close to her face, amazed by the soft glow it cast upon her skin. She handled the cigarette awkwardly, never inhaling but quickly expelling great bursts of smoke, like a child experimenting with tobacco. Her fingers searched the end of her tongue for stray bits.

"Well . . . what is there to tell? When the war came, I was with my mother in Geneva. We had been holidaying for most of that summer. Nineteen thirty-nine. Oh, I hate self-pity, Frederick, I can't stand it. It's so . . . so wasteful. But that was the last truly happy time of my life. And I remember it so well, every detail. I was ten years old, a clumsy spoiled child and quite ugly . . . long braids down to my waist. I was rude to the waiters in the hotel . . . a terrible child, really. Of course I thought I could have anything in the world I wanted, and my father tried very hard to see that I did. I remember . . . there was a boy, a little Swiss who worked with his father on a boat. They took tourists for rides on the lake. I often wonder if he still poles that little boat around the lake. Perhaps with a son of his own now. He was such a handsome little fellow then, in his leather breeches and apron, with a bright red shirt and a little cap. With such sturdy brown legs, standing in the back of the boat like a gondolier. He was so proud to be helping his father. Of course, he paid no attention to me, but I worshipped him and was always after my father to take me on boat rides. I think I must have worshipped that summer too. Those mountains. They surrounded us, guarded us, kept out the rest of the world where real life was going on. And the sky and the lake . . . so blue. You know, I can't remember it raining once that summer, though of course it must have. But my father was worried much of the time. He tried not to show it. He wanted us to have a good time, but at dinner or in the evening, sitting in one of the wicker chairs on the hotel verandah, watching the sunset or reading the papers, he would brood and look terribly unhappy. It was the Germans of course. The newspapers were full of the German business, and he was worried about Grandfather back in Cracow. It was a shame, for this was the first real holiday he had ever taken. But he was restless, he couldn't keep still, and one day, about the middle of August, he said he was going back. I remember going to the train station late at night with my mother to see him off. It was cool, and my father was wearing one of those ridiculous trench coats, you know the sort they wear in films about espionage. It was far too big for him. He had actually lost weight on his holiday, poor man. He held us both close to him and smelled of something. Witch hazel? Is that a scent a man would use?"

"It could be . . . yes," said Landon, listening with a moody tender interest.

"Well, he smelled of this. And held us close and said, Goodbye, my darlings, I'll see you in a few weeks. How naïve we were! Of course, you know the rest. The Germans invaded Poland two weeks later. We listened on the radio. Everyone was listening to the radio and running around in circles, especially the French tourists. We tried to get through to Cracow by telephone, but the Germans had cut the lines. Poland was no longer a part of Europe. We stayed on through the autumn while the hotel emptied. My little Swiss boatman was gone, back to school, I suppose. Everyone was desperate to get to England. After such gaiety it was so sad. One day we got a letter from relatives. There had been an air raid and the shop was hit. Both were in it. My mother, though, to give her credit, was a resourceful woman. We had a little money and we did get out to England. And by the greatest luck we got in touch with my father's people in Montreal and were in Canada before the real war set in the following spring. Oh, we were very very fortunate, Frederick, luckier than most."

"Yes, but it can't have been any picnic," said Landon, seeing Margaret at ten years of age fleeing with her mother across the English Channel. And he was a fat indolent child lying on a rug in the dining room in his father's house in Bay City, Ontario, listening to the great brown Marconi console. How his quick-moving sister hated his sluggish blood! She called him names for lolling about listening to Edgar Bergen and Charlie McCarthy; Duffy's Tavern; Jack Armstrong, All-American boy.

"No . . . it was no picnic," Margaret said after a while, her dark eyes searching the coffee cup for pictures from the past. "And in many ways those early years in Montreal were very difficult. As I said before, my mother did not get on well with my father's people. Yet for a while we had to live under their roof and take their food. But Mother was determined to be independent, and she worked hard on her English and soon got a job in a dress shop. She was very good too, and by the end of the war she was managing it. And right after she went to work, we moved to our own little apartment on Jeanne Mance Street. We were so glad to be on our own. And soon there was a man too. A passionate woman, my mother! Oh, I know it is difficult to think of that old woman we buried today as once being passionate and beautiful, but she was. And my stepfather— Jean-Paul Beauchamp! A very fine-looking man with dark hair and a thick black mustache, quite handsome in his soldier's uniform. Of course the relatives were scandalized. It was less than two years since my father's death, but my mother didn't care a straw for their objections. She was violently in love. Ah—I'm sure my poor father never inspired her like that. I used to hear them—should I be telling you this, I wonder?—I used to hear them on the old couch in the parlor. They thought I was asleep in the tiny bedroom off the kitchen, but I was very much awake and listening . . . a little frightened, I think, by my imagination, but thrilled too in a strange pleasant way . . . There were such groans and cries of delight . . ." Under the glow of the lamp, Margaret shyly smiled at the memory, and so did Landon.

"He was a nice enough man, my stepfather, but a little stiff, you know. Somewhat remote, especially with me. Not unkind certainly but . . . disinterested. He simply had no wish to put himself out. I could never picture him taking me to the films or to a circus. He wasn't that sort of man. But they were married. In a very small chapel on a Saturday morning. None of the relatives came. I remember a slim pretty girl, English Canadian. She worked in the dress shop, a friend of Mother's. And another soldier and the priest, one or two altar boys. Afterward there was a little party in our apartment, and then this girl took me to her parents' house to sleep. They were very kind and gave me ice cream. It was somewhere near the mountain. The homes were large and made of brick. The next day the girl from the dress shop brought me back on the streetcar . . . a lovely summer morning. My stepfather was sitting in an armchair drinking beer from a large green bottle, and my mother stood behind him, with her hands on his shoulders. She was wearing a navy blue dress with white polka dots and white high-heeled shoes. And she looked very happy, was glowing really. They gave me a doll . . . a little black doll . . . what do you call them . . . golliwogs! And shortly after that my stepfather went away overseas and wrote us letters from England. And then . . . Well, my poor mother, it seems, was destined to be an unlucky person, for my stepfather was killed. The next summer in the Normandy invasion. Somewhere near Caen. On the day the Allies landed. His war had hardly started and he was killed. And how my mother wept. Each day she went to the dress shop, and each night she came home to weep. She could not wipe a dish or iron a blouse without weeping. Her grief lasted for months."

"But how sad and how strange too!" said Landon. "My older brother was killed at Caen on the same day. June 6, 1944. Could they have known one another? I wonder." He sat up now, shaken by the oddness of it. But then he always made too much of coincidence, saw something sinister and mysterious, the hidden hand at work, behind such things. He could well remember his mother weeping too. When he came home from school, she was seated at the kitchen table and her face was streaming tears. She was strangely silent, the tears flowing soundlessly from her eyes as she stared ahead and saw nothing, not even him, standing awkwardly with his school books by the small nickel-plated stove. He saw his father too, hands clasped behind his back as he stood rigid at the screen door, looking out toward the garden. He had been suddenly called away from the yards and was still wearing his railroad coveralls.

"I'm sorry," said Margaret. "The war touched so many."

"And you lost two fathers," he said. "That seems particularly cruel."

"Yes, and in a way I lost my mother too," said Margaret. "The war changed her terribly. All that sorrow and pain. Oh, she managed the dress shop all right, and she patched things up with the relatives in a sort of way. They tolerated us. We sometimes went to dinner there on Sundays. After the war I enrolled at McGill in English literature. Conrad was my hero. The Pole who wrote so beautifully in English. And how I wished I were a boy and could go to sea too. And my mother? She turned more and more to the Church. When she wasn't working she was in the church. She became known in the neighborhood as a very devout person. This piety of hers—it held everyone in awe, even my father's people. The shopkeepers gave her special prices. She was . . . somehow special, marked off from the rest of humanity. Some even thought her a saint. But you know—this is terribly sad. My mother never blamed the Nazis for all her unhappiness. It was the Jews. It was the Jews who had caused all this suffering and death. The meddling Jews, she used to say. Everything was their fault. She was fixed absolutely on that point and you could not reason with her. She would grow furious. But my mother came from the country, you know—somewhere deep in the Polish provinces. Feelings against Jews ran high. You see, my mother's family had only been in Cracow a few years when she met my father. But this hatred of Jews was like a poison. And all the time she was receiving the blood of our Savior. It caused so much unhappiness. A friend of mine . . . she made such a fuss." Margaret stopped and looked thoughtful. "Well, it doesn't matter now . . . He's dead too, poor man. All this dying. I'm sure that I'm depressing you. You don't deserve such treatment after your kindness to me. I must stop this talk. And I must go, it's getting late . . ."

She arose and smoothed her dress with the palms of her hands, looking down, avoiding his eyes after so much confession. "You've been most kind, Frederick. I don't know how to thank you."

"Well, perhaps we can have dinner again soon. I mean a decent dinner, no eggs. In a restaurant . . . the works . . ."

"But you have no job . . . the cost."

"Well . . . I'm not broke yet."

"We'll share . . . Only if you agree to that . . ."

"Well. We'll see." He walked with her to the door, touching her lightly on the back, helping her with her coat and wishing her a good night's rest. Later he stood by his bed in pajamas, winding up his old Westclox (he had an appointment the next day) and marveling at his good fortune in finding her.

After this they went out to dinner and the movies a few times, and he continued to cook meals for her in his apartment. She always arrived with a bag of food and out of breath, as if she had taken the stairs two at a time to avoid enemies. For a moment she would stand with her back against the door, clutching her groceries and buckled briefcase, breathing hard, like a fugitive who listens in peril for advancing footsteps. Landon told her more than once, "Margaret, you must stop this foolishness. We're not children. Besides, who cares what we do? The impersonality of the big city. All that guff you read about in *Time* magazine. It's true."

To surprise her one Saturday, he bought a book on Eastern European cookery and tried his hand at a Polish meal. It was a partial failure, the apple dumplings reminding him of that glutinous paste he had used as a child in art classes. But the ragout was surprisingly tasty and Margaret was deeply touched. He noticed the tears as they ate without words by candlelight.

When he returned from New York after Christmas, she was waiting with a gift, a recording of Chopin's Études. It was not his kind of music, some old Benny Goodman would have suited him better, but he was grateful. And since he had nothing for *her* on this blustery Saturday evening, he once again invited her to his table. She was glad to see him. He could sense that as she ran upstairs for a bottle of vodka. Apparently the old woman had liked a nip of this fiery stuff now and again. They drank it chilled, with slices of salted cucumber, an old Russian custom, Margaret told him.

"I feel like Peter the Great," said Landon, leaning back in his chair. They grew quite merry. Margaret played a recording of Slavic dances, fierce hectic polkas and mazurkas. They inspired the performer in Landon, and on stockinged feet he twirled and rounded the room in a crazy imitation of a Greek café dancer. Margaret laughed and clapped her hands. A pounding on the floor halted this party for two. Old Mrs. Harper was applying her cane to the ceiling in protest. They laughed together. It didn't matter, for they were finished. The peppery music had burned through their blood and left them subdued and at ease with each other.

After dinner they sat on the sofa and listened to Chopin. Margaret, wearing a green blouse and skirt, kicked off her shoes and tucked her legs beneath her. She rested her head on Landon's shoulder. "Will you read me some verses, Frederick? Tonight I feel like poetry." How life repeats itself, thought Landon, fetching down a book from the shelf briefly reminded of other older courting days. He handed her the book, a fat anthology.

"You're the English teacher, Margaret. Show me your stuff."

She read "Ode to a Nightingale," and Landon replied with "La Belle Dame sans Merci." Oh, the sweet romantic melancholy of Keats and Chopin! It was too much. It suffused the entire room and entered the lovers' hearts like liquid gold. Margaret touched his flesh and softly kissed him on the mouth. They embraced with passion. "Dearest Frederick," she whispered, "will you love me?"

In the bedroom she undressed before him as bold as a streetwalker. And what breasts and shoulders and deep thighs! And this was his neighbor—the old-maid schoolteacher! With her cloth coats and her health shoes. Her bags of delicatessen rolls and sausage. Her old-fashioned satchel from Lodz. He had examined it one day, a fine piece of leather goods too, pre-war stuff, all hand-stitched. And its owner? An artful lover whose patient fingers and knowing mouth were seeking out the geography of his own body and laying claims to it. Gently Margaret placed him within her. As she received him, she was crying softly, and Landon could not help wondering whether these tears came from the pleasure of his love or the memory of another's.

These tricky erotic memories! They just won't do at all, and by the window Landon smiled down at the street now filling with sheer winter sunlight. Such a tedious season, but in another month these old trees would burst into fresh nascent green, receiving their foliage and dressing for May. Yes—she was a sack artist all right, but burdened by terrific guilt too. Fornication is a mortal sin, and Landon wasn't even a Catholic. She couldn't bring herself to tell Father Duffy, thus compounding her error. Of course, she thought he suspected something, and she was probably right about that. Those Jesuits! Ecclesiastical bird dogs! They could smell illicit tail a mile off. Their priestly testicles twitched and sent warnings to the brain. But what could Landon say to her? This is not the Middle Ages, Margaret. You don't ridicule a person's beliefs. There was enough of that going on already. A terrible dilemma for her and he sympathized. She had suffered similar remorse with his predecessor too, though Landon didn't care particularly to hear about it. She told him anyway, displaying the photograph of a tall spare balding man with frank intelligent eyes. Bushy hair, the remnants of a once-luxuriant crop, sprouted from the sides of his head and grew over his ears. There were horn-rimmed spectacles too. A pipe smoker, handsome in a professorial sort of way. Landon saw in him a remarkable likeness to the playwright Arthur Miller. This was Granstein, former high-school mathematics teacher, former owner of one large balky DeSoto sedan of middle-fifties vintage. A brilliant fellow, according to Margaret; a refugee and survivor of Belsen. He had led an adventurous life before stopping to teach calculus in a Montreal high school. Had he taught her some of those mattress tricks? Landon doubted it. She had known many men. It wasn't just the art she brought to the performance; it was the ease and familiarity with which she played her erotic music. However, Granstein may have added a few tunes to her repertoire. But why was he so jealous of this teacher with the interesting past? Perhaps because he was the only one Margaret mentioned and he guessed she'd been in love with him. The old lady had queered things, and now Granstein was no more; dead, poor man. Of cancer somewhere deep in the entrails. He had survived four years of Nazi brutality, only to yellow and waste away at fifty-two in a Canadian hospital. Just six months before the old lady died. It was awful. Oh, his neighbor was a woman of sorrow all right! And acquainted with grief. She knew the score.

His phone was ringing, pealing brightly, drilling into the silence of the rooms. When he picked up the receiver he heard his sister's voice traveling through the wires from Bay City. His suffering sister! "Ellen? Is that really you? How are things, anyway?" He listened patiently to the dry complaining voice with which his sister published the news of her martyrdom to a world resolutely set against her; bewailing her lot, forever baffled and perplexed by the contrariness of life, always exaggerating the consequences of mischief and burdens. For Ellen rain showers became storm floods and freshening winds always foretold gales.

Lately she had taken to religion and subscribed to doomsday magazines from places like Pasadena, California, and Phoenix, Arizona.

". . . The kids are getting over flu. And Dad's not well." Landon chewed a lip.

"What seems to be the trouble?"

"Oh, it's his hip again. It's giving him trouble. You know how he complains about it. And he wants to get out of that place. He wants to come back here, but you know very well that we can't handle him here. There really isn't room and it isn't fair to Herb. He's shouldered more than his load already . . ." Meaning that I haven't, thought Landon. With his sister it was pointless to inquire about another human being. Ellen always managed somehow to get back to *her* problems. She always wanted to bat. Landon remembered those childhood ball games played in the schoolyard in the spring evenings of long ago. His sister stamping her feet at home plate and the plaintive tones yielding finally to a prancing whine, which climbed like a siren among the swooping bats at dusk. *I do so have another turn. You kids never play fair with me.*

"Yes. Well, I agree, Ellen. It's not that great where he is, but I really don't see any alternatives. He wouldn't be happy here with me. You know Dad and I don't get on for very long."

"Well, I don't know about that," said Ellen. "I think you make too much of that. He's always asking about you. You should come and see him more often."

"Well, I mean to," Landon said. "I don't have a car any more, by the way . . . I sold mine a while back . . . I'm not using that as an excuse, mind you. There are buses, I know."

"Have you found a job yet?"

"No . . . But I'm going to see a fellow today. It's in real estate. Not exactly my line, but then maybe I've reached the end of my line." He laughed and cleared his throat. These feeble jokes! But Ellen had no sense of humor, and anyway, she wasn't listening, was merely waiting for him to finish.

"I wish you'd come up and visit your father, Fred. I might as well come out and say it. I think it's darn unfair to leave us with all the responsibility just because we happen to live in Bay City and you live in Toronto. We have to visit him every week, and I can tell you it's no fun seeing him lying there with his face all twisted and always complaining and asking to be brought home. As if we had the room. And there's never anything to talk about anyway. Week after week it's the same thing. It gets hard on the nerves. Herb's been very patient, but it's been going on now for three years. He's our father, you know, Fred, not Herb's . . . "

"I know, Ellen. Believe me, I realize all this . . ."

". . . Just a visit now and again to take some of the load off us. We haven't a free Sunday to ourselves any more. If the kids want to go somewhere for a drive, we have to go first to see Grandpa. They feel the strain too, you know."

"Yes, well . . ."

"It's darn unfair. I might just as well come right out and say it. It wouldn't hurt you to make the effort once in a while. You haven't been up here for weeks. It's only a hundred miles."

"Okay, Ellen. I've been meaning to, but I'm worried about finding work. I have things on my mind. Still . . . You're right. Absolutely right."

Ellen's tone altered slightly. She was shifting gears. "Have you heard about Wally Beal? We were going to phone you last week, but Herb said he didn't think you and Wally were all that close any more."

"Well . . . What happened? What about Wally?"

"Well, he just dropped dead. A heart attack."

"Christ, no. You don't say?" Landon's own heart began to thump wickedly. Was everyone falling prey to these killing sicknesses? But Wally Beal was his own age. "But this is terrible, Ellen. How did it happen?"

"At the Masons' supper last week. Herb was there. He was sitting just down the table from Wally. He said they were eating their supper and Wally just kept getting redder and redder in the face and then he just keeled over, grabbed hold of Mel

Thurston's arm and just keeled over. He was buried on Monday. I didn't know whether you'd want to go to the funeral or not. Herb said he didn't think you would."

"God . . . poor Wally." Landon felt stricken, but his sister had switched channels again.

"Now, what about Dad, Fred? He keeps asking about you."

Landon was skeptical of that. He had never been a favorite, was too much like his mother to please the old fellow. But persons who had had cerebral hemorrhages sometimes went queer and contrary, attached themselves to people they once had no time for. Often they ignored— even openly disliked—former loved ones. In any case, he should see the old man while there was still time. And poor Wally had run out of time! Wally—his old pal from childhood days—the two fattest kids in town and they were a team. The comedians, his mother used to call them. She was sure they were destined for show business. Major Bowes. The Ted Mack Amateur Hour. It was all waiting for them. Not another Laurel and Hardy or Abbott and Costello, but two fat guys doing the buck and wing, taking pratfalls. The old gags. He had seen Wally just before Christmas on his last visit to Bay City. Landon with a tomato-red toque (knitted by Hattie Wilson for Christmas years before) pulled down over his ears. He was still half frozen as he stood on the main street with Ellen's two kids and watched the Santa Claus parade. The wind whipped up from the harbor at the bottom of the street and watered his eyes, made him shiver deep within his Burberry coat. Booming and tootling past him went the local bands with the high-school majorettes, their heavy legs goose-fleshed in the high white boots, throwing their frosted sticks into the raw air. Tractors and pickup trucks pulling floats for local trade and charity: the chain-saw manufacturer, the Kinsmen Club, Support Pee-Wee Hockey! Herb Reiser was there on behalf of his store, riding a snowmobile atop a float, zippered up in a blue nylon jumper and flight boots, a white crash helmet with goggles on his head. He looked like an astronaut. Wally was one of the clowns, yukking it up on the sidelines in baggy yellow pants with huge red suspenders, the comical shoes flapping loudly on the cold pavement as he joked and passed out candy to the kids, who were packed like sardines against the curb. He didn't notice Landon as he passed. Landon now heard his sister repeat something, a question.

"Well, it's a bit complicated, Ellen. Vera's back in town. That is, she's coming in today."

"What does she want?"

"I'm not sure, to tell you the truth, but I want to see Ginny and get a few things straightened out. They're staying with Vera's sister."

"The one that's mental."

"Well . . . she's had her problems, yes." He had neglected his father lately. Ellen was right about that. But that bus trip was killing, three hours of deadly diesel fumes and stops at every village and town. If he could borrow Margaret's car!

"Ellen . . . I'll try to make it up this weekend . . . no . . . as a matter of fact, I will make it up this weekend, probably tomorrow." Without thinking he added, "I may bring a friend."

"A friend?" asked his sister suspiciously.

"Yes. A lady. I'm not sure if she's free, but if the weather stays fine, she may enjoy a drive in the country." Vera was returning to Toronto, and now he was mentioning the company of another female. These women of his. Ellen had always suspected that he lived a faintly dissolute life and that his marital troubles had sprung from this. He could detect the disapproval in her voice.

"Well . . . Will you be staying for supper then? I'll have to know . . . We go to Food City tonight."

"I don't think so, Ellen. I'll just see Dad and have a chat." He waited, listening hard to his sister's breathing. She was angling for something.

"Are you and . . . this lady? . . . I mean . . . is this something serious? You've never told us anything about it. Of course, you never do tell us anything, do you? We might as well not exist for all you let us in on things . . . And you haven't a job yet either! Well . . . I just hope you don't rush into anything, Fred."

Landon almost snorted. "Rush into anything! At my age!"

"Well, you know what they say," continued Ellen dryly, "there's no fool like an old fool."

"Is that what they say, Ellen? Well, they're probably right." He felt a mounting pressure within, a tightening in his chest. "Look . . . I'm late now, Ellen, and I'll have to say goodbye. Thanks for calling. You can tell Dad that I'll see him tomorrow, probably in the early afternoon, I guess."

"Well, what about lunch?" she asked irritably. "You'll have to have something to eat." He had to get off the line or he would faint dead away. "No . . . no lunch, thank you. We'll eat along the way. Don't worry about a thing. I'll be talking to you."

He hung up the phone and sank into a chair. He knew he must shower and dress for his appointment, but he felt exhausted, weighed down, and immured by old familiar fears. His underarms were damp and his brow felt clammy. He was certain that his heart was pounding violently. *Am I having a* seizure too? he wondered, placing his fingers along his wrist where the blood pulsed, beating out the measure of his life. He tried to pick up the count, but it escaped him each time. His doctor had warned him about this foolishness. Old Horvath, spare and lean as a rake, slightly stooped with age. He must have been nearly eighty, shuffling around his office in carpet slippers, smelling strongly of linament. He had shaken his small white head when Landon confessed his habit. "Not a good idea at all. You miss two or three beats and multiply that by four. You only alarm yourself. Not a good idea at all, mister," he added, laying a flat cool ear against Landon's chest, tapping away and sounding things, bending to his task so that Landon could look down and see the gray scalp beneath the fine white hairs. Landon had been going to him for years but the old fellow could never remember his name. "You should lose some weight, mister," he warned, rolling down the sleeves of his blue-striped shirt and buttoning his vest. "Lose some weight. Twenty pounds maybe. And no fad diets either. Plenty green vegetables and coarse wheat bread. To keep your bowels clear." He scratched out a prescription with his fountain pen. "Take these when you feel tense."

"Tranquillizers?" asked Landon, alarmed.

"Valium. To relax the muscles. You should enjoy yourself more. A big man like you. In the prime of life. Enjoy it. Take a woman for a meal and leave your pulse alone."

Landon knew he was right, yet he foolishly persisted, seated in the chair in the morning sunlight, his fingers seeking assurance from the rhythm of his blood.

*TWO*

Going uptown on the Yonge Street subway, Landon swayed in his seat as the train emerged from the darkness of the Bloor Street tunnel into brilliant sunlight. It dazzled his eyes and struck his hair with sparks of gold. This was mid-morning and the northbound cars were now mostly empty, their whining screeching wheels traveling swiftly like a nerve pain up the spine of the city. As the train hurtled along, Landon's eyes scanned the advertising posters above the windows. These printed appeals for your dollar: correspondence schools, charcoal burgers, investment analysis and advice, sanitary napkins, tango lessons. Something for everyone; a democratic plentitude. His gaze settled on the picture of a young girl modeling panty hose. An exquisite figure if a trifle too thin for his taste. But long-waisted and marvelous slim legs. Unhappily, she had a stupid pouty face, the face of a peevish child. Yet who was looking at her face? Those advertising types knew what they were doing. An old expression arranged itself in Landon's mind. *Put the blocks to her*. Good Lord! He hadn't heard that in thirty years. It was Wally Beal's adolescent cry of desire and possession.

*Freddy? Will you look at that? Boy, would I like to put the blocks to her*! Poor Wally! They weren't putting the blocks to anyone in those days, but they had had their times just the same. Again the train plunged underground, and Landon, remembering, smiled slowly at his reflection in the dark glass of the window. *Well, Andy. De judge say he gonna have to give you six months' hard labor for assault and missbehavious conduc'. Lissen here, Kingfish. Never min' her conduct. I don't even know dis here lady Miss Behavious*. Those corny offensive old gags! But they had bowled over the folks in the high-school auditorium in Bay City. He and Wally on stage in black face with derbies on their heads. What was it called? Spring Frolics 1945.

At Eglinton he stepped from the train and walked toward the escalators, moving at a brisk pace in his flaring oxblood brogues. For a big man he was quick on his feet, and as he walked he leaned slightly forward like a ship dipping its prow into the sea. Standing on the moving stairs, he slowly ascended to the foyer, feeling smaller, more compact and maneuverable in the light gray topcoat recently dry-cleaned for the new season. He was glad now that he had shed the old Burberry, a winter garment. It was a cold day but bright and with a whiff of spring in the weather, a palpable lightness in the air.

On the empty westbound bus he settled himself near the back and prepared for the ride across Eglinton Avenue. He felt uneasy about this appointment. He should have had Butcher make it for Monday when he felt sure he would be ready. These interviews were beginning to wear him down. With each one he felt his self-confidence eroding and crumbling away like soft rock. But had he not read somewhere that Friday was the best day in the week to be interviewed for a job? Some gink had studied the matter: gathered the statistics, done the research, written his paper, and pocketed his Ph.D.; offering his findings to a world already groaning under the weight of such stuff. Anyway, people were supposed to be more receptive on Fridays. Their guards were down. They were looking forward to the weekend. Now Landon drummed his fingers on the window ledge and wondered what this Ozzie K. Smith was looking forward to tomorrow. For that matter, how were things going today? Had he enjoyed his breakfast? Fought with his colleagues? Perhaps he had lost a sale, one he figured was in the bag? Was his wife putting out? Or had she turned her backside to him last night? With my luck, the bitch probably did, he thought.

At Oriole Park he looked beyond the high wire fence to the outdoor swimming pool, now abandoned. Its pale green walls looked naked in the bright air. He had taken Ginny here one day several years ago, holding her small moist hand as they stood in line before the entrance gates. A sweltering August afternoon with hundreds of kids jammed behind that wire fence, splashing and yelling in the soupy green water, which smelled of skin lotion. If you weren't careful, you lost sight of the bobbing ponytail and the small behind in the orange bathing suit. You watched for a flash of color in the churning water and inhaled the odors of toasting flesh. The lifeguards were high-school boys, big brown fellows in red swimming suits. They sat in their chairs high above the water or prowled the edges of the pool, hollering at the kids and watching the pretty girls, their white caps pulled down over their ears. They watched the solicitous Landon too, smelling a rat whenever an unattached middle-aged male wandered near the kiddies' end. Landon saw himself accused of pinching a tiny bottom. He was innocent, of course, but there was the crying child and her bony finger was pointing straight at him. That's the man, Mommy. He's the one. He would be seized by strong tanned arms, hustled along the gangway with the eyes of the crowd upon him. Loathing in their hearts. One elderly white-haired gent still trim in boxer shorts might ball a fist and strike him on the cheek; a glancing unpracticed blow, but painful for all of that. He knew he could be easily rattled under such circumstances. Who knows what the cops could wring out of you if they tried! He could see it happening. He had once thought it would make a good play, if you could get it past the sponsor. But then he had already seen something like it on Kraft Theater. Hadn't Burgess Meredith played the part of the innocent victim? One summer afternoon in Landon's life when he had wished that Vera was along. That would have been at least ten years ago. Long before Ozzie K. Smith. What to expect from *him?* Was he another one of these young wise guys? Landon smiled grimly at his old comic-book slang. He had picked up some of it from Harvey Hubbard, but when all was said and done, he was out of it now. He had been for a long time. His head was filled with old movies and songs. But lately Butcher had been sending him to these queer places. Was he playing some elaborate joke on him? That must be it. Butcher, always grinning with his large yellow teeth, fatter and ten years younger than Landon. He saw himself as a colorful character, a comedian, and when he had first read Landon's file he had stopped in the middle and pressed his full lips together. So Landon had been a writer. A poet, eh! Butcher was interested in this. He himself had once been in show business. A press agent for a rock group. A hectic existence, believe me, and no security. Well—these rock groups! What do they know? You can't keep up with what the kids like. He was much happier helping people like Landon find satisfying work. A more rewarding way to earn your daily bread. The man radiated insincerity and looked like a burlesque comic in his loud checked suits and gaudy shirts, the mutton-chop side-whiskers spreading over his meaty cheeks. It was an outrageous growth, and each week it seemed to inch lower, following the brutal line of his jaw. Soon, Landon had reflected, that tangled brown fungus will cover his face, a small blessing. Butcher claimed a particular interest in Landon's problem. What a shame when guys your age are out of work, Fred! But I still don't understand why you quit your job. In these days of high unemployment that was what? . . . a little hasty? He was right, thought Landon, now regretting his rashness. And why, for that matter, continued Butcher, did you actually settle on sales? Fred—I'll be honest! You don't strike me as being quite—well, aggressive enough. I really wonder if you're sales-oriented. You strike me as a sensitive type. And that's a compliment. I admire sensitive people, believe me. And you've written love poetry? Valentines? That's really fantastic. This man is tormenting me, Landon had said to himself more than once. He should have got up and walked out. But where to walk? Other employment agencies had shown no interest and the Manpower Centre had nothing to offer. He was stuck with Butcher. And Butcher was now sending him to these small gimcrack outfits. The last two had been barely respectable. They were scraping the vat. Meanwhile, Butcher kept after him about the encyclopedias. They are begging for guys, Fred, believe me. And you can make a bundle.

All you have to do is hustle a bit. But Landon argued stiffly against this. No encyclopedias. No door-to-door stuff. I can't face that at my age, he insisted. Butcher had shrugged his heavy shoulders and scratched at his mutton chops, the first note of petulance creeping into his voice. Okay, pal . . . I'll see what I can do. But the market for poetic salesmen is not large, believe me.

He got off the bus in the 2200 block and walked swiftly back to check the store numbers against the address Butcher had given him. The neighborhood was Italian, mostly small grocery and furniture stores, a driving school here and there, a travel agency. Landon stopped to read a poster emblazoned across a window. LET CASA LOMA TRAVEL FLY YOU TO THE HOLY CITY FOR EASTER. Amen to that suggestion, muttered Landon, feeling the cold cement beneath his brogues. Some nervous accordion music stormed from a loud-speaker over the doorway of an appliance shop. Landon hurried on, looking for his number. He spied it next to a discount milk store, a small ordinary place that might once have been a bakery or a butcher shop. He stopped to examine the photographs of properties Scotch-taped to the window. There were several small frame bungalows, one or two shabby-looking duplexes sitting box-like on treeless lots somewhere in the sticks, a corner smoke shop which looked dormant. You could tell they were all losing propositions. This was the bottom of the barrel all right. A white-elephant exchange! Feigning interest in the snaps, Landon peered through the window. What was it, anyway? A front for the Mafia? A bookie joint? He wouldn't put anything past Butcher. Inside, he could see a woman bending over a filing cabinet. Her dark hair was piled high on her head and sprayed stiff as wire, a bouffant style from the early sixties. She was covered by a bright mauve pants suit. Landon lingered, watching her trousered rear without much interest. On the window in white Gothic lettering were the words HEARTHSTONE REALTY: A ROOF FOR EVERY HEAD. As he read the words, the poet inside him frowned. The phrase struck a false note. "A roof for every head," eh! It sounded fishy enough, reminding him of that old Depression slogan "A chicken in every pot." Who had promised that? No doubt someone running for the Presidency of the U.S. of A.! In any case, it was before his time. However, his father would know. He must ask him tomorrow. The old man had spent the entire third decade of the century listening to such promises on the radio. But come to think of it, it probably wouldn't be such a good idea to ask him. It was just the sort of goofy question that would anger him and cause him to scold Landon. There would be the usual shower of scorn falling about Landon's ears. What are you cluttering up your mind with all that old junk for? That's all in the past. You think those were good times? Well, you're mistaken about that, my boy. You're always thinking those times were so great. Well, you're wrong. You should be thinking more about today and what you're doing with yourself. How the old fellow loved to lecture him! But he was right, of course. For him the past was weighted with such heavy bitter memories. A favorite son killed in France and a wife who had fled to California with a failed actor! He must now realize that all those years she did not love him. What a burden to carry into old age! Still, love aside, I must find work, Landon said to himself as he opened the door.

The girl glanced up and smiled as he entered. She was in her middle thirties, an early-blooming type, now fading fast but keeping up appearances, hanging in there with cosmetics and youthful costumes. Heavily penciled eyebrows and vivid crimson fingernails but no ring, though she looked well used. A hard little character with her pile of lacquered hair and her gold hoop earrings. Probably a divorcee, he thought. With a kid in school somewhere. She'd probably been knocked up by some greaseball at the drive-in and two years later found she couldn't stand the sight of him. A hard life ahead of her, but these people somehow survive. The Blanche Halls of this world could afford psychiatrists and trips to sisters in New York. This tough-looking little broad probably ate her lunch from a paper bag and settled for a roll in the hay now and then with one of the salesmen. Certainly there was a frank and merry lewdness in her eye. She knew men and had no illusions about any of them. They were after pussy and that was that. She greeted him with a gum-snapping hello and walked to her desk, swaying her hips and ass nicely. She knew how to use what she had. "You the new guy?" She looked him over slowly, from brogues to golden top, and smiled, a slash of scarlet and large teeth. He felt he was being X-rayed, his muscles and bones sounded for strength, his sex flesh and testicles measured and weighed. And probably found wanting.

"Fred Landon. I've an appointment with Mr. Smith at ten."

"Right, Fred. Take a seat, eh! Ozzie's out right now but he'll be back in a jiff. There's some magazines on the table over there. Or you can look through our current manual."

Landon sat in the inevitable green-bottomed chair with the curving chrome arms. These fixtures from the forties! The cheap outfits seemed reluctant to part with them.

In front of him was a low coffee table, and on it were several copies of *Time* and *The Reader's Digest*, an overflowing ashtray, and a large cracked photograph holder. It looked like an old wedding album, had once been white but now was yellowed and smudged with fingerprints. Most of the plastic envelopes were empty, but here and there was a photograph, another sad bungalow up for grabs. The office itself was narrow and long, lighted by slender tubes of fluorescent along the ceiling and divided by plasterboard walls into several cubicles. Landon could hear phones ringing, sales chatter, a typewriter or two clacking away, someone speaking in Italian behind one of the flimsy partitions. It sounded like an argument, probably wasn't. He leaned forward, resting his elbows on his knees, and flipped through the soiled stiff pages of the wedding album. The prices for these shacks were wild. Who could afford them? He looked up as a tall thin fellow in gray sharkskin and alligator shoes came out of one of the cubicles and leaned his knuckles on the receptionist's desk. A swarthy big-nosed face with prolific black hair and flagrant sideburns. What used to be called in the long ago a sharp character. Landon liked the exotic looks of him, though the fellow threw him a cool hostile stare. New guy on the block. Landon knew the routine. The sharpie, whose name was Gino, asked for some forms, laying on a heavy familiar line with Miss Bouffant. Marking out his claims, thought Landon, an old stag ritual. This bird might be hard to take. Yet, if he got the job, he might have to work with him, learn the ropes from him, take advice. Or shit. Better look innocent and hungry. He turned again to the album and studied the Hearthstone dream houses. After a while the sharkskin returned to his cubicle and Miss Bouffant asked Landon if he would like a cup of coffee. She was nipping out to the dairy bar across the street, a morning routine.

Landon smiled no and continued to thumb through the folder, feeling the weight of these mornings upon his shoulders. They were now a part of his life, and always he was kept waiting in somebody's outer office. It could get you down if you let it. The chrome-armed chairs he had sat in, the news magazines and company propaganda he had browsed through, the potted rubber plants he had watched growing in the tobacco air, the fake foliage he had watched not growing. It was painful to think about. Probably he should have stayed at Caledonia. He might have learned to live with Sugarman and the new regime. But that was a pipe dream. Sugarman wanted him out and he had to follow Cramner. That bastard Cramner!

On the day last August when they fired Cramner, Landon had gone along with his former boss to a place called the Silver Spur on Yonge Street. It was got up like an American frontier saloon, with sawdust on the floor and a player piano in one corner. If you felt like it, you could stand at the long bar with a shoe on the footrail like a cowboy. Landon was nervous about the changes taking place since Caledonia Stationery had been sold to DeVelco Enterprises of Chicago. The new manager, Leon Sugarman, was shaking things up, and the company was moving to a new location in the suburban meadows north of the city. There were rumors of staff changes and cutbacks, but in fact, Cramner had been the only man thus far to go. He had been fired, but he seemed far from unhappy about it. On the contrary. To hear the man talk, he had never had it so good. Leaning back in the chair with his thumbs stuck into the armholes of his vivid waistcoat, he talked about "prospects" and "irons in the fire." He was wearing one of those iridescent suits which shimmer and glow in the dark, and despite the warm summer night there was also this flaming scarlet waistcoat and a broad tie with a fist-sized knot at the throat. He had also been to one of the gentlemen's salons in Lothian Mews, and his fine white hair was brushed forward like a cameo of Julius Caesar. There was some wild attempt to convey youthfulness and chic. Landon thought he looked like an aging nightclub comedian, one of those second bananas who warms up the audience before the star's appearance. But his color was good, and with his spry and sparkish ways he was carrying the day's misfortunes lightly on his chromatic shoulders, kidding the big horsy waitresses who served them in black-net stockings with short skirts and big Stetsons tied to the backs of their heads.

Full of mischief and fizzing good spirits, Cramner winked broadly at the girls, and his faint Scots accent hummed and burred like a plane saw. "Well, Freddy, my lad, I'm finished now at old Caledonia. Well, the hell with that bunch, anyway." He knocked back his drink and wiped the corners of his mouth with a white handkerchief. "I'll tell you this, though. I'm far from finished in the stationery business. Not after thirty-five years, by the Lord Harry, and you can bet the best hat in town on that. I've already been on the phone to friends . . . talked to Jack Harper this afternoon. He thinks it's a bloody shame the way I've been treated. He asked me to come over and see him next Monday and we're going to have a bite of lunch and then we'll just see what's in the wind. And I mentioned your name too, lad . . ." Landon nervously passed a hand across his mouth. What was Cramner up to, mentioning his name to all these people? Cramner leaned in on his elbows and dropped his voice to a whisper. In fact, he was getting tight. Landon himself was feeling no pain but was concentrating fiercely, trying to work out the meaning of his role in this business. *His* name had been creeping into Cramner's conversations with other people. "There are people in this business, Freddy, friends of mine . . . they know what's what . . ." Cramner fought back a belch, tucking in his chin against the wide tie. "And they value experience. And by God we have that, lad. There's no man in this town or in any town in the country who can deny that. You've been with us . . . what . . . fifteen years?"

"Eleven," Landon said absently.

"Only eleven," said Cramner, scratching a cheek. "I could have sworn you came the year Alvin Prescott passed away. And that would have been . . . nineteen fifty . . . seven . . . eight . . ."

"No, Earle," Landon said quickly. "At the end of the month it'll be eleven years."

"Well, never mind, anyway; point is . . . Listen . . . Earle Cramner's in his thirty-sixth year of experience. Right?"

"Yes, right," Landon abruptly answered. He was growing tired of this recital. It had been going on for hours.

"Well then . . ." Cramner waved an arm for more drinks. "I told Sugarman, you understand . . . Listen here to me. I told him that you and I know more about the greeting-card business than any ten men in the country. I also told him that if he's not good and goddamn careful he could find himself out on his fanny with no experienced men on the road. What do young Houle and that bunch know, anyway?"

"What did he say to that?" asked Landon quickly.

The waitress leaned across the table to gather up the empty glasses, her large breasts tremulous and pale in the open-throated satin shirt.

"Another round of the same, lassie," said Cramner, inspecting her handsome chest with a wicked old eye. Landon himself was stirred by the sight of those breasts and forgot his question.

"Now, I'll tell you something, Freddy, and I mean this with all my heart. Maybe . . . just maybe, you know . . . In the long haul, I mean . . . This may all prove to be for the best . . ."

"How do you mean?" asked Landon.

"Well, simply this. Look . . . I was saying to the wife only this afternoon. She's upset about all this, but I said all right . . . what the hell! Why not a change, for goodness' sake? Who says we have to do the same bloody thing all the days of our life? Dear heavens above, a man spends thirty years at one job and never asks himself, Is this the only place for me? Well, when you think about it, it's daft. Do you see what I mean?"

"Yes, I suppose so."

"And I told Sugarman this too. All right, my fine young friend, says I, I've got connections and don't you fear that. And if Freddy Landon decides that he doesn't want any part of this operation either . . . well, you're in trouble . . ." Landon's pulse quickened.

"Well, what did he say to that? I've hardly said ten words to the man since he's been here." Cramner was tapping his fingers along the table and winking at one of the waitresses.

"You know, there's life in the old gander yet, Freddy. We might get something going here."

"Oh, Earle, for God's sake," Landon said, exasperated, "what did Sugarman say?" Cramner shrugged.

"Well, it's hard to read that fellow. They're all a crafty lot, you know. It's in their blood. They're traders to a man and close to the chest about most things, so it's hard to know what the fellow thinks."

"Well, did he say anything about me when you mentioned my name?" Landon was growing irritated by Cramner's drunken vagueness.

"I just told him we might have a few things going . . . He was putting me into a corner . . ."

"Well, what things, for God's sake?" Landon felt his heart leap, a live animal in his breast.

"Well, don't get worked up now," said Cramner. "After all, we've been in the business a long time together, Freddy. There isn't a firm around . . ."

"Never mind that stuff, Earle." Landon's voice had lifted and cracked on a high note. At the next table a couple looked up and watched them.

"Never mind that stuff, Earle, for Christ's sake," Landon whispered. He felt something going sour and queer deep within. "Did you tell the man I wanted to leave and go with you? Out of loyalty or something?"

"No no no, laddie . . ."

"But you hinted . . . Jesus!"

"Now, listen to me for a minute. I never said anything of the sort. I just told the man the truth. And the truth is that we've been close for longer than he can remember. We work well together. We know each other's moves. And that's the truth now, isn't it? Well? . . ." He leaned across the table on one elbow. "Well?"

"Yes . . . yes . . ." muttered Landon. The myths that people create! In the end they are unassailable. Cramner had it in his head that they were a team.

"Well, don't start worrying yourself," said Cramner. "If you want to stay, I'm sure your job is still there. But I'm telling you, Freddy, I've got some irons in the fire . . . So not to worry . . ."

Landon looked away. "Who's worried? Still . . ." His words were drowned in the rack-a-tack music which had started in a corner of the room. It was Sing-along Time and a man in a peppermint jacket was seated at the player piano. A big woman who looked like Mae West with her blond wig and full bosom stood on a platform in a sequined gown and belted out "That Old Gang of Mine." Her large blondness reminded Landon of his mother. The crowd soon joined in, and Cramner, half-turning in his chair, sang a few choruses before his head began to nod like a daffodil, drooping finally to his chest. With the help of the doorman, Landon got him out to the street, where he was abruptly and spectacularly sick. Leaning against a wall, Cramner disgorged several ounces of prime malt whiskey and the partial remains of a Colonel Sanders' Kentucky fried dinner. Although Landon remembered to keep his legs apart, the vomitus still spattered his brogues. Sobered and nervous, he hustled the sick man into a taxi under the suspicious eye of a passing cop.

Cramner was a has-been and something of a fraud, but Landon still felt sorry for the man when Sugarman axed him. Yet it was clear that there was no place for Cramner in the new scheme of things. The company was in bad shape. It had drifted practically rudderless since the death of old Cyril MacCallum. No one had done anything about it, least of all the sales manager, Earle Cramner, who had sat in his office pretending it was still 1950. Now and then he would journey by train to Vancouver or Montreal, staying at the old hotels and joking with the maids. He used to say that he wanted to keep in touch with the customers, but Landon believed he only wanted to get away from the paper work and decisions. Landon was often asked to go along and he dreaded these trips. Cramner didn't know any of the new people and his old breezy general-store gags only baffled the harried department managers with their worries over inventories and quotas. They had no time for that stuff, but Cramner never caught the hint of impatience in their eyes and voices. The man made a fool of himself, and Landon could only stand around helpless and furious. These encounters wore him down, and as always he feared for his blood pressure and heart. On the way out to the street he would catch glimpses of his own hectic color in the counter mirrors of the cosmetic departments; his face a giant beet beneath the flaming mane. Was he Eric the Red, or Leif the Unlucky?

In the club car of the Transcontinental, Landon would watch the sun drop behind the Rockies, marveling at the sky now filled with traveling light as he listened to Cramner's stories, which anyway he had heard before. However, it was impossible to ignore him. His restive energy held you captive and he was never still for a moment. A good part of his life seemed to consist in adjusting his person. He was like a man about to pose for a photographer, tireless and alert, forever folding and unfolding his legs, hitching up a gartered sock that had crept down over an ankle, tugging forward a shirt cuff, or patting his carefully barbered hair into place. Landon knew he was vain and guessed he had once been successful with the ladies. He was really a natty little drummer from the twenties, and he must have gladdened the heart of many a spinster who clerked in country stores.

After dinner Cramner could talk only about those distant seasons when he and old Cyril MacCallum had traveled from the Atlantic to the Pacific, the only two selling men in the company. He was filled with memories and Landon listened through the long nights, suffering headaches from the cigarette smoke and weary beyond words. And of course no one took the train any more. While he and Cramner leisurely rolled through the dark countryside on iron wheels, their competitors swooped down by jet and cleaned out the territories. He and Cramner got the pickings. It had to end, but when it did, Landon still felt sorry for the man. His vanities and mannerisms were annoying, but he had been good to Landon down through the years. He had fought many of his battles for raises and holidays, unafraid to argue with old MacCallum. Landon had often heard their Scots voices raised in anger from the inner office, with Cramner finally exploding through the door, his round face flaming above the bow tie and his high chest puffed forward like a bantam rooster. Leaning over Landon's desk, he would wink and whisper, "You'll get your increase, laddie, and no fear. The old man is a true Scot, but he's always fair."

But what had Cramner told Sugarman? Sugarman appeared to be one of those tough assertive characters whose enormous self-confidence intimidated you. Landon always fared poorly against such people. What would he say to the man? After a sleepless night he had gone to Sugarman's secretary and asked for an appointment. He realized now that this had been a mistake, a strategic error. It looked as though he were seeking a showdown, and he feared a wrong move. You had to be careful. A single sentence, a signature on a form, and your life was changed. Why had he bothered to ask for this meeting, anyway? Sugarman had not even hinted that anyone else would be fired. There had even been a memorandum pinned to the bulletin board: a neat electrically typed message assuring everyone that no further changes in personnel were anticipated. Landon had memorized the words. *You are now in the employ of DeVelco Enterprises. And at DeVelco, people count!* Yes, but for what, wondered Landon glumly as he recalled the memorandum. It had been signed by Leon Sugarman, who now leaned back in his swivel chair and hiked one leg over the other. He had been talking to Landon about his hometown of Chicago and of how the blacks and Puerto Ricans had ruined a great city. This talk of cities had thrown Landon off balance. He had expected Sugarman to be more brisk and to the point. Instead, he was chatty and genial, leaning back in the chair, with fingers laced together behind his head. He was a slick-looking fellow with his wide lapels and colorful necktie. His new elastic-sided high boots were the color of cocoa. Landon guessed he must be in his early thirties, though he was already half-bald, with thick curly sideburns, black as pitch, growing down his jaws; one of those fleshy hirsute types, thought Landon. His own smooth hairless frame shifted uneasily in the chair. Before Sugarman was a plaster model of the new office and plant, now a building in the flatlands north of the city. Now and then Sugarman would spring forward in the swivel chair, unlace his fingers, and grasp a yellow pencil. With this he would poke at the bilious green plaster representing the lawns and fairways of tomorrow or wiggle the pencil through a tiny window to the future location of his own office. Next to the model was a large studio photograph of Sugarman's family. He introduced each member to the anxious salesman. "That's Miriam. She's in love with this city. Only been here a few weeks and already knows half the people on the block. That's Ruthie, a piano player par excellence, and Sarah, the live wire, and little Sheldon. Hey, he wants to be an ice-hockey player. How about that? Follows all the Black Hawk games. Nutty about ice hockey! But listen . . . We appreciate this city. It's so clean. You know you people have a great opportunity to learn from our mistakes . . . Opportunities? . . . Hey, when I think of the opportunities in Canada. This place has just got nowhere to go but up. A tremendous future. Hey . . . and speaking of futures, I'd say yours looks pretty good, Fred."

"Oh," said Landon, alert and wary.

"Well, according to Earle, you two have got something pretty good lined up." His teeth clamped tight, Landon reached up to stroke the hard lump in his jaw. For a brief moment he closed his eyes and listened to the racing pulse in his temple. Otherwise his skull felt quite empty. Beneath his eyelids a white heat burned like sun fire.

"Well . . . you know Earle . . . there's nothing been really settled."

"Is that so?" Sugarman looked frankly puzzled, and a row of wrinkles climbed across his high brow. "Well now, that's funny, because to hear Earle talk we had thought it was pretty much in the bag. As a matter of fact, we've just been waiting for you to drop by and confirm it." He sprang forward again and smartly lighted a cigarillo with a wooden match, using his thumbnail like a country boy. Gray smoke rose from behind hairy knuckles.

"Trying to quit cigarettes." He smiled. "Have one?"

"Thanks no," said Landon.

Sugarman leaned back in his chair behind a cloud of smoke. "Now listen, Fred . . . At DeVelco we understand the meaning of the word 'loyalty.' Understand it and damn well admire it. It's a rare thing any more. Actually . . ."

"Well, I haven't made any decision one way or the other," said Landon, holding his breath.

"You haven't?" said Sugarman, suddenly fidgety. He had taken a slide rule from the breast pocket of his jacket and was now tapping it against his cheek. "Well, we thought," he continued, "that is to say, we gathered from Earle, that it was pretty well settled. You were going to go along with him. Mind you, he never said in as many words, but the implication was there. We just put two and two together . . ." The slide rule rested for a moment against the side of Sugarman's nose. Through the smoke he was sizing up Landon. "And accordingly we made our plans."

"Plans? What plans?" asked Landon, bending forward to hear better.

"Well, yes. You see, we're going to reorganize the sales force from top to bottom. Bring in publicity and promotion. Put it all under the same roof, so to speak. Marketing. We'll automate certain features of our service to customers and reorientate our basic promotional thrust . . ." He leaned back and gazed at the ceiling, talking through the cigar exhaust. Landon listened with a dull ear. Sugarman's voice had taken on the flat impersonal tone of a man who had memorized a company document. Like a tape machine he was now playing it back. As Landon listened (when wasn't he listening to somebody?) it came to him. Blockhead! Fool! Dunce! The old words were too good for him. These people wanted to be rid of him and he had played right into their hands. Must he plead for his job, then? After eleven years, beg to be allowed to stay? But they'd already made up their minds. You could say one thing for Cramner though, the son-of-a-bitch. He never crawls to anyone. Always cocky as a sailor on the town. While Landon lumbers forth with hat in hand. He barely heard his own voice, was only vaguely conscious of interrupting Sugarman.

"Well, I don't know about any of this. It doesn't sound too inviting to me. As a matter of fact—" he groped for the words "—to tell you the truth, I haven't cared much for the atmosphere around this place lately. I don't mind telling you that. Haven't cared for it at all." He noisily cleared his throat. "And I've been making some inquiries of my own too. As a matter of fact, I have a few irons in the fire . . . my own fire, that is . . ." He was floundering, and what was he saying? What irons? And what was he doing with Cramner's tired old expressions, anyway? Sugarman might have been smiling behind his hands, which he now held before his face, palms toward the salesman. He seemed to be chanting something through the smoke.

"I might go in with Earle," said Landon loudly, "and then again I might not." Sugarman's hands were now vigorously pushing back the air. "What's the matter, anyway?" asked Landon sharply.

"You're shouting, Fred," said Sugarman. "There's no need."

"So I am," said Landon. He felt dazed and hot. "Well . . . sorry, but damn it . . ." He stopped and raised fingers to his cheeks. A pair of heating pads. My health. I'm ruining my health with this display.

Sugarman's secretary opened the door. "Anything wrong, Mr. Sugarman?"

Sugarman waved the smoking stump of his cigarillo. "No, no . . . Carol . . . everything's just fine."

With his arm around Landon's shoulders, Sugarman walked him to the door like a kindly uncle.

"Listen, Fred. We don't like anyone to leave DeVelco with bad feelings." He laughed. "It's not our policy to be antagonistic toward anyone, man, woman, or child. It doesn't pay in the long haul." At the door he gripped Landon by the arm and warmly shook his hand. "Sincerity and loyalty, Fred. You can't buy those two qualities. We at DeVelco wish you the very best, and I mean that from the bottom of my heart."

In the washroom Landon fanned himself with paper towels before drinking several cups of tapwater. He surveyed the red face in the mirror, and the red face glared back at him. Bushwhacked by Cramner! Finessed by that cool and crafty Sugarman!

In the afternoon he called Cramner and told him he had resigned.

"A mistake, laddie, if you don't mind me saying so. You should have made more of a nuisance of yourself. Forced the buggers to fire you. That's what I did and they had to pay through the nose to get rid of me. It cost them six months' salary."

Two weeks later, after halfheartedly looking through the sales-help-wanted sections of the daily newspapers, Landon called Cramner again. He tried to sound jubilant and hopeful, though his voice cracked when he asked Cramner if any of his irons were hot. Cramner chuckled and said one or two things looked promising. He expected to hear from Jack Harper by the end of the week. Was Landon interested in the idea of a three–way partnership: he and Cramner to sell the accounts and Jack to do the book work? "We'll keep it small and not try to compete with the big boys. Perhaps in time we'll add a few side-lines, novelties, kiddies' toys, calendars." They could almost do it out of the trunk of a car like the old days. No overhead. No worries. It was his brainstorm and Harper liked the sound of it. They had talked it up over drinks one night until almost dawn.

How did it strike Landon? "I have a little money set aside, you know, Freddy." Landon did not doubt this. Cramner had married into a prosperous family and lived comfortably in his wife's house in Rosedale. "Think it over, laddie, and we'll be in touch." Landon hung up the phone renewed in spirit. He began to feel that leaving his old job was perhaps the wisest move he'd ever made. Actually, he should have done it five years before. Why not gamble a bit and live life to the full? A few lines of Tennyson came to him.

> *and though*
> *We are not now that strength which in old days*
> *Moved earth and heaven, that which we are, we are—*

Good old Tennyson! Landon had borrowed freely from him during his greeting-verse days. And, after all, Jack Harper was a shrewd fellow. With a little luck they just might make it. Landon decided that if they asked him, he would put some of his money into such a venture. Feeling better than he had in weeks, he took Hattie Wilson to dinner. At an expensive Greek restaurant they ate spiced lamb in grape leaves and Landon drank retsina from a hairy flask which, for all he knew, might have once been touched by the lips of some goatherd on Mount Olympus. Hattie settled for bottled beer, claiming that the woody Aegean wine reminded her of the pine gum chewed medicinally as a girl on her father's farm.

When two weeks passed and he still hadn't heard from Cramner, Landon phoned again. One day in the middle of the morning. A woman answered, and she sounded sleepy and a little drunk. She said she was Cramner's daughter-in-law and was looking after the house. She had just won her divorce from that no-good husband of hers, and who was Landon, anyway? As for Cramner and his wife, they had gone to Florida for the winter. Well—he should have expected that. The man was never altogether trustworthy. Still, sitting in the chrome-armed chair in this seedy office, he could only wonder why he continued to be had by the Cramners of this world. Was it his large trusting nature? Or was he merely confusing innocence with stupidity? In either case, he was easily taken in, had all the wrong instincts for survival. He was some kind of vestigial creature, a surviving brontosaurus blinking and groping his way down a superhighway. No need for tears of self-pity, but he should pay better attention to the traffic.

Miss Bouffant returned with the coffee and doughnuts. She placed a styrene cup of the steaming brew and a large sugared bun on her desk and left for the cubicles. A moment later a large black-haired man in a tight-fitting overcoat opened the door. He glanced at Landon and then walked over to the receptionist's desk to study the morning mail.

"You the guy the employment agency sent?" he asked gruffly, without looking up.

"That's right," said Landon, alarmed by the fellow's rudeness. He bruised easily and this guy was a bruiser. You could tell looking at him.

"Better come on in," said the man, walking away toward the back of the store. Landon sprang to his feet and followed, walking quickly and meeting Miss Bouffant returning from her deliveries. He squeezed past her, inhaling the smell of cinnamon and cold air. She smiled wickedly and snapped her rubber cud at him. "Good luck, Fred."

"Thanks."

He passed several doorless cubicles in which men sipped their coffee and talked on telephones or scanned the morning newspapers spread across their desks. In one of the cubicles Landon spotted the sharkskin speaking rapidly in Italian and building some castle in the air with his hands as he talked to an immigrant couple: the man squat and brown in a windbreaker, the woman black-kerchiefed and stony-faced. They looked bewildered. Sharkskin was circling his victims all right, moving in for the kill. Still, it was business. *Caveat emptor.*

Smith's office had a door, and on the back of it he hung his overcoat. As Landon entered, Smith was moving behind a small frame desk. Before he sat down, he broke wind, a fierce brassy emission. "Excuse me," he muttered, pulling open a drawer. "Gas . . . Had to go to a wedding last night. Drank too much beer." Ozzie K. Smith was a heavyset man, about Landon's own age, with a surly pale face and a head of straight black hair slicked down by lotion. Looking at his sleek head, Landon remembered an old radio jingle. *Get Wildroot Cream Oil, Charrrrlee. It keeps your hair in trim.* A razor-sharp part ran high and white along one side of Smith's head. Smith regarded Landon from beneath black bushy eyebrows. He was still canted over and rummaging through a drawer. "Ever sold real estate before?"

Without being invited, Landon sat down. "I'm afraid not." Smith grunted and slammed shut the drawer, laying thick palms on the desk and leaning forward as if to rise. He was obviously looking for something, his eyes searching the desk. Finally he got up and walked to a gray filing cabinet in the corner. He spoke to the files in the cabinet. "I don't mind tellin' you, the last guy Butcher sent me was a real dud. Didn't have a clue about movin' property. Wasn't worth trainin' and that's the truth." He returned with a file folder and sat down heavily, looking awkward and bulky behind the small wooden desk. "Some guys . . . they can sell. Well, what? You name it? Insurance . . . used cars . . . floor lamps at Eaton's . . . any God's number of things. But I'll tell you something, my friend. They can't move property. Property's a special kind of business. There's no way anybody can walk in off the street and start movin' property. Just no way. You gotta be trained. You write a very tough exam for your licence, see! This is a profession, eh! . . . But if you're good and you want to work, you can make money. I got a coupla guys make over twenty a year. No problem. But they work, eh! Nights, weekends, holidays. Other guys? Out playing golf. Watchin' TV. Jazzin' their old lady. These guys are movin' property. It's the only way to get ahead." He leaned slightly sideways in his chair. Squeezing out a silenter, thought Landon. Well, I've done it myself in company.

"You see a guy on your way in here?" asked Smith. "Tall, dark, good-looking guy? Sharp dresser?" Landon nodded. "Gino Bianca. One of the best in the business. Now, he's Italian! Speaks the language like a native and does a large percentage of our ethnic business. This is an Italian community you're in! You speak any languages, by the way?"

"A little French," Landon offered.

Smith sucked his teeth and looked a little sour. "Not too helpful here. I don't suppose we get two Frenchmen a year in this office. Now and then some guy from Montreal gets transferred, but he's usually English anyway. His company pulling out before the frogs blow it up . . ." He studied Landon for a moment. "I'll tell you the truth. I expected someone a little younger. Still . . . don't get me wrong. Older guys can make real money in this business too. Sometimes people want to do business with a guy who looks like he's got years of experience. I know guys sixty who still make a good living on straight commission . . . So what did you do before?"

"Stationery business. Eleven years." Landon bit off the stale words. He knew he sounded abrupt, frankly didn't care. He wasn't sure he wanted to sell houses for this gassy greaseball. And yet it was a job! He could get used to it. "So . . . what happened?" asked Smith. "Butcher said something on the phone about you being assistant sales manager. Eleven years is a long time in one place . . ."

For once Landon was grateful for Butcher's lying tongue. Smith knew only what Butcher had told him on the telephone. He must have impressed the greaseball. Was lying the only way to open doors? He decided to turn the knob a little himself.

"Well, you know . . . New management came in. Americans . . . We disagreed on policy. Basic differences on how the product should be marketed and the company run. My boss and I resigned." It sounded plausible. "Actually, we made plans to go into business. We'd raised the capital, even chosen the site. Many of our old customers guaranteed us business. And then . . ." Landon shrugged. "My boss was stricken by a severe coronary. Complete bed rest for weeks. He's recovering now in Florida, but the doctors have told him to forget about coming back into business. So . . . I decided. Why not try something different? Why not a change? A man does the same thing every day of his life, he grows stale . . ." He was sweating a little after this, but Smith nodded his head.

"That's right. I agree with you on that. Take me! I hustled shoes, cars, half-a-dozen things before I got into property. A man's never too old to learn if he wants to work, eh?"

"Right. That's what I always say."

"Okay! Now, I'll tell you what we're gonna do. It's Fred, is it? Okay, Fred. I like your attitude. You strike me as a guy with a business head on his shoulders. Now, I got a party interested in a piece of property out near the airport. I've been having some trouble with this house. People don't like the noise from the jets, eh! Well . . . you can't have everything. Some people live on truck routes. What the hell? You can get used to anything. You gotta think positive. And the price on this place is good. A bargain by today's values. So this party sounds interested." He fished a card from his suit-coat pocket and held it before his eyes. "A Mr. Lionel Farquerson. It's his day off, and I'm going to meet him out at this property at eleven. You better come along too. You can get the feel of things . . . I'll introduce you as my associate. But I'll do the talking, all right?" Again Landon nodded. Was he hired then? Was he back on someone's payroll? Smith stuffed some papers into an attaché case and moved around his desk, plucking his overcoat from the hook on the door. "Let's move some property, Fred."

In the outer office Smith waved to Miss Bouffant and addressed the door as he walked out. "We're going up to that place near the airport, Jackie. Be back after lunch."

"Right, Oz." Miss Bouffant looked up from a paperback and gave Landon a tremendous wink. On the street Landon fell in step with the real-estate man, squinting against the harsh sunlight. Smith had already put on a pair of dark shades with heavy speckled frames. They walked together to a low bullet-shaped car the color of hellfire. Inside, on the black leather bucket seat, Landon strapped the safety belt to his hip, feeling like a racing driver. Smith sat loosely and unbuckled, hunched against the door like a cabbie. He drove fast and without a word, maneuvering his land rocket through the late-morning traffic. He was obviously proud of his buggy and Landon caught the hint.

"Nice car."

"Thanks." Smith reached for the instrument panel and punched a button. Violin music flooded the car, a veritable tidal wave of sound pouring over and around them from all directions. Smith leaned forward and fiddled with some knobs. "These stereo cassettes are the greatest, eh! You can get all the good music you want. Mantovani . . . Kostelanetz . . . Hell, the radio's no good any more. Just for the damn kids. At home? My daughter drives me nuts with that rock 'n' roll shit." Landon wondered if the man had a hearing problem. His own eardrums were vibrating dangerously, fingers of pain probing his cerebrum.

They sped northward on Dufferin Street, with Smith hunched against his door, lost in his world of soughing violins, while Landon gazed with dead eyes through the tinted glass at a sea-green world of shopping plazas and used-car lots. At the Macdonald Cartier Freeway they circled the ramp and merged into the speeding westbound traffic, traveling smoothly across the gray pavement. Smith poured it on in the outside lane and Landon watched, mildly apprehensive as the speedometer needle brushed ninety. He relaxed only after Smith cut across to his right and pulled off the expressway, moving up on an exit ramp and across a street of filling stations and supermarkets. Soon they were deep in the suburban hinterland, passing ranch-style houses and low flat schools with yellow cardboard bunnies and Easter eggs pasted across the classroom windows. They were near the airport, and overhead a jet streamed through the air, its landing gear already dropped from its belly as it prepared for the runway. Westward, yet another jet climbed the air, trailing a cloud of thick dark smoke. But Landon, submerged in this sea-green light and surrounded by Mantovani's spiraling fiddle music, could only faintly hear its fierce whistling cry. Soon Vera would be returning on one of those big birds! Would she want to see him? Did he want to see her? It was doubtless unavoidable if he wished to speak to Ginny. And he must speak to that slightly addled daughter of his. After all, she was his own flesh and blood, as they used to say. He hadn't seen her much in the past few years. She had grown up without him, and at times he felt he knew her hardly at all. But she just might have had it with Vera's domineering manner and be set for rebellion. And rebellion she couldn't handle. He knew this much about her. She would fuck it up for sure. If either of those two characters in the cowboy outfits were giving her the sexual business, she was in for trouble. She was bound to forget the pill some Monday or Thursday, and then she'd be up the pipe and there could be an abortion or God alone knew what. Enough to drive you mad if you dwelled upon it.

Smith had stopped the car against the curb near a new church, a hexagonal-shaped building of dark red wood and glass. On its roof a slender tall cross pierced the sky like some sacred lance. Smith had shut off the motor and the Mantovani. He seemed a little jumpy.

"Okay, Fred, now listen . . . The house is just around the

corner, and I'll tell you the truth . . . this is a tough one. Because of the airport noise, eh! It's been for sale a long time now, and the head office is getting flak from the owner. He's threatening to put it into somebody else's hands. So we got to move it, right?" He was looking dead ahead through the curving green windshield, his hands still clenching the steering wheel. "It's not a bad house either . . . In fact, it's a very good house. Excellent material in it. Only ten years old. Normal wear and tear. And the neighborhood is good. Churches . . . schools . . . shopping . . . a good thirty-five-to-forty range. There's no cheap building around here . . . Well, look at this street! Normal people live here. They're not bugged to death by the fuckin' jets. Everybody has to put up with a little inconvenience . . . Me . . . I live near the freeway. Off Kennedy Road. There it's fuckin' trucks. All night long. Well, it's part of life today, right? We're not living in the horse-and-buggy age."

"Right," said Landon, looking out the window and feeling sorry for Ozzie K. Smith. He's psyching himself, thought Landon. Like a boxer before a fight. He remembered feeling like this himself outside the offices of new buyers in department stores. Getting ready to do business. Preparing to persuade, lure, inveigle, cajole, lie if necessary. He listened, nodding his head as Smith went on about the inconveniences of city living. On the wide church lawn he could see the signs of new life. There were patches of green amid the bare brown grass and rotting snow. In a flower bed near the front steps a purple crocus bloomed. Awakening life. The abiding seasons and reviving sun. The vision refreshed him. Another jet whistled eerily above them, passing so low this time that Landon could easily discern the lettering along the fuselage. AIR CANADA. Perhaps it came from Paris, where the lime trees are in bloom, thought the greeting-card poet, who had visited the fabled city only in books and films. As the jet passed over, the car windows trembled and knobs buzzed along the instrument panel.

"Those fuckin' planes," said Smith, watching the big jet disappear. "I made this appointment for eleven because I was told it's fairly quiet for the next half hour around here. I checked it out. With a friend at the airport. He works in the control tower out there and is *supposed* to know about these things. So I asked his opinion. As a favor.

I don't want any national secrets, I said, I just want to know if there's any time in the day when it's reasonably quiet around here. And he laughs at me, the bastard. Quiet? he says. In the daytime? Oh, come on, Ozzie! You must be crazy. Better show your customer the fuckin' house at two o'clock in the morning. Oh, very smart! Anyway, this is the best time, according to him. But Friday's a bad day too. I tried for Sunday morning, but this Farquerson is a religious guy, I guess. Says he never misses church. Probably a Catholic." He quickly patted both side pockets of his overcoat, one of his elbows digging into Landon's ribs.

"Did I remember that fuckin' list of neighborhood churches? It must be in my case." He lightly bounced a fist off the steering wheel. "Okay, Fred. Now listen. This is what we're going to do. I'm going to introduce you as my associate! We'll say you've come along from the head office. Customer relations, that sort of shit. You don't say anything. Just nod your head and look . . . wise . . . like you got your pants on straight, know what the world's about." He glanced at his watch. "You understand, this is important to me, Fred?"

"Sure," said Landon, feeling oddly criminal. They could be planning a heist, a bank job. In his black goggles and rocket car, Smith definitely looked like a gangster.

"That's just great," said Smith. "You're all right, you know, Fred. I think we're going to work well together. For once Butcher didn't crap out. You've got maturity, I can see that. The quiet serious type. People who don't push. These young guys. Like Gino, eh! They're always pushing . . . pushing . . ." He hammered the steering wheel a little harder. "They never let up on you . . . But guys our age. We know when not to push. And that only comes with time. You understand what I'm talking about?"

"Sure."

"I'm talking here about being a gentleman. And that's the problem, you know. There's no fuckin' gentlemen around any more." He was looking out his window, still tapping the wheel with his fist. The poor bastard has his problems too, thought Landon. Lying awake at night listening to the trucks and worrying about his job. He was probably being leaned on by the head office. And sharkskin was outselling him, pushing hard, moving in on him. Across the street a woman reached up to adjust the drapes on her wide front window. She was watching them. If they didn't get moving, she might call the cops. They must look suspicious to these hausfraus. Smith may have been thinking the same thing, for he checked off a final tap, a quick finishing jab to the knobby black wheel. "All right. Let's move property." He twisted the ignition key and gunned the rocket's engine. "I'm going to move this fuckin' house if it's the last fuckin' thing I do." Landon, pretending not to hear, coughed into his fist and looked out his side window.

They turned the corner onto a dead-end street, and Smith pointed, making a pistol with thumb and forefinger. "That's it ahead. The last one on the block." It was a two-story white clapboard with a broad window across the front and a carport tacked onto one side. It looked ungainly and incongruous sitting amid the other low-roofed ranch styles. Was it a builder's whim, a blow struck on behalf of variety in suburban design? A laudable idea, but the house seemed somehow half-finished, as though the builder had grown weary of his notion halfway through, thrown up his hands in futility, and said the hell with it. Worse than its pathetic individuality, however, was its unkempt appearance. Whoever lived in it had either ceased caring or was an outright sloven. The paint was scaling from the wallboards, and the carport, exposed to the street, was a hopeless clutter of toys, bicycles, garbage cans, and old boxes. A street-hockey net, its twine rent by large gaping wounds, leaned against the side of the house. The lawn was as bare as a schoolyard, and on each side of the front walk a skinny faltering crabtree struggled for life, tied to wooden sticks by rags and enclosed within a circular wire fence. Smith parked the car on the sloping driveway and placed his hands flat upon his thighs. For a moment he seemed intent on fueling his bloodstream with deep draughts of oxygen, releasing the air with a whistling sound as it passed through the stiff hairs in his nostrils. Although it was the stroke of eleven, there was no sign of the prospective buyer. When he stepped from the car, Smith almost stumbled over a plastic orange toy tractor. He grunted, stooping down to pick up the toy and carrying it to the carport like a tired returning father. He deposited it among the litter and walked back toward Landon.

"Jesus. This job isn't hard enough, eh! You'd think these people would clean this place up a little bit, wouldn't you? I mean . . . they're trying to sell the fuckin' thing. Look at it! A pigpen. And wait till you see inside . . . A nice lady, but oh boy . . ." They walked across the pale dead grass, past the For Sale sign to the front walk, and stood on the steps before an aluminum door with a curving H beneath the glass. Smith had plucked off his sunglasses and his dark eyes were smoldering with hostility. "And the head office expects me to do a job for them. They don't come out and see what I got to put up with. For all they know this is the fuckin' Taj Mahal. Nothing to it . . . And the jets aren't enough, eh! I got to convince some guy he's not buying a landscaping job. And the inside? It wouldn't surprise me at all if the place needs fumigating . . . It's got a bad smell. It's the first thing you'll notice . . . I don't know what it is . . . The kid's diapers, maybe . . . Christ . . ." He stabbed the doorbell with a pudgy forefinger, and Landon shifted his weight from leg to leg, always embarrassed by another's rage and terror. "You'll get your share of these dogs too, believe me," Smith muttered, his face now dark with surging blood. When the door opened he managed a weak smile at the lady of the house, a frazzled-looking woman in her late thirties wearing turquoise slacks and a Charlie Brown sweat shirt. Smith cleared his throat. "Morning, Mrs. Harmon. O. K. Smith from the real-estate office. I called on the phone. I said we'd be dropping by with a customer." The woman looked at Landon with alarm but slowly opened the aluminum door.

"Gosh, I'm sorry, Mr. Smith. I couldn't remember whether you said eleven or twelve. And Harry's out of town on business. I'm afraid the place is a little messy. I just don't know where the day goes. With the four kids, I mean. By the time you get three of them off to school . . ."

"Yes . . . Well . . . don't worry about it . . ." They entered a hallway, stepping over rubber boots and galoshes. From some part of the house a television blared away. "I Dream of Jeannie." The woman kept looking anxiously at Landon, hugging her arms against her chest, just covering most of Snoopy's head. "Gosh . . . Look at me! I'm wearing one of the kids' sweaters. I'm afraid you really caught me . . . I could change. It'll only take a minute. . ."

"That's okay, Mrs. Harmon. Don't worry about it," Smith said, touching Landon's arm. "This is Mr. Landon, by the way. He's from the head office and he's come along to assist us in the transaction. The head office is interested in seeing that you get full value."

"Oh," the woman laughed, covering her mouth with a hand. "Oh . . . I thought this man was interested in buying the house . . . oh well . . ." She seemed relieved. Well, come in please. And excuse the mess . . ." They followed her into the living room, where a little girl in Dr. Dentons sat cross-legged before the television set. Jeannie was tormenting her husband by making dishes and cutlery disappear at a dinner party. Each burst of canned laughter was deafening. The woman squatted down beside her daughter, the sweat shirt riding up her narrow white back. "Now, Sheri Lee honey. These nice men have come to sell our house and we're going to have to turn the television off so we can hear each other." The child remained trance-like, staring dead ahead as Jeannie hid in a water pitcher. The woman looked up at Landon. "We have to play it loud. Because of the planes, you know." She looked at the child again. "Now, honey,

Mommy's going to have to turn Jeannie off." She rose and walked three steps toward the television, when the child suddenly came to life, screaming, "No, Mommy . . . no . . . no . . . no . . ." She began to beat the floor with her little fists. Her mother smiled and looked helplessly at the two men.

"Well, let's turn it down a little, anyway. Maybe we could go in the kitchen," she said to Smith, but he had gone to the large streaked window and was looking out.

"They're here," he said. "They've just arrived."

"Oh gosh," said Mrs. Harmon and fled from the room. Landon looked through the window and saw a tall thin man step out of a green compact, unfolding himself like the petals of a high bloom. His wife was made of heavier clay, a plump matronly woman in a checked coat, and she was working her way out the other door, thrusting both feet onto the sidewalk and heaving herself up with difficulty. She had short tubular legs, looked to suffer from phlebitis or varicose veins, and walked with painful slowness in flat brown shoes. They looked to be in their late forties. Suddenly the large front window began to rattle ominously and another jet passed overhead, moving the pictures along the wall and causing a small glass deer to dance in a tray on top of the TV.

"Damn it all," Smith said, slapping his leg with the attaché case.

"You shouldn't say bad words," little Sheri said, still gazing at Jeannie. On the sidewalk the Farquersons watched the jet sail off into the blue, the man stretching out his long neck like a crane. They began to move toward the house, the man walking slowly behind his wife, with his hands clasped behind his back and his long deadpan face registering neither surprise nor

wonder at anything under the sun. Ahead of him his wife wad-
dled like a ponderous duck, frowning slightly as she took in the
surroundings, a large leather purse hanging from the sleeve of
her coat.

"I'll tell you the truth," said Smith, scratching at the part on
his oiled head. "I expected someone a lot younger than these
two. This could be tough . . ."

They went to the hallway, where Mrs. Harmon reappeared
as magically as Jeannie out of a bottle. She was now wearing a
print dress and had passed a brush through her poor dry hair.
When the bells chimed, Smith opened the door like the man of
the house. The Farquersons stepped into the hallway, the
woman blinking and sniffing the air, which smelled of something old and rancid. Nidorous! Was it years of bacon grease
behind a stove or just the deadmeat odors of the Harmons
themselves, their own peculiar effluvium, which their pores
exuded to a curious world? Landon had noticed it standing
next to the little girl. But Mrs. Harmon had doused herself
with perfume and now stood smelling of lilacs in May-time.
Smith performed the introductions, and Mrs. Harmon
abruptly excused herself, hastening to the living room and her
daughter. The sound of the television ceased and was followed
by a wail and a resounding slap. Landon caught a glimpse of
the poor woman dragging her screaming daughter into the
kitchen. A door slammed. Smith rubbed his hands like a man
opening a sideshow. "Well, folks . . . Shall we get started, then?
There are several features to this dwelling that I'd like to bring
to your attention." They began their inspection, starting in a
cluttered basement that smelled of damp cardboard. Smith
helped Mrs. Farquerson down the stairs, with Landon following

this cumbersome vessel of sluggish fluids. Her husband mildly warned her of the hazards of a missed step. In this long lean fellow Landon recognized a kindred soul, a man with no taste for combat, an agreeable type who found it hard to say nay. His wife, however, was a tougher case. She resisted pressure easily and moved about the large gray room with a critical eye, listening to Smith's spiel and not saying much. When she pointed to a large frost crack running the length of one concrete wall, Smith chewed a lip and looked pained. Farquerson, however, was not a man to hurt anyone's feelings. He figured it could probably be fixed with a little elbow grease in the right places. He drawled like a prairie farmer and shyly claimed to be handy. He didn't mind puttering around a house in the evening. For the first time that morning O.K. Smith looked hopeful.

They made their way to the main floor, standing in the middle of rooms and staring at ceilings and walls, peeping into cupboards and closets. In the kitchen a sinkful of dirty dishes brought a stitch to Mrs. Farquerson's brow. Clearly she was buying the house and Smith had to make his pitch to her. They walked along together, with Smith sweating some and mopping the back of his neck with a white handkerchief as he talked. Landon and Farquerson fell in behind and said little. Let the dealers deal. Negotiation was not their forte.

Upstairs in Sheri Lee's bedroom there was some interesting art work on the walls: crayoned stick men and great balloon figures. Smith said that something could be worked out. Hearthstone might consider redecorating these rooms or they could knock a couple of hundred off the top. Any way you looked at it, thought Landon, following Farquerson into the master bedroom, Smith was probably thinking of his reduced commission. He was doing his best too, firing all guns in a regular broadside. But his adversary, this stout heavy-beamed vessel, only heaved and yawed in the swell. And remained afloat, impenetrable dreadnought. Actually, Landon was faring better with her husband. They stood by a window overlooking the ragged front lawn, where they could just see Sheri Lee, now standing in the shadows by the edge of the carport, kicking uselessly at a clump of frozen mud and sniffling. But where was her mother, that distracted woman? Probably hiding in a clothes hamper, suffocating in lilac fumes! After a moment's silence Farquerson suggested that the grass looked pretty well worked over. She'd need a lot of work, this place. Still, the price was darn good by Toronto standards, and she was close to his work. The new plant was only a couple of miles away. Up the highway, as he put it. He told Landon that he was a machinist from Saskatoon, Saskatchewan, and that his company had recently moved to Toronto. He passed a large heavy hand across his jaw and gazed out at the sun-filled street with his clear hazel eyes. "She's a busy place though, ain't she? . . . I mean, after Saskatoon a fellow notices the difference . . ." Landon agreed and secretly sympathized with the man. The slow shy type. The man they played jokes on at parties. The fellow who gets up from his seat and sees—too late—the rubber turd! And it was no picnic being uprooted like this in the middle of your life; told to move halfway across a continent and dropped into the booming onward rush of expressways and high-rise developments. The man had probably left behind a solid brick home somewhere on a quiet street with trees. Lifelong friends too. Rituals. Roots. A way of life. But at least he had a trade, and Landon asked him if there had been no other machinist jobs available in Saskatoon. They walked along to another bedroom, and Farquerson said,

"It's the pension plan, Mr. Landon. I got me twenty-two years in the pension plan and it's a dandy. The union done real well by us. I can't afford to quit now. Fact is, I'd be a darn fool if I did. Lose a lot of benefits. Anyway, there's only another ten years now and I'll be out. They're letting our people go now at fifty-five."

"Is that so?" said Landon. Then he had only thirteen years left too.

"We'll go back then, I think," said Farquerson. "At first the wife and I thought of an apartment. But dash it all, I like to tinker, you know. Don't really see how I could stand living in one of those big white sugar cubes. Get on a fellow's nerves, I'd think. I often wonder as I drive by. I wonder just what a fellow does in those places. In the evenings, I mean. I guess he must watch the television or listen to the radio. I don't know . . ." He fell to musing on the subject. Landon liked this big amiable fellow and admired the tensile strength of the man. He was taking things as they came. He was doing the best he could. And he was a mark. Even Landon could probably sell him this chicken coop. But then probably anyone could. He was a lamb waiting to be fleeced, probably expecting it. Guys like this filled your fountain pen before they signed. Smith would pick his bones clean and leave the rest for the mortgage-company buzzards. But Smith had to sell the place to Farquerson's wife and he was having a poor time of it. Landon could hear their voices below. As he and Farquerson were leaving the room, another window-shaking, ear-blasting racket began as a CP 707 burned the air above their heads. At the window the machinist bent low, his eye following the path of the big plane as it arched away into the sky, its engine exhaust fanning out darkly behind and settling toward earth like a fallout. Farquerson spoke slowly. There was a hint of apology in his voice. "She's a good price, Mr. Landon, but I sure don't like those big fellows passing by so low. No sir . . . I don't like that at all." Landon bit his tongue to keep from agreeing with the man as they descended the stairs. In the hallway Smith was standing with Mrs. Farquerson, who looked up at them with her blinking-owl eyes. "Well, what do you think, Mother?" asked Farquerson. His wife was working on leather gloves, concentrating on the job but listening too. "I don't like those planes, Lionel. I was just telling Mr. Smith here."

"Exactly the way I feel," said Farquerson, delighted to be in agreement with someone. He was glad the tour was over.

"I was just saying to Mr. Smith," said Mrs. Farquerson, "I'd be afraid to sleep in my bed at night on account of those planes. Didn't I once read about an accident? It happened somewheres in the States . . . In California, I think. This big jet plane just took the roofs off of several houses before it crashed. A terrible thing. Oh, I think a number of people were killed. It happened four or five years ago. Well, you remember reading about that, Lionel?"

"I believe I do, yes," said Farquerson, again passing his heavy slow hand across his jaw and glancing sideways at Smith, who looked flushed and stern. He had lost and Farquerson felt sorry for him. "I like the house in many ways, Mr. Smith. She's got plenty of room and I could fix her up. She needs a little work here and there, but that's not a big problem. But those darn planes . . . Well . . . there just isn't anything a fellow can do about them." In the silence that followed, Landon inspected his brogues.

"Say," continued Farquerson, "I don't know if you fellows read that piece in the paper. Oh, a few months back, I think it was. You remember the one, Mother. We had a good laugh about it. I think it happened somewhere in Germany. Anyway

. . . this fellow is living next to this big airport, see! He's an artist or something, and he's driven half-crazy by the noise of these here jets. So . . ." Farquerson began to make a wheezing sound somewhere in his thin flat chest. To Landon it seemed the beginning of a chuckle. Why he was going to tell a funny story to cheer up O.K. Smith! ". . . So this artist fellow. He rigs himself up this sort of a crossbow thing. And he shoots dumplings at these big jets. Can you imagine? Dumplings?" Farquerson chuckled and clicked his false teeth. "Well, I guess it was some kind of a protest thing, but dumplings . . . Imagine that!"

"Yes, well," said Smith wearily. "Dumplings or apple pie, you will not find a better price on a two-story within fifty miles of this city. This house is a genuine bargain and you better believe it. I got twenty years in this business!" He sounded slightly peevish.

"Oh, we believe you, Mr. Smith," said Farquerson. "It's a bargain for sure. I told Mr. Landon the same thing upstairs. And I could fix her up too. But it's those jet planes. I can't fix them . . ."

"Well now, I think we'd better be on our way, Lionel," said Mrs. Farquerson flatly.

"Right you are, Mother." Farquerson stuck out a hand and Landon shook it. "Nice to have met you fellows and I'm sorry we couldn't do business." He shook Smith's dead hand. "And you can tell the little lady that I hope she finds herself a buyer real soon."

Mrs. Farquerson had already opened the door and was marching down the walk past the sick trees. Farquerson followed, looking back once to wave. "Sorry to have put fellows to all that trouble." Smith nodded his head.

"Forget it, Arch," he muttered as he closed the door. He turned to Landon. "Well, the fuckin' planes beat us, Fred. I might have sold this dump if those fuckin' planes had held off. Well, what can you do?"

"Can I watch the television now?" They both turned to see the little girl staring up at them.

"Yes. Go ahead!" said Smith, not looking at her. He was busy buttoning his tight-fitting topcoat as Mrs. Harmon emerged from her hiding place, looking mildly bewildered, patting her hopeless hair. "Oh gosh. The people have gone, have they? Well . . . Any luck?" She laughed.

"Afraid not, Mrs. Harmon," said Smith, reaching down for his attaché case. "But we'll have better luck one of these days. If I could get someone over here on Sunday mornings."

"Gee, Harry's going to be so disappointed. He was counting on this. We got to find a new place by the end of the month. We need the money for a down payment." She looked at Landon. "Harry's company's moved up north." Everybody is moving but me, thought the salesman. "The company wants him living in the territory he covers."

"Yeah . . . Well, we all have our troubles, Mrs. Harmon," said Smith. "Me . . . I can't sell your house."

"That man said dirty words, Mommy," explained Sheri Lee, pointing at Smith's stomach.

"Well, never mind now, honey."

"That man said f-u-c-k."

"Now, that'll do, Sheri Lee. Just shut it up."

Smith frowned at the child. "Well, we'll be in touch, Mrs. Harmon. You'll be hearing from us. I guess the jets beat us this morning. Maybe a younger couple could get used to the noise.

"Oh, you do get used to it. We've lived here for six years now. We hardly notice it any more." She smiled at Landon.

"Well, goodbye for now," said Smith at the door. "We'll be in touch." They walked across the sad grass carpet to the car. Another silver plane boomed overhead. Smith looked up, shielding his eyes with a hand. "Bastards. Cocksuckers." They watched it disappear into the haze of the inner city sky. "What time is it, anyway?" said Smith, snapping on his black glasses. "Let's have a drink."

They drove through the suburban streets in silence. A heavy brooding stillness had descended upon Smith and he sat hunched over the wheel, lost in hard meditation. Not even Mantovani was called upon to exorcise the devils. Outside the windows of the car the sea-green world floated past like some weird underwater city. They were drifting through it like Captain Nemo in his bathysphere. At the Dufferin Street ramp they left the freeway and drove south to a parking lot adjacent to a long gray building of concrete blocks. Over the entrance a neon sign blinked faintly in the sunlight. KING KONG INN. LIVE ENTERTAINMENT. TOPLESS A-GO-GO. FROM SIX. Inside the front door a man in shirt sleeves leaned across the reception desk reading a newspaper. Once inside, Smith paused before a full-length wall mirror. Taking a small red comb from an inside pocket, he began to mold his stiff hair into place, bending slightly at the knees. The hair scarcely needed any work at all, yet he kept at his design, using his left hand to augment the comb's work. Probably a habit from youth, reflected Landon, staring at the frosted glass panel of the door upon which were written the words FLAMINGO ROOM. Beneath the words a pale pink bird stood on long legs amid the bulrushes. The pallid creature bid you welcome with one limp wing extended. When Smith had finished reworking his glossy top into shape, he opened the door and they walked past the sick bird into a long bare room of tables and chairs. Although it was the lunch hour, the room was empty, except for a pink-jacketed waiter and a bartender. They stood together at a long bar, watching a soap opera on a color TV that was mounted behind the row of liquor bottles. The walls of the room were got up like some swamp or tropical lagoon; but a strange colorless world which had somehow survived without benefit of sunlight. Everything looked etiolated. An old crocodile snoozed by a gray log and looked not very dangerous, while dozens of the skinny pale birds stood around in forlorn unease beneath a sky of eggshell white. Had the artist dipped his brush in plasma? wondered Landon, as they sat beneath a pair of the mournful waterfowl. The waiter glanced over and then walked across the cement floor, slapping the round serving tray against his thigh like a tambourine; a short perky fellow with a puckered comical face.

"Afternoon, gents. What'll it be?" Smith ordered a bottle of Hunt Club and a shot of rye. He also wanted three hard-boiled eggs. Landon settled for just a beer. Nothing was said until the waiter returned with their order, placing the drinks and a plate of eggs before them, whistling softly through his teeth. Smith knocked back the whiskey in one gulp and drank deeply from his bottle of beer.

The chesty little waiter was halfway across the room when Smith called out to him. "Hey, not so fast, Jack. Let's do this again." The waiter looked back, shrugged, and walked to the bar holding up two fingers. Smith, flushed a little from the sudden drink, began to peel an egg, first cracking it against the edge of the table and then lifting off bits of shell, dropping them onto the plate. After a moment he said, "Well . . . you win some . . . you lose some!" He salted his egg. "But the head office is going to be hopping because I didn't sell that bastard house . . . Still, what can you do?"

"Well, there isn't much you can do," said Landon, remembering a line he used to use when he had failed to convince. "If people don't want to buy, they don't want to buy."

"Exactly," Smith said, bending forward to bite the cap off his egg. "That's exactly right." He chewed vigorously. "Just try telling Lavery that though." The waiter returned with the fresh order and departed, still whistling. "Have an egg, Fred," said Smith. "They're all right." To be sociable Landon took one, though he didn't care particularly for the hard-boiled variety. He enjoyed shelling them though and remembered doing it for his mother on summer days of long ago when she was preparing a cold supper, sometimes singing quietly to herself. *I'll get by as long as I have you.* No doubt dreaming of Clark Gable. Smith had finished his second whiskey. "I'm going to tell you something straight off the top, Fred. If you get into this business, you're gonna have to take a lot of crap from people. So you better get used to the idea. I don't mean only the people you work for, like Jack Lavery and me. And don't be fooled, Fred. I'll ride you if you're not producing. You'll also take crap from the people you sell to. In this business everybody wants something for nothing. They all want a fucking dream house at three-and-a-quarter percent. You can't do business that way." He drank some beer. "I been in real estate now . . . ten . . . eleven years. Before that, used cars . . . sewing machines . . . you know . . . At first it was good, eh! I mean, the early sixties were boom years. Lots of credit and people wanted property. The Italians! Hell . . . I sold whole streets to them . . . I moved a lot of property for this company and you can believe it."

"I believe it."

"You better believe it. I worked day and night. Weekends. I made some nice money . . . Two years ago they gave me this branch. Nine guys I got to watch now . . ." He cracked another egg. "But I don't know . . . This managing deal isn't really for me. I can do it. Don't get me wrong. But . . . I mean, you not only got to worry about your own quota but the quotas of nine other guys. It's not worth it . . . And Lavery is always pushing . . . Always pushing . . . Now I got a hotshot in the office who thinks he can do the job better than me. He speaks the language, of course. An advantage. I can't learn fuckin' languages at my age. I can't go back to school now. I mean, what the fuck do they want from me? I'm forty-eight years old." Two men in work clothes came in and pulled up stools to the long bar, ordering beer and setting their yellow hard hats on the seats beside them. Smith raised his hand for another round.

"It's Friday. What the hell!"

Against his wishes Landon accepted another beer. He would have enjoyed a sandwich and vainly looked around for a luncheon menu. Smith asked him if he was married.

"Yes . . . That is, I was," Landon explained. "Divorced. About ten years now . . ."

"No kidding? So you're on the loose, eh! You didn't jump back into the water?"

"No . . . I stayed on dry land."

"Ha . . . Smart man . . . Any kids?"

"Yes. One . . . a girl. She's seventeen now."

"And your ex has got her, eh?"

"Yes."

"Yeah. It's always the way. The woman always gets the kids. She's got the tits and the judge knows it. I got buddies who've been divorced. They see their kids on Sundays if they're lucky . . . God . . . my own kid . . . The oldest one. She's fifteen . . . I'll tell you the truth, Fred, I think she's getting laid. This creep she's going out with. Hair down to here. Has his own car. She's never home. But what can you do? I raise my voice to object and my wife beefs. Don't make a scene. My wife believes in all that psychology shit. You mustn't upset them. But sometimes I'd just like to blast some-body . . . You can't control kids any more. Nobody's listening . . . Sometimes I lie awake at night just listening to those fuckin' trucks on the freeway and thinking of my daughter getting it in the back of this monkey's car. And I just keep saying to myself, What the fuck's the point of it all? I know it isn't healthy. So I get up and make myself a drink and have a sandwich and watch a movie . . . When Norma comes in, I don't even look at her. I keep saying to myself . . . I got two more just coming of age . . . Jesus. But don't get me wrong! I enjoy my family, and I'll tell you the truth, I'm glad I'm not divorced. I don't envy you guys . . . ."

"Nothing to envy," said Landon truthfully.

"Divorced guys are lonely. I know, I've talked to lots of them. They all tell you the same thing. They wish they were back in the middle of it." He sipped some beer and then brought out a long brown billfold, leafing through some plastic envelopes until he came to a color snapshot.

"That's the family. Two years ago at Marineland."

"Handsome people," said Landon, studying the five tanned figures. How many times had he been shown such mementoes?

In the club cars of trains and in the shadows of saloon lighting, he had stared at the celluloid faces of women and children, these families of glassy-eyed strangers. Smith pointed a thick finger.

"That's Norma there. She was just thirteen then, but big, eh! I mean, she developed early." He finished his beer. He must have a hollow leg, thought Landon. "But what about you, Fred?" Smith asked. "Do you worry about your daughter much?"

"Just about all the time," said Landon. "It's the price you pay for having a child."

"Too fuckin' true," agreed Smith, belching. "Let's eat something!"

They ate ham sandwiches and nibbled at a plate of potato chips. Smith ordered more beer, insisting that Landon join him. When they rose to leave, Landon felt a little muzzy from all the hops and yeast. It appeared for a moment as if the old crocodile on the wall had opened an eye in mysterious wonder.

Outside they stood beneath a white sky, the sun having retreated behind some high clouds. The day was now chill and sharp. Although the weather cleared his head, Landon felt oddly depressed by the sun's absence. The morning's promise of spring now seemed hasty and premature. Perhaps next week, the sky seemed to say. On Dufferin Street the traffic stormed past, heedless and wanton. Smith didn't appear to be affected at all by the booze. He sniffed the carbonated air and adjusted his dark glasses.

"Where can I drop you, Fred? I have to go back to the office." Landon didn't want to inconvenience him but this was the middle of nowhere.

"Well, I live downtown."

"How be I run you to the subway, then?"

"Yes. Perfect."

At first Landon worried about Smith driving with all the booze inside him, but he soon forgot his anxiety. Smith handled his big machine as though he had never seen a bottle of whiskey, and they sailed into the heart of the city with the entire cast from *The Sound of Music* serenading them from atop the Alps. At the subway Smith reached back and pulled some papers from his attaché case. "Here. . . You better look at these over the weekend! This thing by Wilbur P. Wade is full of crap, but there are one or two good hints in it. These are copies of the various borough bylaws regarding property and property trans-actions. And this booklet has some typical questions from the real-estate examination you'll have to take. It's like a driver's test, eh! You have to know certain things before you can get a licence." He dropped another booklet on Landon's lap. "That's a phrase book. Hungarian . . . Portuguese . . . Italian. It helps if you can say a few words. Makes the stiffs feel at home."

Landon felt a stirring in his bowels. "Does this mean I have the job?"

"Well, it's yours if you want it. It's no picnic, believe me. You'll work your ass off, and don't expect any favors from me. I'm telling you this, Fred, because I like you. You're not some fresh-faced young punk. You've been turfed out on your ass by a bunch of new guys. I know that. It happens all the time. But you're still going to have to move property if you want to stay on with me. I got quotas to meet. So—as far as I'm concerned, you can come in Monday at ten. We'll try you out for a few weeks. See how it goes, eh!"

"Yes. Sure!"

"All right . . . Bring along your social-security and medical-insurance cards. All that stuff. Give it to Jackie. That's the girl in the front office. And don't get any ideas about her! Gino's laying her these days and I don't want any squabbles in the office. I got enough problems as it is."

"Well, there'll be no problem there," Landon said. Without thinking he added, "I have a lady friend of my own."

Smith guffawed, probably at Landon's old-fashioned phrasing. "Well, good for you, Fred. Hang in there. And we'll see you Monday morning."

"Yes. Right," Landon said, getting out of the car. He watched it disappear around the corner as he stood on the sidewalk before the subway entrance. It came to him then that he hadn't inquired about certain things. Like salary, for instance. Perhaps it was a straight commission job and you had to sell a house to eat. A tough life. And did they give you a car? It was typical of him to forget to ask, and the beer hadn't helped. Anyway, it was a job, and in the subway he felt mildy elated. It wasn't the rosiest position in the world, but it would get him out of bed in the morning and hustling. Perhaps he needed the pressure of selling to eat. It might toughen him up. Those years at Caledonia had softened him. Now he was swimming in a sea of sharks and he'd have to learn to bite too. But there would be problems. Smith he could live with, but how long would that unhappy man last? If the sharkskin took over, he could probably expect trouble. Meanwhile, though, he was working and his days with Hearthstone Realty needn't last forever. He could look for something better in his spare time.

In the subway car he shuffled the booklets, stopping to glance at a yellow one. *Selling a Dwelling is Fun* AND *Profitable. The*

*Secrets to Successful Realty by the King of Realtors, Wilbur P. Wade.* Landon turned a page. *Mr. Real Estate Agent! Here are the* DO'S *and* DON'TS *of selling real estate by America's Number One Realtor, Wilbur P. Wade.* There followed the reprint of a *Reader's Digest* article which described how Wilbur P. Wade had sold an entire subdivision in one week. It had happened somewhere in Arizona. Plenty of time for that stuff, thought Landon. The phrase book was more fun, and he smiled at the strange words. Languages had come easily to him in high school. French . . . German . . . Latin. He had even studied a little Spanish once. Adult education. In an extension class, he sat with a dozen other lonely souls. All looking for companionship on winter evenings. The teacher, Miss Delado, wore long skirts and black stockings. Her hard-heeled shoes clicked like castanets on the floor.

"*Buenas noches*, students of Spanish." And they chanted back like fifth graders. They read from *El cuento de Ferdinando*. The story of Ferdinand, the little bull who would not fight but preferred to smell the flowers beneath the cork tree. Ferdinand Landon. He turned the pages of the booklet, savoring the richness of other tongues. *Come ti piace la mia macchina?* How do you like my car? *E veramente bella.* It's very nice. Or as the Hungarians put it, *Hogy tetszik a kocsim Nagyon.* He could learn Polish from Margaret. Just in case a homeless Pole appeared on the horizon. He was suddenly anxious to tell her the news. And wasn't it nice to have someone to share such tidings with? He would tell her this afternoon when she got home. Perhaps they could have dinner together to celebrate. Other things could wait. Or could they? He stuffed the booklets into the pockets of his coat and folded his arm across his chest, settling back for the crosstown ride.

At Spadina station he climbed to the narrow cement pathway and walked to Madison Avenue, standing for a moment in fatigue and indecision. With mild alarm he realized that the long climb had tired him. He was out of shape all right. All that beer at the King Kong Inn had left him with a headache too, and now its blunt throb was sounding against his temples. It would be nice to lie down for an hour.

He walked east on Bloor Street to Huron and south past the small park where he had sat on a bench listening to the young man who wanted to tamper with the world's water supply. In the park the weak grass struggled through the patches of melting snow, and months of dog droppings now lay exposed, soft and faintly rank in the March air. The place was a canine latrine with enough protein discharged to feed half the world. In another few weeks the poodles and spaniels would drop their load and rub their bums along the green, scorching the poor life out of it. Could something not be done? A letter to the editor. *Dogs Defiling Our Parks*. Sign it "Outraged Citizen." Or perhaps "Slippery Soles!"

Down the street a hundred yards away a familiar figure was bidding farewell to a leggy young redhead. Tommy Rossiter with another one of his girl friends! Landon groaned and hastened across the park. Not Rossiter now! Not with this headache!

Rossiter, all five-feet-six of him encased in an ankle-length coat of brown leather, did not see Landon and crossed to the other side of the street. He had seen Rossiter two weeks before. In front of the Foreign Students' Union where Rossiter was giving a talk on the contemplation of Wu, which he explained to Landon was nothingness in the Taoist tongue. Lately he had become interested in Oriental religion. He had also sunk a few dollars into an import-export business run by a friend. Incense sticks, ironwrought candelabra, prayer wheels, tarot cards, reed mats for kneeling. There was money in it and they were thinking of opening a shop on Yorkville Street. Landon felt it was only a question of time before Rossiter lost his grip altogether.

In the early sixties, when Rossiter and his wife lived next door to Landon, the interest had been in Pete Seeger records and the civil-rights movement. Those hectic evenings when Landon had sat drinking beer, listening to Rossiter quarrel with his wife Sandra over the black man's rights in Alabama. Later he lay in bed listening to the sound of blows which came through the walls as Rossiter and his wife fought the final round with bare knuckles. Those two—they always reminded Landon of a childhood poem which he recited in bed as he listened to them. How did it go?

> The gingham dog went "Bow-wow-wow!"
> And the calico cat replied "Mee-ow!"
> The air was littered, an hour or so,
> With bits of gingham and calico.

Still, Rossiter had some magical power over pretty girls (Sandra had been a knockout). He seemed to cast a spell over them, and that at least was worth envying. *His* forties continued to be green years, and he was always threatening to come around with his latest chick, usually some wide-eyed student from the university. Standing in front of the Students' Union that day, with his Gestapo coat buttoned up to his chin, Rossiter had danced around and flicked jabs at Landon's arm. His boots had six-inch heels and his long brown hair was pulled back into a ponytail. He was delighted to see Landon. "Hey, Freddy man . . . The last time we met you were pounding the pavement . . . looking for work. I guess you haven't found anything yet, eh! Well . . . times are tough. It's no disgrace to be unemployed. You remember what I said. Work . . . work . . . who needs it? Let the johns do the work. Drop the nine-to-five scene. Cut your expenses."

He neglected to mention that his wealthy brothers sent him a large check each month to stay away. But he loved to talk. "A single man doesn't need much to live on. A room . . . a meal a day, a chick. Books are free at the library. Give your inner life some breathing time."

"Yes. Well, unfortunately I'm not a religious man like you, Tommy." Rossiter had laughed, showing brown teeth.

"Oh Freddy, you've always knocked me out."

"I don't know that I could spend the rest of my days in meditation." Landon was smiling, and Rossiter had whooped like a madman, turning around completely as he balanced on one leg. After a moment, however, he stopped laughing.

"Well, that's not so funny either, when you think about it. You're right, you know, Freddy. I am a religious man. That's why I could never hack the straight bit with Sandra and the sweet hearth. What a drag! I was listening to another drum."

"Of course." Landon had glanced at his watch. He had to see Butcher. But Rossiter insisted on talking about his latest job: an attendant in a steam bath. It was only temporary, of course, but meanwhile the sights were fantastic. Still, life presented problems, and soon he was fumbling for Landon's hand and squeezing it. Were there tears in his eyes too? Yes—Landon recognized the old symptoms.

"You were always solid with me, Freddy. I mean that from the bottom. You never put me down when I split from Sandra. Man, you were the only one . . ."

"Well, Tommy, it was your life. It wasn't for me to say . . ."

"You mean more to me than those fucking brothers of mine. What the fuck do they know about life, anyway? Getting and spending, we lay waste our powers. What do they know about that?" Landon had felt embarrassed. Rossiter would not let go of his hand and the tears had started. They were dribbling from the corners of his eyes, running down his cheeks. "You were the only one, Freddy, and I was taking so much shit from all sides. The bastards put me through the mill, you know. They ground me to pieces. It broke me down. How much is a human being supposed to take? I spent a year of my life in the hospital. They had me sewing baseballs up at Oak Ridges."

"I'm sorry, Tommy." He was too, and he had walked away with a heavy spirit. Poor Rossiter! But he led such a melodramatic life. With his coeds and his Eastern philosophy, his tears and shredded nerves, his business ventures and bad teeth. This bohemian lust for novelty. It was bound to get you down in the end. But he looked terrible, was going to the dogs. Like this little park. Landon smiled grimly at the poor joke, but he was glad to have avoided Rossiter.

In front of the Essex Arms, Landon hesitated. It was the end of the week and he needed groceries. He should walk across the street and pay Kneibel a visit, though he seldom shopped there. Kneibel's prices were too high. He couldn't compete with the supermarkets and was always complaining of falling business. Sometimes Landon felt sorry for the German and bought a few things. He could see him now, sitting in his deserted shop, reading a newspaper. A long day when you wait for nothing. Still, if he walked over, he would have to listen to complaints about business and the usual accusation that the neighborhood was anti-German. Then Kneibel would overcharge him. The grocer didn't appear to like Landon. With this headache I can do without his complaints, thought Landon, and climbed the stone steps to the entrance. In the lobby he fished from his mailbox two advertising circulars and a scribbled note from his daughter.

> *Hi Daddy: Sorry we missed you. We're going out to the airport now (2:30) to pick up Mother. There's a bash at Aunt Blanche's tonight. Please come. I'll be expecting you.*
> *Love, Ginny*

Why, he had just missed her! He read the note once more. What did she mean by we? She must still be traveling with Logan and Chamberlain. It sounded like a law firm. He frowned. He could do without one of Blanche's parties right now. They were always vaguely unsettling, particularly to a troubled soul. Landon always found their forced gaiety somehow desolating. Now he wondered what Blanche was into. What kind of people would turn up to represent her latest interest? The Rosicrucians? Women's Lib? The Society of Friends, perhaps? Certainly it was no place for a serious talk with anyone, let alone your own daughter. However, he guessed he must go.

In the apartment he swallowed two Anacin and drank a glass of water. He considered taking a short nap. It would probably be beneficial to his headache. He could study Wilbur P. Wade's guide to real-estate success until he felt drowsy. On his way to the bedroom he passed a small square room which he had once upon a time called his study. He had moved his books and typewriter into the room, and he had bought a desk and cane-bottomed chair, placing them near the narrow tall window which looked out over the alleyway behind the building. The idea had been to resume his writing in this little box-like room. What went wrong? Nothing. Everything. There were periodic selling trips to interfere with a regular writing schedule. There were too many books and magazines to read, too many movies to see. The late shows on TV were nice too, especially with toasted cheese sandwiches and beer. And in the early hours of the morning the alarm clock had rung its crazy head off, awakening the neighborhood but clanging uselessly by Landon, who was buried beneath the pillow in dreamland. When all was said and done, he had lacked the character necessary for the job. Now he didn't care much for this little room. It depressed him, and he kept the door closed most of the time. The dull green walls seemed to give off an odd smell: the faintly unpleasant odor of emptiness and disuse. Or did failure have a smell? After several months he had moved the books back into the living room and hidden away the typewriter in the hall closet beneath a stack of musty scripts. The desk and cane-bottomed chair had remained, along with a daybed he had bought in the hope that Ginny might sleep there when she visited. On three or four weekends she had come from the boarding school and slept on it, yawning into his kitchen the next morning with a face swollen from sleep. He served her corn flakes and coffee. Now too the room contained the recently purchased easel and painting materials set up by the window to catch the hard narrow light. What was he doing spending money on such things? He hadn't touched the canvas in weeks; the paint wells were crusty and split by cracks, the coated brushes lay stiff and unused like dead fingers. He hadn't bothered to soak them in turpentine after painting. He had just got up and walked away from the canvas. Now he forced himself to stare at the thing. What it was he frankly couldn't say. A mass of seaweed seemed to dominate the picture and in the middle of this stringy greenness (Landon's very own Sargasso sea?) floated a lurid yellow eye. Or was it a fried egg, sunny-side up, adrift on a raft of spinach? In either case it should be put away, forgotten, excised, destroyed. Margaret was convinced he was a creative man. If not in painting, then in words. Yet even allowing for the abuse of that term in modern times, he doubted now whether it was true. He did have a flair for words, knew their power and respected it. He might have made it as a TV hack, churning out police dramas or those depressing situation comedies. If he had fought a little harder, taken off his shoe and hammered it on the producer's desk. He had once seen this done in Basil Johnson's office by a stout bearded fellow from New Brunswick. A violent man of principle, and he won his point. Landon had taken pleasure in watching Basil shrink into his blue blazer. Yet would ten years of hacking TV scripts have been any better than ten years of hustling greeting cards? Perhaps his life would have been more glamorous? That wouldn't be difficult. There would have been more money. More women too.

In the bedroom he smoothed the spread with the flat of his hand and lay down, looking up through the window at his own familiar patch of sky. The drumming behind his temples was growing fainter, and slowly he felt his body relaxing, the coils unwinding as he cast loose the moorings and drifted out onto the wide dark sea of sleep. And dreamed again of his daughter. Ginny was dressed like a Cuthbert Hall student in pine-green jumper with black stockings and Oxfords. A necktie was knotted at the collar of her pale green shirt, and her braids fell from behind a beret. It was no costume for a young lady in her eighteenth year. She was standing in a meadow beneath an old crabapple tree. Landon stood some distance away and watched his daughter disrobe. First she threw her beret up to Ralph Chamberlain who was perched like a naked monkey in one of the gnarled branches, his pale flanks gleaming like bronze in the light of a lurid yellow eye which passed for the sun in a green heaven. In this meadow near Bay City, Landon had played as a child with Wally Beal. He recognized the place all right, though he hadn't been back in thirty years. Black-and-white cows used to seek the shelter of that old tree during the heat of summer noons, lying down to flick their tails at the flies or munch a scabby windfall. He and Wally had shagged stones at them, bouncing the rocks off their rumps; town kids ever alert to flee should the slow melancholy beasts charge. When Landon looked again, Ginny had disappeared and Vera was standing beneath the tree, as naked as Eve on the first morning. She was chewing a sour apple too. She beckoned to Landon and performed a slow dance suggestive of carnal favors; then she lay down and hid the apple between her thighs. On a twisted limb overhead, a satyr grinned and danced on cloven feet, piping a tune on his reed flute. Landon ran toward them, amazed at his sudden nakedness and peering down uncertainly at his *penis erectus*, which flip-flopped against his sad belly. When he reached Vera, she grabbed his meat, but as he embraced her she disappeared in a puff of yellow smoke. Above him the satyr laughed wickedly and shied a hard apple at Landon's tool.

He awoke to discover his bashful neighbor no longer bashful but warm and naked and next to him. "Why, Margaret. This is marvelous." She touched him. "And what's this? Were you dreaming of me, Frederick?"

"Why, Margaret darling, this is really grand."

"I think you find me bold."

"Well yes, but I love your boldness. You've taken me by surprise. Oh, happy day . . ."

"Do you love me, Frederick?"

"Yes, I do, Margaret, I really do."

"Say it to me, please. Tell me you love me, darling."

"Yes, God, I do, Margaret . . . I do I do I do . . ."

Through the window, open half an inch to admit the dubious air, Landon heard the honking and squealing of traffic on Spadina Avenue. Across the city a tide of human life ebbing homeward through the clogged streets and the frantic crowded subways. People pushing other people, while Landon found some temporary peace and love in the afternoon.

# THREE

The night was overcast, though earlier Landon had watched from his window as a big yellow moon peeped over the roof of the Research Library, rising quickly to disappear behind the clouds. Now Landon, a solitary pedestrian, walked south from the streetcar stop on St. Clair Avenue following the descent of Russell Hill Road. He had decided to go to Blanche's party after all. He would stay an hour or so. Enough time to ask Ginny about her plans and perhaps arrange lunch with her on Sunday. He could also see what Vera had on her mind. He'd be home in plenty of time for a good night's rest and an early start with Margaret in the morning. She had gladly offered her car, though at first she was shy about going with him. He had finally persuaded her to meet his family.

The curving flagstone pathway led to a doorstep lighted by a yellow coach lamp. A knocker of heavy rich brass yielded up its light against the dark door. Behind the leaded windows figures stood or moved about like shadows on a screen. Landon heard the music from the party: the high fluting notes of some reed instrument mingling with the metallic twang of bows engaging wires. The strange music arose, uncoiling into the night air like a cobra from its basket. On the doorstep Landon listened to these sounds from the mud banks of the Ganges. Vera used to stand on her head listening to this stuff. Her days of Yoga and the Five Steps to Proper Assimilation. He ignored the lion's-head knocker and pressed the doorbell, unbuttoning his spring coat and glancing down to his blue broadcloth shirt and the gray suit he had bought for a wedding in 1966. Hopelessly conservative, but he couldn't wear the tight-fitting clothes now in fashion. He had to shop around to find suitable duds. The trousers were always too snug around his legs and under the crotch. He had always preferred loose-fitting garments. In the office Cramner used to enjoy a standing joke at Landon's expense. He never tired of asking the others where the biggest dance hall in town was. In Freddy Landon's pants, of course! Lots of ball room there! Cramner! Now toasting his skinny shanks in the Florida sun. Boring strangers with his tales. After a moment the door opened and a thin tanned young man stood staring out at Landon. He was handsome enough in his white bell-bottoms with his brilliant-orange satin shirt open at the throat. His dark hair was long and beautifully groomed. A gold charm hung from one earlobe. He was barefoot. It took a moment for them to recognize each other.

"Why, Uncle Freddy . . . it's you!"

"In the flesh, Howard," said Landon, stepping into the hallway. "How are things, anyway?"

"Why, just super, Uncle Freddy . . . My God! We haven't seen you in ages. Where have you been hiding? We've heard all sorts of stories. You're living with a Russian woman or something? . . . Let me take your coat . . ."

"Thank you, Howard . . . You're looking fit."

"Yes. Mother and I have just been back a week . . . From Bermuda. We've been down there for a month. A fun place. Ginny said you might come. I'm awfully glad to see you. You know how fond we are of you. Mother still talks about how you helped her through her crisis with dear old Hughes. They're together again, by the way."

"Is that so?"

"Oh yes . . . Mother and Hughes have been seeing each other again. Oh, it's been going on now for six months or so. He spent two weeks with us in Bermuda . . ."

Howard folded Landon's coat across his arm. "I think Mother is getting over the sex thing now, you know. For a few years it was a real bitch. But now . . . Well, it's no longer such a big deal . . ."

"No, I suppose not."

"Yes. I think Mother's now looking for a companion more than anything else. That's where old Hughes comes in. They always did get on fairly well, you know . . . Mother's not getting any younger either. And I have my own life to live."

"Of course."

"I have my own apartment in Sutton Place, but it's only a bachelor and there's no room to party. Oh, here comes Mother now . . . I'll take your coat upstairs." Blanche walked toward them on silver slippers, wearing a long dress of midnight blue. Bermuda or not, she was still as pale as an Easter lily. A strand of cultured pearls enriched her poor neck. She looked older than Landon remembered, but the eyes still flashed with their old antic energy. She opened her thin arms to him.

"Freddy, dear boy, you did come." They embraced, and Landon inhaled the perfume of old violets pressed between the leaves of books. A maiden aunt of his once smelled like this. "Freddy, it's been ever so long since we last saw you."

"Well, Blanche, I'm out of your league now."

"Nonsense. You're never out of my league, dear boy. I'm hurt that you didn't come to see me more often. You know I've always thought of you as a special friend." She held him at arm's length and cocked her head to one side like a bird. "At one time I thought we might be lovers. Does that shock you?"

"Why, Blanche, you should have hinted. I'm not a subtle man."

She laughed. "Oh, Freddy. Our old talks. Do you remember? It all seems so long ago now. The utter past tense. Well, well . . ." She patted his arm. "And Vera will be so pleased you've come. We must have a talk later, you and I. Come along now and meet some people. They're mostly Howard's friends. People from the theater or advertising. He seems to know people in everything. I have such trouble remembering names any more."

They walked arm in arm toward one of the crowded front rooms and Blanche stroked his sleeve. "I'm so glad Vera and Ginny have decided to stay here with me for a while."

"Is Vera planning to stay in Toronto permanently, then?" asked Landon.

"That's my impression, though she hasn't confided in me. She never has, as you well know. Vera, I'm afraid, has never valued my opinion on anything. However . . ."

They stopped at the entrance to a room thick with people who milled about holding cigarettes and glasses. The Oriental music wound its way through the smoke and noise, and a single drumbeat echoed off the walls. Many of the people were handsome and a few of the women were beautiful. Landon could not help noticing their edible bottoms blooming forth from wide-belted hip-huggers. Several of the men were barefoot like Howard or wore sandals. A few of the blacks looked like tribal dignitaries in their brilliant robes and dashikis. One fellow's enormous Afro-style haircut blazed forth from his head like a black nimbus. A few others were dressed like zoot-suiters from the forties with long coats and broad-brimmed velour slouch hats worn low over eyes darkened by shades. Landon owned an old album of 78s and on its cover Dizzy Gillespie was dressed like these cats.

Blanche, rising on her toes, looked around. "Oh dear, I can't see anyone I know. Everyone's so young . . ." Landon squeezed her hand.

"Don't worry about it, Blanche. I know my way around. I'll get myself a drink. You see to your other guests." He was looking through the smoke, searching hard for Ginny or Vera.

"But it's so rude to leave you like this, not knowing anyone, and I can't see Vera at the moment. And Ginny's gone out for some ice. What a sweet child! I wanted to phone but she insisted on going. One of her young friends went with her. Ralph somebody or other. An attractive young man."

"Yes, I've met him," said Landon.

Blanche touched his arm again lightly. "Perhaps I should mind my own business, but Vera and Ginny have had words tonight."

Landon turned toward her. "Oh? What about?"

"Well, perhaps it's nothing, but I heard them quarreling before the party. In one of the bedrooms upstairs. It's about the young man. You probably know Vera's feelings on young radical people . . ."

"I don't think the subject ever came up."

"When Ginny showed up at the airport this afternoon with the young man . . . Well. When they got here, Vera hit the roof. Insisted that Ginny wasn't to see this young man again. Vera can be very determined, as you know . . ."

"Yes, I know."

"I've sometimes wished I had her strength . . ."

Howard appeared suddenly, a frown creasing his handsome face. "God, Mother! There are people at the door. I mean, they're *your* friends!"

"Yes, yes, dear, I'm coming. Do look after your Uncle Freddy now and introduce him to some of your nice friends . . ."

But after she left, Howard, who appeared to be in a temper, excused himself and disappeared into a large adjoining room where people were shuffling around to some slow jazz. Landon wandered alone toward the bar and asked for a drink. The white-jacketed barkeep clunked two ice cubes into a glass and splashed some Bell's Royal Reserve over them. Landon waved off the soda bottle, preferring to take this premium firewater straight. It was a nice change after Old Troll and he sipped it with pleasure as he stood on the edge of several groups, looking for a familiar face. He always had trouble at parties; had never managed the knack of maneuvering into conversation with strangers. What to say? How do. Fred Landon's the name. Nice party. Full stop. He guessed he was more of a listener. A drink or two always helped though, and he asked for another. He thought the bartender smirked a little when he poured out a double. Probably thinks I'm a boozer, thought Landon. An alcoholic freeloader in a baggy suit. Somebody's bachelor uncle. In his head Landon told the fellow off. Fuck you, Charley!

He could not see Vera, and so he edged his way past people into the other room. He remembered Sunday dinners here with Hughes standing at the head of the table in his gray slacks and blue blazer, carving up the rump roast or tenderloin. Sometimes Blanche, already four drinks up on everybody and feeling rascally, would fondle Landon's knee beneath the table, while Vera, not bothering to hide her boredom, listened to Howard talk about his latest friend. A large airy light-filled room now thick with smoke and noise. In the heated dimness couples circled one another with their arms outspread and their eyes closed. The mildly pleasant slow jazz had given way to a frantic recital on the electric organ. Some madman was using his fingers, or was it his toes? Perhaps he was thumping the keys with his member! Some part of him, at any rate, was charging up and down the keyboard with demonic energy. For a moment Landon saw the organist overcome by powerful feelings, attacking the instrument with both hands and feet, pulling out all the stops with his teeth. Now and then there were searing howls: cries surely from a tormented soul. Landon thought he remembered enough of his Dante from university to wonder whether a traveling shade from the Middle Ages who wandered through this room might not believe himself in Hell. The dancers, some young, some not so young, warily circled one another, lost in private reveries, their faces fixed and suggesting serious ritual, while their bodies jerked as though scorched by fire.

To Landon it seemed a strange gloomy circle of spastics, kindled to some old tribal thing by the organ man's savage rhythms and shrieks. Everywhere you looked there were signs of this residual primitivism. Perhaps not a bad thing, if it didn't get out of hand. However, most things do nowadays, thought the real-estate salesman. Moderation is not this century's strong point. As for this ridotto, it might be more appropriate in the forest after a day's successful hunting. If the young could barely get away with it, there was something excessive and asinine about a middle-aged man sweating and puffing in his tight pants.

Landon looked across the dancers and spotted Vera's hatchet-like profile; the sharp little upturned nose that just spoiled an otherwise attractive face. She was talking to a tall gray-haired man named Bill Craig. Landon remembered him as a friend of the family, a lawyer who handled Blanche's money and straightened out her marital tangles. Still a bachelor, he had always been sweet on Vera. Landon studied his former wife. She had put on a little weight these last few years (who hadn't?), but it had done her no harm. When they were married she had really been too thin, a severely sculpted girl, dark, nervous, and rigidly intense. These extra pounds softened the edges and enriched her womanliness, made her legs and bosom fuller and more inviting. The jet hair still shone deeply, scissored across the brow into those forbidding Joan of Arc bangs that she had worn all her life. Everything from top to bottom spitefully correct to the last millimeter. Perfection in dress was a lifelong habit with her and Landon had always admired it; admired it with the extravagance of a person who never quite succeeds in putting everything together. For him something was always missing or not right. If his suit was freshly pressed, his shoes would appear scuffed. A shirt collar might fit perfectly, but the sleeves would somehow protrude three inches below a coat cuff. Ten seconds on a chair would wrinkle the seat of his pants.

Yet Vera could muscle her way through a theater crowd or a subway rush hour and emerge with every hair in place. And now he stood watching her eighteen years after the wedding bells. He had to admit that she looked superb; cool, implacable, and, as always, unsmiling. Vera had no sense of humor. Not her fault, of course, but a serious handicap nonetheless. It must have caused some tension between her and Ginny. He used to enjoy watching his daughter when she was just a little girl. She was a great mimic and could imitate all the television personalities; Skelton as Clem Kaddiddlehopper and Lucille Ball as a wacky housewife, all the Disney characters and comedians on Ed Sullivan too. Sometimes they did this nonsense together, and it always annoyed Vera, who found it silly. Probably she felt left out. Landon leaned against the wall and nervously lighted a cigarette. Before him, the woman he once believed he loved; now a handsome well-nourished forty-year-old North American female in a perfectly tailored Peck & Peck outfit. Had anyone got into her scrupulous pants since him? There must have been a few discreet affairs, but maybe not. Vera was oddly sexless, one of those persons whose manner suggests that sex is no very big deal. He doubted that she had ever really enjoyed it with him, though there had been a few inspired moments. And she had always spoken with distaste of New York men. Once, after three martinis, she told him that they were all either fairies or perspiring and overweight businessmen from New Jersey who were all packed too tightly into their suits. They smoked foul green cigars and fumbled for your knee under the table. Landon enjoyed hearing such things. And she was a fussy dame. He could remember how she perfumed her armpits before their lovemaking. She also complained about his personal habits, which she considered gross. Not without cause either, for sometimes he allowed his socks to ripen on his feet. Or farted in bed. Or forgot and left his pared toenails on the bathtub ledge. Minor irritations certainly, but maddening to a fastidious type. But she was an attractive woman in her chill proud way and there was something rather fine in this hauteur. Landon had been thinking of this when they last met on Christmas Day in the Palm Court of the Plaza Hotel in New York. Their first family Christmas in years and one of the saddest days in Landon's life. It had been Ginny's idea, and he and Vera had reluctantly gone along. The three of them sat on green chairs and ate bread and butter and drank tea like the English. The Palm Court was filled with old ladies clinking their cups and whiling away the afternoon. The waiters in their starched white jackets and green cummerbunds walked among the tables and potted ferns. In a corner near an enormous Christmas tree a man in tails tucked a fiddle beneath his chin and sawed away at "Greensleeves," accompanied by a languid pianist. Listening to them and glimpsing his own face in the wall mirrors, Landon felt a terrible sadness steal over him. That afternoon had been so painful! Three wills and each pulling in a different direction. The three of them sat stiff-faced over their cups of tea. Vera wanted to have dinner in the dining room and had reserved a table. Ginny found the Plaza old-fashioned and stuffy and, after failing to persuade her mother to try a new restaurant in the Village, lapsed into a childlike sulk with an elbow on the table and a fist mashed hard against her cheekbone. Meanwhile, Landon had bought tickets for a Ranger game, characteristically forgetting that his daughter no longer had crushes on hockey stars. No one saying very much and the day another small failure in three lives. Still, Vera had looked magnificent, and she even managed to insult a waiter, no small feat in New York.

In Blanche's dining room the violent music ceased and the dancers drifted into groups in darkened corners. Landon thought he recognized the smell of cannabis or hashish burning in bowls and cigarettes. When the lawyer left Vera's side, Landon walked across the room and touched her lightly on the elbow.

"Hello, Vera."

"Well, Fred!" She turned toward him and smiled thinly, inclining her head to one side and folding her arms across her chest. "I'm glad you came along. Blanche said you might. And how are things going?"

"Things are not going badly, Vera. And how about you? How's New York?"

"Well, I've left New York for good. Or haven't you heard? I'm coming back to Toronto to live."

"Yes, I heard that." Landon dropped his cigarette into an empty beer bottle, where it smoldered and fizzed away, sending up a cloudy gray smoke signal.

"What happened to Manhattan, the Bronx, and Staten Island too?"

"I beg your pardon?"

"Sorry . . . The words to an old song."

"Of course, it would be . . . You and your old songs. I remember how you used to sing them in the bath. Did I ever tell you how much that used to irritate the hell out of me?" She was still smiling.

"Yes. Many times."

"But you really do have such an awful singing voice, Fred. I mean, it sounded like hell. But it always amazed me. You always knew the words. I could never understand why anyone would go to the trouble of remembering the words to a lot of silly old songs."

"What about Rudy Vallee?" asked Landon. "And Bing Crosby? They did all right. I only needed a manager."

Vera laughed. "Oh yes . . ."

"And New York isn't what it's cracked up to be, then?" asked Landon. Vera's smile vanished.

"New York is too expensive and it's too bloody dangerous any more. The crime is unbelievable. You've probably read about it in the papers. It's a national scandal. They steal every-thing that isn't bolted down. It's literally worth your life to go out in the streets after dark. A single woman isn't safe anywhere any more. Everyone I know has bad nerves. And why wouldn't they? You never know when you'll come home and find your place broken into . . ." She handed him a small lighter and he snapped open a flame beneath her cigarette. She inhaled deeply and then turned her head to blow forth the smoke in a round funnel.

"And speaking of criminals and other undesirable types, do you know where our daughter is at this moment?"

"Well, Blanche said something about Ginny going out for ice."

"Yes . . . And did Blanche tell you who Ginny was going out to get this ice with?"

"Yes. Ralph Chamberlain."

"You've met Mr. Chamberlain, then?"

"Yes. He came around yesterday with another young man. They were bringing Ginny from the airport."

"And what do you think of him?"

"What are these questions, Vera? Every time we meet it's the Interrogation Hour. I only met this Chamberlain for an hour or so yesterday. He appeared to me to be highly intelligent. An impatient angry fellow and a little too arrogant for my taste, but then he has several bees in his bonnet."

"Well, I've seen his type plenty of times before in the States. Bloody rabble-rousers. He's a disgrace to his country."

"Nonsense."

"Well, I think he is. And what about Ginny?"

"Well, what about her, Vera?" He felt an old familiar irritation arising within. These questions were so trying. "She's too young for any serious romance. He's just a boy friend . . ."

"Oh yes . . . Just a boy friend. Fred? You don't really know your daughter, do you?"

"Our daughter, Vera, our daughter."

"All right, our daughter. But the fact remains that you don't know her."

"That's an opinion, not a fact."

"Oh shit, I know what I'm talking about. You weren't around last summer when she got this hero-worship look in her eye. Last summer it was a guitar player from some godforsaken coal-mining town in Pennsylvania. He played the guitar in some village hangout. He was just a skinny hungry-looking kid of nineteen with pimples on his face. He claimed to have a weak heart and it kept him out of the army. It didn't keep him from being another one of these radical revolutionaries. He was all for burning a few buildings down to show us how good citizens should behave. Of course, Ginny was fascinated by him. One evening she brought him around to the apartment for dinner. God, it was awful! He just sat there eating my food and drinking my wine and sneering at everything. The books on my bookshelves, the drapes on my walls, everything. And argued. Mister Know-it-all. I defended my way of life. Christ, it makes me mad when I think about it. Why the hell should I have to justify my way of life to every little skinny half-baked radical who comes along? The boy grew very abusive and I had to ask him to leave. He was the poor boy from the slums, of course. And if there is one character who will set the Virginia Anns of this world off and running, it's the poor boy from the slums and his story. And oh how it works on teenage girls who've had private educations and have credit cards at Bergdorf Goodman. They feel so awful, so guilty about having had these advantages. And this hard-luck story is exactly what Chamberlain has been peddling her. She's given him money. Oh, you can always get to the little Ginnys of this world with that line. They positively cringe with guilt."

"Maybe so," said Landon, "but what about this guitar player from Pennsylvania?"

Vera stabbed a wooden ashtray with her cigarette, sending a brief shower of sparks into the heavy dark air. "Now, that was no joke. The silly little bitch was chasing this Ernie Monroe all over Manhattan. I was going out of my mind. This boy was mixed up with all sorts of people, drug addicts, student radicals, Black Panthers. I'm sure she was at parties where they used God knows what kind of drugs. Coming in at all hours of the morning, and there was no talking to her. She just wouldn't listen to me. Fortunately, Monroe lost interest in her after a few weeks."

"I didn't know anything about this. Why didn't you call me?"

"And what good would that have done? You're up here, 350 miles away. I suppose you would have flown down for an overnight stay and straightened everything out. Oh, you'd have come, all right—one of your twenty-four-hour wonder visits. And you would decide that it was time you and Ginny had a little heart-to-heart talk about certain things. So you'd have taken her to dinner. To some sweet little place in the Village, all quaint and romantic. And you'd have had your little heart-to-heart by candlelight and wine. And you'd have talked about—oh, everything under the sun, except the one thing that mattered. At all costs you'd have avoided mentioning anything that might remotely involve a difference of opinion. You and Ginny would then have congratulated yourselves on what a splendid relationship you have worked out between you. Then you'd have flown home, saying to yourself, What a good daddy I am in spite of this nasty divorce. And Ginny would have told her friends what a super daddy she has and how he's so understanding."

Landon's ears were scarlet, but in his heart he knew she was right. "Well . . . you were never one to mince words, were you, Vera?" Landon examined her face. She was beginning to age around the eyes. And she was edgy. This decision to return to Canada must have been wrenching. And this business with Ginny! The travel fatigue. It was dangerous to irritate her when she was like this. She was now speaking in a slow measured way, weighing each word and investing it with a slight Oxonian flavor. It was always a bad sign when she began to sound English.

"Right now, Ginny doesn't like me very much. I've seen this approaching for the past year or so. I suspect it's perfectly normal for teenage girls to dislike their mothers at some point, so I'm not greatly disturbed. But we've had some nasty arguments lately. Some of them have been quite brutal. Still, deep down I think she respects my judgment, and to me right now that's far more important than her affection. Now, with you, Fred, it's different, isn't it? You simply can't bear to disagree with anyone for fear they'll dislike you. Even for a few minutes . . . Do you remember when Ginny was small? You could never bring yourself to discipline her, could you? Even when she was being absolutely horrid. It was always I who had to endure the slammed door and the I-hate-you-Mommy stuff . . . Do you remember that?"

He remembered all right. Vera had always played the heavy, though Landon couldn't help thinking that she often enjoyed it. There was a broad streak of authoritarian cruelty in her nature. But she was infuriatingly right. He had been a loving but a bad father. He felt a tightness, a swelling in his chest, and solemnly he crunched an ice cube between his teeth.

"It was nerve-racking, that Monroe business," said Vera. "That's why it's so distressing to see it starting all over again with Chamberlain . . . It's really intolerable."

"Oh Christ, Vera," said Landon suddenly. "The girl's only seventeen. Isn't she entitled to a few crushes at her age?"

"Crushes!" Vera sounded exasperated. "God, I think you're still living in the forties, Fred. You probably think that young girls who have crushes these days still hold hands at the movies or have milk shakes at the corner drugstore."

"What you're saying, Vera, is that you don't trust your own daughter."

"What I'm saying is that behind all this funny-girl front is a very mixed-up young lady who is extremely impressionable." The music had started up again. It was something altogether wild, a flight into abandonment. And Vera wouldn't shut up.

". . . And the world she's living in . . . It's simply too fast for her . . ."

"Too fast for me too, goddamnit," said Landon, pulling a handkerchief from the breast pocket of his suit coat and mopping his neck and brow. "This damn place is giving me a headache. I wonder what lunatic chose the music. Howard probably . . ."

Vera surveyed the dancing couples. "I don't know how Blanche can allow these people in the house. It's quite unnecessary."

"Quite . . . quite . . . quite," muttered Landon. "Jesus. . ." Again he felt suspended between tiredness and anger. He shouldn't have come to this circus. These electric moanings and groanings were too much if you weren't used to them. And in the midst of it all, there was Vera's tongue; flaying his spirit with the cord of righteousness. And this tightness in his chest. It depressed him. It could be something serious. Had Wally Beal felt such constricting pressure mounting in his chest before he collapsed at the Masons' dinner? But perhaps this was only what they called tachycardia? He had read about this somewhere. But damn those popular magazines. He couldn't remember whether the article said this tachycardia was serious or not. He did recall that the article prescribed deep breathing and a soothing thought. But where were restful thoughts to be found in this madness? Always polite, he bent an ear to Vera's words and tried to think of Margaret.

". . . And now that we're back in Toronto," Vera was saying, "Ginny will be seeing more of you, and I want you to promise to help me. She's left Columbia, as you know. Now this doesn't greatly disturb me. She was far too young for college last fall anyway. I tried to tell her that. And Columbia has far too many radical types to suit me. She's much better off up here. What I would now like to do is find her a job, anything that will keep her busy for a few months and take her mind off these political things. She could even do some charity work if she really wants to do some good for her fellow man. I should imagine there's lots of work at the United Appeal for volunteers."

"Yes, I should imagine." Landon held his breath, silently counted ten seconds, and then fifteen. At thirty he exhaled, thinking how terrible it must be to die by drowning. Thrashing around in that dark water while strange marine creatures swim silently by, ignorant of your struggle for life; holding your breath until that last awful second when the body must inhale and the water streams through to flood the lungs. The choking and gasping after simple air. And Virginia Woolf walked into water weighted down by a stone. A sickening thought, and Landon felt himself grow dizzy. But it could have been the air in the room. It was now thick with smoke and laden with a dull heavy sweetness.

"In the fall," said Vera, "I should like to see her at Trinity. I know she'll like it there. I've already been in touch with Simon Aspell and he doesn't see any problem at all. Her marks are good . . ."

Half-listening, Landon continued his deep breathing, though he supposed that this was not the ideal place for a man in search of oxygen. It was like jogging near a freeway. Great for the heart but killing to the pulmonary system.

". . . Now, I want you to help me with this, Fred. Ginny's very fond of you and will probably listen if you talk to her.

Moreover, if both of us agree on something for a change, she's bound to consider it more seriously. Are you listening, for God's sake? What are you making those odd faces for?"

"Sorry. Yes, I'm listening . . . I'm always listening."

"Well . . . Will you help?"

"I'll do everything I can to help Ginny, of course."

"Helping me now is going to help Ginny in the long run, believe me."

Again Landon felt the tightness. Were there iron hoops encircling his chest? He had read that medieval churchmen used such devices to extract confessions from heretics. What were they called? Dominican bracelets! Another useless fact. And these hoops around his chest? Were they not fashioned by Vera's will? By her powerful assertiveness? "I know she'll like it there." People like Vera are so confident in their manipulation of other lives. Whence cometh such confidence? How can they be so sure they know what they're doing? And why could he not offer some resistance here instead of standing around like an overheated boiler about to explode. Apoplexy! That could be his fate. It would be just like him to croak from something sounding old-fashioned and musty. Vera could then tell Ginny that her father lived quaintly and died quaintly too. But he must get away and breathe some fresh air. He excused himself and shouldered his way through the dancers toward the kitchen, opening a door which led to a back staircase. He climbed slowly, grateful for the muffling of sound as he mounted the wooden steps. These old houses! You couldn't beat the walls in them.

On the first landing he stopped before a door. He remembered a bathroom here; Harvey Hubbard had used it as a hideout when Blanche was on the warpath in the bad old days.

In the bathroom he turned on the spiggots full blast, and the water poured from the taps, swirling around the beryl-colored basin, a tiny pool for his hungry hands to swim in. There was a choice of soaps: a scented white cake for the ladies, and for the gents a brown biscuit darkly flecked and granular to the touch. Landon sniffed its perfume. Oatmeal soap. His sister used to peddle this stuff door-to-door for Avon. Selling glass cannons loaded with deodorant and miniature antique cars filled with cologne. After thoroughly soaping his face and hands, he rinsed them in the green water and then pressed his face into a towel. This act of cleansing was sometimes a meditation for him. The face in the mirror looked back, a heavy face now charged with a brooding sadness. But the flesh was still firm and the blue eyes reflected an amiable light. Then there was always the hair, abundant and rich and still youthful. Vanity, vanity, all is vanity, saith the preacher. Nevertheless, thank God for the hair. But why the sadness? He had started the evening feeling not bad. After months he had landed a job. At the Essex Arms was a woman who whispered in his ear of love. Yet now he felt overcome by dismal thoughts. He guessed it must be Vera's resoluteness. She tried so hard, wouldn't relax. It oppressed him to think about it, because she just might be right. This might be the way to handle your life. As for Ginny and Chamberlain? No more than a schoolgirl crush. His advice (who was asking?) would be to underplay the whole business and not come on too strong, as people put it nowadays. He realized that he was up to his old trick of arguing with Vera in absentia. Still, he must talk with Ginny about this. And what could he say without putting the girl on guard? All experience is valuable but don't rush into anything without thinking of the consequences. It sounded so pompous. But what else to say? You can't force people to do what they don't want to do. Not any more. They laugh in your ear. You can only hope you'll be lucky.

He walked across the room and unfastened a latch, swinging open the small portal window. He stood there breathing deeply, enjoying the cool unstained air. Below him the sound of music and laughter reached out to the garden. On the gravel driveway by the garage Blanche's Mercedes coupe crouched, its silver flanks gleaming in the dim moonlight which filtered down through the stiff leafless trees. Landon, sniffing the air like an old dog, heard the crunch of footsteps on gravel and the sound of voices approaching the house. Even before he saw the two figures walking up the driveway, he recognized his daughter's laughter pealing into the night. After a moment he saw them, each holding a cardboard bucket against their chests, the ice cubes sparkling like gems in the light from the windows. They walked toward him, slowly enjoying the night. Somehow Landon felt ill at ease standing like this, watching them approach. It seemed peculiarly indecent. But what did he expect to see? Would Chamberlain buss his daughter on the cheek before delivering the ice? Give her a quick feel in the azaleas before rejoining the party? Landon winced slightly. No man in truth can bear the thought of his daughter being touched by another man. Was that Freudian nonsense or ancient human knowledge felt along the bones? What about these dreams he'd been having, for instance? He shut the window and walked away, turning on the faucets once more, twisting around their handles till the water gushed and swirled against the green sides. If there were any shenanigans going on below, he couldn't hear them. If you can't hear it, it's not happening. The old ostrich trick and a family trait. His sister used to turn the taps on full blast while sitting on the john. The water stormed from the pipes. In the old bathroom in Bay City. The gushing taps covered the noise of her water tinkling into the bowl. Or worse yet, a maidenly fart. Now the face in the mirror regarded Landon with pursed lips. It seemed to be whistling a tune Landon hadn't heard in years. How did it go?

> I love you, a bushel and a peck,
> You bet your pretty neck I do.

Downstairs he wandered among the weaving bodies, looking for his daughter; old Lear, stooped and gray, in search of his Cordelia. By chance he plucked a full glass of something from a chair just before a woman sat upon it. He put the glass to his lips and gingerly sipped the liquid. No telling what people consumed at these circuses. Was LSD tasteless? Landon freaked out on acid, hallucinating wildly. And what visions would enter his bushy head? But the drink seemed to be only Scotch and water. As he looked up, he spotted Howard coming toward him. Howard, barefoot in the park, was linked arm in arm with a handsome young man who seemed dazed. Howard himself was extravagantly stoned, crazed with happiness. His dark eyes snapped with malicious humor.

"Dear Uncle Freddy. Are you having a good time?"

"Fine, Howard," said Landon.

"Do you smoke, Uncle Freddy?" asked Howard. "Would you like some grass? It's very good stuff."

"Thanks no, Howard, I'm driving. Have you seen Ginny, by the way?"

"Not lately, I'm afraid. About an hour ago, actually. She was with that yummy-looking man."

"Yes. Well, I have to move along now, Howard. Enjoy yourself . . . As if you had to be told . . ." Howard whooped with glee.

"How we miss your witty tongue, Uncle Freddy. You'll come around and see us more often from now on, won't you? Mother talks about you all the time."

"Yes. Well, we'll see how things work out, Howard."

"Come along now, Duane," said Howard, taking the young man's arm.

"Come and see me too, Uncle," said the young man as they wandered away.

Landon finished his drink and was looking for a place to set the glass when a familiar voice tinged with a phony English accent said, "Can I get you another, sir?" He turned in time to receive his daughter's peck on the cheek. "How's my pop, anyway?"

"Your pop's fine. Where have you been? I've been looking for you." Ginny had brushed her thick blond hair and now wore it tied by rubber bands into a ponytail. In her polka-dot granny dress she looked like a Mennonite.

"Ralph and I went out for ice."

"Oh yes. The political scientist."

Ginny pulled a face, lowering her voice and sounding mock-serious.

"Oh yes. The political scientist." She laughed. "You call him the political scientist and Mother calls him your new friend. And is your new friend coming around tonight?" Her imitation of Vera's slightly snooty voice was almost perfect, and Landon smiled a little, even though he knew it was wrong to make fun of her mother like this. Ginny looked up into her father's face and wrinkled her nose. "You don't look so hot, you know. Are you feeling okay? Your love life's not getting you down, I hope?" How pert and American she had become these last few years!

"Yes, I'm all right," said Landon. "It's been a long tiring day. I got a job though."

"Hey, terrific! Doing what?" She was busy scanning the room, the light dancing off her spectacles.

"Same thing, I'm afraid. Selling. I guess I'm hooked for life in the old shell game. Too late to change now." He smiled. He must guard against this play for sympathy. He watched Ginny's face, seeking some clue to her estimation of him. In some ways Ginny was very much her mother's daughter. In spite of a fundamental ineptness of her own (Landon's maladroit genes!), she admired successful people; new-world pragmatists who got things done. More than once he had detected in her an underlying pity for his own modestly lived life. He had once heard her on the telephone talking to a friend about him. "My dad's in sales. He's really assistant to the sales manager and does most of his selling now on the telephone. He has these important accounts all over the country, and he just sits in his office and phones people all day. He never has to leave the office." But after all, a little teenage boasting about fathers was natural. Now, though, he could see nothing in her face except amusement. After a while Landon said, "It's in real estate. Not much, but it's a job, and maybe something better will turn up later on . . ."

But Ginny was now waving her arm. "There's Ralph now, Daddy. Over here, Ralph," she called. "Daddy, I'm so glad for you, really." She reached up and pecked his cheek again.

Chamberlain approached in his dude-ranch outfit and drooping mustache.

"Evening," said Landon.

"Hi ya," said Chamberlain, sticking his hands into the back pockets of his jeans, elbows flared out as he looked around.

"Where's your friend?" asked Landon. "Did he not come along?"

"Which friend is that?" The boy was springing up and down lightly on the balls of his feet, looking over the room; the dead-end kid who's just arrived at the fancy-dress dance.

"The Texan. Or Oklahoman . . . the big fellow?" asked Landon.

"Oh, Logan . . . No, he couldn't come. Had to visit his chick or something. She's got the flu, I think." He turned to Ginny. "I gotta go soon, Gin. I'm flat out."

Rude little bastard, thought Landon. He seems to have a grudge against everyone over twenty-five. Landon was soon frozen out of their conversation, and so he stood listening to the party swirl around him. What a crazy babble assaulted the ears! But there were some interesting sights, if you could bear to look. In the far room a fat woman was now doing a belly dance in the middle of the floor. Why always the fat ones? he wondered. But she had an enthusiastic audience and they were clapping their hands in encouragement. In one corner a couple lay curled upon a divan. The girl's long hair hid both their faces, but from Landon's view the fellow seemed to be smoking her ear. For some reason Ginny and Chamberlain were talking about their grandfathers. Those wise old men! Landon was stung by jealousy. Grandfathers! They are always *persona grata* with the young. Encrusted with wisdom by time and nostalgia, fossilized into legend. Of course, they are always exempt from criticism. And why not? They are out of it now. They don't threaten, so the young can afford to be generous. It's the fathers who get it in the neck, he reflected with a twinge of bitterness. Yet for a time he had felt the same way about his grandfather. His mother's father—old Ulf Lindstrom, who spent most of the fine-weather days of his life in a Boston rocker, sitting amid the vines and leaves of Dutchman's-pipe, which clung to the verandah of the old white house outside Bay City. In bad weather he moved the rocker indoors and sat by the front window, looking beyond the trees and the highway to the meadows and the edge of Georgian Bay. And his Blue Moon Cabins and Tourist Court. Largely abandoned by all but impatient honeymooners from the towns to the north: gawky young men with their nervous brides who couldn't wait to get to Toronto or Niagara Falls. Old Ulf! Rocking away the afternoons, scanning the fields with eyes as blue as a summer lake, marking the passage of the seasons and God only knows what else. And because he said almost nothing and looked thoughtful, I guessed he was an old sage, reflected Landon, smiling. It wasn't the first time he'd been fooled.

He remembered the rides to town in the slope-nosed '37 Ford coupe, the old man's right hand, speckled by liver spots, resting on the crooked gear lever. The old plush seats smelled of stale bread. And Landon's grandfather, his first hero! With a shock of bright blond hair standing upright over his brow, making him look younger than his years. He dreamed a whole life away while the cabins grew moldy with emptiness and were finally overtaken by the field mice and raccoons. Now and then the old man cracked a wry joke or whistled "Heartaches" like Elmo

Tanner. Or bird calls. Half the birds around flocked to the verandah in search of mates, only to find an old man blowing into his hands. And the tourists passed by in their post-war Fords and Plymouths, heading for the new motels down the highway. People wanted running water and clock radios. You couldn't expect a commercial traveler to crank a pump handle after a day's business. Not that the old man wasn't warned. Landon's father had told him often enough. Persuading, arguing, finally throwing up his hands and leaving the house. As a boy, Landon had lain in bed listening to his mother and father talk about Granddad's tourist court. His father's fierce intelligence, his hasty energy. Where did he get it from? And he paced up and down the living-room floor on legs fatigued from climbing on and off freight cars all day; the proud hectoring voice, the voice of the schoolteacher he always wanted to be.

"Why doesn't he get off his backside, for the love of God? I just don't understand it. He's missing the chance of a lifetime. He's sitting on a fortune. If he'd only take a chance. That highway—after the war he'll be surrounded by supermarkets . . . gas stations . . . new housing developments. He's sitting on a gold mine. Why doesn't he do something about it?" His father's vision!

And Landon's heavy blond mother, looking up from her novel. "Oh, Jim. Leave him alone. You know what he's like. He hates to gamble. It's his nature and he'll never change. You can't change people if they don't want to change." Those lines delivered in the slightly fruity voice of a Barbara Stanwyck. Or whoever she had seen the night before at the Royale Theatre. Not that she was out to mock him. She would never do that. It was just that unconsciously she played out her life in other guises.

This talk about old Ulf had been through the reels many times and the part was familiar to her. She played the long-suffering wife of the prosaic husband, wasting her life away in a backwater hick town. How could he, with his books of science and mathematics, possibly understand the poetry of life, the rich music of existence? All she could do was wait for the handsome drifter, the writer temporarily down on his luck, wearing his black jacket and wide-brimmed fedora and bearing an uncanny resemblance to John Garfield. And she settled for Charley Ames! Those talks about Grandfather Lindstrom, with Landon's father always checking his temper against these phlegmatic Lindstroms, stepping out onto the back porch with a book beneath his arm. Something large and self-educative. Fantastic! *The Stars and Planets: A Guide to Their Movements.* Hunkered down against the clothesline pole with the book propped against his knee, lighting a homemade cigarette. His poor father! He married Joanna Lindstrom when she was nineteen and wore her blond hair bobbed in the flapper style. Landon had seen pictures, old faded snaps in which his mother stood on the running board of a Marmon or Whippet, next to some young blood. She was easily the fairest in Bay City and had many beaus, as she told Landon years later. But she chose his father because he sounded like a serious man and seemed so much more mature than the others. Landon, half-listening to his daughter amid the noise and music, pondered those old events. His mother must have been tempted by Jim Landon's serious manner. Blithe spirits are often attracted to grave ones, perhaps confusing solemnity with profundity, hoping maybe for some counterbalance to their own skittish natures. Take this Chamberlain, for instance. Landon found himself studying the pale intent face, the heavy Savonarola nose and thin lips, the dismal mustache. The face of a fanatic. Those dark scowling good looks proclaimed spitefulness and vanity. He knew he was attractive to women and liked to sulk around them. No doubt Ginny took him for a deep character, whereas he might just be a grudging type, bad-tempered and bratty, stirred only by indignation. Now he looked a little stupid. From sleepiness, probably. Tense faces like this need to remain alert or they slacken into coarseness. Chamberlain listened now without much attention as Ginny rattled on about her grandfather and how he had played with her as a little girl. He had taught her things, some of them beautiful and true. All this, of course, was nonsense, make-believe. The truth was that her grandfather never had much time for children. That tense moody man was too engrossed in his library books and silences. Later Landon came to believe that his father had secretly resented his children. They had helped to burn him out, and because of them he missed the main chance. After Billy's death he could scarcely abide young people. In their presence he felt reproached by life's plain contrariness.

Ginny was talking to him. "And what do you think about that, Daddy?"

"About what? Sorry."

"About going up to Bay City and seeing Granddad this weekend. I haven't seen him in ages." But Landon didn't want Ginny in Bay City this weekend. Especially with this sour little refugee. With Margaret coming along, there would be questions enough from Ellen.

"Well, Ginny, I'm going up to Bay City myself tomorrow," he said. "I want to see your grandfather."

"But that's great," she cried. "We can all go. I could make sandwiches . . . We could have a picnic. It's a super idea."

Landon wasn't so sure. "I don't know about that, Ginny. Your grandfather's an old man and he's had a serious stroke. I don't think he should have too much excitement all at once. It could tire him out . . ."

"But, Daddy, I'm sure he'd love to see me. He doesn't see me every day." She was suddenly animated by this charge of enthusiasm. She loved planning things, organizing people's days for them. She just might make it someday as a travel agent, Landon thought. "Ralph. You should get out in the country anyway. Get some fresh air. You haven't been anywhere in Ontario but this crummy old city. You look like a ghost." Ralph made a sour face.

"How can I go anywhere without a car?" Even though he didn't approve of Ginny's idea, Landon disliked seeing enthusiasm killed by whining. He felt like kicking the boy's ass. But Ginny was not to be scared off so easily.

"Don't worry about a car. We'll borrow Aunt Blanche's car. Or somebody's car . . ."

Landon made one last effort. "Since you're back in Toronto to stay, Ginny, you'll have lots of time to see your grandfather. In another couple of weeks spring will be here. The countryside will be green . . ." Ginny looked at him with a frank light in her eye. Was there not merriment behind those Ben Franklin glasses? And was she not about to erupt into laughter?

"Are you not going up alone then?" she asked, smiling. Oh, these females! With their sensitive antennae that probed the air and sounded the vibrations, forever pursuing the heart's secrets.

"No," said Landon, "I'm taking along a friend."

"Well, don't worry about it, Daddy, for goodness' sake," Ginny said quickly, squeezing his arm. "I'm dying to meet her, but Ralph and I can go up by ourselves. Perhaps we'll see one another there. We're only going to stay a little while . . . Hey . . ." She tugged at his arm as though persuading a sulky child. He was forced to look at her. Sometimes this hearty chumminess of hers was trying. "Hey look . . . If you'd rather we didn't go tomorrow . . . we can arrange another Saturday."

But after all, his reason was feeble. Why shouldn't the girl visit her grandfather? And hang Ellen by her inquisitorial nose!

"No. Never mind. I'm sure it'll be fine."

"Well, good, then. It's settled." She reared back and looked around the room, poking Ralph. "Come on, Ralph. Don't look so down, eh!"

"I'm tired, Gin."

"I know, baby. And you've got to be going soon. And . . . oops . . . here comes Mommy dear . . . I think she's half loaded, Daddy. What do you think? You know, she'd better watch herself. She's been hitting the old juice a lot these last few weeks. A couple of drinks before lunch. A couple of drinks before dinner . . . She always used to talk about Aunt Blanche and her *problem*. Well . . . she'd better watch it. Aunt Blanche seems to be in better shape now than dear Mommy." Landon suddenly felt irritated with his daughter. How the young hate to be rebuked for their infirmities! Yet how quickly they seize upon others'! Catch them at moments of weakness and plunge home the dagger. But now Vera came up to them, smiling brightly.

"Well now. And here we are again. Our own little family happily reunited. Isn't it delightful!" She immediately linked arms with Landon and Ginny and pulled them toward her. This show of feeling was unlike her. She must have been into the sauce. "And what are we talking about, pray? Plans, I expect. Or the great problems of life, perhaps. The overpowering mystery of it all. Are you giving these young people a few proverbs from your vast collection, Fred? Or are you being a good modern grownup and listening to their point of view? The now generation."

Ginny had now linked arms with Ralph and pulled him closer. She looked pained. "Oh, God, Mother. Please let's not be theatrical. You sound like a parent in some funny old Broadway play."

"Do I, darling? Theatrical, you say! Oh, surely not . . ." She paused. "I should have thought that you were the only theatrical one in the family tonight. That entrance you made. Superb, I thought. Though this sort of dress is not to my taste. Quite frankly, my dear, I think it makes you look old before your time. Like the little old lady who lived in the shoe."

Ginny blushed. Vera had struck home and drawn blood. Through Landon's veins coursed the poison of vanity.

"And do you know what we're doing tomorrow, Mother? We're all going up to Bay City."

"Really? How nice for you! A family picnic, is it? Well, a little early in the year, I should have thought. Still . . . You could always have lunch at your Aunt Ellen's. A charming woman. How is she, Fred, by the way?"

"Daddy's taking a friend up with him, Mother."

"How nice for Daddy! How nice for you all! I'm sure you'll have a splendid time." Vera was gripping them tightly.

"What's her name, Daddy?" asked Ginny, deadly persistent. Landon felt the heat rising from the soles of his shoes.

"Her name is Margaret, Ginny," he said with dull annoyance in his voice. Vera looked at him.

"Now, Fred. Tut tut. Females will be females, you know. These little games. Is that not so, Virginia Ann?" The cattiness. The bitchiness. How he sometimes longed to be away from them! Even Margaret. Often gossiping about some other lady teacher! How he would have enjoyed pressing his face against the cool stones of a monastery wall; summoned by the bells to the company of cowled men. Perhaps it was not too late to join the Trappists. He could hoe turnips or tramp grapes in his bare feet; live with people who had mastered the art of keeping their mouths shut.

"I'm tired, Ginny," said Ralph. "I think I'll split."

"Okay . . . I'll borrow Aunt Blanche's car and take you home. Ralph's just getting over a bad case of mono. Good night, Mother . . . night, Daddy."

"Now don't be late . . . please," said Vera. "I want you back within the hour . . . And mind your aunt's car."

"Yes, yes. Good night, all . . ." She skipped out, dragging Ralph by the arm. "See you tomorrow, Daddy," she called. "We'll probably be leaving after lunch."

Vera watched them go, then turned to Landon. "You'll excuse me if I say good night, Fred. It's been a tiring day."

"I'm sure it has." Vera looked around the room.

"If I could find Blanche, I'd have this house cleared out. It's nearly one o'clock. Look at the place, for God's sake. Ashes on the floor, drinks spilled all over the carpet. Where does Howard find these people? I wonder."

"An excellent question."

"Some of them seem unusually depraved."

Most of the people had left now, but a few lingered on, standing in groups and talking religion or politics, the two final subjects of all drunks and sadheads. Someone had found a recording of jazz blues, and now the sound of a sleepy tenor saxophone drifted through the house. Vera suddenly surprised Landon by touching his sleeve.

"You will remember our talk, won't you, Fred? Ginny's going to be all right, but she needs direction. I want that little shit-disturber out of her life. I don't want to have to go through another Ernie Monroe scene."

"I'll do what I can, Vera, of course, but you can't push people too far. They'll only react. A firecracker may explode in your face."

"Just talk to her, please. That's all I ask."

"I'll talk to her if I can ever nail her down to one place."

"Well, please try." He could feel the pressure of her fingers through the coat fabric. She hadn't touched him in a long time. It must be years now.

"I'll say good night now, Fred."

"Good night, Vera." She walked a few paces and then turned. "I hope you have a pleasant day tomorrow."

"Thanks." She left Landon wondering about this display of amiability. Had Ginny been correct yesterday when she suggested that Vera still felt something for him? No. After all these years—impossible. But how to explain this geniality!

In the hallway Landon rummaged in the closet for his coat. Behind a rack of old suits he discovered a tall cylindrical basket containing umbrellas and a few of Hughes Ritchie's old walking sticks. But where was his damn coat? Of course, one had to be idiotically optimistic to expect simple civility any more. But these people! At one time you could ignore their self-indulgence and childishness; their ridiculous aping of English gentry life. Their riding to hounds in the hills north of the city, and their tea and cucumber sandwiches in the late afternoons. You could even forgive their basic mental slackness, their crippling stupidity. At least in those days they manifested a chilly courtesy. Now that too apparently was gone. They might still open the door to greet you, but four hours later everyone is pissed and a man can't find his coat. But then he suddenly remembered. Howard had spirited away his coat to one of the upstairs bedrooms. Landon groaned. If he remembered correctly, there were at least ten bedrooms above him.

He climbed the wide staircase to the first landing, leaning his heavy weight against the handrail and making slow progress. Upstairs was total darkness. Why not a light to guide the forsaken traveler? He tried the first door, found it locked, and proceeded along the hallway, trying each door like the village constable on his nightly rounds. The third knob turned to his touch, and the door opened quietly on well-oiled hinges. Inside, a fog of sweet thick smoke clung to the air, slowly drifting out through an open window. Landon peered into the semi-darkness and was immediately startled by the sight of a nude figure darting for shelter behind drapery. He slammed the door shut, though not before he glimpsed a flash of white buttock and a thin naked shank.

"Sorry," he bellowed into the gloomy hallway. Behind the door he heard a giggle.

"What is it, Uncle Freddy?"

"I can't find my damn coat, Howard." He seemed to be speaking too loudly. Like a man locked up in a closet. "Where did you put it?"

"Next door. It's on the bed. Someone must have turned out the lights." Howard was beside himself with mirth, and now another voice had joined in on the fun.

"Thank you very much," said Landon, with all the exaggerated courtliness of the offended man. But of what use was irony in these grotesque situations? At the next door he pressed an ear to the old wood and listened so hard that his ear rang. But he could be interrupting anything. It could be mad hilarity or some solemn sexual rite in which fantastic couplings were engineered with all the dedication and gravity of a championship chess match. He hesitated with his hand upon the doorknob. Sexually this was an enterprising age. Soixante-neuf! The Prussian Hook! The Old Peach Basket! Mere child's play. The times demanded above all else *originality* and technical advance. You had to be original or you were nothing. Laughed right out of the sack. *Do you want to be a sexual nobody*? threatened one advertisement in a magazine. Well, obviously not. This was important. Bookstores devoted entire walls to sex manuals. Some of it was ingenious stuff too. Even reading the instructions wore you out. Landon had visited these shops on lower Yonge Street, standing on his corns with other middle-aged gents, thumbing through these booklets. Many of the customers were gray-haired men who wore fatigue on their lined faces. Lonely rooming-house masturbators who studied these exotic recipes for love, beneath naked light bulbs. Thinking about that could be a desolating experience. Why were his thoughts in such a sexual turmoil? It must be Howard and his damn games. Now Landon opened the door and faced an empty dark room. Switching on the light, he could see that the bed had been used and some hasty attempt had been made to remake it. A search for his coat forced him to his knees, and grunting beneath the bed on all fours (the bizarre positions one finds oneself in!), he finally found it: a rumpled ball. He ironed out the wrinkles with the flat of his hand and checked out, walking on his toes past Howard's room.

At the bottom of the stairs he saw Blanche. She seemed to be resting before attempting the climb; standing with one arm on the handrail, staring hard at the carpeted steps. Yet she could be either drunk or sick, and Landon called to her as he moved quickly down the stairs, stuffing his arms into the wrinkled coat. At the sound of his voice, she raised her head and her eyes sought his face.

"Why, Freddy, dear boy! Where have you been?" She looked exhausted and ill. "I was looking for you earlier."

"Are you feeling all right?" asked Landon.

"Why yes. I'm all right now. All that noise. It gave me a headache and I lay down for a nap. Missed most of everything, I'm afraid." She smiled weakly at him. "And I had hoped that tonight we might have a serious talk, you and I . . ."

"These parties of yours, Blanche. They're the last place to get serious about anything."

"Quite right. And why do I bother? . . . Well, to please Howard, I suppose." She looked down to the carpet again, as if studying her slipper. Somehow the sight of the small blue-veined foot in the slipper was painful to Landon. "Yes, to keep my boy happy!" Blanche said softly. "But he's not happy, Freddy, that's the problem . . ." She was holding back some enormous weight. "He's so depressed most of the time. I don't know what to do for him any more. He says the most dreadful things . . ." She leaned her head against Landon's chest and quietly sobbed. "I know he's not well . . . And he won't have anything to do with Dr. Lawson any more. Goes into a fit of rage when you mention it. He's called the doctor some terrible names . . . Oh, Freddy, he phones me up in the middle of the night . . . He says horrible things . . ."

"Yes, Blanche . . ." He could feel her frailness beneath the gown. She was never a sturdy person, now seemed merely tissue and bone.

"In the middle of the night he says he's going to . . . do away with himself . . ."

"Oh, Christ . . ."

"He says he's vile and doesn't deserve to live . . . He phones me three or four times a week. Oh, Freddy, what's one to do?" Landon held her tightly. This odd troubled soul. Yes. The question is—what is one to do? Exactly. How to work out a life? But the trouble here was deep, perhaps beyond anyone's powers to deal with. And what, after all, can you say? In the circumstances words are useless, even dangerous. Sometimes all you can do is hold a person. Suddenly Blanche pushed him away with her hands against his chest. She looked up at him with bright wet eyes.

"Freddy, I'm so sorry. This is foolishness. You see, I've been trying very hard lately."

"I'm sure you have, Blanche." Under the hall light she looked haggard.

"Yes, I have. I really have. But you see . . ." She stepped back from him and fingered her pearls, looking away. "Well, I shouldn't have drunk anything tonight. I don't know why I'm so damn stupid about these things. The doctor told me. And I took some pills, you see . . . But never mind that." She paused, looked over Landon, and seemed wryly amused by something. "Please don't misunderstand, but this has been a bit of a strain. With Howard. And now . . . I love Vera and Ginny and I'm delighted they're here . . . but Vera makes me nervous. She always has . . ."

"Yes, I know."

"Oh, never mind. Forget what I said. She's my sister and I love her very much, I really do. Ginny I adore, of course. Please forget what I said. I'm sorry." She looked away again, as if studying some abstract problem. "Isn't it odd how often I say I'm sorry? Hasn't it struck you as funny? It seems I'm always apologizing. That's what Harvey used to tell me." She brought her hands together. "Well, never mind . . . You must run along now, dear boy. You look tired . . . But you will promise to drop in and see me sometime soon."

"Of course, Blanche. And very soon. As a matter of fact, I'll phone you next week."

"You will?"

"Yes."

"Well, you're a lovely man. We shall drink tea. No gin or whiskey . . . There now . . . I'm feeling better already."

"Good."

Landon bent forward and kissed her cheek, inhaled again the old familiar mustiness. Now she looked at him anew, holding both hands, the maiden aunt.

"And we're told that you have a new friend." She paused. "I hope she's kind to you, Freddy."

"Yes. She's very kind, Blanche."

"Good. Excellent. Now I'll say good night. And God bless you."

"Yes. Good night, Blanche."

On the lawn Landon looked through the branches of the trees to the black sky. The moon had long gone to bed and the starless night was now streaming with darkness. The branches of the old trees stirred and creaked in the frost. It was still winter and Landon prayed for spring.

*FOUR*

The expressway bristled with fast-moving traffic, cars hastening from the city to parts unknown. At least unknown to Landon, who watched them whiz by from inside the heavy steel carapace of Granstein's DeSoto. Another cold bright morning, and the sunlight struck the surfaces of cars and glinted malignantly off the frost-whitened roadway. Before Landon's own eyes the DeSoto's rich ruby hood gleamed and flared like a fine old jewel. Earlier Landon had fetched a cloth over it, buffing away like a Saturday suburbanite. But the old car had given him trouble, stubbornly refusing to start. It was the same old business, and in the raw dampness of the garage Landon's breath smoked the air as he monkeyed with the haywire ignition. Beside him Margaret sat impassive as stone. She seemed preoccupied, even depressed. Yesterday too after their lovemaking she had lapsed into this moody silence. A funny dame. Perhaps her time of the month. But he was mildly irritated with her too. She might at least have had this car fixed by now. Like him she was a procrastinator. Two in the household and nothing would get done. A person should mate with someone who has different deficiencies. Balance one another's shortcomings. Spread around the misery and blame. After a while, though, the old car came to life and Landon had pointed it northward.

Now, tooling along the expressway at a conservative fifty-five (no Ozzie K. Smith he!), Landon ignored the blare of horns from behind. Overhead the early-morning blue was shading off to whiteness in the north. There was snow in that sky. A brisk wind stiffened the flags on the roofs of small factories and office buildings. Here they were widening the expressway. The construction crews had left their bulldozers and giant rollers by the roadside for the weekend. And what great weapons they were for wounding the earth! Landon looked out at them, now standing idle, frozen into silence like petrified monsters. And as for this particular patch of Canadian geography—it resembled a bombed-out area more than anything else. The land was cruelly blasted and scorched. All necessary, of course. According to the authorities. You couldn't be old-fashioned about these things. These enormous cars needed room! But how much was enough? wondered Landon. Eight lanes? Ten? Twenty? And suppose in thirty years some smart dick discovers a cheaper, more effective method of moving people? Of what use will these superhighways be then? Perhaps long-range bowling alleys! Concrete runways for roller-skating marathons in aid of charity. Bah! The damn country was imitating all the worst American mistakes. A thick-headed people. They'll never learn. As he cautiously mounted the northbound ramp toward Highway 400, Landon relaxed. The traffic thinned out, most of it streaming westward. Beside him Margaret calmly gazed out the window at the dreary little factories and plants strung along the highway like beads on a cheap necklace. He glanced over at her.

She didn't get out much, and even though this scenery was nothing to write home about, it was a change.

On Saturday mornings they usually went shopping at the Kensington Market. Now he realized how much he missed this weekly expedition. He truly enjoyed that old street market, the last of its kind in Toronto. On fine mornings it swarmed with life. The cold winter cement rang under your heels. Here he felt something like the generating pulse of life, felt its rhythms traveling along his blood. The modern soul! How starved for authentic experience! He often thought of this as he walked along Nassau and Baldwin streets. Those open-fronted stalls of merchandise. The racks of coats and dresses. The religious pictures and books. The handbags and watchbands. Stands of fruit and vegetables, and cocks crowing in the middle of the city as they looked out from their lath coops with yellow eyes. He loved to watch the people too: the West Indian women who knew what they were doing as they shopped for beans and rice and sweet potatoes, the college kids and young married couples still sleepy and looking for bargains, the old immigrants pinching the fruit under the owner's eye. And he enjoyed watching Margaret handle the cheeky vendors. She was a shrewd buyer and could be serious to the point of severity. She took no guff from anyone, got wonderful deals. He marveled at her. She was happy here, and beneath the kerchief her eyes shone and her cheeks glowed in the frosty air. The market reminded her of childhood days in Cracow, and she was often terrifically animated, grabbing his arm and pointing out a good buy. On these Saturday mornings he saw another side of her. He amused her too, playing the fool in his cowhide ranch jacket with its burled wool lining and the tomato-red toque pulled down over his ears, making her laugh by ordering strudel in a mock German accent. The strudel they ate as they walked along the street, and he warmed her hands with his breath, sometimes holding them between his woolen mittens or putting them inside the jacket where she could feel his grateful heart.

Together they carried the groceries back to her apartment, and she ran water in the kitchen sink, washing the vegetables and letting them drain on a wooden board. In the living room Landon sat in one of the overstuffed chairs, sipping a glass of schnapps or Alberta Grey Cup vodka, watching the cat sleep in front of the small black hearth which had once burned coal. By his ear the radiator hissed and knocked, and the cat awakened, stirring and stretching, extending her claws. The place was dark and cluttered, the old rose wallpaper browning and loose at the corners. The rooms were filled with religious items; a small-scale Lourdes, Landon often thought. The lumpy brocaded sofa was crowded with cushions bearing Biblical messages. On the walls hung cheap tapestries vivid with the blood of Christ. He had seen these on sale at the market. There were plaster Virgin Marys holding candle stubs and crucifixes everywhere, including Margaret's bedroom, where a slender sly-looking Christ figure gazed down upon the old iron bedstead. The dark dining room smelled sourly of furniture polish and emptiness. A fine copper samovar rested on a sideboard, and there were pictures of bearded old-world relatives on the walls. To Landon the total effect was overpowering and claustrophobic. It oppressed the spirit. Margaret was slowly weeding out this stuff, but Landon sensed that she was taking her time. Perhaps discarding these ornaments pained her in some mysterious way. The old woman had been a miserly soul, and so the place was filled with strange junk. Margaret showed him old Christmas presents: boxes of clothes and linens put away for a rainy day. There were night-dresses and bath towels and pillow slips which had never been used and were now yellow with age. It was creepy. One morning Landon thumbed through a stack of old magazines, *Colliers* and *Liberty* and *Saturday Night,* turning the musty damp pages and sneezing as he read the advertisements for Kaiser cars and Ipana toothpaste. On the square brown phonograph scratchy 78s whirled furiously and Polish dances leaped into the dry electric air; spirited music, to challenge the drabness of a February morning. In the kitchen Margaret hummed the tunes and prepared *piroshki,* lifting the batter from the oil with a long-handled wooden spoon. The smell of those cheese turnovers bubbling in the hot oil left Landon dizzy with joy.

In the DeSoto he whistled a melody from one of those old polkas and wondered where he was going with this neighbor of his. She was a good woman. He was certain of that. Perhaps a little eccentric and set in her ways, but basically sound. He still didn't know a great deal about her. He only knew that she had made him happy these past few months, and he liked to think that he had returned the favor. Was it not greedy to ask for more? She was eager to please him and that was always nice. Today, for instance, she had dressed for him. Normally she was not particular about clothes, could even be dowdy and neglect-ful like an absent-minded spinster. He sometimes wondered if she might not have a bit of her old lady's skinflintedness in her nature. Although she was always generous with him, he knew she was close with a buck. And in dress and manner she clung to the past, her mother's pre-war Poland. After thirty years in Canada, she still dressed like an immigrant. But now there were signs that she was stirring from these old ways. Perhaps it was her mother's death that did it. The old woman must have been a powerful figure. Anyway, Margaret was looking fine today in a pair of new slacks and a heavy knit sweater. Her hair was pulled back and kept in place by a yellow bandanna, and there was a trace of blue eye shadow on her heavy-lidded eyes. She had bought a rather sporty-looking winter jacket too, a hip-length coat of black-and-red-check wool fastened down the front by small wooden pegs. No doubt she had caught one of the winter sales downtown. Well, it only made sense. But in spite of these American frontier duds, she remained somehow alien in appearance, a visitor to the new land, got up like the natives, all right, but persistently apart too. An aura of the old world still surrounded her and gave her—what? A presence! It somehow hinted at respectful remoteness. She could be the rancher's new wife, the foreign woman from the city, bowling over the boys in the bunkhouse, but no fooling around, mind. That little lady can take care of herself. His whistling made her smile.

"You seem to be in an excellent humor now," she said, looking across at him. She was probably remembering his earlier troubles with the car. The day had then boded ill. But now there was no irony in her voice. When all was said and done, there was a sweet decency about her.

"Well yes, I feel pretty good," said Landon. "Getting out of the city helps, I guess. I'd forgotten what it's like to be on the road on a Saturday morning. No wonder people take to their cars on the weekends, put up with the hellish traffic. It's hard to beat this feeling of freedom. You can see how the automobile has taken hold of our imaginations. It answers such primitive needs for freedom and mobility." He paused. No lectures this morning, please. "And then there's the new job, I suppose. I feel I'm back on my feet. For a while there, my confidence was shot."

Margaret half-turned toward him, crossing her legs and propping an elbow against the back of the seat like a man, a fishing companion swapping yarns. "And your wife coming back has not upset you as much as you thought it would, then?"

"My ex-wife, Margaret. And the answer is—I don't think so. It's strange . . . She can still keep me off balance. She has a way of seeing through me that is . . . uncomfortable. But as they used to say in the Old West, I think the town is big enough for both of us." Margaret frowned slightly. Was there a jealous streak in her character?

"I'm glad for you, Frederick," she said. "And I hope your daughter visits you often." She clasped her knee with both hands, lacing the fingers together. "It's so hard for me to imagine you with a grown daughter . . . well, almost a woman now."

"Why is it so hard for you to imagine?" he asked.

"Oh, I don't know. You hardly seem married."

"Well, that's not surprising. I haven't been married now for years."

After a moment Margaret asked, "I wonder if she would like me?"

"Who? Vera?"

"No. Your daughter."

"Oh yes, I think so. After she got to know you. At first though, I think . . . well, she might feel a bit intimidated."

"Intimidated? By me? Why?" Margaret appeared unusually interested in this. It seemed important to her. Landon hesitated.

"Well, sexual jealousy, you know . . . You're a sexy woman, Margaret. You try to hide it, but it comes across. Other females must sense it, feel the rivalry."

"Oh, nonsense, Frederick," said Margaret flatly, looking away across the brown fields. She was not pleased. This sort of talk made her uneasy. Outside the bedroom she was shy as a nun about sex. But Landon knew he was right about Ginny. She would feel sexually out-classed, a bit resentful. It was only natural. Now if he were seeing a thin flinty type with stork-like legs! But with Margaret, Ginny would sit in the corner and look glum, crossing her legs and folding her arms over her chest like a pouting child. She would loosen up after a while, but it would take time. Oh yes—he felt certain he was right about this. Yet Margaret was so touchy about her sexual powers.

"Of course, I could be wrong about that," he said. "Ginny is a lot like her Grandmother Landon; like me, I guess."

"Like you?" Margaret looked at him again.

"A romantic character, I mean," said Landon. "A dreamer. And always full of these sudden enthusiasms which sputter out so quickly and leave you feeling horribly depressed, really low. My mother was like that. She was always taking up something and then just as quickly abandoning it. Fortune-telling, soap-opera contests, amateur theater at the local high school, you name it . . . One year she took it into her head to supply the household with vegetables. I don't know why. I guess she'd read one of those books by some horn-rimmed dame in a checked shirt. You know the kind. How to get away from it all and live on roots and bear meat for ten cents a day. Anyway, my poor mother slugged it out for weeks. An enormous garden, planting, hoeing, weeding. I can still see her in those wide rubber boots with the thick red soles. She bought them especially for the job. And she hacked away at the damn weeds until she just got fed up. The whole thing got her down, became a terrible millstone. Finally, she drew the kitchen curtains, even on sunny days. None of the rest of us were farmers. By the end of July the weeds had taken over. Our back yard looked like those vacant lots you used to see on corners in small towns, choked with weeds and tall grass. My father made a little joke about it one evening at supper. But he wasn't very good at making jokes, had all the wrong touches. A more lightweight character might have got away with it. But my mother hit the roof; she left the table and wouldn't speak to any of us for days. Oh, she was in a real snit over that. In the fall my father got an old fellow with a horse to come around and plow up the whole business. We sowed grass seed and put in a bird bath. It seemed to make more sense." Margaret was listening closely, watching his face. Her serious expression told him this wasn't a joke. She was no stranger to people's eccentricities. Somehow they had to be respected.

"Do you know?" he said finally, "she once took up the trumpet!"

"The trumpet!" Margaret had to laugh at this, and Landon joined her.

"Yes, it's true, bless her," he said. "There used to be this all-girls' jazz band on the radio. It was during the war, and they played for the troops, went on tours. They were mildly famous for a while and now I can't even recall the name. It was Billie Jean and the Jeannettes, or something. They weren't all that bad either, as I recall. Anyway, my mother studied the trumpet for weeks. I don't know what she had in mind. Maybe she thought she could run away and join this band." Those few weeks when the stillness of the old house was shattered by these sudden blasts of noise. It could have been a lost elephant trumpeting for the herd. His mother raised a small callus on her lip but never mastered the scale, only these great unearthly alarms.

"And of course there were always the movies," said Landon. "She lived for them, went several times a week. Sometimes she took Ellen and me. Billy was away, of course . . . All those great old tearjerkers from the days of the big studios . . . *Casablanca* . . . *Mrs. Miniver*. And they kept bringing back *Lost Horizon*. I think for years my mother was in love with Ronald Colman . . ."

"And your father?" asked Margaret. "Did she not love him?"

"Oh yes, I think she did. Once . . . But toward the end. During those last few years . . . Well . . . After Billy's death, something just went out of the whole thing. They were like strangers going their separate ways."

"How sad."

"Yes, it was sad; painful, really. And then of course Charley Ames came along. I'll say this for him: at least his timing was good. Look . . . does this family-history stuff bore you, Margaret? I mean, you can always tell me to shut up."

"But please no. I want to hear . . ."

Landon found some of it not easy to recall. But after these many years he was perhaps grateful to someone for listening. Once he had started to tell Vera and then something had happened. A telephone had interrupted him or a visitor. She had never asked him to begin again. Now he stared out the windshield at the long straight road and the whitening sky.

"Charley came to Bay City right after the war. He was an American from somewhere in the Middle West, Nebraska or Iowa, a farmboy who had just picked up and gone West during the Depression. Thousands of young people did this sort of thing in the thirties, you know. From all over America; Canada too, I suppose. They headed to California for a crack at the big time. Trying to make it on their smiles. And Charley must have been handsome too in his day. As a matter of fact, he did get some bit parts in a few pictures. But mainly he worked at odd jobs, and then the war came along and he joined the navy. After the war he wandered around for a while and ended up in Canada, in Bay City, where he had a cousin. He got a job there managing the old Royale Theatre. It's an odd thing, when I think about Charley and my mother. My mother was a big woman, a blond, and good-looking too. In a sort of raw-boned Scandinavian way. But I always thought she would have gone for one of those sleek Latin characters with the little pencil mustache and the black slicked-down hair. As it turned out, she went for Charley, and he was big and blond too, looked enough like her to be her brother. Managing the Royale should have been an easy touch. The only show for miles around and no television in those days. People bored half out of their minds. But somehow Charley managed to run it at a loss. I suppose he was really too good-natured to be a successful businessman. On Saturday afternoons he used to take tickets at the door and half the kids got in free. Either they sneaked by him or he just never bothered to look. Actually, he was just a big overgrown kid himself, full of jokes and stories. He never seemed to take anything too seriously. Maybe he was just what my mother needed after twenty years with my father, who was all business. And of course Charley had been around. To Hollywood of all places. He'd seen Bogart, Gable, Jean Harlow in the flesh. Naturally my mother was his best customer at the Royale, and they soon took to standing outside after everyone had left. Talking about the movies, I guess. I suppose he filled her head with stories of the people he'd met, the places he'd been, these glamorous reminiscences. He was full of it, you know, but amusing. He could make you laugh. Pretty soon Charley was reminiscing inside the Royale, and one night the two of them were seen leaving together. It was very late . . ."

"And your poor father!" said Margaret. "Did he not guess that something was going on?"

Landon smiled. It was so like her to sympathize with the quiet one who waits at home. Yet his stern moody father had been far from blameless. It helped if you saw it from the other side too. How many times through the years had he turned over these thoughts in his mind! And to what good purpose? It was all finished now, ancient history. "Well, my father . . . He kept to his books, you know. Back from the railway yard, bend over the sink and wash away the day's dirt. Then head for the pile of library books on the hall table. That was his world. But he must have guessed something the night my mother invited Charley for dinner. It was a bold piece of strategy when I think of it. She was probably trying to deflect any criticism by making Charley appear a good friend, a pal to the whole family. Of course it didn't work. My father couldn't stand Charley, and he must have seen how excited my mother was. It's hard to hide the fact that you're in love, particularly if you're the actress type. And I remember my father telling Charley to stop one of his stories because of Ellen. It wasn't a bad story at all, just some innocent Hollywood gossip about a party in which everyone swam nude. Oh, he rattled off some famous names! We were all fascinated. Except Dad, who was shocked. He asked Charley to stop.

Charley didn't seem upset. He just shrugged and went on to something else. But he was never invited back. And then one day . . . Well, I came home and my father was sitting at the kitchen table, reading a book. He'd finished his supper and was reading this book by H.G. Wells. And he said, 'Your mother's gone away, Fred. With Charley Ames. I don't think she'll be back. She left letters to you and your sister. They're in your bedrooms. Your supper's in the oven.' Oh, he was a very cool customer."

"Ah . . . And how did you feel, dear Frederick? Were you shattered by all this?"

"Well, I don't know how I felt, to tell you the truth . . . Shattered? I don't think so. My mother had gone, all right. Vamoosed across the continent to California. And yet I think what I really felt was a kind of relief. The tension in the house seemed to have lifted. There was peace. It was easier to breathe. I've never been much good in an atmosphere of quarreling and back-biting, Margaret. I suppose I like people to get along. Perhaps if I could take a little more rough weather . . . Anyway, this letter my mother left . . . I must tell you. It was a gem. Purple notepaper with little yellow flowers at the top of each page. And scented too. My mother was an awfully sentimental soul. And this damn letter began, 'Dearest son . . .' Now, my mother never called me "dearest son" in her life, but there it was in her large sprawling hand. There must have been twenty pages. Oh, it was dramatic stuff, Margaret! Real Twentieth-Century Fox. I can still remember some of those lines. 'Your father and I—whatever was between us once is gone.' 'Life is stifling me.' 'Now that I have found someone to share my dream with . . .' etc., etc. It wasn't my mother talking at all; it was Bette Davis.

Still, she waited it out. There were all those years when she must have felt like getting away. But she waited until we were old enough to look after ourselves. And then when the opportunity came—she took it. I don't blame her. Maybe I did at the time, but I don't now. It caused quite a stink in the town too. Things like that are taken for granted today. Nobody looks twice when the little suburban housewife runs off with the storm-window salesman. But this was Bay City in 1948, and mind you, it caused quite a stir. My father had to put Ellen in a boarding school in another town for the rest of the year. She was taking it pretty hard. I was in my last year at the high school and I found quite a lot of sympathy. I became almost popular. Fellows who wouldn't give me the time of day offered to loan me money. Even the gym coach went out of his way to be considerate. No more punishing flips on the parallel bars or three extra laps around the track for fat Freddy. My father and I bached it in the old house and we got along not too badly. When I think of it, we probably ate better than we had for years. My mother was a terrible cook. But now the ladies of the town all rallied to our side, you see. Many of them were my mother's old rivals, now middle-aged, with hair nets and varicose veins. Oh, my mother never had many girl friends in that town. So the ladies came to the door with their tuna-fish casseroles and their graham-cracker pies and with big smiles which said, 'I told you so.' Oh, they were glad to help out. It tickled them to see us in this fix. People love to lend a hand when they know you've been shafted."

Margaret looked thoughtful. She was weighing the contents of his story in her mind, trying to calculate its consequences. "And did your mother find happiness with this man, then?" she asked.

Landon thought for a moment. "Hard to say. She must have been a little disillusioned. About as close to Hollywood as she got was the drive-in theater where Charley works as a projectionist. In Anaheim. Not much glamor in that. But Charley's very good to her. He's really a devoted husband. And she knows she can't come back, so I guess she's settled down like most people to make the best of it. And really they seem to be doing all right. They live in one of those mobile homes in a trailer camp."

"You've visited them, then?"

"Yes. Once. Years ago when my marriage was starting to crumble. Well . . . had crumbled . . . collapsed is perhaps a better word. Anyway, I wanted to get off somewhere and think, so I took some holidays and went out to California." He stopped and pointed toward the sky. "Look now, Margaret . . . We're going to have a little snow . . ." It was true, but he was also anxious to divert her attention. He didn't feel like talking about that trip to California. The journey had exhausted his spirit. Perhaps it was his own troubles, but for the first time in his life he thought he might be cracking up.

"These unhappy marriages. And the breakup of families." Margaret said it almost to herself. Perhaps she was contemplating her own past. A lonely life, but at least no one else had been hurt. Landon suddenly felt the need to justify.

"She still likes to keep in touch. She writes now and again, and there's always a Christmas card. She's very fond of Ginny, who has been out to see her a few times. They seem to get on well together. Ginny is really the only grandchild Mom can claim. My sister won't have anything to do with her. Mom used to send Ellen's kids these presents at Christmas. All kinds of California junk, sweat shirts with corny slogans on the front, rubber balls that talked back when you squeezed them, just the sort of stuff kids love. But Ellen kept sending it all back, sometimes unopened, and after a while Mom got the hint . . . Now look. We're going to be in for it . . ."

Overhead the sun had disappeared behind the clouds, and the DeSoto, like a ship entering thick fog, was suddenly plunged into another world, the snowflakes storming against the windshield as the long wiper blades went to work. It reminded Landon of the first night they had sat together in this car. And the near-accident on Queen's Park Crescent. That snotty cop. However, this was only a squall and wouldn't last more than a few minutes. But visibility was almost nil, and Landon reduced speed, wiping away at the fogging windshield with a handkerchief. He hadn't a clue where the defroster switch was located and this was no time to be exploring the dashboard. On his left, maniacs still passed him at the same furious speed, their taillights piping hot as they touched the brakes behind slower drivers. They were now on the upper reaches of Holland Landing and here they began the long descent into the valley. They were soon through the little blizzard, but across the fields it was still snowing. The lemon-colored sun was struggling to pierce the clouds, sending forth a queer yellow light through the falling snow. Beyond was blue sky where the sun had broken through and now sent long shafts of light to strike the fields. The intense black earth was powdered by snow and lay steaming in the sunlight. Beside him Margaret was awed by the beauty of this foolish weather. Nature was making a bungle of the day, couldn't make up its mind what to do with it. Yet it was freakishly beautiful, even inspiring, and Margaret was captive to this spectacle of land and sky, marveling, as only an urban soul can, at strange weather.

"It's so lovely, Frederick. That sky—I've not seen one like it in years."

"Yes. This is old winter's parting shot. It should be milder after this. That's the old country boy speaking." He laughed. Above them the traveling clouds boomed forward, torn here and there by jagged strips of blue. And behind the clouds the sun rolled along like a mighty hoop, slipping out from time to time to blaze fiercely.

The sun had also been blazing on that day twelve years ago when he landed at the airport in Los Angeles. For that matter it never stopped blazing all the time he was there. A merciless cauldron of fire, pouring light and heat upon him as he stepped from the gangway of the aircraft into this California glare. And he was far from well, overwrought and filled with great heaping emotions, fleeing from one unhappy marriage to observe the ruins of another. In the air-conditioned terminal the perspiration froze on his neck and brow as he embraced his mother, seen at last after so many years. And oh God—what a sight! She had put on weight, perhaps fifty pounds, and her hair, piled high on her head, was now bleached white. In the pedal pushers and sleeveless sweater (those slack heavy arms), she looked like an aging swinger. You saw such women at discotheques, attempting each new dance, trying desperately to keep up. If her first husband could have seen her! Charley was there too, still handsome, jowly, and tanned, his stomach held in by elastic-waisted pants and on his back a multicolored shirt from Hawaii. To Landon they looked like two giant children, and maybe they were. Perhaps that was the only role to play in this make-believe world.

They drove away in Charley's yellow Dynaflow, the top down and the warm rank air rushing at them from all sides.

Landon's hair, greatly stirred, seemed to be standing on end. Those myriad confusing freeways were ovens in which the baking heat shimmered over the hot glittering metal of automobiles and delivery vans. The air was laden with exhaust fumes and the hot dry wind seemed to carry bad news. And that blazing malignant sunlight. It struck everything, harshly illuminated this fractured landscape, bursting off the pink stucco buildings with their Moorish fronts, and the endless signs of motels and gas stations. It took some getting used to. Of course, everyone wore dark specs, hiding their eyes from this cannibal light. But even behind the sunglasses Landon couldn't get a hold on the place, and after a week he still felt adrift on alien land. Even the vegetation perplexed him. The skinny brown shafts of the palms, the goofy ginkgos and monkey trees, with their odd tubular fruit. All apparently growing out of cement. But then they could have been synthetic. Someone told him they were now installing artificial trees along some of the highways.

In the toy kitchen of the trailer, Charley poured orange juice and Gordon's gin into tumblers, moving around with a quick deftness. Even Landon's mother, whom he remembered as being physically awkward, moved about with surprising ease. It was something to watch these two behemoths brushing past one another without colliding. But the place gave Landon trouble, and forgetting to stoop, he often bumped his head on cupboards and doorways. In the tiny yard they sat behind a low wire fence on folding aluminum chairs. His mother had planted flowers, geraniums, and Indian peas, and these she sprinkled each afternoon, bending over them with a hand on her wide hip, as she waved a green plastic watering can back and forth. On both sides of them stretched rows of these wheeled homes, their jangled steel television antennae glinting in the hard light. The air seemed electric, ever crackling with radio music or television noises, often acrid with the smoke of barbecues. And there was so much to talk about that conversation was difficult. No one knew where to begin or what to say. Too much time had elapsed, and Landon knew the moment he arrived that this trip was a mistake. His presence only reminded them of another life across the continent. He came bearing old memories, old ways of getting by.

Because Charley worked nights at the Star-Burst Drive-In they slept late, awakening to drink their fruit juice in front of the morning show on TV. Like a good guest Landon adapted to the routine. In any case, there was nothing else to do. Walking anywhere was impossible, there were no sidewalks. And he didn't feel brave enough to drive, though Charley offered him the Dynaflow. By noon his mother had poured the first gin of the day, mixing it with Orange Crush or Tab. In the afternoons the three of them sat in front of the TV, drinking and watching the game shows. Landon, muzzy from the sweetened gin, watched the contestants: the sport-shirted men shuffling around and grinning while their perky little wives flirted with the M.C. before taking home the roomfuls of furniture and the trips to Alaska. They ate dinner early, his mother serving huge helpings of spaghetti and meat balls or barbecued ribs and chili; everything washed down with tumblers of red wine, which Charley brought home in plastic gallon jugs. At first his mother seemed embarrassed by all this drinking. She always apologized as the ice cubes rattled into the glasses. "Now, we don't do this all the time, do we, Charley?" she would say. "But your visit is such a special occasion, honey, that we just have to celebrate. We've just got to let our hair down a little bit." Landon knew better but kept his mouth shut. It was none of his business. And since he hated anyone to feel uncomfortable on his account, he joined in, often secretly pouring his drinks down the john or near the beds of geraniums.

Charley liked Landon but he was conscious too of their special relationship. Thus, he practiced an extraordinary politeness. It amounted to a kind of courtly deference. Standing solidly by Landon's side, he would gravely agree with everything Landon said, laying a heavy hand on his shoulder and absently kneading the muscles. This was his honey Jo's younger son and nothing was too good for him. One afternoon he brought out an old photograph album and showed Landon some faded brown pictures. In one of them Charley stood arm in arm with several other smiling husky young fellows. They were dressed in lion skins and each carried a spiky club (papier-mache, Charley told him). The snapshot had been taken on the set of an old Tarzan picture. Charley had been one of the cavemen, a non-talking part but something anyway. It was one of Johnny Weissmuller's first pictures. "You probably don't remember him, Freddy," said Charley. He was a champion swimming star before he went into the movies. A helluva nice guy." Landon remembered him all right.

One day they took him to Disneyland, only half an hour's drive away. There Landon sailed down the Mississippi on a sidewheeler, squeezed against the upper-deck railing by kids and grandmothers, watching some rubber crocodiles browse along the shore. His mother and Charley were keen to point out the highlights, the Wild West Show and the Wonderland (they came here often), but try as he might Landon could summon no enthusiasm for the place. In fact, he was utterly depressed by it all, though to be a good sport and not ruin their day he grinned till his face ached.

Several nights a week his mother went along with Charley to the Star-Burst, and on his last night in California Landon accompanied them, pushing himself up the narrow stairs behind his mother. In the projectionist's booth Charley, wearing old-fashioned rimless spectacles, threaded the giant reels through the machine while Landon's mother laid out the sandwiches and a six-pack of Dr. Pepper. Landon guessed that, for an ardent moviegoer like his mother, this was as close to heaven on earth as you were likely to get. In fact, however, she often complained about modern films. They were too sexy and there was no story to most of them. And where were the grand old stars of yesteryear? The Spencer Tracys and Gregory Pecks? The Walter Pidgeons and Gene Tierneys? While Charley warmed up the big black machine, examining its parts like a physician, Landon looked down through a small window to the parking lot filling with cars. They came down the ramps from the entrance gates and turned slowly, pointing their snouts up toward the great blank screen. On the loudspeakers a song called "Moon River," and off to the west a raw orange sunset over the Pacific Ocean.

The Star-Burst featured motorcycle and beach-party films, and as the evening passed, his mother fell asleep in her chair, leaning back with her lips parted slightly and her plump thighs spread. In the judo sandals her toenails were mauve. By the light of the whirring machine, Charley read a paperback novel and sipped his Dr. Pepper. Landon looked past him and saw the air abounding with insects, swimming in the stream of white light which poured from the booth. No—the visit had not been a good idea, and the next morning he boarded a plane for Canada.

They left Highway 400 at Crown Hill and drove westward on a quiet road. As they approached Bay City, Landon felt moved by old deep feelings. Here were his roots, his beginnings! The sky had cleared and now enveloped them in brilliant blue. On either side of them the gray-stubbled fields lay waiting for April rain. At one time the cemetery had marked the limits of the town. Now it was pressed from all sides by motels and used-car lots. There were also an Esso and a Texaco station and an A & W. Colonel Sanders was there too, his big ol' Kentucky smile revolving on a giant bucket mounted high above a chicken take-out store. Next to the cemetery was the Blue Moon, his grandfather's old place. Years before it was all by itself out here and people said his grandfather was crazy to build next to a graveyard. Undoubtedly they were right. The land must have been cheap then, or maybe old Ulf just set out to fail on purpose. That would be like him. Customers were not to be encouraged. They interfered with serious meditation. Now, slowing down, Landon could see that only a couple of the larger cabins remained, partly hidden away among the pines. The Blue Moon was now an L-shaped concrete block motel with a large sign in the shape of a new moon hanging over the entrance. The word "vacancy" still sputtered a blue electric signal. The old verandahed house was gone. To be expected, of course. It was falling down years ago. Landon, deeply stirred, touched the brakes and pulled off the highway, hearing the fat tires crunch along the gravel of the motel parking lot.

"Margaret, we're going to stop here for a moment," he said. He switched off the engine and they sat in silence, listening only to the cooling tappets ticking away beneath the hood.

"What is this place, Frederick?" Margaret asked finally, looking across at him.

"This was my grandfather's place," said Landon. "Well, not the motel of course, but those cabins back there through the pines. There used to be a dozen of them. My God, I haven't stopped here in twenty-five years. I usually just pass by. Let's go and have a look."

They stepped from the car. After two hours of sitting, it felt good to stretch the legs, and Landon arched his back, putting stiffened joints to work. He took Margaret's hand and they walked across the gravel toward the pines behind the motel. It was nearly noon, and in shelter from the wind the sunshine felt hot upon their backs.

Behind the motel they climbed hand in hand down a slight bank and jumped a shallow drainage ditch. The two square-cut log cabins were painted black and trimmed with pale blue. The window shutters had new moons carved into their wood. Nearby was a stone-and-brick barbecue. Someone had stacked the pine-log chairs and picnic tables against one of the cabins. That damned homely lawn furniture! Landon's grandfather had sawed and nailed it together by hand. They were hungry for the rustic look back in the thirties. And so you got this junk. Nevertheless, it had an odd appeal. Like the taste of green apples. In the shadow of the trees a final patch of snow lay wasting, partially hidden from its enemy the sun, clinging stubbornly to form, to life. The long gray grass was dusty, pressed flat in places after months beneath the snow. Landon pointed through the pines to the glinting blue of water.

"That's Georgian Bay out there, Margaret. Part of Lake Huron, the Great Lakes, the old explorers' routes. Sam Champlain came up this way over three hundred years ago . . ."

They walked across the brown dead needles and stood looking off toward the water.

"There used to be a path down there," said Landon. "God knows where it is now. Overgrown, I guess."

He took her arm and they walked along. There used to be some fine large trees here. They stretched almost down to the shores of the bay. Now it was a field of burdock and dead goldenrod, with only a few forlorn spruce and Scotch pines. Here he had gone on Sunday afternoons in March with his mother. They had picked bunches of violets and trilliums. You weren't supposed to pick the trilliums and they didn't last indoors. But his mother always said that after months of winter any flower was welcome, and so, for a few hours, the house waxed with these unfortunate blooms. However, they soon fell limp and died. Margaret linked arms with him and pressed her cheek against his shoulder. She knew he was affected by the place, touched deeply by old memories. By the open door of a motel room a young girl stuffed bedclothing into a laundry cart and wheeled it along to the next room. Looking across, they noticed a man observing them from the office doorway. He was a short heavy-looking fellow and stood with his hands in his trouser pockets. Probably the owner, thought Landon, and he's wondering what the hell we're doing down here.

As they turned back toward the motel, Landon said, "I've had some happy times here, Margaret. I've never really been back for any kind of visit. That is, beyond a couple of hours with my sister and father. We don't seem to hit it off any more, and so I usually just talk a little and run. There's been no reason to stick around . . ." He stopped. Margaret was listening but looking ahead toward the man. Landon watched her as they walked. The wind was still brisk and tugged at her bandanna. Strands of dark hair had escaped from under its folds, and now and then she absently passed a hand across her brow. The wind gave her face fresh color. Landon hesitated for a moment before he spoke. "Margaret . . . This may strike you as an odd idea but I'd like to stay here . . ."

"Here?" She looked at him. "But I thought you were most anxious to see your father."

"No no. Not stay now but come back. Spend the night here. We could check in now. I'd like to catch up on some of this. Show you around the town where I grew up. You can't do much in an afternoon." He was greatly excited by the idea and Margaret smiled at him.

"So . . . You've lured me into the country for a wild weekend . . . To seduce me . . ."

"Yes. That's it . . ." He was delighted with her and, putting his arm around her waist, kissed her cold cheeks. What if that man was staring at them? What did he care? Had he not spent too much of his life worrying about what others thought?

"But how will this look?" asked Margaret. "I don't think I'm prudish, Frederick, but . . . Surely your sister will think it strange?"

"Of course she will, and let her," said Landon quickly, turning once more to look at the cabins. "It's cold this time of the year, but if we could get heaters . . . Maybe we could stay in one of those old cabins . . . I noticed some firewood." But he quickly shrugged off this thought. "Well, perhaps that's not such a good idea. They've not been used all winter." Margaret held his hand tightly against her waist as they walked. She seemed to be thinking hard.

"Of course, you know that I'd spend a weekend anywhere with you, Frederick." She paused. "But I wonder if this is wise . . ."

Yes. He could see her point. How would she appear to his family? A woman whom they'd never met was now shacking up with him in a motel on the edge of town. He was putting her in a tough spot. But the idea had such visceral appeal for him. He didn't feel like leaving Bay City for a while. And staying at Ellen's was out of the question. He'd be a nervous wreck by the morning.

"Well, why not?" he said. "I'll think of some excuse for staying." But he was suddenly angry with himself. "Christ no . . . why should I? If I feel like having some . . ." He was going to say fun, but it sounded too calculated; there was a hint of the one-night stand about it. "If we feel like enjoying ourselves, why shouldn't we? We're not children." He was conscious of having said this before. "Oh hell, let's do it, Margaret. And tonight . . ." He squeezed her waist. "Tonight I'll treat you to a bottle of wine and a terrible Chinese dinner from the Flying Dragon. They used to deliver. We can have it right here if you like . . . Tomorrow I'll show you around the town. The old swimming hole . . . the tree I fell from and broke my arm in the year nineteen-oh . . . all that old Tom Sawyer stuff. Oh, I'll bore you to death, Maggie, I promise . . ." God bless her, she laughed at his foolishness.

"A terrible dinner and a promise to bore me," she said. "It sounds excellent, but I've brought nothing."

"Never mind," said Landon, "we'll pick up some things in town. Toothbrushes and sexy nightgowns . . . net underwear for me . . . the works. I'm buying."

"But you have no money for such things." She looked so serious he had to laugh. "No buts, now . . . We haven't really done anything yet to celebrate my new job. After all, I've now returned to the land of the working. On Monday morning I have to move some property, as O. K. Smith puts it." The thought temporarily dampened his spirits, but it was only a brief shower. The sun came out again and, laughing, arm in arm, they climbed the bank toward the man who still stood looking at them with his hands in his pockets.

"Good morning," said Landon cheerfully. The man returned the greeting without much enthusiasm. He was short and bullet-headed with no neck, or so it seemed. It really appeared as though his head (a formidable weapon!) had been hammered down into the thick torso. He frowned at them from behind a pair of thick-lensed tortoise-shell glasses. These bifocals and the thick shaved head gave him a look of military sternness. He seemed vaguely familiar to Landon.

"My grandfather used to own this place," said Landon. "Years ago, of course. We were just looking around."

The man nodded but didn't appear interested in Landon's forebears. For no good reason Landon found this irritating. He had better get down to business. These cranky ones always brightened up when you mentioned money. "We'd like to rent a room," he said.

The man looked at him with suspicion. Yes—there was mistrust in those boiled-raisin eyes. Wasn't it a little early in the day to be renting rooms?

"Say, what about a cabin down there?" asked Landon.

"One of those?" said the man, disbelieving his ears. He pushed the glasses back on his nose with a forefinger. "There's no way I'm going to rent you one of those." There was a bullying tone in his voice. This was the schoolteacher, used to lecturing pupils, and always right. This type always chewed his cabbage twice. "This time of the year," he said. "You'd freeze to death down there. My wife . . . It would take her all day to clean one of those up. I'd have to chop firewood. Oh, there's just no way . . ." Schoolteacher! It came to Landon. Of course! Those bifocals and the short packed figure. It was Gibson, the science teacher! What did the kids use to call him? Fireplug Gibson. Yes—that was it. In those days he taught zoology and chemistry, squinting with effort over his beakers and flasks, his lips pulled back and the long teeth exposed. He looked like a beaver on its hind legs. Knifing through those frogs and snakes, peeling back the flesh for a gander at the digestive system, the tiny reproductive parts. And those deadly laboratory gases they cooked up! Landon couldn't take it. He preferred to conjugate Latin verbs. And here, after all these years, was old Fireplug, still carrying on, though grayer and stouter. He must have bought the place after he retired. The Blue Moon had passed through several hands since his grandfather's time. He waited for Fireplug to finish.

"Well, anyway, it was only a thought. We'll take a room up here."

"Right now?" asked Gibson, looking doubtful.

"That's it," said Landon abruptly. He had never liked this little bugger. A regular martinet, always hustling the kids along the hallway, scolding them for lineups at the drinking fountain.

Gibson, hands still in pockets, hitched up his trousers with a great jingling of coins.

"You'd better come in and register, then. But you can't move in yet. The beds aren't made up."

"No problem there," said Landon loudly. Two could play this game.

"You'll have to come back at three o'clock."

"We'll be here," boomed Landon, following him into the office and signing his name on the registry card. Gibson examined the card, holding it a few inches from his nose, before asking for the rent in advance. Landon forked over the bills. Now that he had decided to stay for the night, it was typical of him to be uncertain about the whole thing. Perhaps it wasn't such a good idea after all! And what would Ginny think? He had forgotten that she was coming up here today. Still, he was stuck with his idea now.

They left the parking lot, the DeSoto's rear wheels firing stones at the office door. Landon drove into town in a mildly unsettled state. They ate lunch at the Flying Dragon, where Landon, chewing on an egg roll, stared at the dragons slumbering on the walls. They looked more playful than menacing, and they reminded him of those sleepy birds and beasts in the King Kong Inn. These Chinese restaurants! There was one in every town in the country. He often thought about these young Oriental waiters. Spending their lives far from fellow countrymen in these dotty small towns. In his traveling days he had stepped from the train onto the street of some godforsaken prairie hamlet where the summer sun parched the juices from you and the winter wind froze the blood in your veins. And there was the Star Cafe, where you could always get a bowl of wonton or a pot of scented tea. The January noon hours he had spent warming his fingers on those tiny cups, inhaling the fragrance of orange blossom or jasmine and listening to the cowboy songs on the jukebox. But the numbing loneliness of those places! It must take a severely disciplined mind to endure the estrangement. With only games of Mah-Jongg and gobang played in the kitchen on Sunday nights, while the wind shrieked and the snow flew. Ah well—perhaps not a bad life.

From the street the house had not changed much since he was young. The street itself looked much the same, with its sensible red-brick houses and its maple trees. But another generation had come here to live, and the older people, the parents of Landon's friends, were now mostly gone to apartments or senior citizens' homes or the cemetery. Landon parked in the street and sat looking at the white frame sun porch which his father had built. In the weeks after his mother's flight. His father, studying the plans for home improvement in *Popular Mechanics*, bending back the magazine's spine until it cracked and lay flat on the kitchen table. From here he made his notes in a lined five-cent scribbler. In the spring he worked furiously, hammering, sawing, planing boards; half-opened books on woodworking and plastering always underfoot. In the end a carpenter friend came along to help him finish the job, and Landon painted the walls and ceiling. They hauled down books from an upstairs bedroom and brought out the old living-room sofa with its fat plush seats in which you sank deep, buried to your armpits. And there was a floor lamp with a painted cardboard shade—pickaninnies dancing on the levee or something—an aunt had brought it back from Florida. His father had several sisters and they were always sending him ashtrays with humorous warnings about smoking, glass balls in which you could stir up a minor blizzard, wooden wall plaques carved with fat little Bavarian men in short pants. *Ve grow too soon oldt. And too late schmardt.* But Landon remembered that floor lamp, a solitary island of yellow light, with his father reading beneath it. On summer nights the moths beat against the window screen, slipping through to circle dizzily inside that crazy shade.

Landon's brother-in-law had built a spacious new garage in which to house his boat and station wagon. And inside there were workbenches and shelves for tools and padlocked cupboards in which Herb kept the rifles and hunting knives he used in his relentless war on the natural world. His brother-in-law wasn't fussy about Landon, though he often gave him the grand tour, especially after he had bought something new. Sometimes he seemed to forget that Landon had once lived in the house.

"Now, Margaret," said Landon. "Ellen is a fine girl. She has the best heart in the world and she means well. But you may find her a little nosy. And sometimes she comes on a bit strong, if you get what I mean . . ."

"I think I do, yes."

"She can be an oddly unlikable person," he said.

"Oh, Frederick. You're doing all you can to make me dislike the poor woman before I even meet her. Now stop worrying." She patted his knee.

"If she's still on this religious kick," he said, "the end of the world in seven days and all that stuff . . ."

"But you mustn't worry about any of this. You think I've lived a sheltered life? It isn't so . . . Some of my relatives are very

. . . strange. Old Aunt Anna in Montreal . . . Oh, come. Let's meet your sister . . ."

"Well, don't say you haven't been warned," he said, getting out of the car. "And we'll not stay long. I just don't feel like taking any guff today. A cup of coffee, that's all. I want to get over and see Dad . . ." He knew he sounded peevish but couldn't help it. For some reason he always got huffy before meeting his sister.

On the doorstep he rang the bell, listening to the chimes sound the first seven notes of "Bless This House." Through the glass he could see Ellen moving quickly down the hallway, all nervous energy and dressed to kill in a yellow pants suit. For the past couple of years she had been working part-time in a fashion shop and she dressed for the job. To Landon the effect was somehow comically at odds with her character. Ellen was really a stern little Presbyterian, and in these clothes she looked falsely got up and fundamentally ill at ease. They were altogether too jaunty for her severe and downright nature. But she was a true Landon, quick and dark like her father. And full of bustle, easily discouraged, a born pessimist. Billy had had this crotchety vitality too, Landon thought, watching his sister open the door. Ellen looked Margaret over as she offered him a cool dry cheek.

"How are you, dear?"

"Fine. And, Ellen, I'd like you to meet a dear friend of mine, Margaret Beauchamp . . ."

Ellen smiled and said hello. "This is a nice surprise, Fred." They followed her tight little trousered rear into the living room.

"Hey—what's the occasion?" asked Landon. "You're all dolled up." He looked closer. Yes—she was wearing, of all things, a gray wig. A permanent "permanent." He considered making a joke but thought better of it.

"It's just a bridge party at Kay Swanson's this afternoon," Ellen said, sitting down and patting the gray stiff curls.

"And where's Herb and the kids?" asked Landon.

"Herb's working today. There's a year-end special on snow-mobiles. He's been worked off his feet for the past week. The kids are over at the Cowleys'. They're just getting over flu—what a time we've had!" Landon breathed deeply as he entered the room. This used to be what they called the parlor, a square dark little room with maroon drapes and an old upright piano, which only his grandfather played. On Sunday afternoons he drove the family from the house with songs from Sigmund Romberg's operettas. *The Student Prince. The Desert Song. Wanting you . . . Every night I am wanting you.* The old man had a bad voice, a cracked tenor, but he played vigorously, his large cheeks sometimes streaming tears as the music moved him.

Now the room was larger and brighter. Herb had knocked out a wall and borrowed some space from the dining room. Landon approved of this, though the room was not to his taste. It was overcrowded, cluttered with things. Besides the end tables and lamps and chairs there was colored glass everywhere: little swans and birds of paradise perching on triangular corner shelves and window ledges. Also several large ceramic vases and pitchers. These great jugs stood on the floor and held dried flowers or feathery fern-like strands which stirred as you passed. Against one wall was a white brick fireplace with its bed of plastic coal, which glowed fiery red when you turned on the juice.

Sitting on the knobby-bottomed sofa, Landon waited for the ache which would soon invade his lower spine. It always did when he sat on this long lumpy surface. They called this stuff French Provincial. How these spurious aristocratic furnishings ended up in the bargain-center living rooms of the middle class! But nowadays common folk hungered after distinction. They craved the trappings of a richly decorated life. What was the first thing some jerk pop singer or movie actor bought with his million-dollar contract? A Rolls-Royce, of course. Landon checked himself. He must stop this internal crabbing and pay better attention. It was so like him to fall silent like this and let the conversational waters lap around him. And Ellen was busy fishing in the waters! Was Margaret French, then? No?—Polish! Well, and wasn't that interesting! What a coincidence! Someone was preparing a Polish meal this week for the Knife and Fork Club, a weekly supper meeting in the church hall at which members cooked dishes from different countries. It was Mr. Gabler's idea. He was the new minister. The aim was to promote tolerance and understanding among different peoples of the world. Ellen had cooked spaghetti and meat balls on Italian Night. But you couldn't prepare a decent meal any more. The chemicals they put in food! No one knew what they were eating. Only this week she had read a piece in a magazine about this. It *was* something.

Landon listened, nodding sympathetically, an arm thrown across the back of the sofa. Here it comes, he thought. Inside, he felt tense as a runner. He knew the magazine all right and he could see several copies on the coffee table in front of him. The editor was a California radio preacher. You could hear him on almost any small-town station on Sunday morning. His message was doom and disaster for the times. Everything was out of whack. There was too much fornicating and boozing and drug-taking. The industrial revolution had gone haywire somewhere down the line. The cities were a mess. And what about this racial business, and atom bombs, and things had come to a pretty pass when you didn't know any more what you were putting in your stomach. It was just the ticket for people disgusted with the failure of their own lives. Middle-aged nobodies and envious old-timers who were out of it now and weren't getting any. Perhaps never *had* got any. The only hope left was the total collapse of everything. Then they could say, There, didn't we tell you so? Landon could see the appeal in such a pitch. Now, watching Ellen in her canary-colored pants suit complaining about the unfairness of everything under the sun, he was reminded of Vera's words: "A little bird pecking at a hard nut." Yes—that was good. And she was still on food. Surely gluttony is the abiding sin of the middle class. Inquire after people's vacations and you receive a list of meals eaten in Howard Johnson's and Holiday Inns. But who was he to talk about gluttony? He knew it was nervousness, but he wished his sister would shut up. However, she wouldn't, perhaps couldn't. And hadn't they had a Polish meal in that funny little restaurant in Vienna? Or was it Zurich? Had they been abroad, then? Oh, Margaret! How he loved her! She wouldn't dream of mocking anyone, hadn't a satirical bone in her body. Instead she actually looked interested. And yes—Ellen and Herb had gone to Europe last fall. A bargain—seventeen countries in twenty-three days! Two coachloads from Bay City had gone. On the charter flight they were served champagne, though personally she didn't drink. The cities in some of those European countries were filthy. The canals in Venice, for instance. People threw their garbage into them. Imagine boating through all that!

" . . . But you people must be starved," said Ellen. "Here I've been chattering away." Landon roused himself.

"Thanks, Ellen, no . . . We had lunch on the road. Just a cup of coffee, if you've made some. We can't stay long." Ellen looked puzzled.

"Can't stay long? Why, what a funny thing to say! You must have something to eat. I was expecting . . ."

"Nothing please, thanks, Ellen . . ." Landon raised his hand like a traffic cop. "Please . . ."

"Well. All right then," she said, getting up from the chair. "What funny people you are!"

From the kitchen his sister continued to talk, peering around the corner now and again to make certain they were still there.

"Well, Dad will be pleased to see you, Fred. I know he gets tired of just seeing us. He never had a lot of friends, as you know. And those few he had have now mostly passed away. He gets tired of us, I think. But it's no picnic for us either. You just run out of things to say when you go week in, week out. After a while there just isn't anything left to talk about."

"How is he, by the way?" asked Landon, leaning forward and cracking his knuckles.

"Much the same," she called from some corner of the house. "Well, his hip gives him a lot of trouble, you know. And he's always worrying about how he looks. But really his face has come back quite a bit in these last few months. It's not nearly so bad now . . . But to hear him go on . . ."

Yes, thought Landon. That twisted face would worry him. He had not been an exceptionally handsome man, but he had had good looks enough to be vain. Those serious eyes and the fine intelligent brow. And women had spoiled him these last few years. One or two had been interested in marriage, but he had had it with women. Now lying there with his suffering mapped out around his crooked mouth. The terrible bitterness in his eyes. It must be awful for him.

"Anyway," continued Ellen, "this will be a busy day for him." She entered, carrying a tray of food. There were coffee and biscuits and sliced cake. Landon looked up.

"Busy? How do you mean?"

"Why, you'll be his second visitors, that's what I mean. Ginny is up, of course. I thought you knew."

Landon helped himself to a piece of sponge cake. His sister was an excellent cook. Her pastries and cakes were delicious and not to be missed.

"Well yes, I knew she was coming, of course. I saw her last night. But I didn't expect her this early in the day. Sometimes these kids surprise you."

"Well, they came about eleven thirty. They just left a while ago. She and this young man. Not a very friendly young man."

"That would be Ralph," said Landon, swallowing hard. The cake had lodged in his throat, and he reached for a cup of coffee. He felt disappointed. He knew it was unreasonable but somehow he had hoped his daughter might have come alone.

"Yes . . . Not a very sociable young man," said Ellen. She was sitting on a hassock, balancing the cup in her lap. "Anyway . . . they came about eleven thirty. Drove up in this foreign sports car. It looked very expensive. I thought at first her mother had bought it for her, and I said to myself, 'Oh, that's trouble. You start giving teenagers presents like that . . .'"

"It's her aunt's car, Ellen," said Landon.

"The one who's had the mental trouble. How is she, by the way?"

"She's okay."

Ellen had turned to Margaret. "Fred's former wife has this sister. I don't know if he's told you about her . . ." So they had Blanche's Mercedes! Well—a car was a second home to kids nowadays. Still, he worried. A fierce anxiety gripped his chest. Flat-out that car could do a hundred and thirty, and maybe Ralph was one of those birds who only came alive behind the wheel of a machine. He felt damp under the arms. An urgent restlessness seized him.

"Did they stay long, Ellen?" he asked.

"Only an hour or so. And then they were off to see Dad. Visiting hours on Saturdays are from one to four, you see. I offered them lunch, but they said they were going on a picnic. Can you imagine? At this time of the year. But they said it was so warm in the sun. They had a basket lunch in the car and I guess they were going down to the park." She turned again to Margaret. "We have one of the prettiest municipal parks in the province. You'd go a long way to beat Bay City Park. Isn't that right, Fred? But this is no time of the year for a picnic. Why, we only got rid of our snow last week."

"Yes, right." He was thinking hard. Perhaps he was only worried about what Ginny might think if she discovered he was staying at the Blue Moon with a woman? Booking in at that motel was a crazy thing to do. What business had he showing Margaret around this town, anyway? That old sad stuff. It was finished. For better or worse, his life lay elsewhere and ahead of him. Margaret sat forward in her chair, listening to Ellen, who was talking about Bay City winters and how long and taxing they were. Landon excused himself and hastened upstairs, taking the steps two at a time. It was impolite to leave Margaret alone like that, though she appeared not to mind. Vera would have seethed. And alone with Landon's former wife, Ellen had always clammed up, her face going rigid as she cast wildly about for things to do, ashtrays to empty or plates to scrape. Well, Vera's chilly silences *were* intimidating. She probably scared the poor woman half to death.

In the bathroom he ran water into the basin and slowly sponged his face. Was he not always retreating to the john when attacked by anxiety? What the hell did that mean? Anyway, in these polished enamel rooms he seemed to calm down. Now he felt quite drenched. Stripping off his shirt he dried his armpits and neck. Then he loosened his belt and dropped his trousers to the floor, taking his underpants between two thumbs and spreading them wide. Cool air circulated around his parts. It was, to say the least, refreshing. When he finished putting on his clothes, he sat on the terry-cloth toilet seat and took his pulse. He made it seventy-six. Even if he was out a beat either way, it was still not bad. For a moment he resisted leaving. Instead he sat surveying the room. When he was a kid, there had been a pull-chain toilet that emptied with a roar and gurgled and sang all night. The old white tub was high and narrow, gripping the linoleum on four ugly paws. Now everything was a mild aquamarine, pleasing to the eye. The bathtub glittered, spotless but for one solitary pubic hair. A fugitive from Herb's lonely balls? Landon shook his head as though to clear it. He must get cracking. See his father. And then flee this town. There was nothing here for him. Perhaps there never had been. He had never before felt so urgently restless about anything. In a few hours he and Margaret could be home and watching an old movie, eating a late supper. He would ask Fireplug for a refund on the room. And he would call Ginny tomorrow and ask her to come to lunch. No—he would *tell* her to come to lunch with her father. And on Monday morning he would put on a freshly pressed suit and a clean shirt and go to work for O.K. Smith. Suddenly his life seemed cleanly etched, its contours bold and lucid as daylight.

Downstairs, he stopped at the entrance to the living room and leaned in on the doorjambs. He smiled at the two women, who were conversing like old neighbors.

"I think we'd better be going now, Margaret. I'd like to get away and see Dad." Ellen looked over at him with eyes opened wide in alarm.

"But you've only just got here. You can't leave in such a rush. I don't see you for months. Why, you've hardly touched your coffee . . ."

"Yes. Well, I know, but I'd like to be off now." Sometimes he could bully her. "I'm anxious to see Dad."

"Well then . . ." Ellen stood up. "I'm sorry you won't stay longer. I was expecting a visit . . ."

"Next time, Ellen, eh!" He bent forward and kissed her brow, holding her sturdy little shoulders in his big hands.

"I'm sorry we have to go so soon," said Margaret. "I hope I see you again." She offered a hand. This old-world courtliness clearly flustered Ellen.

"Well yes, of course." Margaret has her flummoxed, thought Landon. Ellen's like me. Always expecting the worst in people. Common decency dismantles us. At the door they said good-bye, Landon guiding Margaret down the steps with a practiced hand. He was anxious to convey the proper degree of intimacy between them. Ellen, looking her usual worried self, waved to them from the doorway.

In the car Margaret surprised him with anger. "Why were you so rude to your sister?" she asked sharply. "It wasn't necessary at all. She is nervous enough as it is . . . And you make her even more nervous."

"I make her nervous?" Landon was startled.

"Of course. Anyone can see that. She's frightened to death of you."

"Oh, come on, Margaret."

"It is true. Anyone can see *that*." She sat beside him, inert and distant, her arms folded across her chest as she looked away from him out the side window. These spells of sulking, he thought. We're starting to behave like old lovers. Or married folks. The thought mildly depressed him, and they drove on to Greenhaven House in silence.

The old Edwardian house, set back on its spacious lawn among the elms and maples, had once belonged to a man named Carstairs, a lumber baron. When the house was built, the harbor in Bay City was dense with brown logs and the air was strewn with dust from three sawmills. The steam engines, pulling their loads of lumber, raised long harrowing cries into the night. It was all before Landon's time, of course, but his grandfather had talked a great deal about it. Now the Carstairs house had gone to the town for taxes and was a nursing home for senior citizens. The dark high-ceilinged rooms had been whitewashed and hospital beds were wheeled along the hallways. At the back of the house the servants' quarters were now kitchens and linen pantries. Outside, little had changed. Some-one had stuffed orange plastic roses into the Grecian stone pots which flanked the steps to the entrance, and here people hastily stubbed out cigarettes and balled-up candy wrappers. Under the long trees there were park benches painted in pastel colors, donated by the Shriners. A high, thickly matted cedar hedge enclosed the grounds.

Inside the parked DeSoto, Landon took Margaret's hand. "I'm sorry if I seemed rude back there to my sister. I never really thought about it before . . . We've never been close. I suppose the truth is that we get on each other's nerves. But there's no malice between us . . . It's only the usual family stuff."

"Oh, Frederick . . ." She turned toward him and to his amazement her eyes were filling with tears. "I'm so sorry. For-give me. It's none of my business . . ."

"But yes, it is . . . I was unkind and you told me so. That's important."

"No . . . no . . ." She shook her head violently and reached into her handbag for a tissue. "I should mind my own business. Let us please forget it."

"Fair enough, but I don't want you to feel bad about it." He stopped. "Are you sure you want to come in here or would you rather just wait in the car? I'll try not to be too long, but I'll be a while. I can't just drop in and say hello and leave. I've got to spend some time with him. I've really been negligent about this."

"Of course you must spend time with him. He's your father. And I don't want you to rush anything because of me . . . Please."

"I'm not going to rush anything, but I am warning you. He's not himself any more. He can be awfully cranky. They have trouble with him here. They're always complaining to Ellen about it . . ."

"I should like to meet him, Frederick. He is your father."

"Okay, but after this we'll go back to the motel and get our money back. Maybe my idea of staying here overnight isn't such a hot one. I think it would be better if we just went back to the city this afternoon. Tonight I'll cook you a dinner at my place. Okay?" She smiled. He knew she was pleased. She hadn't really wanted to stay. Small-town motels were not her style.

"Okay?" he repeated. "Is all forgiven?"

"Of course, darling."

"Well then, let's see Dad."

In the front hallway of the old mansion Landon sniffed the powerful fumes of disinfectant. They stung the nostrils but covered up the old flesh odors, killed the germs that swam in the septic air. In the large bright rooms the daughters and sons stood around the high beds, sometimes bending forward to hear the words. Just as often they looked away across the room or sharply hushed restless children who tugged at wrists and dragged their shoes along the floor. After a few moments the words simply ran out and there was nothing more to say. To stare at the fatigue and defeat in these old faces was wearing. Yes— Ellen was certainly right about this. When you watched death take its time, it could scrape the nerves raw.

On Landon's last visit his father had complained bitterly about the location of his bed. He wanted to be near the window where he could look out over the grass and the two Persian lilac trees. He had finally got his wish too, for he now lay sleeping in a bed near the tall window. Probably the old man had worn them down with his peevish outbursts. Either that or

someone had died and he had been moved up. A cruel senior-
ity system. It brought to Landon's mind a story he had once
read. It was by Maupassant or Chekhov, he couldn't be sure.
But in this story two men shared a room. Were they not in a
prison hospital? Anyway, they were confined to their beds,
couldn't move around at all. Only one man could see out the
window. And he would tell the other man of the wonderful
sights to be seen from this window. There were trees and flowers and changing skies and passing seasons. On Sundays he
described the beautifully dressed ladies who strolled on the
promenade below with their parasols and dogs. Each day his
roommate would listen, with jealousy mounting in his heart.
He began to covet the other man's bed with such passion that
he contrived to poison him. This he did so cleverly that he
escaped detection and won the bed next to the window. Only
to discover a solid brick wall. Yes—it was a good little trick
story, and once upon a time Landon had thought of adapting
it for radio or TV. It was another of those things that he had
never gotten around to.

Now he stood by the bed and watched his father sleeping. His
mouth was open, but the damaged face was turned away from
the eyes of visitors. He was still wearing his reading glasses, and
his thin legs were drawn up under the sheets. He had dropped
off over the crossword puzzle and his long gray fingers still held
the folded newspaper. Even in sleep, the face lost none of its fundamental tension, its wrath at life's cheating ways. Bitterness had
scored this face terribly. Staring down at his father Landon felt
deeply moved, felt his eyes filling. The old Lindstrom sentiment.
Forever seeking the moment to surface. Yet he must not weep.
His father was only disgusted by tears and would show him no

mercy. He warned himself to be careful with this fierce old man. Leaning forward, Landon touched his father's arm, felt the frail bones beneath the sleeve of the nightshirt. The old man was nearly eighty.

"Hey, Dad. It's me . . . Fred. I've come to see you."

At once his father's eyes opened. Like a light sleeper, he was not easily startled, and without moving his head he stared out the window.

"Is that you, Fred? I've been waiting for you. Your sister said you'd be coming." His voice was not strong but his mind seemed all right. Ellen had said that there were lucid days. At other times he didn't know you. Landon looked down upon him.

"Well, how have you been, Dad?"

The old man now turned his head and looked up at his son. "Well, here you are then, eh!" He lay the palms of his hands flat upon the bed and struggled to rise, lifting himself slowly, grimly. Landon sprang forward to help. "It's all right. It's all right," his father whispered irritably. "Just put some pillows behind me there. They never give you enough pillows in this place." As he sat up, his nightshirt fell open and Landon could see the ribs and the sunken dugs with their tufts of whitened hair. He was painfully thin, had deteriorated badly in these last weeks. Landon's hands trembled as he helped his father. The old man's skin smelled sourly of used bedclothes. But sitting up, he quickly plucked off his glasses and rubbed his eyes with thumb and forefinger, massaging the temples as well. The vigor and physical briskness of his former days were best displayed in these old habits, and even at this late hour had not entirely deserted him. Landon could now see that his face had almost healed. There remained only a trace of asymmetry in the jawline. It really wasn't bad at all. The blue eyes were cloudy but filled too with angry light.

Landon asked again, "How have you been, Dad?"

"How have I been?" His father looked affronted by the question, and his weak voice gathered a peculiar querulous strength. "Well . . . look at me! The picture of health, eh! I'm used up . . . finished . . . that's how I am . . . And this face of mine . . ." He touched his cheek.

"But your face looks fine, Dad. There's nothing wrong there." But his father was looking past him toward Margaret. He was frowning. His look suggested that he didn't want any strange females around his bed. Landon regretted bringing her.

"Dad, I want you to meet a friend of mine who came along. She asked to meet you. This is Margaret Beauchamp." Margaret shyly said hello, but the old man only nodded to her and turned again to his son.

"Well, how are you getting on now?" he asked. "Have you found another job?" It was so like him, thought Landon. Everything else was brushed aside while he zeroed in on the only questions that mattered to him. Have you made a success of your life or have you botched things? Are you working or looking for work? The old Depression questions. And for a change Landon was glad to be asked.

"As a matter of fact, I have, Dad. It's in real estate. And that's big business now . . . With all the building going on, you know . . . The company is small but it's expanding all the time. It could be a great opening for me." He stopped, feeling the shame that arose from glamorizing a mediocre job. Besides, his father was hardly listening. He was thinking of other things.

"That father-in-law of mine," he said. "He could have made a fortune in real estate thirty years ago. Right after the war he could have bought up that south end. Developed it. Expanded . . . It's *criminal* what he let slip through his fingers. I told him, but he wouldn't listen to me. I just wish . . ." He was growing fretful and he adjusted his body's weight, leaning over hard on one fist and fetching a shallow breath. "I just wish that he could *see* with his own eyes what's happened down there since the war. I'd just like to look at his face when he sees what he missed out on . . ." He looked up sharply at Landon. "Well, you made your mistake too, didn't you? All the time you spent on that writing. That took a big chunk out of your life right there. Put you behind the rest of them and there you were in your twenties too. That's when a man has to be moving up in his job. When he's got the energy. I warned you then too. I told you how many writers make a decent living out of it. Oh, I've read the lives of writers, don't you fear I haven't. There wasn't one of them that didn't go in for dope or alcohol or women. And most of them starved to death or bummed off their friends. I told you all that, but you weren't listening. You and that wife of yours. You both wanted the glamorous life . . ." Some glamor, thought Landon, faintly smiling. Some life! "Science is the thing nowadays," said his father. "If you'd have got into something in science, you'd have been all right. But I guess you weren't much for science, were you? Well, you could have taught high school or something. English or social studies. That's steady . . ."

"Margaret teaches," said Landon softly. His father's lectures! They still humiliated him. Still left a dull wound in the heart. But he could live with them. He mustn't argue and annoy the old man.

"It's steady," said his father, staring ahead at nothing. "I should have gone into it in 1924. Instead of which I got married . . ."

"Is there anything we can get you?" asked Landon. "Anything you need?"

His father's voice assumed a rasping tone. All this talk was wearing him down. "Can you get me anything?" he asked. "You can get me out of this damn place, that's what you can get me. Lying here all day with these foolish women. Look at them! All they do is watch that television. And there's nothing on it educational. It's all junk, and they just sit there and gawk at it all day. I can't do my crossword. The noise is terrible. I make them turn it down. I tell them . . ." Next to his father's bed sat an old woman in a wheelchair. She was watching the soundless TV and paying Landon's father no mind. Perhaps she couldn't hear him. The braided gray head afflicted by some nervous disease was never still but waggled continuously on the thick short neck. The old face was full of years and patience. In front of her on the buzzing white screen a deodorant can with a head and limbs alarmed a housewife in her kitchen. Landon's father wanted out.

"But, Dad, you know that neither Ellen nor I can take you. I mean, you need professional medical help. A full-time nurse . . ."

"I need my *family*," the old man whispered passionately. He had grown pale and Landon feared for him. He seemed terrifically agitated. But it was always like this, thought Landon. He never had any patience with me. As a teenager I used to get on his nerves. I couldn't help it. Moping around the house, thinking about girls. Splayed across the chairs and chesterfield reading muscle magazines. My heavy formless presence always got to him in the end. And sitting in his chair, he would finally throw down his book or newspaper and leave the house, walking swiftly away down the street. Perhaps I reminded him of her. And here, years later, he was being scolded like a child.

"What did I raise you for? And all by myself those last few years. I worried about *you*. Now I'm stuck here with a lot of women." What a misogynist he had become!

"Dad, I'm sorry . . ."

". . . Yes yes yes. You're sorry . . . You're always sorry. That's what I remember most about you, Fred. That phrase, I'm sorry." He added spitefully, "If Billy had lived, I wouldn't be in here."

"Well, maybe not," said Landon, feeling a stab of jealousy. "But don't be too sure. It's not as easy as it used to be. . ."

His father looked at him scornfully. "How do *you* know how it used to be? You were just a kid during the Depression. You didn't have a thing to worry about. I did the worrying in my house . . ." A nurse began to distribute glasses of fruit juice from a tray. She approached Landon's father, smiling. "Would you like some, Mr. Landon?" The old man shook his head angrily, and as the nurse turned away, he leaned toward Landon.

"I don't speak to that woman. And I don't trust her. She's not going to feed *me* anything."

"Why is that, Dad?"

"She doesn't like me, that's why. She has it in for me."

Landon shook his head. "Oh, come on now, Dad."

"I'm telling you, she has it in for me. She hurts me."

"How?"

"When she rubs my back. Oh, she hurts me then. Yes, she's got it in for me all right . . ." Landon glanced at Margaret, who looked away in sympathy. But she had endured years of senile temper. How do people manage it? he wondered. Patience. Charity. A cheerful heart, he guessed.

"Say, Dad. They tell me you've already had a visitor today. What do you think of Ginny? A big girl, eh!"

"Who?" His father had stuck on his glasses again and was now studying his puzzle, frowning at it.

"Ginny! Your granddaughter! She came to see you, didn't she?"

"Yes, the girl was here," old Landon said abruptly. "But I was sleepy. She came right after my lunch. I always have a nap after my lunch. She only stayed a few minutes. She talked a lot. I was . . . tired . . ." Landon could see her with the old fellow. She must have burned off his ears with her chatter.

"Well, she's young, you know . . . Enthusiastic about things . . ."

But his father interrupted him. "You see that old woman over there?" They looked across to a bed where a small gray figure lay sleeping. "Ninety years old," said his father acidly. "Ninety years old and she can't move her bowels any more. That's something that I can still do, thank God. But her . . . They have to dig it out of her." Landon winced. "Do you think it's pleasant to lie here and watch them do that? Hear her groan every morning . . ." He returned to his puzzle. Landon frantically searched his mind for something to say to his father. The grumpy old man looked very very feeble. But he wasn't dead yet and his voice was sharply virulent. "Well, you're the big word man," he said finally. "Mediterranean wind. Seven letters . . ."

"What's that, Dad?" Landon leaned over his father's shoulder. He had always enjoyed crosswords. "Let's see . . . How about sirocco? I've always liked that word."

"No," the old man said testily, "there's got to be a T in it somewhere."

"Let's have a look," said Landon, bending forward and thinking hard. "What about mistral? That's the name of a wind somewhere, I think."

"Never heard of it," said his father. "How do you spell it?" Landon spelled the word for him and with his ballpoint pen the old man tapped out the squares of the puzzle. Then suddenly, with a groan, he threw down the paper. "I'm too damn tired to do any more of this. Where's your sister? Why doesn't she come to see me?"

"But she does come, Dad."

"Once a week she comes. And she lives ten minutes away . . . Don't anyone talk to me about raising a family . . . It's not worth the trouble and the worry . . ."

To Landon's surprise, he was touched on the arm by a nurse. "Excuse me. You must be Mr. Landon's son. Mr. Fred Landon?"

"Why, yes."

"There's a telephone call for you, Mr. Landon. You can take it in the hall."

"For me?" Landon hurried from the room, following the square-shouldered little nurse to a table in the hallway. The telephone lay on the opened guestbook, and he lifted the warm receiver to his ear. It had to be Ellen on the other end.

"Yes? Hello." Immediately he heard his sister's voice.

"Fred?"

"Yes. What is it, Ellen?" He hated surprise messages.

"Now listen, Fred . . . Something's happened, but don't get yourself all excited. I'm sure it's nothing too serious." His sister's thin voice was lightly tensed, mildly inspirited. It must be bad news.

"Well, what's happened?" he asked quickly.

"Well, the police called here a few minutes ago."

"The police?" Landon felt the rush of heated blood to his head. Like a blind man he mechanically groped for the arm of the chair and sat down. His sister was talking.

"Now, don't get excited, Fred, but it seems that Ginny and her friend are in jail." Ellen sounded excited. These grim tidings! They were right up her alley.

"In jail? For God's sake, why? There's not been a car accident, has there? Is she all right?"

"Oh yes, she's all right. But the police wouldn't say anything to me. They made the call because Ginny told them you were in town and she told them that Herb was your brother-in-law. Of course, they know Herb. They did it as a favor to Herb, I guess . . ."

"Yes, yes, Ellen . . ." His sister's explanations. Her ready grasp of the irrelevant. It could vex him to madness.

"What did they say, Ellen?"

"Well, they want you to get down there right away. I guess they'll have to be bailed out or something . . ."

"And they didn't say anything more? Didn't tell you why they were there?"

"No . . .They just said for you to get down there."

"Well, of course, I'll be down. I'm on my way now. Is the jail still in the old courthouse?"

"Yes. Right off the main street. The same place."

"Okay, Ellen, thanks. I'll be off now."

"How's Dad today?"

"He's all right. Goodbye, Ellen." But his sister would not let go. Apparently she wanted a piece of the action too.

"Do you want me to phone Herb? He knows most of the policemen in town . . ."

"No, no, please . . . I'll handle it."

"Are you sure? Because it's no trouble . . ." Landon hung up on his sister. On quick light steps he returned to his father's bedside, breathing hard.

"Dad . . . I've got to go now. I'll try to get back to see you soon. Right now something's come up." The old man's eyes had clouded over. He was close to sleep, yet he whispered something, and Landon bent closer. 'What's that, Dad?"

"My face?" his father murmured. "How do you think I look?"

"You look fine, Dad. Really . . ." He squeezed the dry gray hand. "I have to go now. I'm very sorry. God bless you . . ." He left. It wasn't enough time. He knew it. But Ginny was in jail. In jail! His daughter! What could they have done? Outside, he tightly gripped Margaret's arm and they walked across the lawn, leaving footprints on the damp grass. In the car Margaret asked him what was wrong. She looked very grave. Landon looked flushed, even ill. In the rear-view mirror he could see his hair was awry. He had absently run nervous fingers through it while talking to Ellen. He told Margaret the news.

"Darling Frederick, I'm sorry. I hope it's nothing serious."

"Yes, me too," said Landon. Oddly enough he wished Vera were here, though he would never call her. The kids were in jail in *his* territory. She would see it as further bungling on his part. And she would be more angry than anything else. What's that little bitch gone and done now? That would be her line. Yet somehow, crazily, her bad temper always diminished the anxiety of these emergencies. Tragedy fled before this awful wrath. While his poor spirit only grieved and fretted. As they drove along the empty back streets, Landon tried to get a grip on this thing. Well, it was a shock. Your daughter in jail! But at least she wasn't hurt. That little bastard Chamberlain was behind this.

"Margaret, I'm driving you back to the motel." He was insistent. "Then I'll go down to the jail and see what's happened here." She didn't argue, and they drove to the motel in thoughtful silence. However, in the parking lot Margaret inexplicably began to weep. With her elbow on the armrest of the door, she covered her eyes with her hand and sobbed, the tears flowing over her fingers and down her face.

"Margaret? What is this, for God's sake?" asked Landon, amazed. "I can work this out. It can't be anything too serious . . . Why don't you go in and wait for me? . . . Lie down . . . and rest." She reached in her handbag for another tissue and held it tightly against her eyes. Frankly he hadn't counted on this. He had thought she was a bit tougher. "Come on now, Margaret . . ." She turned to him.

"I'm sorry, Frederick. Acting like this. It's just that I'm frightened . . ." She *was* frightened too—he could see the fear in her swollen eyes.

"There's no need. Look . . ."

"No, listen, please . . . Listen to me, Frederick . . ." Her eyes had fixed on the dashboard clock. It was out of order, had stopped on some long-ago day at ten past nine. Margaret spoke slowly, measuring her words. "I must tell you this . . . Before you go to your daughter . . ." Landon felt a thickening across his scalp. Something terrible was about to descend upon his head. A message from the guillotine! Margaret had stopped weeping and her voice was ominously calm. "Dearest Frederick . . . I'm sorry to tell you like this, but I can't keep it to myself any longer. These last couple of weeks have been terrible. But I've been to a doctor . . . and there's no mistake. I'm carrying your child."

*FIVE*

Carrying his child! Was it possible? Of course, it was possible. Anything was possible. He had said so himself and more than once. She was with child. *His child*. And in these freewheeling fuck-happy days when safety is only a swallow away. With Vera in the fifties it had been at least understandable. Those antediluvian times; the late rubber age when rolling on a condom was an unromantic nuisance. But with Margaret he had never bothered. Yet a moment's thought (who was thinking?) might have reminded him that she was an old-fashioned devout Roman Catholic. The sacraments in Latin and love by the calendar. Jesus! And at forty-two must he start again? The seven ages of man once more brutally thrust upon his sloping shoulders. And she was forty! A dangerous age to have a child. But abortion was out. She would never agree to that, and anyway the idea revolted him too. No—this must be lived through. The responsibility must be borne. But a child! Another Landon on the way—fiery-headed and with Slav blood in his veins. *His* veins. A son for Landon? *Landon & Son. Greeting Cards to the World*. But it could be a girl, dark and serious with a rich deep spirit, full of religion like her mother. He felt a sudden flood of tenderness for that woman. Her tragic face when she told him. How frightened she must be! He longed to comfort and be comforted. But what happened to the simple life I woke up to this morning? he wondered as he turned into the courthouse parking lot.

The old courthouse, its gray stone face weathered by the years! The adjacent buildings were long gone, demolished for a parking lot, now mostly empty in the late afternoon. There was plenty of room among these rows of metered posts for Granstein's DeSoto. At the far end of the lot, in a space reserved for police vehicles, stood Blanche's Mercedes coupe. At least there had been no accident, then! He walked slowly toward the courthouse. It still stood in the midst of all this change and talk of redevelopment. The old building had been saved by the local historical society, according to Landon's sister (who had sent him a clipping from the town paper). At least for a while it had been spared the wrecker's deadly swinging ball. And so it stood, massive, stolidly ugly, earnestly Protestant, casting its Victorian shadows over the town. He supposed it was worth preserving, if only as a curiosity, a reminder of colonial sycophancy. Once a year as a child he had gone through those wide front doors, holding his father's hand, awed by the somber vestibule with its Union Jacks and its portraits of whiskered Boer War heroes. In the afternoons the wooden floors were sprinkled with a strong-smelling powder and swept clean by a one-armed man. His father paid his taxes in cash, shoving the large bank notes through the clerk's cage without a word, waiting bone-still for his receipt, rigid with anger. Outside, he would mutter, "Those tax-gathering thieves. Not one of them does an honest day's work." Could he have dreamed in those far-off times that one day he would enter in search of his jailed daughter? He went around to the rear of the building, past the grim iron-grilled windows, and stopped before the entrance to the police station. Over the doorway hung a frosted white globe with the word "police" printed on it in black paint. Landon remembered this. It glowed at night like a white moon. On Halloween the kids used to throw stones at it, hooting at the cops. He pulled open the door and was struck in the face by a wave of stale heat. It must have been ninety in the place. The room was large and harshly illuminated by a bank of fluorescent tubes along the ceiling. This strident light—it was like an atomic blast! Behind the long high counter a typewriter clacked away in the friable air. Seated at one of the desks behind this counter was a burly blue-shirted figure wearing rimless glasses. He stabbed the type-writer keys with thick fingers. Landon recognized his own search-and-peck technique. The cop was in his late fifties, freck-led and ruddy, his balding head fringed by reddish hair. There were yellow sergeant's stripes on his shirt sleeve.

"Be with you in a minute, sir," he said, briefly looking up from his work. The voice was robust, assertive, and gruff, richly laced with Gaelic. It was, above all else, a bossy voice, pleased with itself and used to being obeyed. Another Celt immigrant, thought Landon, leaning his elbows on the old-fashioned counter. And so many of them become cops. Or pushy little greeting-card salesmen like Earle Cramner. But they were, after all, descendants of war-like clansmen. A physical domineering people who thrived on combat. Cramner loved to bully you.

The big freckled policeman seemed in no hurry to finish his job, and Landon wondered whether he should sit down on the long slat-backed wooden bench. How many people had sat on its yellow rubbed surface waiting for bad news? And it had to be bad news. You didn't come to such a place for laughs. He looked at a wall calendar which advertised chain saws and tractors. A little girl with a head of blond curls sat cross-legged, grinning at the camera and holding up two pups. It was so like these big tough cops to go for that stuff. What was that old proverb from Eastern Europe? He had read it somewhere, marked it down in his mind for future reference. *Beware of the man who weeps at his dog's funeral, for he will slit your throat in the next war*. The wry Slovak mind! They were probably thinking of the Germans.

The policeman was finishing up his work, hammering a single key, underlining something. He finally pushed himself away from the desk, the swivel chair wheeling backward on its casters. When he stood up, he was powerfully built, though turning broad with fat. A wide black belt held in his stomach, but his hips had thickened and his backside was almost comically enormous. Only yards of polished blue serge could cover such a heroic arse. And even typing messages he wore the gruesome-looking sidearm strapped to his waist. When he removed his glasses, the heavy face looked less avuncular, more belligerent.

"Now, sir . . . what can I do for you?" He moved stiffly, the joints beneath that flesh resisting motion. He could have been arthritic. And Landon was so anxious to make himself clear. His role was that of the worried parent whose child was in trouble. It happens to the best families. And you weren't dealing with the usual riffraff either. He was probably above the national average in intelligence and education. Most of the time he had fine sensitive thoughts in his head. All this he wished to convey by the lines of worry on his respectable brow.

"My name's Landon, Sergeant. Fred Landon. I live in Toronto and I'm just up for the day. Visiting my father in Greenhaven House. I got a call there from my sister . . . Mrs. Herb Reiser. She said you were holding my daughter and a friend of hers. What seems to be the trouble? Is she hurt?" The sergeant laid huge calm hands upon the counter.

"No, your daughter's not hurt, Mr. Landon, but she is in trouble. It's narcotics . . ." Landon couldn't be sure he understood. But then there were many matters difficult to comprehend today. And he was having problems with assimilation. Today it was somehow decreed that his system was to receive a series of psychic shocks, electric jolts of varying intensity. But the circuits of his consciousness were already dangerously overloaded. And in this blazing dry heat he felt parched, bleached. He must have paled visibly, for the policeman regarded him not unkindly.

"We've not put your daughter in the cells, Mr. Landon. We thought someone might be down for her shortly and she looks like a decent lass. I'm afraid she might have got herself mixed up in some trouble here though."

"What were they doing? What's the charge?" There was hoarse urgency in Landon's voice, but the desk sergeant would not be hurried.

"I'll get the report for you, sir," he said, walking slowly back to his desk, the great hams bobbing inside those shiny voluminous pants. He talked as he moved. "They were caught speeding an hour or so ago. On their way out of town. They were driving an expensive car, I understand . . ." Landon thought he detected a hint of mild disapproval in the sergeant's tone. Kids driving around in twelve-thousand-dollar cars. It probably offended his Scottish sense of thrift and good management.

"Yes, it's a Mercedes-Benz," said Landon. "Not mine," he added. "It belongs to my daughter's aunt. That is . . . my former wife's sister . . ." These clumsy explanations. And he was at it again. Soliciting sympathy.

"Well, we've impounded it for the time being," said the sergeant, making his slow awkward way back to the counter, studying the papers as he moved. He fitted reading glasses on his nose and spread the papers on the counter. There were several carbon copies. He cleared his throat and frowned at the papers, began to read. Landon listened to the courtroom jargon, trying to catch hold of the key phrases: "Arresting officers Burnett and Simmons apprehended suspects at approximately three ten p.m. . . . Radar detected excessive speed in violation of Bylaw 1006 . . ." Landon looked down to the dirt-filled cracks in the floor as he listened to the drone.

". . . A search of the suspect's person resulted in the discovery of six cigarettes believed to contain marijuana or some similar narcotic in violation of Section Three, Subsection One, of the Narcotics Control Act . . . A further search of the vehicle disclosed a quantity of marijuana in a small plastic bag. After telephoned consultation with authorities at the R.C.M.P. detachment at Millwood, defendants were charged under Sections Three and Four of the Narcotics Control Act. Appropriate charges have been read to the accused before detainment. To wit. Under Section Three, Subsection One. Except as authorized by this Act or the regulations, no person shall have a narcotic in his possession. And Section Four, Subsection Two: no person shall have in his possession any narcotic for the purpose of trafficking."

"Trafficking?" Landon looked up and searched the heavy face. "But that's a serious charge, isn't it?"

"Very serious, sir."

"You don't think they've been selling this stuff? . . ."

"We don't know what they've been doing with it, Mr. Landon. But we found enough to make us wonder. The R.C.M.P. advised us . . ."

"Where's my daughter? What about bail? They don't have to stay here all weekend, do they?"

"No. We phoned Mr. Loomis. He's justice of the peace." The sergeant gathered up the papers and tapped them into order against the counter. "You know . . . normally we'd let them out of here, Mr. Landon. We get a lot of youngsters these days who are having problems with narcotics. Even in a small town like this. And usually we just ask them to sign an order of appearance and let them go home. Then they show up in court in a day or so. It's almost as common as liquor offenses nowadays. But your daughter and her friend had a fair little amount of stuff in that car. We couldn't take the chance . . ."

"How much is a fair little amount?" This was bad business all right.

"Well . . . several ounces."

"What's the bail, then?"

"The J.P. has set five hundred for your daughter and a thousand for the young lad. He's an alien, you know." Landon sensed a dig at his failure to keep track of his daughter's companions.

"Yes, I know. Can I see my daughter now?"

"Yes, certainly. She's in the next room. I think she's comfortable enough." He came around the counter, first opening the small wooden gate and then leading Landon to a door, swinging it open and standing to one side. "There you are now."

"Thank you, Sergeant."

Ginny looked up from the wooden bench where she was lying on her side reading a book, one arm tucked behind her head like a pillow and her knees drawn up to her chest. When she saw her father, she swung her feet down to the floor and sat up, hunching her shoulders forward like a schoolgirl. "Hello, Daddy." This voice he remembered. From her childhood days. It was low, cracked, full of doom, and delivered with the eyes cast downward. It was a voice calculated to inspire pity in the hardest heart. God knows, she looked pitiful enough in the faded patched denims and plaid sneakers. There was also a blouse of some color—was it peach or ocher? No matter. It contrived to make her look pale, washed-out. Or perhaps the gray prison air had already infected her skin. And there was a drab olive sweater, the sleeves tied together at the throat and worn across the shoulders like a shawl. Landon had seen such clothes on old women in their gardens in the evenings. This daughter of his—she wrung the pity from him! And here in this dismal room with its metal gray footlockers and folding chairs. It must have been the policemen's changing room. A damp sour smell seemed to rise from the stone floor and cling to the tobacco-colored walls. Landon briefly wondered what the cells must be like in this old tomb. And his daughter! With a plea for understanding and forgiveness in her eyes, widened now in innocence behind the glasses. He walked over and sat down beside her on the bench, grateful to be off his feet. He knew he was punishing her with this silence. It was not like him and she knew it. She couldn't figure him out this time, and her blank downward gaze was evolving into a frown of puzzlement. Soon she would pout. Landon picked up the paperback she had been reading. *Spirits Rebellious* by Kahlil Gibran. It was annotated, with whole passages marked in heavy dark pencil like an undergraduate's textbook. Landon read: *If the flames of my sighing soul had touched the trees, they would have moved from their places and marched like a strong army to fight the Emir with their branches and tear down the monastery upon the heads of the priests and monks.* For some reason the words irritated him. What was she doing in jail reading this guff? Did she not realize how serious matters were? He didn't know what he expected from her, but these vague sentences and the thick stony silence of the room exasperated him. He found himself staring at his daughter: the soft plump throat, the hair pulled tightly into a ponytail and fastened by rubber bands, just as it had been when she was seven years old and he had taken her to the museum to see the yellowed bones of dinosaurs and the Egyptian mummies. The emptiness of those Sunday afternoons after he delivered her to Vera. It maimed the soul. And this neck with its loose strands of hair, thickening with vulnerable adolescent flesh—his flesh—Landon's blood and bones. He struggled against strong feelings and vowed to be firm with her.

"Ginny? This is bad business. You're in deep trouble here."

"Yes, I know." She continued to stare ahead, hunched over and with her hands lost between her knees. This too provoked him. It was the old business of the childish sulk.

"Well, what's the story, then? How the hell did you get into this mess? You should know better than to get mixed up in this sort of thing." He knew he was uncharitable. He hadn't heard her side of things. But he felt tremendously put-upon this day. Forces were converging against *him*. "I'd like an explanation, Ginny."

She turned to him, and her eyes were shiny and wet. She was blinking back tears. "Oh Daddy. I thought you'd understand. I could always talk to you. You always understood . . ."

"You mean, I always agreed with you. There's a difference, Ginny." He paused. "Have you phoned your mother?" Ginny looked away and hunkered down again into a slouch.

"Yes."

"What did she say?" He could well imagine.

"What does she always say? I knew this would happen sooner or later, et cetera, et cetera. Then she called me a silly little bitch and hung up."

"Hung up?"

"Yes."

"Well, she's worried, you know. Upset. You've caused her a lot of grief this last year. She's told me about it."

"Mother won't be happy until she has me in a convent."

"Well, you could be in worse than that if these charges against you are proved . . ."

"But it's so stupid . . . Grass isn't as harmful as alcohol. It's been proven . . ." He ignored this.

"What about all this stuff in the car? The truth now, Ginny. Is Chamberlain a pusher?" He lowered his voice. Would they bug this dingy room?

"No. Of course not," Ginny said. "How can you say such a thing?"

"I can say it very easily."

"Well, it's not true."

"What's he doing with all this marijuana, then? It's not going to be the easiest thing to explain."

Ginny turned toward him with hands pressed together as if in prayer. These prayerful hands she tapped against her thigh as she whispered, "Daddy, it's all a terrible mistake. Ralph would never push grass. He knows what happens if you get caught doing that. He knows people who've been caught."

"Well, they should make excellent character witnesses at the trial." But he instantly regretted this flippancy. She was trying to explain. "All right now, Ginny." He took her hand. "What was he doing with this stuff in your aunt's car?" She took his hand gratefully and looked toward the floor as if the history of these errors were engraved in the stone. She talked slowly.

"We left Toronto this morning. And then as we were driving along, Ralph said, 'I'm going to pick up some grass. It's good stuff and it's dirt-cheap.' A friend of his was leaving town and needed the money. So we picked it up, and Ralph was super happy. He'd never seen so much stuff before and it hardly cost him anything. He only wanted it for himself. Or to give to friends. He wouldn't sell it or anything like that . . ."

"You don't have to sell it to be charged with trafficking, Ginny. Did you know that?" She closed her eyes and rocked her head back and forth.

"I know, I know. And isn't it crazy? I mean, if you give a drink of booze to a friend of yours, no one charges you with trafficking . . ."

"Well, never mind that for now. Whether the law is idiotic or not is beside the point here. You can't defend yourself in court on the grounds that the law is silly. Why, in God's name, did Chamberlain leave it in your aunt's car? It seems criminally stupid."

"Ralph was afraid to take it back to his rooming house. There's a lot of heads there and the police have been watching the place. Besides, there're no locks on the doors. People just walk in and out of your room. It's like a dormitory. You can't hide anything. So Ralph was going to leave it at a friend's tonight. He figured it would be safe in the car until then. He says the police never bother people in expensive cars."

"Another of your friend's illusions. He should write them down, publish them in a book. Perhaps call it *A Paranoid's Proverbs.*"

"Daddy, please . . ."

"All right. But all this is very bad, Ginny. I can never forgive Chamberlain for getting you into this . . ."

"Everybody picks on Ralph." She looked away from him, her face frozen into sullen loyalty. For a moment Landon leaned back against the wall and studied his daughter's profile. The eye and cheek were straight from old Ulf Lindstrom, but the nose was a Hall nose, sharp, even child-like. Such a nose made frowning difficult. If Vera could get away with these severe expressions, her daughter couldn't. The peculiar chemistry by which the Landon and Hall genes had intermingled (what an alphabet soup that was!) had left Ginny unmasked. She had no angry eye in her head, and this guileless face with its sharp little nose could register only the sulks. She would probably carry this artless girl-bride's glout into womanhood. It was too bad. He knew she was angry and disappointed in him, yet he persisted.

"What do you see in this fellow, Ginny? He looks to me like a troublemaker. And he's got you in an awful jam here."

"Ralph is no troublemaker," she said matter-of-factly, leaning forward, elbows on knees and prayerful hands resting on her chin. She looked like the tomboy left behind by the gang. "The trouble is that Ralph's an idealist." She stopped as if to let the room absorb this fact. "Nobody understands him. He's really very deep. He has principles and he sticks to them. You don't meet many people—well, I don't, anyway—who do that . . . Stick to principles, I mean. Ralph's left his country and his parents . . . friends, everything, because he wouldn't serve in their lousy army. I mean, that takes real courage. To leave everything like that. And now he's up here in another country. And the people haven't exactly been friendly, you know. He's taken a lot of flak when he's gone looking for a job and things."

"How does he support himself? Does he have a job?"

"He gets a little money from home. His mother sends it. Not much. And he's worked at a lot of jobs. He worked at this hamburger place last summer, but he got sick and had to quit. He's writing a book now."

"A book? What kind of a book?"

"A book on everything. That's what he's calling it. *The Book of Everything*. I mean, that's just a title for now. He may change it later on. And he and some other guys are trying to get some money to make this movie. But nobody'll give them any support because their ideas are too revolutionary. Ralph says Canada's no different from the States. Look at the way we treat our Indians. And if you've got money you're okay. But if you haven't . . . Everything is all screwed up. That's what his book's going to be about. I mean, look at the Great Lakes . . . how dirty they are. And Ralph heard this guy on TV. This French scientist Cousteau, who photographs fish and seals. He only gives the oceans fifty years . . ."

Landon listened to his daughter. Yes, the trouble was that even the lunging rage of a Chamberlain had to be considered, weighed, examined. The times demanded it. They forced peculiar bedfellows upon you. You had to move over, make room for their opinions. This Chamberlain! With his scowling dark good looks and his grudging airs. His beefs and passions and ideals. Probably he saw himself as an author, movie producer, university lecturer, department-store autographer of books, a TV star, a Renaissance man of the twentieth century. And all before he was twenty-five. Well, he wasn't exactly dreaming the impossible dream either. It happened all the time. Nowadays it was useless to put a check on your ambitions, take stock of your limitations. You could always turn on the television and find someone only half as clever making twenty times as much money peddling his opinions.

"All right now, Ginny," said Landon. "We'll put all this aside for now. Chamberlain may have some very lofty ideals, even admirable ones. And for what it's worth, I happen to admire his stand on the war. But this is not the place or time to discuss ideals. First we've got to get you out of here. Did your mother say anything about the bail money? It's fifteen hundred dollars." Ginny made one of her sour faces.

"No—but she'll be here. She didn't say so but she will be. Only I'm not going with her."

"Why not, for heaven's sake?"

"Because I know damn well she'll bring only the bail for me. She won't bring any money for Ralph. She'll let him sit all weekend in this crummy place. Well, I've got news for her. If Ralph stays, so do I . . ." She hugged her arms now and bent over, studying the floor. "I just will, that's all . . ."

"Well, I think you're being very foolish about that," said Landon. He looked at his daughter's rounded back. "And don't be too sure about your mother. I don't think she's a malicious woman."

"Oh Daddy. That's just it. She *is* malicious. She'll come up here all righteous and snorting fire and give me a lecture and then plunk down the money for me and let Ralph rot here. I mean, I know her."

"Maybe she won't come at all," said Landon.

"Oh, she'll be here, all right." Ginny said this quickly. "She'll be here." She seemed so sure of herself on this point. The old Hall arrogance asserting itself after all. But then perhaps this kind of thinking just accompanied a lifetime near money. Someone would always turn up with the bread. Revolutionary ideals aside, Ginny didn't expect to spend the weekend in this Victorian fortress eating hamburgers and drinking coffee from Dixie cups. But maybe her mother was finally fed up with this behavior? Maybe she would leave them here for the weekend? A brutal lesson. He shuddered at the thought.

"I think I'd better try to raise the money," he said, "though fifteen hundred is a big bite."

"Never mind, Daddy. We can stay here all weekend. I don't mind, really."

"Of course you mind. And please forget the martyr role, Ginny. You're not here on some civil-rights thing. There are no great principles at stake. You're here on a criminal charge."

"Well, I'm not leaving without Ralph. He's down there all by himself. It isn't fair . . ." Landon stood up, heard a bone crack in his knee.

"Well, I'll see what I can do." Ginny stood up too and he looked down at her. She seemed to have been shriveled by the experience. Her face, normally full, had shrunk. She looked ten pounds lighter. He touched her face with his hand. "Are you all right? Have you had anything to eat?"

"I'm not hungry, Daddy, though I could use some coffee."

"I'll see what I can do. Meanwhile, sit tight. I won't be far away." He wanted to say more, wanted to tell her to be more careful with her life. But now he could think only about getting her out of here. It was conceivable that Vera wouldn't appear at all. Or if she did, she might only cough up the five hundred for Ginny. In which case, a nasty scene. He had better see to it. But how could he raise fifteen hundred bucks at six o'clock on Saturday evening in this hick town? Herb probably had this much in the bank or could get it. But Landon would never hear the end of that. No—he wouldn't borrow a pin from his brother-in-law. He smiled at Ginny and kissed her on the brow. "Take care now. I'll be back."

In the blinding light of the main office, the sergeant was eating his supper, leaning over his desk with elbows out as he bit into his hamburger. Landon smelled the French fries and coffee. There were two other policemen now in the room, younger men sitting on the edge of the desks with their big black thick-soled boots dangling over the sides. Were they Burnett and Simmons, then? They drank coffee from paper cups and regarded Landon with friendly interest. This was a lively Saturday night and they were enjoying the company. Landon cleared his throat. "I wonder, Sergeant, if I could see the young man?"

The sergeant poked a French-fried potato into his mouth. "All right," he said briskly. He sounded more formal than before, and as he stood up, he frowned at the remains of his supper. Probably showing the younger ones how it's done, thought Landon. Or I'm disturbing his eats, always a serious business with a big man.

The jail stank of moldering stone and Lysol. Under the bare light Chamberlain looked morosely handsome in his stiff denim suit. He sat in the corner of his cell with his knees pulled up against his chest, not saying much. Landon did the talking, holding on to the iron bars and listening to the sergeant breathe behind him.

"I'm going to get you out of here," said Landon, feeling shy with the boy. Words were difficult. "I'll get you a lawyer," said Landon, "so don't worry about staying here for the rest of your life, eh!" Chamberlain hugged his knees.

"Look, I'm sorry about getting Ginny into this . . . She's a good kid . . . She's okay . . . I told the cops that." He sounded irritably sincere.

"Yes, well . . ." Landon looked around at the sergeant, who stood rocking on his heels, with his hands behind his back. He was staring down at the floor. "Well, just . . . sit tight and I'll see what I can do . . ." said Landon. "You can't stay in this place overnight. Christ . . ."

Outside, he walked into an early spring evening. It was clear and cold, and under his shoes the sidewalk felt like a slab of ice. In the Flying Dragon he changed three dollars into quarters, dimes, and nickels and, holding the heavy silver in his fist like an offering, walked to a public phone on the next street. In the booth he stacked the coins on the metal counter and drew out his address book, circling Blanche's number with a pencil. But either no one was home or no one was answering, because all he got for his trouble was a long stuttering buzz in the left ear. Next he tried Harvey Hubbard, the only person he knew who might be able to lay his hands on fifteen hundred bucks at short notice. But no one was answering Harvey's phone either. Still, this was Saturday night, wasn't it? And Harvey was now a bachelor, something of a swinger. He had several lady friends. If he's entertaining one now in the sack, he'll hate me till I'm dead and buried, reflected a gloomy Landon. The constant buzzing was giving him a headache. He decided to call Margaret, dialed the motel number, and was grateful to hear a human voice. He told her about his troubles. She had been lying down and sounded sleepy. "Are you okay?" asked Landon.

"Yes, I'm fine," she said in a drugged voice. "But I'm worried about you. All this trouble."

"Oh, it'll straighten itself out, I hope. Have you had anything to eat? You could order in some food."

"I'm not really hungry." A thick silence passed between them. It was awkward. Landon felt tense but could think of nothing to say. His skull was a gourd with only a few dry beans inside; a poor instrument for graceful musical games. Yet he spoke her name and said he loved her. Did he?

"Oh, Frederick. You don't have to say that. What I said this afternoon. About the child. I wouldn't want you to feel you are under any obligation . . ." The voice was pleasantly languid and stirred Landon.

"Listen . . . Don't talk that way." He felt a tremendous wave of feeling surge through him. What was this feeling? Impossible to identify. It couldn't be labeled. Neither could it be ignored. "Margaret, all this has caught me a little off balance. But I'm not really unhappy about the child. It's complicating, yes . . ."

"My darling, I am *very happy* about the child. I want you to know that. I didn't think it would ever happen to me. I'm very happy. But I don't want to ruin your life."

"Now, don't talk that way. We'll have to see about all this. I want to be with you as soon as possible, but first there's this business with my daughter. It's a mess, I'm afraid. I don't know if her mother's coming up here or not. I can't reach anyone by phone. And I'm trying to get in touch with a friend. To get the money."

"Could I not help, Frederick?"

"Well, unless you have fifteen hundred dollars on you."

"No . . . but there's money in my bank . . ."

"Mine too. But how do I get it out tonight? Look . . . wait for me there. I'll keep trying Harvey's number, at least for a while. I shouldn't be too long."

"I'll wait for you. Don't worry about me."

"Are you sure you're all right?"

'Oh yes, I'm better now. I'm glad you called. I feel better for that."

"All right. I'll be along when I can, then."

"Goodbye, darling."

"Goodbye." He held the dead phone in his hand. Yes—things in general were desperate. Could he build a new life with this woman? It wouldn't be easy. Rearing another child! Was he not a little past those tiresome games of piggyback and hide-and-go-seek? Papa Landon crouched low behind the sofa, hiding from three-year-old eyes! It had been a long time. He would be an old man before this child grew into adulthood. Yet companionship through declining years? It was not to be sneezed at. He might never have another chance. The city was filled with bachelors, divorced guys, widowers. Most of them were younger, richer, handsomer. But even the old ones competed now. Lean dry old men with their mod clothes and sideburns (there was Cramner!), some sporting white goatees like European professors. They swallowed their vitamin E tablets and received their hormone injections; gamely trying to keep up. And he had had poor luck! For most of his life the women he found desirable wouldn't give him the time of day. The others he had mounted with an open wandering eye, mildly bemused and longing for better things. These last few years had been no joke. It would probably get worse. Fears of a crabbed and lonely old age often drove people into unholy alliances. He could finish his days with a hag, some sharp-beaked crone (another Vera?) who would nag him into an early grave. He shook off these miserable thoughts and again dialed Harvey's number. Still no answer! Where was the man? Away for the weekend? Perish the thought. He felt a little faint and opened the folding glass door for air. He should have eaten something. He could try a cousin in Hamilton. Raymond Landon, Uncle George's youngest son. As children they had visited each other during summer vacations. Raymond was a skinny black-haired kid with pimples and a big dick. He smoked British Consol cigarettes and taught Landon how to jack-off one memorable August. Behind the billboards in vacant lots near the steel works. They knelt like acolytes before the girdle ads in the mail-order catalogue, a fine red dust settling over everything. Somewhere a war was going on. Landon's own brother, only five years older, was bayoneting sandbag dummies at Camp Borden. The shipyards were busy. A swooning Landon heard the hammers pounding steel and the riveters' guns drilling into the dry summer air. That Raymond! Full of dark Landon intensity and capable of great rages. And there was a kinky side to him! Ultimately unlikable. He once anointed Landon with Crown Brand corn syrup and staked him to an anthill. One of his Indian phases. With crayoned war paint on his cheeks and brow, he danced half-naked over Landon's white body. Then left him to the ants. Now he was married to an Italian girl and had four handsome strapping daughters. He worked at Stelco. In the blast furnace or something. But Landon hadn't seen him in years. Now, in the phone booth, he decided to take a walk. It might clear his head. In a little while he'd try Harvey again.

Dusk was settling over the town and someone had flicked on the street lights. This fine wide main street—he had always enjoyed walking along it, and had once been a part of the Saturday-night promenade, when the town's youths walked up and down looking for girls. Now the street was oddly deserted except for a car or two. Most folks were now at home, eating supper or waiting in front of the TV for the hockey game. At the main intersection the traffic lights hummed and blinked at the empty street. A few teenagers straggled into the Flying Dragon for their Cokes and chips, but Landon had the street mostly to himself. Above the courthouse the sky was the color of new zinc, and the trees stretched dark stiff fingers toward the light. Landon, the solitary wanderer, stopped in front of a men's clothing store, the Stag Shop. He peered into a window of coats and hats, saw reflected only a beefy gent of middle years dressed in a cowhide ranch jacket and nondescript odd pants. He should have been more particular about clothes before visiting his father. What a sight for those old eyes! He hurried on, walking down the sloping street like a man fearful of justice.

In the harbor the hungry gulls wheeled in the pale sky above a government ship loaded with buoys. The buoys were freshly painted and lay on their sides like giant tops. Soon they would be carried up the lakes and dropped into the water, navigational guides for the big ore and grain freighters. Landon wouldn't have minded sailing with them either. Perhaps even bobbing about in the lake too, listening to the lapping water sounds, watching the ships' lights glide by in the night, a sea gull on his head for company. The Not-So-Ancient Mariner. The sun had set, and to the west a band of crimson cloud lay across the horizon like a long inflamed wound. Landon turned and walked back toward the phone booth. Over the town a full moon rose, blessing all below with light. On the darkened street Landon was his own little island of light as he pressed his back against the glass door of the phone booth, working the telephone once more, almost crying aloud when he heard a voice. He quickly followed the operator's instructions, feeding the telephone with coins, listening to them bong and chime through the machine.

"Harvey? Is that you?"

"Yes. This is Hubbard. Who the hell is this?"

"An old friend from the dead, Harvey. How are you?"

"What? I can't hear very well. I think I got a bad connection."

Landon spoke up. "Harvey, it's Fred Landon here."

"Who? Freddy? Is that you?" He sounded amazed.

"Yes, Harvey . . . How have you been?"

"Well, I'm all right. I'm getting by, you know."

"I've been trying to reach you for a while," said Landon.

"Is that so? Well, I just got home. I've been in the shower. What's new anyway, Freddy?"

Landon fought his shyness. He hated asking favors. "Harvey, I need a friend."

"Well, you got a friend here. What's the trouble? You're calling from a pay phone, aren't you? You had an accident or something?"

"No . . . no car accident. I'll tell you. I'm up in Bay City. Do you know where that is?"

"Bay City? . . . Yes. It's up on Georgian Bay, isn't it? About a hundred miles north of here. Yeah . . . They have this nice park. I've been there in the summer. What are you doing in that place, anyway?"

"I used to live here. I was visiting my father. And my daughter's up here too. But she's in trouble. She and this friend of hers. The police caught them with some pot."

"What? Pop?"

"No, pot . . . grass . . . marijuana . . . drugs . . ."

"Oh . . . oh, Jesus. Is that so? And they've got your kid in the can, then?"

"That's it."

"These fucking kids. What a pain in the ass they are, eh! Am I glad I didn't give that dizzy bitch Blanche any kids. I had enough trouble with Howard. That crazy bastard was always getting into trouble. He'd phone me in the middle of the night from some cop station out in the suburbs. Once there was trouble with this soldier he picked up in a bar. Jesus . . . I always told the cops I was his stepfather . . . I went out of my way to *emphasize* that." Harvey and his stories!

Landon held his breath. "Harvey, I need fifteen hundred dollars to get the kids out."

"Fifteen hundred, eh! A nice round figure. Freddy . . ."

"It's a lot of money, yes." He waited, watching his breath steam the window. "It's a tough time to raise money, but I don't like to see the kids spend the weekend in this place. The jail's pretty awful."

"Well, yes . . . But I'm thinking here. They'll want cash or a certified check?"

"Yes. I'm afraid so."

"I don't have that kind of cash around the place, you understand . . ."

"Well, I didn't think you would . . ." He was putting an old friend in an awkward position. He felt flushed with embarrassment. But Harvey was talking.

"Still, I could probably get it from that tight prick bank manager of mine. You'd have to come for it, however. I got this engagement tonight."

"Well, of course I'd come, Harvey. A couple of hours' drive."

"No, wait a minute . . . wait a minute . . ." Landon waited. Harvey was constructing some scheme. "I got a better idea than that." The operator asked Landon for more money, and he swiftly plugged the quarters and dimes into the coin slots. Harvey talked right through this metallic music, with Landon straining to hear. "I know this lawyer over in Millwood. That's not far from Bay City, is it?"

"No . . . Only about thirty miles," said Landon. "It's east of here."

"Right. This lawyer I know. A guy named Mel Foster. He did some work for me a couple of years ago. A real-estate deal up there. A cottage property. He phones me from time to time . . ."

"Yes?"

"For market advice, eh! I've put him onto a few good things. He owes me a favor. I'll give him a call and tell him your problem. He'll get the money for you. These lawyers! They have no trouble raising dough. Probably he'll bring it over himself and spring your kid. Okay?"

"Harvey, this is kind of you."

"Forget it. You were always okay with me, Freddy. When I had my problems with that screwball dame, you listened. The way I figure it is, we both took a hosing from those broads. They tried to make monkeys out of us. We made our mistakes all right. But it don't mean we have to pay through the nose for the rest of our lives . . . Give me fifteen minutes to talk to Foster and then call him. He's in the book. If he's not home, call me back here and we'll think of something else. Okay?"

"God bless you, Harvey!" Harvey made a barking sound, almost a snort.

"Ha . . . That schmuck bless me? What did He ever do for me? What I got, I got myself. You're talking to a rag-picker's son. I haven't forgotten my beginnings. I know what trouble is."

"I know that, Harvey. I'll say goodbye, then. And I'll try this Foster in a few minutes." He hung up the phone and with two fingers raked the rest of the coins from the counter into a warm moist palm. He was sweating again, felt uncomfortably damp under his clothes. This was such an ordeal. A vexation of spirit. And he had counted on a quiet weekend. Now he felt cheated, deprived, sorry for himself. Still, he appeared at least to be getting somewhere. With any luck at all, he'd have them out in a couple of hours. He decided to tell Ginny.

The hot odorous blast of that police station! It seemed even more stifling than before, and the desk sergeant's face was the color of raw meat. He leaned across the counter, resting on his elbows, scanning the outspread newspaper, his big fists bunched up under his eyes. He looked over his spectacles at Landon.

"Well, now, Mr. Landon. You've just missed them," he said, tucking his hands underneath his arms. "They've only been gone—" he glanced up at the wall clock "—about five minutes now."

"Gone?" Landon knew he looked stupid standing here gap-mouthed. "That's right, sir. Just a few minutes ago . . . But they're waiting for you across the street at the Chinese restaurant."

"Who is they, Sergeant?"

"Why, your wife . . . and a tall gentleman . . . a lawyer."

"They brought the money, then?"

"Oh yes." The sergeant straightened up, placed broad hands on his hips.

"For the boy too?" asked Landon.

"That's right."

"Well, thanks, Sergeant."

"That's all right." The sergeant returned to his paper, and Landon walked out again into the cold air.

So Vera had come after all! Ginny had been right about that. She knew her mother. She apparently also knew her father. And this knowledge, translated into action, meant that he was not to be counted on in a pinch. She didn't really expect him to come through when the going got rough. No doubt he was a lovable old bear of a dad, but in a tight corner it was little hatchet-faced Vera who delivered the goods. But perhaps, though, he should feel grateful. After all, she was learning about life, wasn't she? These valuable lessons in survival. You couldn't discount their importance.

In front of the restaurant he saw the heavy dark sedan, recognized its brutally massive rear trumped up by the fake tire mold. The night before he had seen it parked on the street outside Blanche's house. It belonged to the lawyer, Craig. Beneath the sizzling green dragon Landon stood looking past the printed menu into the restaurant. The four of them were seated at the large round booth near the front. Ginny and Chamberlain looked glum as orphans, staring down hard at their coffee cups. Vera looked masterfully aloof in her light, tightly belted trenchcoat. The helmet of dark hair gleamed above the small pale face. She brought the coffee cup to her lips with both hands, elbows on the table, staring ahead. She was listening to Craig. He had laid out his flat black attaché case, leaving it open on the table like a salesman. It looked as though he were giving Vera a little lesson in the law. He was the helpful friend. And he did look handsomely competent, a package of well-tailored, prudently husbanded strength in adversity. You had to admire the capable good looks. The collar of his TV newscaster's shirt, for instance. It lay softly blue and pliant as tape against the deeply tanned neck. The big square-jawed face looked almost cruelly efficient, unassailable as stone. And clinging tightly to his scalp, this stiff poodle-gray hair, the sideburns flaring modestly and chopped just below the ear. A head of ironstone belonging to a man who swallowed his vitamins and exercised regularly without complaint. Probably his bowels moved with becoming regularity and with no vulgar strain. They made a handsome couple, and looking in at them, Landon felt scruffy and badly managed. Whiskers seemed to be sprouting from his cheeks and the hair was growing over his ears. His hands felt grimy. But what did they want with him? He had no wish to speak to any of them. They could sit there until the Chinaman closed the place for all he cared. He now realized how put-upon he felt. But really his anger was comical. Ginny had done the right thing. She was out of the can, wasn't she? Behind him he heard a voice. It came whiskey-throated and jagged from the big car. Landon walked back and leaned in on the door, smelled the old pressed violets and tobacco smoke.

"That is you, Freddy, isn't it?" said the voice from the dark rear seat.

"Yes, Blanche. What are you doing up here?" Blanche switched on a dim light and Landon could now see her. She sat with her legs drawn up, pale and small against the black ribbed leather seat.

"I just came along for the ride, Freddy. I know that sounds callous, but please don't think that . . . I love Ginny too. But I so hate Saturday nights in that house. I just can't stand to be alone any more."

Landon said nothing.

"I'm sorry for you, Freddy, I really am. This sort of thing is really very hard on the nerves. It's an old story to me, you know, so I think I understand how you must feel. But the child is all right?"

"Oh yes. She's all right." Landon straightened up, watched the dragon's electric tongue spit flames. "I wasn't sure if her mother would come up here tonight." He spoke across the dark glabrous roof of the car. "She didn't say anything to Ginny on the phone." A chill breeze came up from the harbor. It brushed against his face, ruffled his hair. He bent down again to the warm fragrant leather. "I've been trying to raise the money." Blanche clucked sympathetically.

"Freddy, Freddy . . . Haven't you learned anything after all these years? Vera always looks after these things."

"She hung up on her daughter. I couldn't be sure she'd bring the money."

"They play their game, Freddy, but Vera always brings the money. I always bring the money. Money is not the problem."

"Then I've just been wasting my time." He said it tonelessly and Blanche seemed not to have heard him. She was busy unscrewing the top from a silver pint flask. In the sheltered light the splendid little vessel spangled and flashed like a tropical fish. Blanche measured out a brimming capful.

"Here . . . Drink this, dear boy. You look half-frozen." Landon took it to his lips, holding it in both hands like a priest with his Mass wine. He tilted back his head and swallowed the whiskey. It was excellent stuff. "Would you like another, dear boy?"

"No thanks, Blanche. But that was very good." He felt strangely emptied, hollowed out, as though he had nothing inside him but this pool of whiskey washing warmly against his stomach wall like some brackish tidal water. His head seemed remarkably clear. He was sure that if he struck his temple with a mallet his skull would ring like a monastery bell. "I think I'll be going along now, Blanche. Tell Ginny I'll call her tomorrow. In the afternoon."

"Do take care of yourself, Freddy," said Blanche. "And don't be too hard on them. They're not very happy people."

"Blanche, I'm going to pay you a visit one of these days. We've neglected each other."

"Dear Freddy, I hope you're being truthful. I can't bear lies."

Landon raised a hand. "Scout's honor." He walked across the courthouse lawn and over the cold sidewalk to the parking lot.

At the Blue Moon, Margaret was waiting for him, and she ran to the car. In the front seat they hugged and kissed like sweethearts.

Landon was extravagantly pleased to see her, and to him she looked gravely beautiful. She touched his face.

"Darling, you've had such a time. Is everything all right?"

"Yes, I think it'll work out, Margaret." He felt weary, older than his years, yet strangely exalted. Deep within he was stirred by the old hopes which always surround new beginnings, fresh starts. Through the windows of the motel office he watched Fireplug Gibson bend forward to adjust his color TV. They had hardly touched that room, and perhaps he should ask for his money back. "We paid for a room in this dump, Margaret. We could stay here if you like."

But she shook her head. "Darling, let's not. Please. I want to go home."

It was really not a bad idea. He himself had had enough of this damn town, and he'd soon see it again at Ginny's trial. Right now he could use a drink and something to eat. Some music too and perhaps later a little love. All might yet be well and a bleak day partially redeemed. He turned the ignition key and felt it resist. "Margaret, I'm going to take this damn car in one of these days and get it fixed." He tried again and the old motor came to instant life. "There now, you see . . . I've frightened the damn thing."

Margaret smiled at him with sad affection. "You're a good man, Frederick. You don't give yourself enough credit."

"Kind words, Margaret, but I'm no prize, believe me."

The highway stretched before them, empty and gray in the moonlight. As they passed the cemetery, Landon looked beyond the iron railing fence to the rows of stones among the trees. A whole town lay sleeping beneath that cold grass. And now Wally Beal had joined them. Landon too someday. But not just yet. The DeSoto's motor thrummed along, and inside Margaret had leaned against him, hiding her hands in the sleeves of her woolen coat. She had kicked off her shoes too and tucked her broad stockinged feet beneath her. Something was wrong with the heater, and by turns it blew great blasts of hot and cold air over Landon's crotch. There was much to repair in the old car. In his life too. There were many questions that needed answers. He might begin with the Church. What was its position on divorced men, anyway? He felt Margaret's body relaxing as she settled against him into sleep. In the morning he would go along with her to St. Basil's. He would speak to Father Duffy about it.

Through her gripping personal testimony (*Finally Free Bible Study: 7 Weeks to Freedom from Your Past*), Jennifer Kosytal shares God's gift of freedom with a hurting and broken world. Mercy Ministries utilizes Jennifer's powerful message to assist young women on their journey to complete and lasting freedom.

—NANCY ALCORN
MERCY MINISTRIES

Jennifer Kostyal is a dynamic woman of God who has a deep love for the Word of God and a passion to see His Word transform the lives of others. She is a living testimony of how God can take a life that has been scarred and broken and powerfully use it to set others free.

—PHIL ORTEGO
SENIOR PASTOR, SCOTTS HILL BAPTIST CHURCH
WILMINGTON, NC

If you are looking for fluffy, bedtime reading, do not get near *Finally Free*. Jennifer Kostyal has stepped up to the platform with a megaphone in her hand, proclaiming boldly that there is freedom in Christ Jesus for the millions of victims of abuse who suffer in silence. Jennifer's willingness to be transparent, her compassion for those who are hurting, and her ability to speak with frankness on sensitive issues have provided answers to questions long overdue. The book *Finally Free* is Revelation 12:11 in action—"*And they overcame him by the blood of the Lamb, and by the word of their testimony; and they loved not their lives unto the death.*"

—DR. WANDA ROUSSE, SENIOR PASTOR
FAITH CATHEDRAL WORLD OUTREACH CENTER
NEW IBERIA, LA

The response was overwhelming when Jennifer Kostyal looked into the television camera and spoke to people all over the world. Her entertaining ability to communicate life and her transparent approach of using her own history to speak freedom into our future are supernatural. Jennifer is living, breathing, preaching, praying proof that God can take the most broken life and make it absolutely beautiful for His Glory!

— STEPHEN MARSHALL
CHRISTIAN RECORDING ARTIST

The Jennifer Kostyal story (*Finally Free*) is a stellar example of what happens when a person filled with a desperate and despair-filled life encounters the living Christ—TRANSFORMATON! Before you begin to read about her journey, have your Kleenex nearby. You will be touched by the living proof of God's power to take abuse, fragmentation, brokenness, guilt, and shame and change this woman into a powerful exhibit of His personal love and purpose for every person. I could easily see the Jennifer Kostyal story touching multitudes both through her book and the movie version. Get ready to be dramatically encouraged.

—JAMES BURKETT, SENIOR PASTOR
SOUTHWOOD BAPTIST CHURCH, TULSA, OK
DIRECTOR, OKLAHOMA CONFERENCE ON APOLOGETICS

Jennifer unselfishly shares her childhood pain, trauma, and suffering and has emerged as a gifted writer and evangelist who invites thousands to a hope that Christ alone provides. She is a living witness who is clothed with the full armor of God, whose joy and deep love for her Savior is overflowing to all who are blessed to know her.

As a Christ-centered licensed professional counselor, I am dedicated to serving others by integrating biblical truths with the well-proven mental health practices. Day in and day out in my practice, I hear and see brokenness that only God can heal. Jennifer's story and Bible study lead others toward Christ for forgiveness, healing, and ultimately restoration. I am blessed to be able to use her material as a resource in my counseling practice.

—JOANNE G. DAVENPORT, MA, CAS, NCC, LPC
LICENSED PROFESSIONAL COUNSELOR, WILMINGTON, NC

Jennifer Kostyal…energy…joy…laughter…tears…unfolding love that brings light. With a true story of severe abuse, her message is not of surviving but overcoming! She knows where you are at because she has been there too. Let her take your hand…love you and take you to the top of the mountain where joy is clear.

—PAM THUM
CHRISTIAN RECORDING ARTIST

WOW! This book is hard to read, yet hard to put down. It's an incredibly transparent look at the horrors of abuse in any form, and yet there's hope! Jennifer does a great job not only sharing her testimony to freedom but in giving us a "how-to" manual for helping anyone scarred by abuse.

—PASTORS HAL AND LISA BOEHM
SUMMIT CHURCH, ELKINS, WV

The message in the book *Finally Free* is a message that must be heard. Jennifer's statement, "Abuse always follows abuse," is a reminder of the cycle of abuse.

Many victims of abuse suffer in silence. Although the acts of abuse may have long since ended, the images of abuse are all too often reoccurring. *Finally Free* offers hope, healing, and restoration. It will set the reader on a path in which they, too, can be *Finally Free.*

—TOM ARNOULD, SENIOR PASTOR
GOOD NEWS CHURCH, YUKON, OK

*Finally Free* allows us a rare glimpse into a secret world none of us would choose to visit. Jennifer's transparent testimony provides hope for those still grappling with the complex wounds of abuse. When our daughter fell victim to a sexual predator, I struggled to understand her pain. If I had read Jennifer's book years ago, I believe our healing would have come quicker!

Her seasoned wisdom is extremely valuable. I highly recommend this book to all parents. With one in three girls and one in six boys falling prey to sexual abusers, modern parents must equip themselves to thwart the damages of abuse.

—LISA CHERRY, SPEAKER AND AUTHOR OF
*UNMASK THE PREDATORS: THE BATTLE TO PROTECT YOUR CHILD*

A great philosopher once said that the masses of men live their lives in quiet desperation. Jennifer Kostyal's life used to fit that description. *Finally Free* is her testimony of God's miraculous grace and bondage-breaking healing. It proclaims that the masses need not despair.

—REVEREND JASON LANIER
PASTOR OF WORSHIP MINISTRIES
LEE PARK BAPTIST CHURCH, CHARLOTTE, NC

Jennifer has a message of healing our world needs to hear. In her honest and direct style, she bravely unfolds her personal journey from unthinkable abuse to unimaginable wholeness in Christ. If you are one who has been broken by others, read this book and find the hope you need to be truly free. Jennifer's life used to bear the painful scars of abuse, but now it bears the loving fingerprints of God. Through her story, you will realize that yours can too!

—Pastor R. Sonny Misar
Living Light Church, Winona, MN


Jennifer Kostyal is a God-fearing spiritual arrow, piercing denominational traditions to help all who desire to receive salvation. An encounter with her will be an experience of a lifetime.

—Robert Kirkland, Chairman of Deacons
Manhollow Missionary Baptist Church
Hampstead, NC


Thanks to Jennifer's willingness to expose the destructive forces of the enemy, the statistical strongholds of abuse can no longer triumph. *Finally Free* not only shares Jennifer's journey to freedom but provides the hope and a valuable resource in ministering God's amazing grace and mercy to a hurting world.

—Dale and Sarah Hirschman
Ultimate Challenge Ministries


With her intense, unique, exciting, and captivating delivery, whether you are young or old, rich or poor, no matter what you have been through or are going through, Jennifer's testimony of God's ability to heal her broken life will leave you, too, Transformed by the Word.

—Roy and Velma Belon
Jennifer's Spiritual Mom and Dad, Pastor and First Lady of
Palmer Memorial United Holy Church, Chapel Hill, NC

# Finally
# *Free*

# Finally Free

*Living in Peace by Releasing Your Past*

*Jennifer* **Kostyal**

HONOR✠NET
PUBLISHERS

SAPULPA, OK

Published by HonorNet Publishers

P.O. Box 910
Sapulpa, OK 74067
Web site: honornet.net

*Dedication*

To my precious children, Rebekah Renee Kostyal and David Michael Kostyal II. I love you both more than life itself. You have sacrificed much with Mom in ministry, sharing me with so many hurting people. Thanks for all of your prayers before I leave on trips and while I am away ministering to people who need the love of Jesus so desperately. Many nights I walk into your rooms while you rest peacefully listening to Mom's healing scriptures CD, and I am amazed that the Lord has given me such incredible children, such precious gifts. I am so proud of you and know the Lord Jesus is proud of your sacrifice for Him.

David, thanks for the many times you said, "I forgive you, Mommy," when life had gotten out of control before I met Jesus. You taught me unconditional love.

Rebekah, you were the gift from heaven who made me face the "Goliath" of abuse in my life. You are the "princess" I always dreamed of having one day when I played baby dolls as a child.

Dave, my love for you grows every day! All of those nights you held me and kept telling me it would be all right...you were right! Jesus brought it to pass! The prayer you said that day on the living room floor turned my life around, enabling me to see Jesus waiting to take me into His arms. I will forever treasure the night I woke you up to say with tears, "You are the first person to love me like Jesus." I still feel it every day of my life. I love you, Dave Kostyal, and I thank God you never gave up on me! I get so excited when I realize that when our work here on Earth is done, we get to be with Jesus together forever! You are definitely the best present He ever sent into my life.

*Dear Reader,*

Some may ask why I wrote this book. I have but *one* purpose...to let others know that sexual abuse—and abuse of any kind—can be healed through the blood of Jesus Christ. In no way am I attempting to expose my family or any individuals who were abusive to me in the past. In fact all personal names have been changed with the exception of my name and those of my husband, my children, and Roy and Velma Belon.

As a result of my healing, I have been set free from my past, which has allowed me to completely forgive my family. If you have been abused, it is essential that in your healing process that you are able to forgive also.

I want to make it clear that my parents were *not* the ones who abused me sexually. It was solely an extended family member who had married into our family. I have no doubt that my parents loved me. There is not a day that goes by in which I do not sincerely miss them. I pray that as I have been healed emotionally that one day my relationship with them can be healed and restored. I remain hopeful, for nothing is too difficult for God.

Sincerely,

*Jennifer*

*If the Son sets*
*you free, you will*
*be free indeed.*

JOHN 8:36

# Contents

# Acknowledgments

*F*irst and foremost, I want to acknowledge the Lord Jesus Christ. It is because of Him that I am *Finally Free*.

With heartfelt thanks, I would also like to acknowledge my precious husband and children—Dave, David II, and Rebekah Kostyal; spiritual parents—Rev. and Mrs. Roy Belon; and my dear friends and sisters in Jesus—Karen Hardin, my co-author, and Betsy Williams, my editor. Bless all of you for standing with me. Wow! All of you are wonderful, wonderful people in my life!

I also would like to thank my literary agency, PriorityPR Group & Literary Agency, P.O. Box 700515, Tulsa, OK 74170.

*Preface*

"What does Farrah Fawcett have to say to us?" chided the dark-skinned inmate with a toss of her head. She was referring to Jennifer Kostyal who was walking into the prison chapel to stand before the rows of women seated in the audience. Slouched in her seat with arms crossing her chest, the sarcastic inmate had merely verbalized what it appeared many in the audience were thinking. The remark was understandable. By outward appearances, the blond, green-eyed, former beauty queen seemed to have nothing in common with her captive audience. But in the next thirty minutes, their opinion would completely change as tears streamed from their eyes and heads bobbed in acknowledgement as Jennifer related her story of abuse. Although never incarcerated herself, in reality Jennifer Kostyal's past mirrored that of many of the inmates—only now she was free both physically and emotionally.

The female prisoners' reactions to Jennifer's story have been repeated over and over as she has chosen to reach out to women from all walks of life, many of whom have been victims themselves. Statistics bear out the fact that women with a history of childhood abuse are at a notably greater risk of experiencing violence later in life. Nearly two-thirds (62 percent) of women reporting childhood abuse have also experienced domestic violence as an adult in the form of sexual, physical, verbal, or emotional abuse. That statistic in itself is alarming, yet a report issued by the Commonwealth Fund reveals more. The report states that women who suffered a history of violence or abuse were at a much greater risk of experiencing a breakdown in mental health.

In fact, half of the women in the report also experienced high levels of depression.[1]

In a stunning revelation, *Desperate Housewives* star Teri Hatcher announced her own experience of childhood abuse—a secret she had kept, even from her parents, for over thirty years. "It feels like there is a little girl in there that's insecure and needs to be constantly told it's not your fault," she stated. "I think that will dominate me forever."[2]

In our present society, one in four women and one in six men will become victims of some form of sexual abuse.[3] But whether it is sexual, physical, verbal, or mental, the long-term devastation is the same.

Of her abuse Teri Hatcher also stated, "I have so much pain. I'm a woman who carries around all these layers of fear and vulnerability. I'm trying to be my powerful me."[4]

Jennifer Kostyal understands. Molested and raped by an extended family member and raised in a religious cult, she was battered by boyfriends and was on the verge of a mental breakdown. But then her husband prayed for mercy...and mercy came.

---

1 Karen Scott Collins, Cathy Schoen, Susan Joseph et al. "Violence and Abuse," *The Commonwealth Fund 1998 Survey of Women's Health*, May 1999. From http://www.cmwf.org/publications/publications_show.htm?doc_id=235787. (Accessed January 4, 2012.)

2 Teri Hatcher, *Good Morning America*, ABC News, May 3, 2006. From http://abcnews.go.com/GMA/story?id=1917268&page=2ite. (Accessed January 4, 2012.)

3 Centers for Disease Control, Adverse Childhood Experiences Study, *Prevalence of Individual Adverse Childhood Experiences,* http://www.cdc.gov/ace/prevalence.htm . (Accessed January 13, 2012).

4 MSNBC, March 8, 2006. From http://www.msnbc.msn.com/id/11717426/. (Accessed January 4, 2012.)

That prayer, however, marked an entirely new beginning for this real-life desperate housewife.

Abuse isn't something you "just get over." Yet it is possible to overcome the deep-rooted damage, find healing, and walk free from the past. Jennifer did. And this is her story, her journey to freedom.

## A NOTE FROM JENNIFER

As a little child I couldn't wait for the day when I would grow up and the abuse would all be a thing of the past. I remember thinking, *When I'm older, I won't be afraid of the dark anymore. When I'm a teenager, I won't be so scared of people.* But when the time came, I was.

I longed to be older, believing that then the grip of fear that had controlled my life would disappear. But it didn't. Like cancer, it only intensified over time as its tentacles invaded every part of my being. I tried to will myself to be normal, to make the fear go away, but that proved futile. It seemed totally hopeless.

Ironically, as I finally began my journey to freedom, I discovered that in order to be healed from the scars of abuse, I needed to once again become the very thing that had made me susceptible to the abuse in the first place. Once again I had to become vulnerable—as a child with childlike faith. Only this time, instead of looking into the eyes of an abuser, I looked into the eyes of Love himself—Jesus Christ of Nazareth, the living Son of God.

My desire as I share my story is to give hope to others who have experienced abuse, so they can experience healing. As God has healed my heart, I have been able to forgive everyone who hurt me or rejected me during my childhood. Now I can truly say that I love them with the love of the Lord Jesus. I know that Satan meant to destroy my life, but God is using it to set people free. Just knowing that makes all the pain of the past worth it.

Whether you are a teen or an adult reading this book, if you have suffered abuse, you, too, will have to look into the eyes of Jesus with childlike faith. Only then can the wounds from abuse begin to heal and the root of fear be removed. Only then will you be able to look into a crowded room full of strangers and feel safe. Only then will you be able to close your eyes at night and be free from the pain-filled images of the past. Why? Because it takes a miracle. And there is only One who can work miracles. But He can and will work the miracle you need. *Jesus changes everything.*

It's amazing, but it is absolutely true—*anyone* can be healed from abuse, regardless of what kind or how horrific. Human psychology only promises to help a person *cope* with the effects of abuse, but one minute in the presence of Jesus Christ can provide the miraculous. When we cry out to Him for healing, this same Lord—whose power created the world, the universe, the design of our bodies, and the very air we breathe—can, through a snap of His finger, deliver us from the trauma of abuse and set us on the path of healing. Then, as we walk out our journey hand in hand with Him, He will heal the damage inflicted upon our souls (which includes the mind, will, and emotions) and actually restore what was destroyed. In short, He will give us an entirely new life.

I know—because He has done it for me.

*Chapter 1*

# A LITTLE GIRL FROM A
# STREET CALLED "MUD"

*B*y all appearances, we may have looked like the perfect family. Those who drove by the beautiful estate might have noted the Mercedes convertible, the well-manicured lawn, and the nanny in the front yard attending the two young children and assumed that we had everything. They would have been almost right. We had everything but one of the most essential ingredients for a happy family…peace. Peace was something I had rarely known.

With surreal calm after the nanny left for the day, I made my way to the children's playroom.

"I love you, baby," I whispered, setting a coloring sheet and crayons in front of two-year-old David. Turning to eight-month-old Rebekah, I strapped her into the battery-operated swing and flipped on the television to *Sesame Street* to keep them occupied. I looked around the room to assure myself that the children were safe before turning to walk out. At the doorway I turned to look at them one last time. Then, as if on automatic pilot, I made my way to the formal living room.

It's difficult for the average person to comprehend the tormenting images that consumed my mind of harming my children. Not that I *wanted* to hurt them, but terrifying thoughts overtook me that I *would*. All I wanted was for the terror and agony to stop. Thankfully I had no idea where my husband had hid the gun. I might have been tempted to use it.

At that moment I was completely oblivious to the crystal chandeliers and lavish surroundings. I had labored over this room for weeks, working with the finest designers of the city for that perfect look. But it held no joy for me now. Instead my eyes rested on a recent portrait that hung in its gilt-edged frame over the sofa. In an instant a combination of rage and despair exploded from within.

*"It's a lie!"* I screamed, crumpling into a heap on the floor. The portrait of the children and me dressed in our finest mocked me from its high perch. It conveyed the image of a happy, doting mother. The portrait, like my life, was a lie.

Contrary to my surroundings, I hadn't always known wealth, but I was quite familiar with sadness. "Home" for me was on a farm down a dirt road named "Mud" in a very small town in North Carolina. While most children were busy learning their ABCs, I was learning to keep secrets as my childhood innocence was stolen. The molestations began at the tender age of seven and would continue for ten long years. My molester had married into the family, creating easy accessibility. He threatened to kill me if I told anyone. He needn't have worried. Nobody would have listened anyway. Mine was just one more secret in a house of many.

*Chapter 2*

# FAMILY SECRETS

*I* suppose every family has at least one "skeleton" in the closet—some deep, dark secret intentionally stuffed away in an inconspicuous corner. These deceptions, lurking beneath the surface, are like a pot of fear simmering over a low flame ready to come to a boil at the first threat of exposure. As I grew older our family "skeletons" took on a life of their own, emerging from their cloaked hiding places, slowly causing the fabric of our family to unravel.

It all began in the early 1900s when my great-grandfather, Rev. Jeremiah Black, moved to North Carolina and began a religious sect. Although I never knew him, the account of the founding of the family church was told with pride frequently throughout my childhood. By the next generation, my grandfather, Rev. Black's son, started a similar denomination, which now boasts of many churches in North Carolina. This is the religious heritage I was born into—a powerful system that has been passed down through four generations in my family. It is what I was raised to call "church."

Although the Bible was used in many ways to establish the church charter, in reality, the tenants of faith are based only on a handful of scriptures that take legalism to the highest degree.

As a child, all I really understood about our church was that it was a set of rules dictating what I could not do. I could not wear makeup, jewelry, pants, or fashionable clothes. I could not watch TV, movies, or attend concerts. Even our family vacations had to be approved by "the church." Many of the church doctrines,

however, are held in strictest secrecy, only being revealed to members once they are totally integrated into the church family.

To me, religion became nothing more than a set of laws to reach for a God who could only be pleased by performance, yet it offered no grace or hope to attain the lofty standard. As a child I had difficulty understanding the maze of rules and regulations that governed our family. All I really understood was that we had absolutely no control over our own personal life choices.

I remember the humiliation that would swell within me as we attended public school but were so obviously different from the other children. From my classmates I would hear stories about the churches they attended and wondered at their freedom to do "normal" things. *Was it just our church that had these strict rules?*

In elementary school our clothes and outdated hairstyles immediately marked us as different—ultimately making us outcasts. And although the church leaders eased up on the most prohibitive of their restrictions regarding dress by the time I reached middle school, the confusion and ridicule that stemmed from those early years remained a label that defined me.

My mother had been raised by her parents in this way, so it is how my three siblings and I were raised as well. I eventually discovered, however, that my mother hadn't always agreed with the system herself.

My mother, Debby, was the oldest of two daughters…granddaughters of Rev. Black. For anyone looking at her childhood and teen pictures, it is obvious that Mom was a knockout. She had beautiful skin and a figure that rivaled Marilyn Monroe's. Exquisitely feminine, she had curly, long brown hair and gorgeous legs that grabbed the attention of almost every boy, much to my grandfather's dismay. Although she was never allowed to

enhance her appearance due to the strict religious guidelines, it was difficult to conceal her beauty. Eventually—and in spite of her less-than-modern clothing—she caught the attention of one of the most popular boys in a neighboring community, and a forbidden relationship sparked.

Just under six feet tall with jet-black curly hair, Bob was incredibly handsome. His charming, outgoing personality only added to his popularity…especially with the girls. As Mom recounted the tale of their courtship, she shared about having to contend with more than one alluring female who had set their sights on the handsome high-school student. As the attraction deepened between Debby and Bob, they began secretly spending time together, knowing that a dating relationship between a member and someone outside the church was strictly forbidden. The family church exerted an enormous amount of energy to protect our small religious community from exposure to the outside world. Dating someone beyond the "inner circle" was unacceptable. It was of paramount importance that the church and its members were protected from the polluting outside influences.

Although her father kept a watchful eye, he was unable to prevent the growing attraction between the young couple. The relationship between Debby and Bob blossomed from surface attraction to serious interest. Inevitably, it came to the attention of the church.

Humiliated by his daughter's actions, my grandfather attempted to end the relationship between the two. Although used to controlling the entire congregation, he found himself unable to control Mom. In spite of his efforts, Grandfather Black could not convince her to marry within the system like her younger sister had. In one incredible moment, Mom emerged from the restrictive cocoon of her upbringing. She and Dad eloped.

Upon discovery that his daughter had ignored his warnings, Granddad "disowned" her—a common practice in the church

for disobedience on this level. But instead of using this opportunity to start their lives anew and be free from the strict confines of the church, Mom and Dad worked hard to reverse the family shunning. Although her parents refused to acknowledge their presence, Mom and Dad began to worship at the family church in hopes of restoring the broken relationship. Eventually it worked. Over time the leaders and Granddad softened their stand against Mom and her new husband as they watched him accept the tenants of their religion. Eventually all was forgiven and the relationship was completely restored. But while it seemed that all was now resolved, the muscle of rebellion had been successfully flexed to chafe at the restrictive guidelines. It wasn't the last time that Mom and Dad would attempt to buck the system.

*Chapter 3*

# THE CONFINES OF
# DEAD RELIGION

*B*y the time I was in the fourth or fifth grade, my parents had begun to distance themselves from some of the stricter elements of the church. I believe this was due, in part, to my mother's distaste for the restrictive guidelines she had experienced as a child. Back then mandatory fasts sometimes were imposed upon the members—children included. There were instances in which she was made to go without food for days in order to be "purified." But the more outward restrictions were what caused her the most pain as they drew the attention of outsiders.

Well-meaning neighbors and classmates, who pitied Mom for her outdated and restricted apparel, offered gifts of clothing and shoes. Regardless of whether the items were new or used, however, Mom was forced to hand them over to her parents. It is easy to imagine the devastating effect this had on her as each gift was viewed as offensive and condemned as "sinful."

Coming from this painful past, Mom understandably began to embrace change, as did my father. They knew, however, that even the smallest infraction of the rules would bring a heavy reprimand from their superiors, resulting in immediate removal from any position of leadership they held within the organization. It was a risk that they were finally willing to take when they met Rev. John.

Just as my grandfather had started a slightly revised version of the system founded by my great-grandfather, Rev. John's father had also started a small church in a community about an hour

away from our church. While the theology in all these churches was similar, each group had its own doctrinal bent. Rev. John's system had loosened the extreme regulations on hair and dress, which came as a welcome relief. But they had also adopted the belief that there was not an actual hell. This theology eventually split the system into two sects—those who believed in a literal hell and those who didn't, pitting my parents against my grandfather as they chose opposing views.

As my parents embraced Rev. John's friendship, they also embraced his religious system. Almost overnight my sisters and I were suddenly given the freedom to wear more modern clothing and even shorts. I immediately liked Rev. John. His family drove a nice new car, something that impressed me as a child, and his two children wore clothing more in keeping with the current styles. We soon became friends.

Probably the biggest change that occurred from this new relationship, however, came about a year after our family integrated into Rev. John's group. Standing in the pulpit that Sunday, Rev. John began with the morning announcements. I was only half-listening when he came to an item that caught everyone's attention. There was going to be a beauty seminar!

As you can imagine, most of the women from our church and the three other satellite churches in the denomination attended the half-day event, hungry for information. Although I was too young to attend, my older sisters went with Mom. I'll never forget the moment of shock when they arrived home that night. Kathy's long flowing curls had been cut above the shoulders. In fact, after that, the majority of women in Rev. John's church sported short hairstyles as opposed to the traditional bun, which my grandfather's church imposed. It felt like a set of shackles had been removed.

As a child, I was delighted with Rev. John's new leadership, unable to comprehend that in reality, the religion we now followed under his guidance was just as controlling. The only difference was in some of the mandates. Each group still maintained a rigid set of rules and regulations, omitting the single most important ingredient of the Christian faith—a personal relationship with the Savior.

After a couple of years of attending Rev. John's church, my mother and father made the decision to accept the leadership of a small congregation. When the pastor of a sister church—which had been started under my grandfather—decided to retire, my parents took over the leadership role with Rev. John coming in each Sunday to preach. I can still picture that tiny white clapboard building out in the country near our home, far away from the prying eyes of outsiders. As I look back, I never remember having more than twenty to twenty-five people in attendance at our Sunday morning meetings.

As a child, I was expected to sit in one of the first rows of the hard hand-hewn pews. The long-winded sermons seemed to go on forever, and I often focused my attention on the cracks between the floorboards to watch the chickens as they raced back and forth in the crawl space. Their carefree search for food sharply contrasted us as we stoically listened to the fire-and-brimstone messages shouted at us from the small platform.

Although legalism was still the foundation for salvation in this new sect, it was a relief that we could at least cut our hair and wear pants without condemnation—except from my grandfather and some of the other "old-timers" from my grandfather's church who occasionally came to preach. We certainly enjoyed these new freedoms, but they caused enormous confusion in my young mind. Each change in our rules for living left me questioning who was right, who was wrong, and whether I would ever make it to heaven.

When my grandfather would come to preach, my confusion multiplied. His voice carried easily across the small congregation as he stood behind the wooden hand-crafted pulpit. His message

was always the same—a list of strict regulations to attain salvation. As he spoke one particular morning, I remember unconsciously reaching to finger my short hair, which differed sharply from the bun sitting atop the heads of my aunt, my grandmother, and the older women in the system.

As he spoke it took me back to the annual denominational camp meetings that our family attended faithfully each year. Members from various churches around the state—many of which were branches of my great-grandfather's original church—attended. Each time my siblings and I were paraded before the attendees and introduced as founder Rev. Black's great-grandchildren. While naturally we experienced a sense of family pride, the moment was also mixed with shame as we no longer held to the religious dress code, obvious to all since we lacked the prominently displayed bun. I would often leave those camp meetings resolute in the decision to no longer wear pants or cut my hair. But these were vows I would break again and again. Because of this, heaven seemed like the elusive carrot dangled from a long stick in front of me. No matter what I did, I never seemed close enough to reach it.

As my mind returned to the present, I recall squirming in my seat with sweat trickling down my back as my grandfather pounded his message home from the pulpit. The walls of the little room seemed to close in around me from the stifling heat generated from both the weather outside as well as the message. As Grandfather ended the service, we were offered their plan of salvation and the opportunity once again to accept their rules. The penalty for our rebellion was described with vivid accounts of others who had come to untimely deaths from cancer and accidents due to their lack of submission. These seeds of fear were planted in the fertile soil of my young heart and would grow deep roots, penetrating into every area of my being for years to come.

As terrifying as this was, it wasn't long before I would have reason to fear more than just breaking my grandfather's rules.

*Chapter 4*

# THE MONSTER WITHIN

*T*ime seemed to stand still as my oldest sister, Sue, walked into the kitchen of our small wood-framed home to introduce her new boyfriend to the family. Joe was tall with straight dark hair and very good looking. A senior and an accomplished athlete at the local high school, everyone in our small town knew him and expected great things from this young man who seemed marked for success with his good looks, intelligence, and athletic ability. Joe came from a well-respected family, the son of a preacher from the local Baptist church. As he was introduced to me, he looked down and tousled my hair.

"You sure are pretty," he said with a big smile.

Warmth flooded over me as a smile spread across my face. It was the first time in all seven years of my life that I felt someone had noticed me in a positive way. Looking up at him with sweet innocent eyes, I was like a puppy begging to be stroked. Someone had called me *pretty*!

There is a reason why his words had such a strong impact on me. Throughout my childhood, my grandmother and my parents repeated the story of my birth. I was told that they had just cleaned me up when my father came in to see his newest child. The first words out of his mouth were not what you might expect.

"That sure is an ugly baby," he commented as he walked to the bed where Mom held me in her arms.

Not long afterwards, my grandmother came to view the newest arrival. Her comments mirrored her son's.

"Well, Debby, that's the ugliest one you've had yet."

The room filled with laughter each time the story was retold for family and friends during my childhood. I would always laugh along to hide the pain, but my face would flush red with embarrassment. I longed to be beautiful.

Sensing my hurt, there were times when Mom would pull me aside after the family left.

"Jenny, I thought you were a pretty baby," she would confide, stroking my hair. But instead of erasing the pain, it would only make me feel sorry for her. I'm sure it wasn't easy for her to constantly hear the story either.

To add insult to injury, I also heard Dad refer to me as their "mistake." He and Mom had already made the decision not to have more children and were surprised when they learned of my impending arrival. As they adjusted to the turn of events, the next surprise came at my birth when the doctor announced a girl. Mom and Dad had chosen only boy names. Perhaps this contributed to Dad's negative feelings toward me, but these revelations didn't ease the pain I felt at his remarks. Each time he told the story, it reinforced the image in my young mind that I was ugly, a mistake, and worthless.

I cannot stress enough how important it is for parents and adults to understand how their words affect children. Encouraging words instill healthy images and produce positive actions, while damaging words wound the soul. I longed for words of affirmation. This intense need created a dangerous vulnerability for what was to come.

*He's so nice,* I thought as I embraced the warm glow of Joe's words like a comforting blanket. I actually envied my sister for her new boyfriend. Little did I know that being pretty in his eyes would provide the catalyst for what would become ten years of terror and abuse. Feeling ugly and unloved, I was the perfect target for Joe's advances.

Let me interject here how critical it is for parents to understand that if their children do not feel loved, it can provide the setup for this type of predatory relationship. I cannot stress strongly enough how important it is for moms and dads to speak blessings over their children so that they feel beautiful and worthy of love. Their positive words are priceless and shape their little ones forever. When children know that they are treasured by their parents, it creates protective walls around them to help shield them from predators searching for new targets.

Another powerful way for parents to protect their children is to pray God's Word over them on a daily basis. Jeremiah 1:12 states, "I [the LORD] am watching over My word to perform it" (NASB). Because of this, I encourage parents to read Psalm 91 every day, inserting the names of their children. As God watches over this portion of His Word to bring it to pass, a spiritual fortress of protection is created over children as they walk out their lives in this sinful, fallen world.

In my early twenties I read a magazine article on how to recognize the signs of children who are experiencing sexual abuse. The list included bedwetting, depression, extreme fear, being overly introverted, feelings of guilt, and having suicidal thoughts. As I began to mentally check off the symptoms, I realized I had every one!

Inwardly I screamed, *Why didn't anyone notice or care?* The outward signs were all there. Anyone looking should have been able to pinpoint that I was a victim of abuse or that at a minimum, something was terribly wrong. But nobody said a word.

The youngest of four children, I greatly admired Sue, the oldest. Eight years my senior, she was everything I felt I was not. She

was beautiful and yet had a tough, no-nonsense strength about her that I admired. Everyone loved her and I was her shadow. I tried to be just like her—that included in the area of sports.

While in school, Sue had excelled in softball. I adored going with her to games and volunteered to help the team wherever needed. I especially looked forward to the time when I would finally be old enough to play myself. The day of tryouts couldn't come soon enough and in my heart I could see myself handling the ball as confidently as she. Instead, I failed miserably. It was quite apparent that I did not possess the same natural coordination and timing that allowed Sue to excel as an athlete. The coach just shook his head.

"You're sure not like your sister," he stated bluntly, letting me know that there was no need for me to return for the next practice.

Sue was not only gifted in softball, she also excelled in horseback riding. It was she who taught me how to ride. I remember how frightened I was of the huge animals towering over my small frame.

"Don't be afraid, Jenny. You can do it," she encouraged. Even so, I was simply too afraid to become a proficient equestrian. It was just one more area where I fell short.

Fear was my constant companion as it seemed I was always afraid of something. Little did I know that a new level of terror was about to be introduced into my young life.

Sue and Joe married quickly after it was confirmed that she was pregnant. Joe came from a respected family and the wedding was held in the community church. But despite my parents' attempts to conceal the real motivation for the wedding, it was impossible to keep the news quiet in a community as small as ours. The whispers as they entered church—whether real or imagined—became a source of shame for Mom and Dad and our family name.

Although Joe had grown up in the Baptist church, for a season he assimilated into our religious system, completely rejecting his past to appease my upset parents. But soon after the wedding, his attempt at harmony with our family abruptly stopped and he insisted that Sue attend the church where his father was pastor. Needless to say, this added additional tension to the already strained relationship between my parents and their new son-in-law. This wedge also widened the door of opportunity Joe had into my life. While my parents had limited contact with Joe and Sue after this, they didn't mind if I spent time with them. In fact my parents often sent me to Joe and Sue's mobile home located just five minutes from our farm. Had my parents been watching, perhaps they would have recognized the signs as Joe's friendly compliments turned to more.

Joe was so handsome and always kind to me. Whenever he was around, he would take the time to talk with me or compliment me. At first I was thrilled to have someone so attentive as part of our family. During that period, both of my parents held full-time jobs, in addition to their work on our farm, and were very active in the church. Consequently they were gone much of the time. Because of this, it was not unusual for them to send me to Sue's house most weekends and even for weeks at a time during the summer when I was out of school. It didn't take long before a very different side of Joe began to emerge.

Only a few months into Joe's and Sue's marriage, the honeymoon stage quickly dissipated as the most inconsequential incidents began sending Joe into fits of rage, resulting in verbal assaults against my sister. Over the next year I watched her wither before my eyes as he flung his belittling words at her like daggers ripping her self-confidence to shreds. My heart went out to Sue as she endured his tirades, but being so young, I didn't dare stand up for her.

"You—!" Joe screamed expletives one morning as he stormed through the house in search of Sue. I can't remember the offense that sparked his wrath on that particular day—perhaps the laundry wasn't done or breakfast had been late—all I really remember is the fear and torment I saw in my sister's eyes. The tension increased on the days that Joe worked the graveyard shift, returning home in the morning to sleep. This became extremely problematic once they had children. Although Sue tried her best to keep them quiet, inevitably the noise level would increase and Joe would be out of the bedroom and after her.

As the verbal assaults continued, Sue slowly transformed from a strong, confident young woman to a timid and self-conscious one, cowering before her husband. Now with my sister completely under his control, Joe turned his attention to me.

Many times I have listened to my husband's recollections of his childhood—pleasant memories of school sitting at a little desk with new supplies, coming home to a warm house filled with the smell of fresh-baked bread, sitting in his mother's lap as she held him close and read to him, family outings—these are his memories of his close-knit Catholic family. He maintains only happy memories of a mother who catered to her three sons and husband. I often wonder what it would be like to have such sweet memories of childhood. Instead, mine are cluttered with the vivid images of lying in bed at night, every muscle of my body tensing as I heard the floors start to creak in that single-wide trailer.

In an instant I'm back again in that small bedroom as the door swings open and the smell of beer on Joe's breath punctuates the closeness of his body against mine. Closing my eyes, I pray he will go away as he touches my body in a way only meant for married couples. The sickening words that he loved me were so wrong and repulsive, yet in my desperation to be loved I tried to believe they were true.

As the years passed, the sordid ritual continued with familiar frequency. Between the abuse and the religious control, my heart was in a constant state of confusion and chaos. The conflict within me mounted as I was bombarded with rules for being "good and accepted" by day and perverted acts by night. I felt trapped between two worlds that demanded my total compliance. My mind had been violated by the religious system and my body by Joe. Sleep never came easily even after Joe retreated to his own bedroom, for then I was left alone to face the demons of his vile acts that most certainly doomed me to an eternity without heaven.

Our church services only confirmed these terrifying beliefs. Although my parents had chosen to follow the more relaxed mandates of the church's sister system, they had welcomed Grandfather Black to visit on occasion as the guest preacher. Each time his message was the same, confirming my worst fears. His tall frame and stern demeanor made for an imposing figure as he stood before us, pounding the podium until it shook as he forced his point home.

Each time I heard Grandfather speak, it reinforced my certainty that I was going to miss heaven! I wanted to be good and desperately tried to follow the steps outlined to achieve this elusive goal so I could be saved. One evening, not long after Joe had entered my room and began to fulfill himself, I burst into tears.

"Please stop! I want to be saved. I want God to accept me," I pleaded as I tried to shove him away.

"You make me do this," he hissed. "And if anyone finds out, you will be in a trouble."

Keeping his voice low, Joe went on to describe the exact form of "trouble" he meant.

"If your sister finds out, she'll cut off your head and hang you from the clothes line until all the blood drains from your body."

You may find it laughable that I could believe such a statement, but this was as graphic a scene as I could imagine growing up on a farm. In fact, it was exactly how we killed our chickens. I shuddered involuntarily as my mind envisioned the scene he described.

The threat rang over and over in my mind until I finally quieted and let Joe continue, totally convinced I would never be saved.

I was twelve when Joe gave me my first drink of beer. At first I could barely swallow the foul-tasting liquid, but after several sips, I recognized it had a calming effect that helped numb the pain of Joe's invasion. Alcohol then became a staple in our nocturnal ritual until the liquor became more than a numbing agent. It became a necessity.

My introduction to alcohol through beer and then wine progressed to harder liquors as Joe introduced them to me. In time he would buy me any kind I requested because he knew that when I was drunk I would do anything he wanted. All I knew was that it temporarily took away the pain.

It is a sad irony that all the while I was learning to drink "spirits," my grandfather was trying to cast spirits out.

*Chapter 5*

# CHURCH SECRETS

*I*'ll never forget one particular Sunday service in my early childhood. My grandfather had a common topic for his sermons—devils. This particular service was packed. It was a hot summer evening, and we fanned ourselves to move the thick air as he ranted and raved about the devils he had cast out of people. Those around me shouted their praises to God as if the loudness of their voices would somehow ward off the demons my grandfather spoke about. Inwardly, I sensed the meeting was about to turn to the activity I feared most. My grandfather was going to cast the devil out of someone. The whole experience was terrifying to me.

Sometimes in these services, I would hide under the pews to escape the strange sights and sounds of the participants. At the conclusion of services like this, my sister Sue would have to search the building for me. The church was not a large one, so it wouldn't take long for her to locate me and drag me out of the safety of my close confines.

"Don't be afraid, Jenny," she would whisper as she tried to comfort me. "You'll be all right."

But her words did nothing to soothe my fears. Growing up I became so fearful of people and even going to school that on some mornings I would hide in a linen closet to escape. In my young mind, I somehow thought that Mom wouldn't notice and would take my brother and sisters to school without me. Of course it never worked.

I'll never forget my aunt sharing with me an incident that happened during one of my grandfather's services. Grandfather was in full swing on his favorite topic when a large woman in her midthirties walked into the service. Almost immediately she began screaming and fell to the ground, her body writhing back and forth like a snake out of control. Without hesitation, my grandfather walked to where she lay and standing over her body began commanding the devils to leave. The noise level accelerated as his shouting combined with her screams until a wet spot could be seen on the woman's dress that grew into a yellow puddle.

Each time my grandfather preached about demons, I would begin to shake as I remembered the story. *Oh my God, what if that happens to me?* I thought again and again.

My family talked about devils as some might talk about the weather and with great regularity. The thought of such spirit control left me terrified. Today, after having studied the Bible, I understand that according to Luke 10:19–20, believers in Jesus Christ have authority over these foul spirits. Jesus said,

> *I have given you authority to trample on snakes and scorpions and to overcome all the power of the enemy; nothing will harm you. However, do not rejoice that the spirits submit to you, but rejoice that your names are written in heaven.*

As a child, however, I had no understanding that I had any protection from these unseen forces, which were spoken of so prevalently in our meetings and at home.

My older brother picked up on my fear regarding this subject and used it as a tool to torment me.

"Jenny, you are full of devils, aren't you?" he sneered on several occasions when I behaved in a manner that angered him. I believed his taunts and feared that if the church leaders found out, I would be the next one to have to stand in front of the church.

Words were not the only tool my brother used in his playful harassment. And for me his actions went far beyond "play."

*Chapter 6*

# FUN AND GAMES
# AT MY EXPENSE

*E*vidently, in my brother's mind, the fences on the family farm served a dual purpose. All were charged with electricity, which could be turned off and on as needed to prevent the animals from escaping, particularly the bulls that fed in the pasture beside our home.

Scott had a mischievous streak. Five years older than I, he often manipulated situations, as many older brothers might, to bring about my discomfort. Only Scott's practical jokes held a wicked element of control, which he liked to exert over me.

On one particular summer day when Scott was around thirteen years of age, he and I were watering the animals together, going from pen to pen. The electricity to the fences was off as we made our way, squeezing through the posts that separated each area. Pulling the long hose behind us, we filled trough after trough, watching as the animals immediately came our way to partake of the cool fresh water. After filling a trough for the cows located directly behind our house, my brother yelled for me to continue on to the pen that ran parallel to the garage.

Giving the hose a yank, I climbed through and then reached back, giving the heavy hose another strong jerk to pull it underneath the fence behind me. By now my shirt and jeans were soaked from the effort it took to water all the animals. Thankfully we were almost finished.

"Is the fence still off?" I asked warily, noticing Scott's close proximity to the fence switch, which was just inside the garage.

"Sure," he smiled. "It's safe. Come on back."

As I grabbed the fence to climb through, the current shot through my body creating a suction force. I couldn't let go. The juice from the fence coursed through me, causing a burning sensation to travel over my entire being. I could barely breathe. Laughing, Scott ran back inside and flipped the switch off, releasing the power and my hold. I crumpled to the ground, shaking and crying. I hurt. I wanted to hear him say he was sorry, but all I heard was laughter. When I finally made my way back into the house and told Mom, she barely gave it a thought.

"Just get over it, Jenny. You'll be fine," she said, brushing off the offense.

The only boy in the family, Scott could do no wrong and was already being groomed to take over leadership of the church when Rev. John would eventually step down. Since he and Sue were older, Mom and Dad often left my other sister, Kathy, and me in their charge when we arrived home each day after school. This meant that there was usually a two- to three-hour time span when we were left in our older siblings' care without parental supervision. I hated going to Sue's house for fear of Joe, but I was equally terrified of what might happen at the hands of my brother when he was in the mood for a little fun.

Most days after school we headed outside after watching our favorite TV shows, *Gilligan's Island* and the *Beverly Hillbillies*. Sometimes we were joined by our cousins who lived a short distance up the road.

There were always chores to accomplish, but these were mixed with play as we had plenty of room to roam on the forty-five-acre farm. One afternoon as I was walking around the back of the house searching for one of the cats, Scott hollered at me to join him at the corn bin just behind me. The silo was enormously fun.

With the door open for light, we would climb up the ladder and then jump into the soft mound of corn below, sending a cloud of dust into the air. Eventually, after doing this a number of times, the air would become thick, making it difficult to breathe.

This particular day when I had had enough, I found it difficult to climb out of the shifting mound and panic began to rise in my heart. Then, before I could make my way back to the small hatch where we had entered, I saw the door begin to close and the shaft of light that had filtered in through the opening began to diminish. Finally it became pitch-black inside as I heard the latch being shut.

"Scott, that's not funny!" I screamed, terrified of the darkness that wrapped itself around me. "Open the door!"

My screams were met with the sound of the metal rod sliding into place, which was used to secure the door. Inching my way to where I thought the hatch was located, I pounded on the metal walls, begging for release.

"*Please, Scott! Let me out!*" I continued to scream, banging on the walls to get his attention.

"There are snakes in there, Jenny. You'd better be careful," he taunted from the safety outside.

Although there was no logic to his words, my heart began racing at the thought that I was not alone in my prison. Instinctively, I pulled myself into a ball, hoping to become a smaller target for the predators whom Scott insisted shared my space. In answer to my screams, Scott laughed as he ran around the circular bin, randomly hitting the sides with a tobacco stick. I jumped at each strike, never knowing where it would come from next and whether the sound was coming from Scott outside or my cell mates within.

"*PLEASE!*" I begged.

This wasn't the only time Scott played upon my fear, delighting in my torment. Over time I realized that my screams were

fruitless. Finally, I learned to simply shut up and endure until the nightmare was over. It was the same coping mechanism I used when Joe would molest me. I simply shut down. Those times in the corn bin seemed like an eternity. Once I learned to be quiet, I passed the time by continually searching the darkness for the slithering enemies. Finally, I would hear the metal rod scraping back across the door and a shaft of light would pour into the crib as Scott would peak inside.

In a flash, this particular afternoon, I bolted from my position and shot for the opening. Pushing past my brother, I tumbled to the ground. Oblivious to the pain, I scrambled back to my feet and ran as fast as I could for the house. I didn't even look to see if Scott was behind me, terrified that he would grab me and throw me back inside. I had one goal and that was to make it to the safety of my room.

I hit the back door at full stride, unwilling to stop until I felt the soft comforter of my bed beneath me. But once inside, hives began to break out on my skin from the corn dust and the anxiety. Making sure the coast was clear, I tiptoed to the bathroom. Turning on the spout, I waited as the warm water flowed into the tub then sprinkled a layer of white powder on the water. I had learned from Mom that baking soda could ease the itching. As I soaked, I contemplated Scott's behavior. How could he be so nice one minute and so cruel the next? Tears flowed freely down my cheeks and into the water. I didn't emerge from the safety of my small haven until much later when Mom called us for dinner.

As we sat down at the table, my eyes met Scott's for an instant—the humor of the incident still evident in his eyes.

"Mom, Scott locked me in the corn bin," I burst out, angry that he could find amusement in my pain.

"Jennifer!" Mom exclaimed really looking at me for the first time that day. "Your brother would never do anything like that."

There were no words of consolation, only correction. Exhausted from work, she never investigated the incident or gave it another thought. As usual, Scott was above reproach.

Little did I know that the enmity between my brother and me would one day escalate to a level far greater than had been created by Scott's childhood pranks. It would become the dividing factor of my family as he stepped into the pastoral position of the family church and I became his target to destroy—that is, if others didn't succeed first.

Chapter 7

# MY REAL FRIENDS

S wing higher! What is wrong with you, little girl?" the tallest
boy taunted as I glided back and forth on the simple swing
set located in a dirt field just behind our country school. I went
there on occasion after school was dismissed when I was certain
the field was empty. I was comfortable being alone...where no
one could hurt me. Retreating into silence, I found it difficult to
make friends. Usually I just wanted to be invisible. As with most
victims of abuse, I was full of anxiety and even at a young age
began erecting walls around my heart and life to prevent additional pain. In my mind, alone was much better. It was safe.

The insults continued as five or six boys about my age stood
before me throwing out their verbal arrows. I kept my eyes
straight ahead, trying to ignore their presence, but their words
struck deep.

*I'll just keep swinging and it will eventually stop*, I thought
to myself. It was my programmed response—all I knew to do.
But instead of stopping, the harassment became worse as the
boys began spitting big globs of saliva into my hair and onto
my clothes. No one saw or came to my rescue; instead I continued swinging back and forth, showing no emotional response.
Eventually the boys grew tired of their game and left. Once I was
certain they were gone, I jumped off the swing, covered in their
slime, and ran for home. Only then did I allow the painful sobs
from deep within to be released. It was a luxury that afforded
little comfort to the wounds compounding deep in my heart.

I knew all the boys who had participated in the ugly attack—in our small school, everyone knew everyone else. But I never told a soul. With abuse, part of the victim literally dies, leading to a lifestyle of ignoring pain. There is a common misconception that eventually it will stop. But it never does—even years after the abuse has ceased. It takes a miracle to eradicate this level of agony—the miracle of Jesus.

The devil knows that one of the most effective ways to destroy a nation is to destroy the children. When children are wounded and experience no healing, they become wounded adults who will in turn reproduce more wounded children.

It may seem simplistic to say that Jesus heals, *but this simple truth is absolute truth.* He will never deny a request for healing when we sit before Him and say, "Lord Jesus, please heal what has been done to me." I am a living, breathing example that trauma can be turned into victory and sorrow can be turned into joy. I like what Jesus said about himself through the prophet Isaiah:

> *The Spirit of the Lord God is upon Me,*
> *Because the Lord has anointed Me*
> *To preach good tidings to the poor;*
> *He has sent Me to heal the brokenhearted,*
> *To proclaim liberty to the captives,*
> *And the opening of the prison to those who are bound;...*
> *To comfort all who mourn,*
> *To console those who mourn in Zion,*
> *To give them beauty for ashes,*
> *The oil of joy for mourning,*
> *The garment of praise for the spirit of heaviness;*
> *That they may be called trees of righteousness,*
> *The planting of the Lord, that He may be glorified.*
> Isaiah 61:1–3 NKJV

There is no "formula" for healing except to look into the loving, piercing eyes of Jesus, but we can do that through His Word! Those who do will never doubt that He heals. As a child, I would often peer into people's eyes, begging for someone to notice me. Inwardly I screamed, *Can't someone help me?* It was life changing the day I looked into the eyes of Someone who finally said, "Yes, I can and I will." That Someone was Jesus.

Although during my early years at school I didn't have many friends, I loved animals. Raised on a farm I was surrounded by chickens, cats, and cows that I considered my true friends. On warm days I loved to walk through the tall green grass with the animals and watch the reeds sway in the wind. Many times I would lie down in the field on my back near the baby calves beneath the beautiful blue sky. Soaking up the warmth of the sun, we would often fall asleep together. The peace of the fields and the gentle breeze calmed my soul. It was a place where I felt safe.

Our forty-five-acre farm was surrounded by a fence made from round wooden fence posts through which were strung either two strands of barbed wire or plain, smooth wire. Within the perimeter were additional holding pens for the chickens, cows, pigs, a huge vegetable garden, and a corn field. As children, we were assigned the job of taking care of the animals and tending the garden. Summers were especially busy as we were up at first light every morning.

"Time to get up, Jenny," Dad called each morning.

Rubbing the sleep from my eyes and throwing on a pair of jeans and a simple T-shirt, I would head to the garden with a plastic bucket to pick the ripened vegetables.

I hated picking vegetables...especially butter beans. Each day when we were finished, Dad would conduct a "bean check" to

make sure our buckets didn't contain any "flat" beans. "Flat" beans were the ones that had not fully developed. No matter how hard I tried, it seemed I always had a bunch in my bucket. For each one found, I would receive a lecture or quick thump on the head. I remember wondering, *Will I ever do anything right?*

The majority of our mornings were spent picking, each of us working on just one row at a time. The rows seemed infinite. We picked until the sun rose high in the sky and beat down upon our heads. Then we would head home for lunch before starting our afternoon chores, which usually consisted of shelling beans, shucking corn, or blanching the vegetables we had picked that morning. By an early age, we Thompson kids had learned how to work hard.

Each day we moved through the chores as quickly as possible in hopes of getting permission to ride our horses or go swimming in the ponds nearby. The value of hard work is a life lesson I received from my parents for which I am thankful. It assisted me greatly when working my way through college.

Although I did not enjoy picking the garden, growing up on a farm did encourage my love for animals. My affections went beyond our own herd as I embraced every stray that headed our direction. Anytime a hungry animal found our farm, I would sneak to the kitchen and grab a bowl, a piece of bread, and some milk. Tearing the bread into small chunks, I would pour the milk on top and mix the two together. Most often the grateful recipient was a stray cat that had wandered onto our property. They were so sweet and cute. I could sense their unconditional love as they would rub against my legs when I stroked their fur. In many ways they were like me, searching for someone to love and protect them.

Feeding the animals was mainly Scott's job, although I didn't mind helping. It was one of the longest tasks of the day. Each

morning, the animals clucked and bayed in anticipation of their next meal as we moved through the pens.

On one particular day I made my way to the cow pasture with a bucket of feed. Our cows were penned in several fenced areas further out from the smaller animals, which gave them room to graze. As I threw some food into their trough, I caught sight of the cripple. A few days before, one of this young calf's legs had become caught in some barbed wire. The resulting wound had festered and now prevented her from walking from the back pen to reach the feed. Her thinning sides spoke of her eventual fate. My heart constricted within me for the wounded animal that no one else seemed to notice. I walked to where she lay and poured out some of the feed where she could reach it. It brought me so much joy.

Each day from then on, I hauled feed directly to her in hopes that she would recover. It was hard work to both feed and water her in the remote location, requiring several trips through the field that separated us, but I didn't mind. Even though no one else seemed to care about her plight, I did. She was just like me.

Eventually, my father noticed that the crippled cow was getting fat and although she still had difficulty walking, she was looking really good. Amused by my compassionate heart and hard work for her survival, he thought it was sweet that I was helping the wounded animal and never prevented me from continuing my self-appointed task. I could tell he was even proud of me.

One evening after a particularly long day, we gathered around the table for the evening meal. The room was quiet as we filled our plates and began to eat, too tired at first to make conversation. But Dad had quite the sense of humor. He was always making us laugh and meal times were usually fun. Mom was a great cook and the table was filled with her delicious Southern cooking of green beans with fatback, fresh corn on the cob, homemade biscuits, and two kinds of meat—fried chicken and chuck roast.

After several bites, Dad smiled, complimenting Mom on the meal and her beautiful good looks. He continued smiling as he looked at me and announced that the beef we were eating that night was actually my friend—the crippled cow. My eyes filled with tears as I remember her soulful, trusting eyes. I knew this is what we did on the farm, but it didn't make it any easier. I consoled myself with the thought that at least she had experienced a little love in her life. In my mind, that was the most important issue of all. I pushed away from the table unable to take another bite.

## Chapter 8

# RAPED

*J*enny, let's go swimming," Joe said one Saturday as he walked in the front door wiping a trail of sweat from his face with one of his big hands.

Joe often took me places—just the two of us—leaving my sister home alone to take care of baby James who was around two years old. I was nine, and by this time Joe had been sneaking into my bedroom for a couple of years. He had successfully broken my will and had me completely programmed to do his bidding. On numerous occasions as we sat in the living room with my sister and the baby, he would ask me to rub his feet. He frequently created scenarios in which we would have some form of physical contact in front of her. If she knew of his advances, she never let on, but his manipulations were used as much to beat her down as to control me.

I remember an instance years later when my husband once asked me to rub his feet after a particularly long day at work. The request sent me over the edge.

"Don't you ever ask me to rub your feet again!" I screamed, losing control as the memories of the past flooded my mind. "I will never rub your feet!" The very action represented the sum total of things I had been manipulated to do against my will throughout my entire life, and there was no way I was going to rub *anyone's* feet—not even those of the husband I dearly loved. Thankfully, after receiving my healing, this became a non-issue; but prior to that time, it was obviously a hot spot.

During my elementary years, Joe had dealt with my mind and my body for so long that I didn't even try to stay away from him. My family constantly joked about how I was his favorite. They had no idea. If anyone in the family suspected what was really happening, they never said anything and never commented if we went off together. This day was no exception.

I changed quickly into my one-piece suit and headed out the door to join him. It was hot as we drove in his orange Nova, the noise from his muffler interrupting our quiet surroundings. The pond was located about ten minutes from the trailer. In typical fashion, Joe had music blaring as we made our way down the road. He had a good voice and seemed to know all the songs on the radio. I tried to sing along, enjoying the upbeat tunes that were so different from our dreary Sunday morning hymns.

I loved swimming. It was a special reward for us on the days we finished our work early on the farm. Jumping into the water, I relished the refreshing cool against my hot skin, washing away the sweat that had already soaked my suit from the short drive with no air conditioning. The water was clear and I could see small fish swimming near my legs as I waded from the deeper water back to knee-deep level.

Then, as if an alarm had gone off in my brain, I jerked my head up and spotted Joe gliding toward me with an intent look in his eyes. Removing my swimsuit and drawing me into water over my head, he continued through my screams.

"It hurts! Please stop!" I cried, struggling to break free.

Once the act was consummated, Joe seemed to snap back to the reality of what he had just done. Although he had fondled me for years, he had never actually taken the abuse to the point of rape.

"Oh my God!" he stammered, confusion and fear evident on his face.

In one quick movement, he picked me up and flung me into the deep as one might discard an empty drink can. He then waded to the edge of the pond and stumbled back to the top of the hill where he had left the car. This little child, however, could not be disposed of that easily. I didn't know it then, but God had a plan for my life. The very experience that left me crying and broken—that should have destroyed me—would later be used by Him as a platform to tell the world that no matter what devastation people experience, He can make them whole once again.

What happened next can only be described as a miracle.

The shock of the assault and being thrown into the water left me stunned. But instead of sinking, I found myself floating on my back, seemingly suspended in the water. Across the pond I saw a figure walking toward me. I knew it was Jesus. Tenderly, He scooped me up in His strong arms and carried me out of the water to safety. Laying me gently on the ground, he put a finger to my lips to calm the sobs that rushed out in torrents, shaking my entire being.

"Shhh…you're going to be all right," He whispered.

I don't have any idea how long He was with me, and I have no recollection of getting dressed. The next thing I remember is walking up to the top of the hill where Joe sat in the car.

"Want to hold the wheel on the way home?" he asked as if nothing had happened, hoping the offer would erase what had just transpired between us and keep him out of trouble. This time he even let me shift gears, but I was so shaken from the incident that I accidentally put the car in first gear when I should have shifted into third, causing the motor to grind—something that normally would have made Joe furious, but not this time.

"It's all right, Jenny," he said as he placed his big hand over mine to move the stick into the correct position. I hated those hands that had hurt me so many times, but I felt helpless and smiled as if nothing was wrong.

Instead of returning to the trailer, Joe dropped me off at the farm and sped away. For the next several days, I was somehow able to avoid their home. Of course I kept the awful truth of the incident to myself, too overcome with shame and fear of what would happen if I told.

I don't remember exactly how long it was before I saw Joe again, but I remember the sickening feeling that filled the pit of my stomach as the loud noise of his muffler announced his arrival long before he reached our house.

As the rest of the family walked out to greet him, I ran to the bathroom, overcome with nausea. Clutching the porcelain, I vomited over and over between choked sobs. I don't know if anyone heard me, but no one came to my aid. I was all alone with my awful secret.

Despite his momentary fear of being caught, eventually Joe resumed the familiar routine. He couldn't stay away from me. And I couldn't get away from him...that is until finally I became old enough to discover a way of escape.

By age sixteen, I had blossomed both mentally and physically. No longer a child, I had grown tall and slender and began receiving lots of attention and invitations to do things with others, providing the perfect opportunity to stay away from my sister's home...and Joe. At other times I would stay in my bedroom and study for hours, having discovered that education could be my ticket to freedom from the abuse I experienced at his hand. What I didn't realize was that by now I carried the baggage with me wherever I went and in whatever I did. Layer after layer of rejection and pain covered my life. I thought I hid the scars well, but they were obvious to anyone really paying attention. Thankfully someone did, but that person wouldn't find me until I had endured a tragic end to a very special relationship, leaving me on the brink of suicide.

*Chapter 9*

# FIRST LOVE

*H*igh school opened a wonderful new world for me. I went from feeling like the ugly duckling to suddenly people noticing me...especially the guys. During the summer between ninth and tenth grade, like a butterfly I emerged from the cocoon of awkward adolescence to a body that was developed far past my maturity. I learned quickly how to dress and fix my hair in such a way to make a boy's head turn.

Unfortunately, I craved that attention—that is, anyone's attention but Joe's. Inside I was still the little girl who longed to be loved. Yet this desperate need for love and acceptance set me up to become a magnet for abuse in every relationship I entered.

Fortunately during this time, I also turned my attention to academics. Although good grades didn't come easily for me, I was motivated, holding to the hope that a good education would provide a new life for me, away from the abuse and the confining religious system of my parents. My siblings Scott and Kathy were considered the "brains" of the family. They had done very well academically and had graduated from high school with honors. And although it was frowned upon by our church leadership, they went on to pursue a higher education. I was determined to follow in their footsteps.

Until this time I had been an average student and, not surprisingly, had some attention problems, as is common in children who have endured abuse. However, what I didn't possess in natural talent I made up for in pure determination, working for hours to complete difficult assignments. With projects that were too difficult for me, I sought out my peers for tutoring.

It didn't take long to learn that good grades brought positive attention from my parents and the acceptance that I so desired. By my junior year, my diligence began to pay off as I was elected class president and inducted into the Honor Society. It felt so good to be recognized for my hard work, and it brought a sense of value to my life as nothing else had before. I looked forward to the induction ceremony and asked Mom and Dad to attend.

"Honey, we can't," Mom informed me prior to the day of the ceremony. "Your dad and I will both be working."

Although disappointed, I wasn't surprised. I knew my place in the family and had learned from a young age that Scott was Mom's favorite and Kathy's was Dad's. Unfortunately I was Joe's.

It is important to understand that the effects of abuse are long-term. Dr. Dan Allender, stated in his book, *The Wounded Heart: Hope for Adult Victims of Childhood Sexual Abuse*:

> I went through my case files for one year to evaluate the relationship between the reason people came to see me for counseling and the issue of sexual abuse. What I found staggered me. I worked with thirty women and fifteen men during that year. Twenty-six out of thirty women and eight out of fifteen men had been sexually abused (in childhood). (Yet) not one man or woman came to see me because of the issue of sexual abuse, nor did any acknowledge or even wonder if their past abuse had any effect on their current problem.[1]

---

1 Dr. Dan Allender, *The Wounded Heart: Hope for Adult Victims of Childhood Sexual Abuse* (Nav Press, 1990 with revised editions 1995, 2008) 148. Used by Permission of NavPress. All Rights Reserved. www.navpress. com (1-800-366-7788).

Is it any wonder, then, that as abuse against children has exponentially increased in every realm and at every age that we find ourselves caught in a cycle that continues to perpetuate the offense? Once a child's sexual awareness has been prematurely awakened and the seeds of perversion have been planted, there *will* be a harvest. Sexual abuse typically results in outward behaviors of promiscuous activity and sometimes homosexual activity if the child has been abused by an individual of the same sex.

In many cases, the abused becomes an abuser. Our prisons are filled to capacity with those who will attest to this sad truth.

Having been sexually awakened and so desperate for acceptance and love, I was like a sponge. The area that had once been a source of so much pain and ridicule as a child had now become my greatest asset. As I walked through the hallway between classes in our high school, a smile would come to my lips as I noticed guys turn to take a second look. My five-foot seven-inch height and size-six figure was offset by curly blond hair, and I was determined that *this* blonde was going to have fun. Finally I felt in control of my life and sexuality. By my junior year of high school, when one of the cutest, most popular boys in school began to pursue me, I finally felt I was special.

"Hey Linda, wait up," Jake yelled as he ran to catch the best friend of my sister Kathy.

Jake was a senior and the captain of our high-school football team. Our school was small, but football was huge. Of course, that meant the captain's popularity was as well. Although taller at six feet one inch, Jake reminded me of Tom Cruise with his characteristic dark hair and eyes, quick wit, and amazing smile. By all accounts, Jake was drop-dead gorgeous.

"What's up?" Linda responded once Jake reached her side and caught his breath.

"Hey, tell me about Jenny Thompson," he questioned. "She is really pretty."

Jake was friends with both Linda and my sister Kathy. Due to a family crisis, Linda had been living with our family for a few months till things calmed down at her house. She was a sweet girl and well liked by all of us.

"I'm going to tell her you said that!" she teased as Jake continued to ask about me...and she did.

"He said what?" I stammered unbelievingly when Linda told me the news.

"He likes you, Jennifer," Linda commented in an all-knowing, older-than-you fashion. Typical high-school stuff, but I was floating.

Jake usually hung out with the popular girls and to be honest, I only saw him occasionally in the hall between classes. The very next day, however, I ran into him in the school cafeteria. Completely self-assured, Jake took advantage of the situation and began chatting with me. We clicked immediately. I felt like Cinderella had met her prince—and in fact, Jake became my first love.

Through his senior year, we became quite the item and continued dating off and on over the next three years. Most likely because of my upbringing in the church, our relationship remained pure...at least at first. That is until one night when I discovered what my parents actually thought about me.

It was late as I made my way down the paneled hallway for bed. Scott and Kathy had already turned in and the house was quiet except for the voices of my parents as they sat together in the den just off the foyer. For as long as I could remember, Dad worked the farm during the day and then worked the second shift at the boiler plant in the neighboring town. Each evening when he got home from work, he would unwind from his long day by watching Johnny Carson on TV. Sometimes, as she did that night, Mom would stay up and watch with him. During the commercial breaks, they would talk over the day.

I shouldn't have, but that night instead of going to bed I sat down with my back against the wall to listen as strains of their conversation about my siblings and me floated up to where I sat. Although they talked in hushed tones, Dad's baritone voice could be heard clearly.

"I'm so proud of Kathy," Dad commented. "She's so faithful to the church and has never given us a moment's trouble."

In my mind I imagined Mom nodding in affirmation. I had always considered Kathy to be Dad's favorite. She was very beautiful and Dad would often comment about his pretty daughter with the dark curly hair. Since I was blond, there was no mistaking that he didn't mean me. While his comment about Kathy wasn't surprising, what he said next caught me completely off guard.

"That's something that can't be said for Jenny. You know, Debby, she's going to turn out just like Sue, messing around with that football player of hers. She'll probably have to get married."

I cringed at the words not meant for my ears. Sue's situation had always been a source of shame for my parents in the church system, and now I understood that Dad feared the same behavior from me.

Jake and I had been dating for a few months and up until that time, I had never slept with him. To be honest, I had never had a serious boyfriend until then, so by most in the school I was considered a goody-goody. But that would soon change. I knew the moment I got in the car with him the very next night that my resolve had shifted. That night as Jake began to kiss me, I made a decision and lived up to Dad's expectations. Although I had already lost my virginity from the rape, in my mind I was now giving what should have been my virginity to Jake. If Dad thought we were already sleeping together, then we might as well just do it. Because I truly loved Jake and he loved me, in my mind this act cemented our relationship and future together.

Of course, as in any instance of premarital sex, it only created a soul-tie that would later cause us both pain.

When my relationship with Jake was on, I loved going to the Friday night football games. It was the biggest thing happening in our little town and the players were our heroes. I stood and waved my arms, cheering with the full stadium as the team ran onto the field, my eyes always searching out Jake. Sometimes I felt I had to pinch myself. Could this really be happening to me?

Jake was an amazing athlete and possibly could have obtained a football scholarship if our school had been larger. His greatest dream, however, was to be a fighter pilot in the Air Force. After graduation he hoped to go to nearby UNC (University of North Carolina in Chapel Hill) to pursue this dream. I hoped so too, as he would then be close enough to visit on weekends. We both had dreams for the future and I was certain that he would be part of mine.

As the second semester of his senior year sped on, it seemed that daily we heard news from friends in Jake's class of college acceptance letters or scholarships. But so far he had heard nothing. I sensed the tension mounting within him as he waited for some news of his own. Finally his day came.

One morning before school as I stood talking with friends in the hallway, Jake caught me from behind and wrapped me in his strong embrace. Grinning from ear to ear, he twirled me around before sharing his news.

"I'm going to UNC on a full ride!" he exclaimed as he held me close. It was a special moment but frightening as well. I held on to him tightly as if the strength of our embrace would ensure that nothing could come between us. I was tormented by the thought that Jake would go to the university and find another girlfriend. My unhealthy possessiveness had already caused a strain in our relationship, but I refused to let go. From that moment on, I

longed and prayed that when I graduated the following year I could go to UNC as well.

As graduation neared, our relationship continued. It was a dream come true. Jake's home was right near the beach where we spent hours swimming, walking, and talking about the future. An all-around strong athlete, Jake could surf as well, and I loved to watch his lean bronze body shooting across the waves as he made his way back to me.

I knew that what Jake and I had was special, but I could not control my fears that he would find a prettier girl at UNC. I voiced my concern to him as we sat overlooking the breaking waves. Gently turning my face toward his, he looked at me with those dark brown eyes that made me melt.

"Jen, I have never loved anyone like I love you. Don't you worry that pretty little head of yours!" But I couldn't shake the nagging feeling that what seemed so special wasn't going to last.

During that time, Jake worked for one of the local radio stations, taking the late-night-to-early-morning shift, while I worked for his dad in a small grocery store. One evening he called me to see if I would drop by the station when I got off work. Immediately I called Mom.

"Can I go?" I pleaded.

After a pause and a sigh, she gave her consent.

"Don't be out late," she finished as I hung up the phone. Usually Mom would have protested more. I remember thinking, *Boy, she must have had a good day.* She never liked us to be out on those dark country roads too late, so I promised her I would not be long at the station.

Immediately after I finished my shift, I dashed out the door to drive the five or six miles to see Jake. I jumped into my old blue Nova that had been passed down from Scott, to Kathy, and now to me. I loved that old car, but it could not seem to go fast enough that evening as I raced to the station. I was rarely allowed

to visit Jake at work and was breathless with anticipation by the time I arrived.

The offices were quiet as he met me in the dimly lit reception area. In an elaborately planned scheme, he had called my parents to ask their permission to give me a ring. He had also set the music programs for the station, so they would automatically air without his assistance for the next thirty minutes. I couldn't tell you anything about that small reception area. All I saw was Jake as I melted in his deep brown eyes.

He took my hand as he led me over to one of the chairs.

"Jennifer, I really love you. I want you to know that when I go to UNC, I will only be yours," he said as he handed me a small gray box. My breath stopped as I looked at the small container that could hold only one thing.

My hands shook as I opened the lid and lifted out a simple gold band with a cluster of five small diamonds.

"Please accept this ring. Every time you look at it, know it represents that I will love you forever," he finished as he kissed me.

I could feel the dampness on my face as I looked into his eyes and threw my arms around his neck. It wasn't really an engagement ring, but it was a promise for a future together. I slipped it onto my finger—a perfect fit. Driving home that night, I felt—for at least a short moment—secure in his love and that everything was going to be fine.

*Chapter 10*

# STARTING OFF ON MY OWN

**W**eekends were glorious during my senior year as Jake nearly always came home to see me then. Our Friday nights and Saturdays together usually consisted of the high-school football game and long hours walking the beach. The time was always too short and before I knew it Sunday morning would arrive, signaling Jake's return to campus.

At the Sunday morning church service each week, my thoughts were full of Jake rather than being focused on the preaching. I typically spent the time passing notes to one my friends about my romantic weekend rather than listening to Rev. John or my grandfather. As soon as the service was over, I would then read-just my thoughts and turn my full attention back to my studies. My greatest goal was to join Jake at UNC the following fall.

I missed seeing him between classes at the high school and the year seemed to drag by slowly. But finally the cold dark days of winter gave way to the warmth of spring and ultimately the hint of summer. Graduation was nearing. As my classmates and I walked the halls of our high school during our last month as seniors, the air seemed to pop with the excitement in anticipation of our impending ceremony. For me, this season was much more than a transition from schoolgirl to adulthood. In my heart, it seemed as if a painful chapter of my life was finally being locked away. My freedom was so close.

There were only a couple of weeks left as I stood in my room before school one morning. I pulled back the sheer pink curtains and looked out the window of our white ranch-style home as I

had done a million times before. I gazed at the familiar expanse of land in front of me, my eyes dancing back and forth over the open fields and every animal pen. But it wasn't the cows or the crops that filled my sight. It was what I imagined lay beyond the familiar landscape. It was my future. For the first time that I could remember, I had a great anticipation of what was ahead. With the transition, I felt I would finally be free from the memories and abusive relationships that marred my childhood. No longer would I have to tolerate Joe along with his lurid sexual advances. I was crossing the imaginary threshold that would take me to my new life. I smiled to myself as I considered the possibilities before me. I hoped and prayed they would allow me to stretch my wings and shake off the control that had defined my life.

The curtain dropped gently back into place as I turned away from the window. I was going to be late if I didn't hurry. I raced to the living room to grab my books with just enough time to make it. As I walked out the door that morning, my thoughts stayed focused on the present and future to avoid the past. In my naïveté, I truly believed I could leave the abuse behind as easily as I would leave my childhood home. If only it had been that simple.

UNC is the oldest university in North Carolina. With its stately architecture and well-manicured grounds, it is highly respected and sought after. I considered it an honor to be accepted as one of the twenty-thousand-plus students. And more importantly, Jake and I would be together again.

The long-awaited departure date finally arrived. It was a difficult day for Mom as we finished unloading my things into my dorm room and I turned to give her and my dad a final hug.

"Good-bye, Jenny. We love you; and if you need us, call us," Dad said, ready to go. The mood had been tense in the car on

the drive down. Mom had fought back tears as Dad fought back anger from an episode that morning when I had accidentally run over a six-pack of beer bottles.

After we had said our good-byes and they started down the walkway to leave, Mom turned back to look at me again. She was like a mother dropping off her kindergartner for the first day of school. My heart went out to her as they drove off.

Although I had been anticipating this day for months, now that my parents were gone I sensed the familiar feeling of depression creeping over my thoughts. I was just a country girl who had been deposited into a big-city college. What was I doing here? *At least I have Jake*, I consoled myself.

I only *thought* I was heading to a secure future with Jake. But like most fairytales, mine crumbled. Our relationship, with its foundation of immaturity, simply could not withstand the weight of my impossible expectations. Within weeks after the start of the semester, the strain from my insecure possessiveness began to show. And although my constant need to be affirmed was enough to smother any relationship, things were further complicated when I discovered I wasn't Jake's only love. He had found a new and exciting interest...cocaine.

*"What are you doing?"* I demanded as I noticed Jake's increasing camaraderie with the drug heads of his fraternity.

"Baby, a few social drugs won't hurt anything," he responded, brushing aside my concern.

My heart sank. It felt as if someone had sucked the life out of me as my legs started to give way. This couldn't be happening to us. The peer pressure and party atmosphere common in many universities had taken their toll as Jake embraced a habit that I deplored.

During the years Joe had molested me, he had been addicted to more than just pedophilia. He eventually turned to addictive high-inducing drugs. I hated Joe and the substances he used, which seemed to embolden him. Although I drank, I vowed in

my heart I would never become a drug user or marry anyone who was. But this was Jake and my previous black-and-white judgment wavered at the thought of losing him.

Although I hated what he was doing, I still adored Jake. I was convinced that I could be his "savior" and help him overcome his new habit. Only Jake wasn't looking for my help and lashed out at my constant mothering.

It was early in the evening one day as I made my way across campus to Jake's fraternity house. The air was brisk and I pulled my coat closer to keep out the cold during the twenty-minute walk. It was a relief to be done with classes for the day, and even though there was always more studying to be done, I wanted to see Jake.

My repeated knocks on his door were met with silence. *What a stupid idea to try to surprise him*, I berated myself. *I should have called first.*

Just as I turned to leave, I heard his voice down the hall coming from another room. But before I even reached the door, I was met with the sounds of the Grateful Dead mixed with laughter. I knocked once and then louder.

"Come on in," came a voice I didn't recognize.

As I opened the door, the pungent odor of marijuana mixed with the scent of other drugs assaulted me. I stood still for a moment waiting for my eyes to adjust to the dark room, finally recognizing Jake among the partiers.

"Jake, I need to talk with you," I stated, trying to maintain my composure.

"I'll be right back guys," Jake called back, giving me a look of disdain.

I looked into the glazed eyes of the man I loved and felt nauseated. It was like looking into the eyes of a stranger.

"What are you doing here, Jennifer?" he demanded once we were out in the hall. In my naïveté, I had expected Jake to leave

his friends and come with me, but I realized that all he cared about was getting back into that room for another hit. I was devastated.

"Please stop hanging out with these weird deadheads," I pleaded, hoping to connect with the Jake I knew. In an instant his anger flared and he pushed me against the wall.

"Jennifer, I am sick of your lectures and I will not stop partying just because of your set of rules for me," he barked in a voice too loud and slightly slurred. As he turned to head back to his friends, I grabbed his arm.

"Please don't go," I cried.

"I have had enough of you and your smothering behavior. It is over, Jen. Just leave me alone," Jake screamed, finishing with a string of profanity.

Pushing me harder against the wall, he abruptly turned to go back into the darkened room without a second glance. Sliding to the floor, I cried there for about an hour, thinking surely he would come back out to check on me. He didn't. When I finally stood to leave, I was a mess. My makeup was streaked down my face, my emotions were shattered, and I felt completely alone on that immense campus.

I was devastated at the loss of our relationship. Jake's rejection of me stirred the old feelings of worthlessness and ugliness that had marked my early years from abuse. My emotions began spiraling downward. Over the next several weeks, I ate very little and missed most of my classes. I longed to sink into the oblivion of sleep, but slumber rarely came. When it did, it usually included unwelcome images of the past, which left my heart racing.

Only a size six when I first entered college, my weight dropped drastically as did my grades after our breakup. I was on the verge of being expelled from the university. In my dorm room on campus, I pulled the dusty Bible from the bookshelf searching for hope, but the words seemed empty. After a lifetime in our

religious system, all I had were rules to live by. I had never learned how to apply the scriptural promises in the Bible to my life. As a result, the words did little to ease my pain. Closing the book, I slid it back into its place, completely unaware that I had shelved the one tool that could truly bring me hope.

For a second time I read over my grades for the spring semester. I shook my head in disbelief. I had failed most of my classes. In order to remain in college, I would now be forced to enroll in summer school to resurrect my failing GPA. After reviewing the courses offered, I finally settled on a drama class—figuring an easy ace. But the depression from my failed relationship with Jake clung to me like the heavy moisture-laden air just before a storm. The day of the first class I reluctantly pulled myself out of bed, barely sliding into a seat before the professor began.

As he began his introduction, I briefly looked over my summer "prison." The dreary walls of the basement classroom fit my mood perfectly. Only half listening to the professor as he espoused the basic skills needed for acting, I mused how I had been using those talents all my life due to the abuse. In self-preservation, I had already mastered how to turn my emotions on and off at the blink of an eye. And I could easily transform myself to respond to whatever situation in which I found myself. I knew in an instant that I would do very well in this class.

The professor droned on as I shifted to find a comfortable position on the hard plastic chair. I was completely oblivious to my fellow classmates, in my own little world, absorbed with my familiar emotional wounds. For anyone looking, I was a walking billboard plastered with the words, "Emotional Wreck!" Fortunately someone did notice.

A pretty African-American coed, Vickie was well dressed with shoulder-length hair and a megawatt smile. Energy and happiness exuded from her as she walked across the room to introduce herself, and it wasn't an act.

"Hey there," she said with a small wave. "I'm Vickie."

I just stood staring at this beautiful girl in front of me, immediately conscious of my disheveled appearance. The night before the class I had attempted to win Jake back one more time, showing up at his dorm for what was an almost-repeat performance of the night we broke up. Jake was emotionless, remaining firm in his resolve and reducing me to tears once again. Running back to my dorm room, I cried myself to sleep, not bothering to change out of my clothes or wash my face. Now standing in front of Vickie, I was still in the same crumpled clothing and hadn't even run a comb through my hair that morning. Somehow Vickie saw past all of it.

Almost immediately after introducing herself, she began talking about a Bible study she attended with some other students from campus. Although I was attracted to her warmth and bright smile, my guard went up instantly.

*Not again*, I inwardly mumbled.

I had had religion forced down my throat all my life, and college was finally affording me the opportunity to break out of its restrictive confines. I studied Vickie as she continued to talk up the Bible study. I had to admit, she didn't look or act like the people who attended my church.

"I don't mean to pry, but you seem very sad," she said, looking straight into my eyes. Part of me was drawn to her kindness and the other part wanted to run. Trust was an element that didn't come easily.

Before she turned to go, she invited me to the study group. I hesitated briefly as I contemplated the invitation. Ultimately, I had nowhere else to go.

"All right. I'll come," I said as I wrote down my phone number on a small scrap of paper.

Now walking down the sidewalk on my way back to my apartment, I debated the hasty decision. My emotions waged war as I wrestled with what I should do. Although I was scared to go, inwardly I desperately wanted help and longed for the joy Vickie seemed to possess. A conversation of pros and cons played in my head the entire walk from class. But after arriving back at my dorm room, I realized I was more interested than I had imagined as I waited for the phone to ring with her call. But Vickie had another call to make first.

"Mrs. Belon, I met this white girl who is really messed up," Vickie commented to the Bible-study leader, her spiritual mom. "Can I bring her to Bible study tonight?"

Velma and her husband, Roy Belon, were in their late thirties and lived just five minutes from the campus of UNC. Both business professionals, they each held prestigious full-time jobs by day but felt their true calling was to the students at the university who needed Christ. For the past two years, they had opened their home to any student who was willing to come to their weekly study. But their commitment to their call went far beyond the once-a-week meeting. I would soon learn that their door was open to anyone at any time who needed their help.

"Bring her, baby. God is not a respecter of persons," Velma answered without hesitation.

Although the study only met once a week, it just so happened that this was that day. Vickie called and we arranged to meet at her dorm that evening. I was filled with both anticipation and anxiety on the five-minute ride to the Belons' home. I was about to become one of the biggest challenges they had ever encountered.

*Chapter 11*

# THE BLACK FAMILY THAT ADOPTED THIS WHITE GIRL

We pulled into the driveway of the beautiful light-colored brick home that rested atop a crest overlooking a wooded area of Chapel Hill. As we stepped out of the car, I noted that there were already a couple of other cars parked in the driveway.

We had barely walked through the door when I was greeted by Mrs. Belon. She had become like a mother to most of the kids in the group. With a warm smile, she pulled me into a strong embrace.

"I'm happy to have you here. You'll be all right," she said with a knowing look.

It was a statement of truly prophetic proportions. But in my mind at that moment, it seemed impossible.

After everyone had arrived, we gathered in the den spreading out to claim a chair or ottoman. The room was so inviting. I settled into a soft brown leather couch across from the fireplace and listened as the voices of the others joined in song. Five other students made up the loosely formed circle—all of them, along with the Belons, were African-American. Having grown up in an all-Caucasian community and church, this was the first time I had been in such an environment, yet I felt completely at home and welcomed. I had been around preaching, the Bible, and a list of religious rules all my life, but what I encountered that night was something completely different than I had ever experienced in the churches from my childhood. What I found that night was love.

Roy Belon's gentle but firm voice was a striking contrast to the pounding delivery I had grown accustomed to in the family church. His message was short but gave opportunity for discussion within the group as he, Velma, and the other students talked about the meaning and application of the Scriptures in our personal lives. I merely sat as an observer during the dialogue, mesmerized by their words. Up until that time, the only "application" of the Bible I had ever heard about was what I *couldn't* do—never what I could do or what God wanted to do for me.

As the discussion concluded, the Belons prayed for each of us individually. Although they had never met me before, their prayer included every area of my life that was hurting. I glanced at them in amazement. I was instantly hooked.

For the next nine months, I attended the Bible study faithfully and a close bond developed between the Belons and me. Emotionally needy in so many areas, I looked to them for counsel, prayer, and friendship—not to mention parenting.

They were the first people I could remember who didn't judge my clothes, makeup, or actions. They simply accepted me, even in my messed-up state. And they knew a God who I never knew existed. Even more to my amazement was the fact that these two Christian leaders had a television in their living room! This was all very difficult to comprehend from the mixed-up set of rules I had become accustomed to.

When Roy and Velma taught from the Bible, I sensed an indescribable love and power. I was drawn to their words, yet also confused. It just seemed too simple.

"Jesus loves you. You can invite Him into your heart," either Roy or Velma would stress at the end of each study, never wanting to miss an opportunity for the participants to make this important choice.

As I attended each week, I grew more comfortable with their invitation, but I was still leery. Salvation by simply confessing

Jesus as Lord had been labeled false doctrine in our family church. The peace I found at these gatherings and in their home, however, was undeniable. Eventually I began staying after to help Velma clean up the kitchen. She thought I was just being kind. In reality, I prolonged my stays as much as possible because I dreaded leaving behind the peace that permeated my heart when I was there.

Even after all the dishes had been washed and the food put away, Velma would stay up and talk with me, sometimes into the wee hours of the morning as I began to open up and share the wounds of my heart with this sweet woman. Although she would have to be at work early the next morning, she never rushed me to leave. As long as I wanted to talk, she was willing to listen and provide counsel.

"Honey, you take this chicken and sweet-potato pie with you," she said one night as I finally stood to leave.

"Mom" Belon would never let me leave without sending me home with an armload of food in an attempt to fatten up my tiny frame. Although I was oblivious to it, I hovered close to becoming anorexic, and Velma had made it her personal mission to make sure I didn't cross the line. She spent hours prior to each week's study preparing her mouth-watering specialties, including homemade rolls, collard greens, and of course, southern fried chicken. It brought new meaning to the words "comfort food" and I loved eating there.

As time went on, I found myself making more and more excuses to be at the Belons' home. They always welcomed me with open arms. Many a night I fell asleep on their couch in the safety and comfort of their care. I hated returning to the emptiness of my little apartment—a place that would soon become a den of terror.

*Chapter 12*

# SUPERNATURAL ENCOUNTERS

*A*lone in my small apartment, I glanced at the clock over the counter. It was well past midnight. Over the past several nights, this had been my pattern as I studied late in an effort to boost my grades. UNC is a difficult university and it took all my effort to stay in it, especially during the immediate days following the breakup. Since our introduction, the Belons had helped me get my life back on course as I shifted my focus from the failed relationship with Jake back to my studies.

I shook my head and rubbed my eyes, trying to focus on the paper in front of me. I had several assignments due and needed to keep working but eventually succumbed to exhaustion as I crawled into bed, too tired to even change out of my clothes. Although I had a roommate, that night she was at her boyfriend's. It was too quiet for my taste, but the typical feeling of panic I often felt when trying to fall asleep in the apartment alone never materialized that night as I fell asleep almost instantly.

Between the practical jokes from my brother and the years of molestation, fear and nightmares had been commonplace. Typically when I did fall asleep, the slightest noise would rouse me. Subconsciously I was always listening for the unwelcome intruder. Tonight I was about to experience the most terrifying one yet.

I don't know how long I had been asleep, but I came awake wrestling with a dark and hideous figure. His strong arms

grabbing my shoulders pinned me easily against the mattress. This was no dream—the figure was very real.

"*In Jesus' name, get away!*" I screamed.

The most sinister grin crept over the evil being's face as he replied, "You don't have that power!"

Terrified, I fell from the bed, gasping for air as I continued fighting with this demonic force. Finally breaking away, I ran to the phone and dialed the Belons—my lifeline.

"Get in the car, baby, and come to our home," Velma encouraged. I didn't need to be told twice as I raced out of the apartment with little more than my car keys and purse. It was after that frightening experience that I moved in with the Belons and witnessed my first answer to prayer.

## HEAVENLY INTERVENTION

I had just concluded the second semester of my sophomore year and had made the dean's list! Yet my overall GPA had been greatly affected during my freshman year after the breakup with Jake. During those months, I had become so distraught that I completely flunked out an entire semester and had been put on academic probation. Although the probation had been erased with my rising grades, in my heart, I wanted that failed semester totally removed from my record.

"We serve a God who can do anything," Velma encouraged and prayed with me that the semester would be expunged.

Bolstered by her prayers, I went to my academic advisor with my request.

"That would be highly unlikely," he stated, shaking his head. "Work hard and keep your grades up. That's the best you can hope for at this point."

But my advisor didn't know the power of prayer.

The Belons later told me how they would frequently pray, calling out to God to bless this new spiritual child in their lives and to have that bad semester blotted out. Although the advisor did little to encourage me, he did instruct me on the necessary steps to follow to petition the removal of the disastrous semester. I followed his instructions and the Belons continued to pray. After submitting the request to the school review board, several weeks passed before I returned to visit my advisor.

"Miss Thompson, I must tell you that in all my years as an advisor, I have never had a student successfully petition to have a semester removed from their transcript—until now."

I jumped up from my seat with an ear-to-ear grin and shook his hand, expressing my gratitude for his help—and then ran out the door and drove directly to the Belons'.

"God answered your prayers!" I shouted, amazed at the miraculous results.

Roy and Velma were excited, but not nearly as excited as I. They were used to getting their prayers answered, but this was a completely new experience for me.

Outside of class, I spent most of my time with them. To their credit, if they grew tired of me they never showed it. Instead they treated me as if I were their own daughter. We spent many evenings attending revivals at various small African-American churches in the area. When the organ would begin to play and the drums began beating in their unique style of worship, I could feel God's peace settle upon me and was able to praise Him as never before.

I received the Gospel in large concentrated doses during that short season, and it was a good thing. I didn't realize it then, but I was about to be thrown back into the lion's den.

## Chapter 13

# MISS CONGENIALITY:
# A MAGNET OF ABUSE

*D*ad lost his job," Kathy informed me in a frightened voice. It was 1985 and my brother, my sister Kathy, and I were all attending college within the state. They attended Wake Forest University while I was in Chapel Hill. The fact that we were all in college was a source of pride for my parents but a daunting financial obligation. My sister and I had both qualified for financial aid, which helped somewhat, but my parents picked up the tab for the remaining amount.

It was toward the end of my sophomore year that Kathy called with the distressing news.

Six weeks from retirement at the local boiler plant, Dad had been informed of the closing and his subsequent layoff. Although some of the workers were transferred to another plant, Dad was not among them. At the time of his release, he had accumulated six weeks of paid vacation, yet the company refused to honor it, while also stripping him of his retirement and future financial stability.

The impact of my sister's words shook my world as the reality of the situation became all too clear. Scott, who was on full scholarship, wasn't as severely affected by the news. For Kathy and me, the results were more unsettling. We would both have to drop out of school.

I packed slowly, heartbroken at the sudden turn of events. Leaving school was like abandoning my future. But leaving the

Belons was worse. I was leaving my spiritual mentors and my friends, the ones who had helped hold me together when my world was falling apart.

At the end of the semester, Dad drove to the Belons' to pick me up. Tears streamed down my face as I reached to give them both a hug. It was an emotional good-bye, and I could see the concern in their eyes as they watched their young protégé preparing to exit their protective care. In typical fashion, Velma sent me out the door with a hug, a prayer, and a sweet-potato pie. Not quite ready to leave the safety of the Belons' fold, I was now like a young lamb being separated from its shepherd.

Not long after, I met Jeff.

Leaving Chapel Hill was, in essence, more than just returning to my parents' home. I was returning to the religious stronghold from which I had just begun to break free. Without the constant presence of the Belons in my life, a feeling of despair seemed to push out all the peace and hope I had experienced under their guidance and teaching. The emptiness was overwhelming. In an effort to regain the feeling of security I had experienced, I began to seek out love and acceptance in all the wrong places. This led to a pattern of drinking, soft drugs, and promiscuous affairs.

Much to my parents' dismay, I was reticent to return to the family church. I had tasted the freedom of true Christianity, and while I wasn't particularly living as a devoted disciple since returning home, I was unwilling to totally reenter my parents' controlling religion.

Despite our financial struggles, I was determined to return to school and began searching for any avenue that might bring in the needed scholarship money. That is when I discovered the world of beauty pageants. I was drawn to the glamour, beautiful

clothes, jewelry, and makeup—everything I had been taught against as a child—not to mention the potential for scholarship money awarded to the winners.

"Mom, please let me enter," I begged as I shared with her the opportunity that lay before me. She just stared at me as I outlined the various aspects of the pageant. She wasn't at all encouraging in this new endeavor. In fact, no one in my family encouraged me as I made the decision and turned in my application.

"You'll never win," Daddy stated afterwards in a matter-of-fact tone. "You know, Kathy felt the competition was so stiff that she didn't feel she could win. So you shouldn't even try." In spite of his words, I pressed ahead with my plan, hoping against hope.

"And the winner…the new Miss North Carolina Fourth of July is…Miss Jennifer Thompson!"

It was an unbelievable moment. Not only had I taken the title in the first beauty pageant I had ever entered, but I won Miss Congeniality as well. Afterwards, still standing on the stage, my sister Kathy came to give me a hug, her new boyfriend in tow.

"Jennifer, this is Jeff," she said, completing introductions.

In his late twenties, Jeff had already established himself as a well-respected businessman in the city. As a trophy of his accomplishments and thriving company, he drove a late model Porsche and lived in an elite section of that city. I was already aware of who he was since his father was a preacher in what was considered a sister church in our religious system.

As my sister completed the introduction, Jeff reached out to remove the contestant number off my hip as he whispered in my ear, "It's so nice to meet you."

As our eyes met, I knew exactly what he meant. A slight thrill ran through me along with a titillating sense of power as his

gaze and appreciative smile slowly traveled the course of my evening gown.

There were no boundaries in our family. Kathy was gorgeous and the apple of my father's eye. He could never deny her anything. Even though I had just won a beauty pageant, in my mind when it came to my sister, I would always be the ugly duckling and she the beautiful swan. Add to that the fact that as siblings we were bred to be competitive with one another. At that moment, I sensed the thrill of a new contest.

It is important to understand that the perversion of sexual abuse typically results in one of two scenarios. Women either unconsciously insulate themselves in obesity to prevent further sexual advances, or they go in the complete opposite direction, craving continual acknowledgement of their sexuality in order to stay their insecurities. The latter often results in lustful, promiscuous affairs.

As Kathy led Jeff off the stage, I watched as he turned back to give me a wink. The competition had begun.

Accompanying my new title was an array of jewelry, clothes, speaking engagements, and a feeling of local celebrity status, which I completely relished. Then one day after I had just completed a title obligation and was driving along the highway to return home, a storm suddenly blew in from the ocean. As the intensity increased, I fought to see through the pounding rain and struggled with the wheel as gusts of wind slammed into the car. At one point I almost jerked the vehicle off the road as a flash of lightning snaked directly in front of me. Terrified, I was convinced it was the hand of God judging me because of my participation in the pageant and the expensive ruby-and-sapphire earrings I was wearing at the time.

My heart raced as I pulled the jewels off my ears and cried out to God to forgive me for my "sin." The very next Sunday, I was back with my family in their church.

I hung my head as I stood broken before my parents and the congregation, repenting of my sinful ways. I had to. If I didn't, I believed it was just a matter of time before God was going to kill me because I wasn't following Granddaddy's rules. The system had always taught me that. Yet the pulsating fear and my penitent heart didn't last long.

Within a month after the pageant, Jeff took a step to remove my sister—his current live-in girlfriend—from the scene. Under the guise of concern, he went to my parents to express his fear for my sister's health as her drinking had turned out of control, often resulting in blackouts. Kathy was considered the "good girl" of the family. She had lived by the rules of the church system, was a distinguished Moorehead scholar nominee, and had been the president of her class in high school. Once in college, however, she had been introduced to alcohol, which turned into an addictive relationship that had grown beyond her control.

As Jeff discussed Kathy's out-of-hand substance abuse with my parents, they agreed that immediate steps were necessary. Before I knew it, arrangements had been made and Kathy, Jeff, and I were heading in his Porsche to Atlanta to have Kathy institutionalized at one of the best rehab centers in America. My sister believed Jeff loved her and was truly trying to help her. Because of this, she willingly entered the institute.

After the long seven-hour drive, we pulled up to the clinic. While Jeff checked Kathy in, I gave her a long hug and said goodbye. I'll never forget the look on her face as she turned to wave one last time. Even though she was still stunningly beautiful, she had aged far beyond her years. At one time she had had so much going for her, but alcohol had stolen much.

Once Kathy was settled, Jeff and I walked back to his car for the return trip to North Carolina. Already past seven o'clock, it would be well after midnight before we could make it back.

Without fanfare, we stopped for a quick bite to eat and then jumped back on the road.

As we talked during the course of the drive, I studied Jeff's profile. Handsome and confident, he seemed to know everything. The conversation flowed easily from one topic to another.

We had been on the road for almost five hours when he commented, "Hey, Jennifer, do you mind if we pull off for the night? I'm having difficulty keeping my eyes open."

I figured it was a ploy, knowing what I had seen in his eyes the night I met him at the pageant. But to my surprise, Jeff remained a gentleman...at least that night. While we stayed in the same room, we remained in separate beds.

"Good night," he said as he gave me a hug of consolation for my sister.

I did love my sister and felt sorry for her current condition. However, my need for love and attention had a compelling appetite, begging to be fed.

*Chapter 14*

# SLEEPING WITH THE ENEMY

$S$ince leaving school, I had been working at the Carolina Power and Light Company in order to save money to return to college. But soon after having Kathy admitted to rehab, Jeff offered me a job working for him in the city. Logically it made sense. I could work for him during the day and go to school at night. To further entice me, he offered an enormous salary—double what I was currently making. It was an offer I couldn't refuse.

After I accepted the job, Jeff pursued me relentlessly. The hint of physical chemistry that had sparked between us at the beauty pageant roared to life. Jeff showered me with gifts of trendy purses, clothes from the finest boutiques, and extravagant jewelry. On a couple of occasions he invited me to go with him to the Bahamas for unbelievable weekends. It was an amazing whirlwind affair and within three months, I was head over heels in love. I became not only Jeff's new secretary, but also his live-in partner.

What started out as a relationship that I believed was one of respect, however, quickly transformed into something I was all too familiar with—abuse. Once Jeff recognized that he had won my affections, a different side began to emerge that would erupt without warning.

"Jennifer, why don't you stop by the barbeque place on the way home and pick up dinner?" Jeff suggested after a tiring day.

Not long after moving in with him, I recognized that his personality had an obsessive component. His house, car, and life were meticulous. Opening the door to his pantry, one could see every can was neatly stacked onto the other. His closet was the

same, every piece of clothing color coordinated and in place. I should have heeded the warning signs of his compulsive behavior that were beckoning for my attention. Instead, I shielded my eyes, allowing myself to focus only on the extravagant things he did for me. The disastrous outcome was inevitable.

Entering the restaurant to pick up our meal, I made a last-minute alteration, replacing Jeff's request for coleslaw with potato salad. Containers in hand, I hurried back to the car, hoping to arrive home and have the table set before his arrival.

The sound of the garage door lifting signaled his return.

I finished the last-minute preparation just as he walked in. Glancing over at the table, he set down his briefcase. As I walked over to give him a kiss, I felt the back of his hand slam against my head, knocking me to the floor. His black Italian loafers connected hard in the small of my back, sending shooting pain up my spine.

"I told you to get slaw and you bring home that fattening potato salad!" he berated. It was the first time he had hit me, and Jeff was immediately remorseful for his actions…at least for the moment.

Overnight he transformed from the doting boyfriend lavishing me with gifts and everything I wanted to an obsessive abuser, questioning my every move. His paranoia over my schedule and other friendships eventually resulted in physical assaults that left me covered in bruises, cuts, and broken bones that couldn't always be hidden. A girl can only put so much makeup on her face.

Several months later, after working late at the office one evening, Jeff suggested a special surprise as he took me out to a very expensive restaurant in the city. It started pleasantly as the low lights and soothing music took the edge off of the long day. Jeff was relaxed as we lingered afterwards drinking wine. It was like old times. But as we stood to leave, Jeff noticed a handsome gentleman looking at me. I knew better than to say anything but

sensed his outrage as we got into the car. The entire drive home, the silent tension seemed to mount.

Once inside the townhouse, Jeff's rage erupted like a volcano as he pinned me to the floor. Screaming obscene names in my face, he began pummeling my sides and head with his fist. Then he grabbed one of my pinkie fingers, bending it back until it snapped like a matchstick. Thankfully the bone breaking made him come back to his senses and his anger quickly subsided. Then—as was typical—he became extremely repentant for his actions just moments before.

"You broke my finger," I cried, holding it as pain pulsated through it.

"No, I didn't. I just sprained it," he insisted as he grabbed it and tried to pull it back into position. The pain from my finger and where he had hit my face was excruciating. He put his arm around me and promised to get counseling—something I had begged him to do. Now pleading with me to forgive him, he helped wash the blood off my face and then insisted that he take me to the hospital. I was shocked and deluded.

*Maybe he has changed this time,* I convinced myself.

As we walked inside the clinic, the contemptible "Mr. Hyde" had transformed back into the kind, concerned "Dr. Jekyll," taking complete control as we stood at the admittance desk of the emergency room. I'll never forget how easily he explained away my injuries as a result of slamming my finger in the car door.

After he stepped away from the desk, the admittance clerk, who noticed there was no bruising around the finger to corroborate the story, whispered a warning, "I know he did this to you. You need to get out."

"No, he didn't," I lied, unwilling to look the clerk in the face. My hands began to shake as I turned to see if Jeff was watching.

There was no time for further discussion as Jeff walked back to the counter and escorted me to one of the waiting-room

chairs. He then became absorbed in the television hanging near the ceiling as I contemplated the clerk's warning. I knew he was right. The only problem was, I didn't know how to get out.

A few days later, Jeff and I went to visit my parents, the bruises—now turning from black to yellow—still obvious on my face.

"How could you let a man beat on you?" Dad questioned when we were alone. "We didn't raise you this way. You never saw me hit your mother. Why would you let him do this to you?"

Uncontrollable anger filled me in that moment and I responded in a voice as cold as ice.

"After all I've been through, a man hitting me is a piece of cake," I spat out before turning to walk away.

My father appeared to have no idea what I was referring to and seemed perplexed at my response. Later my mother also pulled me aside to express her concern and begged me to leave Jeff. But in my warped reasoning, I felt their attacks were aimed at me rather than my boyfriend. Rather than reinforcing the wake-up call from the hospital clerk, it actually served to bring Jeff and me closer together.

Only a victim of abuse can understand what I am about to say. The reason I would not leave is that I didn't feel I deserved any better. Sadly, this mentality is prevalent in the lives of most victims of abuse and exacerbates a dangerous cycle.

For those who don't become abusers themselves, most remain victims their entire lives, being drawn from one abusive relationship to another. Take my friend, Susan, for example. Susan is a beautiful, highly intelligent professional who is vice-president of a large marketing firm. In her early twenties she met and eventually married Doug. Good-looking and attentive, Doug made Susan feel as if she were the most important person in the world. However, within the first year of marriage, the façade crumbled as Doug turned abusive both verbally and physically. From a Christian home that shunned divorce, Susan chose to stay with him until the beatings became so severe that near death, she was eventually hospitalized. While the doctors were able to save her life, Doug had stolen her ability to bare children. Susan finally pulled together the courage to leave him and walked out with little more than the clothes on her back, a couple of suitcases, and no self-esteem.

Determined that she would never again give her heart to a man, Susan threw herself into her career. She remained true to that vow until almost fifteen years later when she met Jason. Her past experience with men had resulted in a myriad of walls being erected around her heart, yet Jason patiently wooed her. His gifts of flowers, elegant dinners, and patient acceptance of her need for time eventually thawed her heart until Susan said yes and walked down the aisle for the second time—this time believing she had found the man of her dreams. Within six months, the marriage crumbled as Jason's attentive caring turned to obsessive manipulation. Insisting on knowing her whereabouts at every given moment, he eventually prevented her from leaving the house without him...even forbidding her to go to work. Once again, Susan found herself in the divorce court, her self-esteem shattered.

Finally, almost ten years later, Susan embraced love again—this time with a man who seemed more gentle and compassionate than any she had ever met. Divorced and with a daughter in high school, Nick eventually shared with Susan stories of his ex-wife. Sensing he was another individual as wounded as she, Susan let her defenses drop. She immediately related to the pain he had experienced as he revealed the hurt of a cheating spouse who had abandoned him and his daughter.

Tapping into her need to be needed, Susan convinced herself that Nick and his daughter simply needed a godly woman to step in and help make their house a home. Nick's dream to return to school eventually became Susan's dream. She agreed to marry him and became the primary breadwinner as he worked to

complete his law degree. Finances were uncomfortably tight, but they were working toward the goal of a bright future together—a future that dissipated after Nick graduated. No longer reliant upon her salary, Nick's gentle nature turned to explosive verbal displays that became more and more common until eventually they turned physical. Once again Susan had attached herself to an abuser.

Tragic and real, Susan's story is not an isolated incident. It reveals the repetitious cycle that follows multitudes of abuse victims. No matter how many times others tell them that they deserve better than the "losers" they attract, the pain of the past becomes a magnet attracting continued abuse. This cycle will continue until two things take place. First, the spiritual cycle must be broken in the name of Jesus Christ, which we will cover in more detail later. Second, the abused must learn to reeducate their minds to see themselves as people of value. Until those who have been abused rise above the erroneous mentality that they deserve the beatings, healing will forever be an allusive dream.

The Bible offers hope and instruction:

> *Do not be conformed to this world (this age), [fashioned after and adapted to its external, superficial customs], but be transformed (changed) by the [entire] renewal of your mind [by its new ideals and its new attitude], so that you may prove [for yourselves] what is the good and acceptable and perfect will of God, even the thing which is good and acceptable and perfect [in His sight for you].*
>
> ROMANS 12:2 AMP

It is not the will of God for His crowning glory of creation to be abused, cursed, or beaten. However, the old messages that play in the minds of the victims of abuse—the ones that beat down their self-esteem and value—have to be destroyed forever.

In my case, abuse had cemented in my mind familiar thoughts that sprang up without warning: *Jennifer, if you tell anyone, the person will hate you and you will be in trouble. You are the one who made me do this to you. Just be quiet and it will be over in a little while.*

It took years for me to discover that I wasn't who or what those sick men had decreed me to be. Instead I have learned to renew my mind by believing that I am who and what the Word of God says—I am fearfully and wonderfully made, created in the image of God himself. I am of infinite value to Him, which He proved by sending His only Son to redeem my life. I did not make anyone perpetrate those perverted acts. *They* made the choice to act out their own sick fantasies and rage.

Dear reader, if you have been abused in any way, you can be healed through the power of the Word of God, which is "alive and full of power [making it active, operative, energizing, and effective]" (Hebrews 4:12 AMP). It does not matter the degree of damage that has been inflicted upon your body or soul, it can be completely erased as you renew your mind to what God says. Unfortunately as a young adult I didn't yet know of God's amazing gift that was available to heal my hurts. As a result I endured the physical and verbal abuse.

"How can you love him?" Mom would ask, concern filling her eyes.

I never had an answer. I didn't know. At that time I didn't understand that abuse is cyclical. And that cycle included my mom.

## Chapter 15

# THE CYCLE OF ABUSE

*T*he weight of the secret I had carried throughout childhood grew with age, commanding acknowledgement and release. The empty threat of Joe's words no longer paralyzed me to silence. Now as an adult, I felt compelled to finally open up with my mother about the years of sexual abuse. I didn't know how or where to begin and stammered as I tried to share with her the horror that had been my childhood.

The words and tears spilled out as I finally gave voice to the dark secret that I had locked inside.

"You need to keep this very quiet or you could destroy your sister's entire family," Mom whispered in hushed tones, her voice void of emotion. There was such finality in her words that it let me know that this topic was not to be broached again.

The shock of her words and lack of concern shook me to the core. I had expected to hear a response such as, "Oh, honey, it is awful that this has happened to you." Instead, her words only intensified the feelings of betrayal, abandonment, and confusion that had become my constant companions.

According to Jan Frank, author of *Door of Hope: Recognizing and Resolving the Pains of Your Past,* "Adults who tend to go through life wearing blinders, often have shut out their own abuse and cannot see the obvious indicators regarding the protection of their own children."[1]

---

1 Jan Frank, *Christian Counseling Today* (1998, Vol. 6, No. 1). 34.

As it turns out, the cycle of abuse began during my mother's own childhood. This came to light when an extended family member once let it slip that a visiting preacher had abused my mother when she was young. Although I never discussed it with her, I can only assume that in her pain, like me, she told no one. Her lack of response to my admission of abuse was obviously the result of her own victimization of religious and sexual abuse as a child. Yet her advice to just press ahead and forget it, as she had, was a recipe for continued grief. The pain of abuse cannot be masked, pressed down, or covered up. This course of action only prolongs the pain as it festers. Eventually, it will rise to the surface, demanding attention much like a splinter that pierces deep beneath the skin.

I want to make it clear that although it was painful at the time, I in no way hold anything against my mother for her reaction. It is a common response of many parents who have no knowledge on what to do or how to bring relief. Through my experience, I have come to understand that if we do not deal with issues and patterns that reside within our families, they will ultimately be passed to the next generation in a perverted cycle. My mother had no way of helping me deal with my abuse because as a victim herself, she had never been taught to deal with hers.

Typical of most women who have been abused, I always forgave Jeff. After each assault he would quickly return to being a sweet and caring lover, promising me the world. With the more severe assaults, it was not uncommon for him to fly the two of us to a ritzy resort in the Bahamas and pamper me for days. Like most controllers, he knew what to say and what to do to win me back. He had an uncanny ability to key in to my woundedness and to use it to his advantage. One example was in my relationship with my family.

"Bless your heart, Jennifer," he commented after one of our visits with my parents. "You deserve to be treated so much better

than this." Jeff could hone in on the smallest comment from my family that put me down and use it to bolster his position and my need for him. The irony of his statement missed its mark as I turned to him for comfort and the acceptance I craved.

Jeff's obsession over my whereabouts increased exponentially as the months wore on until he finally demanded to know where I was twenty-four/seven. I found myself entangled in a web of attachments with him both professionally and romantically from which I couldn't escape. When I would finally gain the confidence to make some feeble attempt, he knew exactly how to intimidate me back into fearful submission.

"I'm leaving," I threatened after yet another beating, trembling as I said the words. I was filled with disgust at the life that had become my own and knew something had to change. But Jeff had heard the words before and knew how to turn on the charm to woo me back into his arms and a false sense of security. He also knew how to intimidate. That same night as we went to bed, Jeff placed a shotgun on the mattress between us. It was an unspoken threat that said far more than words ever could.

Over and over I begged him to get counseling until he finally agreed to go with me to church—his parents' church. Their congregation held very similar core beliefs as the church in which I had been raised. It was a familiar system of rules and laws, void of the saving grace of Jesus. In a strange sort of way, I took comfort in these services and their familiar rituals, which lulled me into complacency. I couldn't see how my life was careening out of control until I received a wake-up call in the form of handcuffs being slapped onto my wrists.

*Chapter 16*

# GETTING OUT

*J*eff was incredibly smart and—although only in his twenties—had done very well for himself. So well, in fact, that the State Bureau of Investigations had been keeping their eyes on him due to the wealth he had amassed in such a short time. We were living the high life. Jeff traded in his Porsche for a new Mercedes 560 SL sports coupe. He also owned a beautiful new navy-blue, wood-paneled Jeep, which we used when we drove through the country and farmlands that he and his parents owned. This was some of the same land on which he threatened to bury me if I ever told that he had abused me.

Jeff's passion was fourfold: the finer things in life, beautiful women, control, and speed—the latter resulting in a temporary suspension of his driver's license.

One mild evening after working well past dark, Jeff closed his briefcase with a yawn, suggesting a quick dinner before going home. We went to one of our favorite restaurants and then he drove me back to the office, so I could pick up my car. The evening had been wonderful and I wanted to enjoy the mood that was between us.

"Honey, let's leave my car here tonight and I can just ride with you in the morning," I suggested. Jeff nodded in agreement and pulled onto the main street from the parking lot.

It turned out to be one of the worst decisions I could have ever made.

Almost immediately Jeff caught sight of a policeman traveling the opposite direction. Instantly his paranoia kicked into

high gear as he turned onto a side street and floored the sedan. Whether or not the officer had really been looking for him is unknown, but as Jeff squealed the tires and gunned the engine, the squad car turned to follow.

"Get in my seat," he screamed as we sped down the street, the speedometer already topping over seventy miles per hour. Still without a license from an earlier offense, Jeff knew that if he were stopped, the police would have him without a battle.

Without thinking of the consequences, I grabbed the wheel and inched under Jeff's five-foot-ten-inch frame. With some maneuvering I finally positioned myself in the driver's seat and took control of the vehicle.

"*Go, go, go, go!*" he continued screaming against the many sirens that were now trailing us. In shock, I stared in the rear-view mirror at the squad cars in hot pursuit. There were at least three and escape seemed impossible. Despite Jeff's demands to keep going, I brought the vehicle to a stop. Almost instantly we were surrounded.

"Jeff Dawes," the officer smirked, sensing victory as he peered into our stopped vehicle and saw the look of horror on Jeff's face.

Once clear of the car, the officer asked us to get into the back of his vehicle. Only then did the possible consequences of my foolish actions begin to make their way into my mind.

"If you think I'm going to jail for you," I hissed into Jeff's ear, "you are mistaken. I'm going to rat on you right now. I am *not* going to jail."

"Let's pretend that you were trying to get me to the hospital," he whispered back, as he immediately detailed an elaborate story.

Like a fool, I fell for his plan.

Once we reached the jail, they put me in a holding cell while Jeff immediately went to work contacting a bail bondsman. After making the call he returned to where I was. Ironically, they put

him in a cell beside me where we could talk. A drama ensued as
he began vomiting, pretending to be sick to support our story.

In the end, Jeff hired an attorney to represent me. When the
case came up before the judge, I never had to say a word. The
case was settled and I was only charged with reckless driving.
Although Jeff saved us both from a prison term, our relationship
was racing toward disaster.

Not long after on a Sunday morning as we were preparing to
leave for church, I looked up and caught that familiar glint in
Jeff's eye. I didn't know what I had done, but I knew I was in for
another beating.

The moment I saw him coming into the bedroom, I took
off. Jeff chased after me, grabbing for my clothes and hair and
blocking my exit. I pleaded for forgiveness, having no clue what
had provoked his wrath. But there was no mistaking the evil
intent in his eyes, which sent fear surging through me.

Cornering me in the master bath, he grabbed both sides of my
head and slammed me against the towel holder, shattering the
ceramic fixture into fragments. Blood dripped down my face and
my head was spinning from the impact, but somehow I stayed on
my feet and wiggled past Jeff, desperate for freedom.

"I'm going to kill you!" he screamed, lunging for me but
missing.

I tore out of the bathroom and into the hall. Snatching the
wireless phone, I punched 911 without slowing as I headed
upstairs to another bathroom. From experience I knew it had a
deadbolt and the thickest door in the house.

"Help me!" I screamed into the receiver. "Somebody please get
here!"

On the other end of the line, the operator was working for
more information.

"Ma'am, please calm down and tell me what is happening,"
she repeated over and over.

I made it into the bathroom and slid the deadbolt into position just as Jeff hit the door. It thumped from the weight of his beating and kicking, his obscenities filling the air.

Gasping for breath, I slumped to cold tile floor against the thick door.

"He is going to kill me this time! Please send the police before he breaks down the door," I finally managed.

"You—!" Jeff continued ranting obscenities and informing me what he was going to do to me once he broke through. Somehow he heard my voice pleading with the operator. As the realization hit that I had the phone, Jeff cursed loudly before running out of the room, screaming like an enraged animal.

By the time the police arrived, my face was a display of red swollen handprints. Blood had dried in my hair and on my cheeks and mouth, and my clothes were torn. Jeff was nowhere to be found. This time he had beat me good.

"This is heavy duty," one officer commented as he surveyed the disarray of the house from the chase. As he walked into the bathroom, I pointed to the broken towel holder on the floor, detailing the fight.

"Ma'am, you should be dead," he replied, shaking his head in amazement.

My head was bleeding again from the wounds. Jeff had also bitten me in several places—the imprint from his teeth evidence of his work on my fingers.

During the course of our relationship, Jeff had beaten me many times, but this time I knew he would have carried out his threat to kill me. As the officer continued to look over the evidence, my mind returned to a recent incident in which Jeff's anger had exploded in the same bathroom. On that day, he had grasped me by the hair and held my head under water until my skin was blue from lack of oxygen. When he finally released me, I fell to the ground gasping for air.

I shook the memory from my mind as the throbbing pain from the beating pulled me back into the present. I determined then that Jeff would never beat me again.

Ironically our tumultuous relationship finally ended not because I finally gathered the courage to leave, but because Jeff kicked me out.

Although the police encouraged me several times, I did not press charges against Jeff from the assault. But I was determined that he would pay for the pain he had inflicted on me. By nightfall he was back at the condo as if the events of the morning had never transpired.

Our relationship was so messed up. In my heart I believed I loved him, yet I also wanted revenge and planned my attack in the one area I knew would hurt the most—his manhood.

Not long after, as Jeff left on a short business trip, I began to accept the advances of a mutual acquaintance. It made little difference to me that others noticed my behavior or that this man was married. Jeff learned of our weekend fling almost immediately after his return.

He was devastated and in spite of my vow that I would never let him beat me again, he did. At the end he picked me up and threw me to the ground, ordering me out of the house. I should have welcomed my freedom, but instead I begged for forgiveness. I had only wanted to inflict pain, not leave. I was still in love with him.

"Get out! You're nothing, Jennifer," he yelled at my back as I walked out the door. "Do something with your life. Get your education," was the last thing I heard as I piled my belongings into my car. As it turned out, his last piece of advice was the only good thing that came from our relationship.

With nowhere else to go, I went back to my parents' home to heal. Eventually, after licking my wounds, I took Jeff's advice and returned to school full-time to complete my education.

Where my relationships had all failed, there were two areas in which I knew I could gain the praise and success I desired. And so resigned to the future before me, I launched all my efforts to accomplish these tasks—burying myself in school and the religious system of my parents.

# Chapter 17

# MY KNIGHT

*Y*ou'd make a great teacher," Jeff had one time stated offhandedly. As I contemplated my future, the thought resurfaced. *Why not?* I thought as I changed my previously undeclared status to that of an education major. Shortly after, I began immersing myself in my studies again. Working and living with Jeff, I had at least saved enough money to attend school full time. Now with no boyfriend, I focused entirely on my studies and was soon turning out straight A's. Approximately eight or nine months after our breakup, I had accumulated enough credits to begin my senior year.

Outwardly it might have appeared that I had finally pulled my life together, but actually I was like a chameleon, a champion when it came to playing games to fit in. People who have been abused as children have to learn how to play these games to survive. Attending school was no different. I just did the best I could and did what I felt others expected of me to gain their approval. For now I was working to please my professors. Noticing my grades and serious achievements, several had suggested graduate school. With no other prospects for my future, I was seriously considering this option as I climbed into the car one morning early in my senior year. At the moment I had to take care of a more practical need—my auto insurance.

After talking with an agent and completing the necessary transaction, I turned to leave as one of the female agents stopped me.

"Are you dating anybody?" she questioned out of the blue.

I stopped in my tracks. Where did that come from? This woman didn't even know me.

"No, I'm not interested in men. I'm going to grad school," I responded almost without thinking.

"Well, I know this really nice guy and I think you would make a good match," she continued.

I thought dating was the last thing on my mind, but before I knew it, I had responded in a manner that really took me by surprise.

"Well, you can give him my number if you want."

Before leaving, I jotted down my number and handed the slip of paper to the woman, then headed back to campus. I contemplated the exchange on the drive but quickly dismissed it after I returned to my busy routine of classes and papers.

Two weeks later, while at my parents' home, the phone rang. Goofing around I ran to answer it with a sarcastic comment, "I'm going to pick up this phone and it will be the man of my dreams."

"This is David Kostyal. May I speak with Jennifer?" said the unfamiliar yet warm voice on the other end.

My words caught in my throat at the unexpected caller.

"Speaking," was all I could squeak out after my smart response just moments before.

"A friend of mine told me about you, and I would like to take you on a date."

My mind raced back to the day at the insurance office. I hadn't been on a date in months and was uncertain what I wanted to do. In the end, the determining factor was his voice—confident but gentle. After what I had experienced with men, gentle was definitely on the menu.

"Well, I'm in the middle of finals and I don't do anything during finals but study. Why don't you give me a call in two weeks."

"Great, I would like to do that," Dave responded.

Being a man of his word, he called me back in exactly two weeks and we set a date for dinner.

As I got ready that evening, I fumbled with my hair and my clothes. I was nervous. Part of me wanted to begin dating again, while the other part was content to remain in solitude.

With the chime of the doorbell, I opened the door for my mystery date. At first glance, one thought jumped to my mind: *Who dropped this Greek god onto my doorstep?*

Dave was six feet six inches tall with dark hair and dark brown eyes, his well-toned physique evident in the light jacket he wore. After a quick introduction to my parents, we said good-bye and he took my arm to escort me to his vehicle. Instead of letting me walk around on my own, as I had experienced with most men, he opened my door and waited until I was completely settled before gently closing it and walking around to join me on his side. I was impressed so far.

Dave drove the short distance to our reservation, an upscale seafood restaurant at Wrightsville Beach, a sharp contrast to the older model truck in which we rode. As Dave talked during the drive, I studied the truck, his face and clothes, gleaning little information. I didn't have a clue what Dave did for a living but learned later that was the way he wanted it. Tired of women who were interested in him only for his money, this self-made millionaire had left his new Mercedes at home.

As we talked throughout the meal, it dawned on me that Dave was probably the kindest, sweetest man I had ever met. It was easy to carry on a conversation with him and surprisingly, I found myself enjoying his companionship. There was only one problem. On several occasions during the evening, he kept referring to his old girlfriend!

After the meal as he drove me to my parents' home, I sighed as I offered a piece of advice, "Dave, you need to call this woman. You are obviously still hooked on her."

I could tell by the look on his face that my words had cut deep. I hadn't meant to hurt him, but it seemed obvious that a relationship with this handsome man was not feasible at this time. In any event, I rationalized, I was headed for grad school.

"It was really nice meeting you," Dave commented as he walked me to the door. "May I call you again?"

Surprised, I lifted my head to look into his eyes. He really was good-looking.

"Thank you for dinner," I replied momentarily avoiding the question. I could feel Dave's anticipation for my response, but I really didn't know what to say.

"Do whatever you want," I said as I walked inside and closed the door. I sincerely doubted he would call me again.

"How was your evening?" Dad asked from the sofa as he and Mom watched Johnny Carson.

"He sure is good looking, but he is hung up on another woman. I'll be surprised if he calls me again," I answered as I headed for bed.

I completely underestimated Dave Kostyal.

Within two weeks Dave had called to set up another date. As before, he was every part the gentleman. He opened my doors and took my hand to assist me as we walked. It was obvious that he really desired to please me and it felt nice.

I was also very cautious. I had learned from experience that if something looks too good to be true, it usually is. I found myself almost looking for the battery that surely was operating Dave. Anyone as kind and handsome as he was couldn't possibly be real.

Eventually, Dave began to open up about himself. I learned he had earned a masters degree in forestry at Duke University. After graduation, he went to work for a timber firm where almost immediately he became one of the top producers for the company. Each year, Dave made them hundreds of thousands of dollars buying timber and managing their crews. Eventually he

came to the next logical step after padding the pockets of the company through his sweat.

*Why don't I do this for myself?* he determined, launching the David M. Kostyal Timber Company.

Dave was raised in a middle-class Catholic home and was taught hard work, ethics, family values, and faith from a very early age. He graduated valedictorian from his public high school before heading to Duke on full scholarship for both his undergraduate and graduate degrees.

By the time we met, he had already owned his company for five years. Now at thirty, he was quite the catch. Completely debt free, he already owned his own home and a new white Mercedes Benz—which he let me drive on many occasions.

If I said I wanted something, he immediately purchased it for me. One example was the new cell phone he gave me long before cell phones were popular. It came in handy as we talked for long hours on the phone almost every night.

I was beginning to release my caution as I began to consider that Dave Kostyal was the real deal.

One evening as we were driving over the Cape Fear River Bridge, one of the classic songs by Elvis Presley came on the radio. As the famous crooner sang the words, "I can't help falling in love with you," Dave looked over at me.

"That's exactly how I feel right now," he said as he took my hand.

To be honest, I felt the same way but said nothing. Inwardly I was terrified that one day this perfect man would find out about my past and run as fast as he could. My fears were compounded as Dave opened up later on with another confession.

"Jennifer, I've saved my virginity for the woman who will become my wife."

Dave hadn't even kissed me until after we had been on several dates. Now I understood why he had never pushed me past a simple kiss. When he said those words, I cringed.

*I can't even begin to tell you all the men I have been with in my life,* I thought to myself. I then responded, "You're lying. You're telling me that you went to Duke University and even played football for them and you've never been with a woman?"

His face said it all as Dave turned his head for a moment to brush off my words. At that time, I didn't realize how dear his stand for purity had been all his life.

"Well, I'm not a virgin, Dave," I finally replied without elaboration.

Undeterred, he took my face in his hands and looked me straight in the eyes as he said, "Jennifer, to me you are beautiful and you are pure, and I don't need to know anything else."

His words were like an arrow piercing my heart. I wanted to smother his face in kisses and cry all at the same time. Sitting there with him, remembering my past, I felt like Mr. Gentlemen and Miss Tramp. It was probably in that moment that Dave Kostyal won my heart.

From then on, all I thought about, dreamed about, talked about was Dave Kostyal. I had finally met my knight in shining armor. All my life I had wanted someone to protect me, love me, and tell me it would be all right. Dave did that and more. But there was a part of me that he had no idea existed, and I hid it very well.

## Chapter 18

# CONFESSION TIME

"*D*ave, honey, are you listening to me?" I asked as I noticed his eyes take on a faraway gaze. Normally very attentive, for the past couple of days he had seemed preoccupied. Immediately my insecurities kicked in as I began to imagine the source of this new development. As much as I tried to convince myself that it was probably business related with Dave's upcoming trip to Florida, my heart toyed with the thought that maybe he was having second thoughts about me. This man was too good for me anyway.

Although we hadn't dated long, I could tell that something had changed and it made me nervous. I decided to do a little sleuthing.

"What's the matter?" I probed. "Did something fall through with the deal in Florida?"

Dave shirked off the question and tried to give me a reassuring smile, his reply evasive at best. Although we had dated just a little over three months, Dave had already asked my parents for my hand in marriage. Although I knew he was serious about the relationship, I also knew that realistically it could be months before we took that final step that would lead to marriage. I could tell that Dave didn't want to discuss the matter, so I dropped it. But that nagging feeling in the pit of my stomach would stay with me for the next several days.

"Hi, babe, I'm back," Dave announced through the receiver. "Can you stop by after class today? I've missed you."

Even though he had only been gone for three days, I had missed him as well. However, between the nagging feeling that had persisted and the mounting projects demanding my attention so I could graduate, I found myself rather short with him, drumming up my excuse.

A wave of guilt washed over me as I heard the disappointment in Dave's voice. He had been nothing but good to me.

"On second thought, just let me know what time," I responded in a quick change of heart.

Still feeling the pang of guilt, I stopped at the nearby bakery to pick up a loaf of Dave's favorite cinnamon bread before heading to his house. But as I pulled into the driveway, I felt the same initial irritation that I had experienced over the phone. The house was completely dark and it appeared Dave wasn't home.

*I sure hope I haven't made this twenty-five-minute drive for nothing,* I thought as I closed the car door. Smoothing my dress, I walked to the door, while the list of work waiting for me at home continued eating away at my patience.

As I pressed the doorbell, I heard its sound echo through the house and then silence. I tried again, shaking my head, but still there was no response. Just as I turned to leave, Dave opened the door. As he greeted me, an alarm sounded in my head. Something was wrong. In his line of work Dave's dress was typically casual, but now he stood before me in a suit. I had never seen him dressed up like this before and briefly wondered why.

*Perhaps he's heading to a funeral,* I contemplated as he leaned down to give me a kiss.

"Here's your favorite," I said, handing him the loaf of bread. "I'm really sorry I was short with you on the phone earlier. I guess finals are getting to me," I finished, glad to be with him again.

"Please come in," Dave responded in a serious tone as he held the door for me.

Stepping into the entryway, I noted a beautiful small table in the living room covered with a flowered-print tablecloth. The reflection of the light from two tapered candles danced on the walls, giving the room a warm romantic glow. The soft melody of classical music played lightly in the background as Dave led me to the table and a small peach-colored box.

"Open the box, Jennifer," he said.

I reached for the box with trembling hands. It dawned on me that this was probably more than a Whitman's Sampler. Inside was a beautiful coffee cup with a lid that said, "Our love is forever."

"Open the cup," he continued, intently watching my expression.

As I lifted the lid, Dave bent down on one knee. Inside the mug was another small box. As I lifted the lid, the flame from the candles reflected in the stones.

"Will you do me the honor of becoming my wife?" Dave asked with tears in his eyes.

"Yes!" I screamed without hesitation, breaking the quiet of the moment.

Standing to his feet, Dave hugged me, swinging me through the air.

"Thank you," he whispered as he kissed my lips.

While in Florida, Dave had had the two-carat diamond ring custom made by an exclusive jeweler. It was the biggest, most gorgeous thing I had ever seen. I held my hand up to examine it more closely. The reality of the moment played out like a fairytale as I considered my upbringing. I had grown up on a farm where we cropped tobacco for our school clothes. My dad had always worked two jobs. Although I had always said I wanted to date guys with money, the truth of what was really happening

seemed far beyond my wildest dreams. I couldn't believe this was happening to me!

Later that night as I lay in bed, my joy was short-lived as I considered the enormous task before me. Dave had to know the truth about my past—at least some of it. As I contemplated what I would say, I wondered how he would respond when he realized just exactly what kind of woman he had asked to marry him. I would put if off as long as possible, but I knew that eventually I would have to come clean.

"Dave, we need to talk," I said as we sat on the sofa in his living room.

It had been almost three weeks since Dave had proposed. I had imagined this scene almost every night since with varying outcomes. I had no idea how he would react to the news I was about to share. I could see the question in his eyes as he turned to give me his full attention. Before I could talk myself out of the inevitable, I continued.

"For most of my childhood, starting at age seven, I was sexually abused by my brother-in-law, Joe," I said in a monotone voice. "I just thought you needed to know that." I quickly concluded my rehearsed speech and waited for his response. I couldn't have been more surprised.

Dave's shoulders hunched over as he began to weep for the loss of my innocence. For several minutes the only sounds in the room were his sobs. When he could finally speak, it was in no way condemning.

"Baby, I hate that you went through all that," he finally managed as he reached to wrap me in his protective embrace. But instead of finding comfort in his words, I was appalled.

"I've dealt with it. I just wanted you to know," I said pushing him away.

Years later remembering the conversation, Dave said it was like talking with a statue. I was stone cold. At the time as Dave sat broken before me, I kept thinking, *I'm fine, get over it. I have.* The walls surrounding my heart had become an impenetrable fortress. My response should have been a severe warning to my husband-to-be as he struggled to absorb this news.

Contrary to my words, I had in no way dealt with my past, but it had certainly dealt with me all my life. Erroneously, I believed that because my knight in shining armor had arrived on the scene, I would be protected and would never again have to address the unresolved hurts of my childhood.

For the next couple of years, the issue remained buried. I was thankful that Dave didn't bring it up again. But like a dormant virus, it was simply waiting for a catalyst to bring it to life.

*Chapter 19*

# THE HAUNTING
# OF THE PAST

*A* little over a year after Dave proposed—after I had completed my student teaching to finish my degree—we said our vows in a beautiful historical Catholic church in downtown Wilmington. Our wedding was at high noon and my gorgeous gown and his black tux were stunning in that immense sanctuary.

In spite of my cold response after the revelation of my past, the relationship had continued. Dave never pressed me for details and never changed his opinion of me. When I was with him, I felt like the most special woman in the world. For once in my life, I finally felt safe.

Yet because I had never dealt with the layers of abuse that had been heaped upon my life, it was only a matter of time before the façade of our happy union began to erode as the present collided with the past.

"Wake up! You're okay, Jennifer," Dave repeated as he gently tried to shake me out of the familiar nightmare. It wasn't the first time our sleep had been disturbed by the tormenting images of my childhood, which invaded my dreams.

My heart gradually began to slow as my eyes adjusted to the darkness; and the reality dawned on me that, at least for now, the demons of the past were gone.

"Are you all right?" Dave asked, concerned.

"Of course, I'm all right," I spit out, still unwilling to allow him into that painful part of my inner soul.

Nighttime had always been terrifying for me. As a child I didn't fear the "monster in my closet" but the one that would come through my bedroom door. As an adult I was harassed by fearful images of the past and the unknowns of the future. Even in sleep, there was a part of me always on high alert, perhaps making me more vulnerable to the constant nightmares.

Although now married and in my late twenties, I was every bit the little girl on the inside, still screaming for help. Years later, after I had begun my journey to healing, the Lord began to peel back the layers of this painful part of my past. It took the power of the Holy Spirit to remove the terror from the horrific memories—being awakened in the middle of the night by squeaking floors, the foul scent of beer breath, and groping hands. I had been scared for so long.

If this describes you, stop right now and ask the Lord to anoint your dreams and give you peace. You can use this prayer, if you like:

> *Father,*
>
> *I ask You to give me sweet sleep and peaceful dreams. Help me wake up healthy, happy, and rested for You have not given me a spirit of fear, but of power and love and a sound mind. I know that You are a good Daddy who hears my prayers and that You watch over me even as I sleep. I thank You that nightmares are a thing of the past and not a part of my future.*
>
> *In Jesus' name. Amen.*

Occasionally now, when nightmares slip back in, I realize that I have the Word of God to hold on to and to give me power to

stop the enemy's harassment in the middle of the night. I open
my Bible to Psalm 91 and personalize several of the verses:

> *I dwell in the shelter of the Most High and rest in the shadow*
> *of the Almighty. I say of the Lord, "You are my refuge and*
> *my fortress, my God, in whom I trust. ...I will not fear the*
> *terror of night, nor the arrow that flies by day."*
>
> (VV. 1–2, 5)

If nightmares are an area in which you, too, have been harassed
because of the past, I encourage you to turn to the appendix section on sleep. There I have included scriptures for meditation and
an additional prayer for peaceful dreams and slumber.

Another thing with which I had to contend in the early years
of marriage was in the area of intimacy. What is often very difficult for adult survivors of sexual abuse to admit is that their
bodies react to physical intimacy in a manner distorted from
what God originally intended. The bodies of victims of abuse
have been programmed to respond sexually from a young age. It
is possible for a child to climax even in abuse, so it totally warps
the beauty of what God created sexuality to be.

It took years of renewing my mind in order for me to truly
enjoy the sexual union with my husband and not be hindered
by the memories that were programmed into me as a little girl. I
remember one night after Dave and I had been intimate; I wept
for hours. This time the tears were not from pain but joy. That
night, for the first time in my life, I saw sexuality as a righteous
act and not a sick perverted way for my body to react to a man's
touch. I went into our marriage programmed to perform sexually. I never knew what "making love" truly meant until I was
thirty-one years old and allowed God to heal my mind and heart
from the distorted views of love and sex that had been planted
there. Again, I have included a section on sexual intimacy in

marriage in the appendix if this is an area in which you have been challenged.

If you would have asked me about children when Dave and I first married, I would have told you that I didn't want to have any of my own. I suppose in my dysfunctional mind I felt I was protecting our children from experiencing the horror that I had been subjected to. I loved being married and was completely content being Dave's wife. I thought that was enough. Although I knew he wanted children, he never pressed me to reconsider.

Then one day in the grocery store, I mistakenly turned down the baby aisle and everything changed. The rows of diapers, baby food, and cute little sippy cups stirred something deep inside me. All of a sudden I admitted what I had long tried to deny: I wanted a baby.

"Do you want to start a family?" I ventured that night over dinner.

The surprise on Dave's face was evident, but he didn't skip a beat in his response.

"I'd love to," he replied.

Catholic premarital counseling had been beneficial in many areas, and this was one of them as we began to monitor my monthly cycle and the most likely date for successful conception. Within a few weeks I was craving cheeseburgers for breakfast.

We were spending time with Dave's family in Pennsylvania when an over-the-counter test confirmed what I already sensed in my body. Excusing myself from one of the family gatherings, I drove to the store as I contemplated how I would share the news with Dave.

As I walked through the aisles of merchandise, my eyes landed on two particular items. I smiled as I carried them to the counter,

knowing they would assist me nicely with my announcement. The transaction completed, I asked the clerk to wrap the two items separately.

Later that day when Dave and I were alone, I asked him to join me on the porch of the beautiful resort where we were staying. The weather was gorgeous as we looked across the manicured grounds of the hotel and the mountains across the horizon. It was perfect.

"I have two presents for you," I smiled as I handed him the first package.

Inside was a Precious Moments figurine of a mother with two children. Dave seemed appreciative of the gift, but I could tell he didn't grasp the message I had hoped to convey. The next gift was a little more explicit.

"You're not!" Dave exclaimed as he held up the pair of baby booties. I nodded in affirmation as Dave's surprise was replaced with joy and then concern. Before my eyes, Dave immediately transformed into the nervous father.

"Sit down, sit down, Jennifer," he exclaimed as he took my hand. Just as he had proven himself to be an amazing husband, I knew Dave was going to make a terrific father. I only wished I had as much confidence about myself.

Over the next eight months, I ate everything I wanted, when I wanted it. Sixty pounds later after giving birth to a beautiful ten-pound baby boy, I regretted my lack of self-control. But nothing could take away the joy brought about by our new son.

Both of our families had come to the hospital with the news of the arrival of David Kostyal II. It was a joyous event. Dave cried so hard that you would have thought *he* was the one who had given birth! Afterward one of the nurses had to remind him that as the mother, I also needed a little time to hold the baby!

I was fanatical about childrearing and prior to the birth as well as afterward, I read everything I could get my hands

on…anything that would teach me how to be a good mother. Little did I know, all the parenting books in the world could not have prepared me for what was to come.

Psychologists suggest that when painful events of the past are not dealt with, they will eventually emerge in some fashion during a time of crisis or significant change. That is why major events—even happy ones such as marriage, relocation, a new job, or the birth of a child—can become triggers of emotional collapse. This was certainly true in my case.

David II was just two or three days old when Dave came to bring us home from the hospital. I was more than a little apprehensive to leave the assistance of the skilled nurses to take on the sole responsibility of our infant son.

Ever the loving, considerate husband, Dave pulled the car up to the exit to prevent me from having to walk any further than necessary. We waved good-bye to the nursing staff as Dave, with one hand under my arm, maneuvered me to the car as I held our precious bundle.

It was March and the temperature was cold as I settled the baby and myself in the car.

"Dave, it's too cold in here for David. Can you please warm it up?"

Immediately in response, Dave reached down to adjust the thermostat. Within minutes the vehicle had warmed considerably, only now I felt it was getting too warm for the baby.

"Dave, you've got to get this temperature regulated!" I exclaimed, my frustration far exceeding what was appropriate. For the remainder of the trip home, I fiddled with the thermostat as I poured out words of anger on Dave. Childbirth had been the catalyst that had unwittingly stirred the wounds of the past. I felt compelled to provide our child with the safety and protection I believed I had never received. No child of mine was going to have anything but a perfect world.

*Chapter 20*

# CRISIS BREWING

"Calm down, Jennifer," my mother said in a quiet but authoritative voice as she walked into the room where I was striving fruitlessly to quiet baby David. In an instant she had summed up my precarious mental state, reaching over to take the baby from me.

"Get him to shut up! Just make him shut up!" I pleaded irrationally, completely overcome with the frustration of a situation beyond my control. For the first time in my life, I had an understanding of what might push some parents to shake their babies.

From the time we brought him home from the hospital, David had been very colicky. He cried incessantly, leaving my emotions frazzled and my body begging sleep. Fortunately Mom had come to stay with us for a short time after his birth, but even with her help, I was not responding well to the situation.

During the long episodes of crying, I tried everything to calm David down—walking the floor, holding him, and patting his back. Bizarre, frightening images began creeping into my consciousness of just how I could get him to really stay quiet. I shook my head to dismiss the unwelcome mental pictures, but they were never far from my thoughts. They terrified me, yet I was too afraid to share them with anyone who might be able to help.

Finally, after approximately three months, the colic passed and David settled into a more normal routine. Because the frightening images seemed to have stopped as well, I ignored what had transpired and threw myself into being the best mother possible. But there had been a subtle shift in the previous peaceful balance

of our home. Prior to childbirth, Dave had been the recipient of my complete attention. Now I gave everything I had to baby David. He became my entire world.

If David woke up at 1:00 a.m. and wanted to play, then I got up and played with him. Then we would go back to sleep until noon. My over-mothering was a major sign that I was very out of balance and needed help. But my mother was the only one who recognized it.

"Jennifer, let him cry himself back to sleep. You are too intense," she chided, trying to introduce some equilibrium to my mothering skills. "You cannot let the baby dictate your schedule this way."

How could she or anyone understand the crisis building within me?

"I just want my child happy," I responded, confident I was doing the right thing.

I ignored her advice and continued reading my parenting books, determined that no harm or danger was going to get near any child of mine.

Inevitably, my out-of-balance mothering drove a wedge between Dave and me.

"You show me no attention," he complained one evening as he returned home from a long day at work. The house was a mess, there was no dinner on the table, not to mention the lack of activity in our bedroom since David's birth. Dave had a right to be frustrated, but I lashed out at his words.

"This is a helpless child. What else am I supposed to do?" I argued defensively.

The more Dave complained, the harder I worked at being the "perfect mother"—and the longer he began to remain at the office.

We had been married only two years at that time. Outwardly, it may have looked like we had the perfect marriage, but the danger signs were increasing rapidly. In our own personal pain,

we ignored the warnings—that is until the ultimate crisis erupted with the arrival of our second child.

David was fifteen months old when the desire to have another baby surfaced in my heart. What began as a contemplative thought eventually birthed into a compelling desire until I finally went to Dave to discuss it. Our relationship still bore the scars of strain as I struggled to comprehend the balance between wife and mother. I hesitated for as long as possible, fearing a negative response.

"I would love a house full of children, Jennifer," Dave replied as I approached the question later that night. Dave never ceased to amaze me. Despite the difficulties of the past several months, he had remained caring and forgiving. At times, whether from exhaustion or just dysfunction, I hammered him with irrational arguments, bringing strife into the marriage. But Dave refused to be baited, always taking the high road to restore peace.

Dave may have wanted a house full of children, but in my heart I knew I could only handle two—and that the next one would have to be a girl.

"Jennifer, it might be a boy," David repeated as he had throughout the pregnancy, trying to spare me from disappointment. In the hospital between contractions, I continued thumbing through the pages of my Bible, trying to decide between the New Testament spelling *Rebecca* and Old Testament spelling *Rebekah*.

"Honey, which spelling do you want to use?" I questioned completely undeterred.

For the last nine months, we had worked to prepare David II as well as our own hearts for the introduction of a new member

to the family. Pouring over the newest parenting books, I followed their suggestions of having the new baby give gifts to David as well as including him in some of the doctor's visits and other appropriate preparations. The second pregnancy seemed to speed by.

"Congratulations!" Dr. Mason finally spoke as the baby slipped into his waiting hands. "It's a girl!"

Already I could envision how fun it would be to dress our new daughter in frilly pink dresses. Dave knew my thoughts.

"Wonderful, now you can stop dressing my boy," he quipped good-naturedly, referring to my habit of buying velvet knickers, scarves, and other cutesy, less masculine baby clothes for David.

We both cried as we held our perfect baby girl.

"She's so beautiful, Jennifer," Dave said as he touched her tiny fingers. "I'm afraid to hold her, she looks so fragile."

Weighing two pounds less than her older brother at birth, Rebekah did seem incredibly small. Tears formed again in my eyes as I held her close. Little did I know that there were many more tears to come…but they would not be tears of joy.

Chapter 21

# SPIRALING OUT
# OF CONTROL

*M*y transformation was probably most confusing to little David as it quickly became apparent that the mommy who went into the hospital to have a baby was not the same one who returned.

"Mommy's too tired to play right now, honey," I replied as David pulled his toy truck over to where I sat with Rebekah on the sofa. Although we didn't experience the season of colic with her that we had with David, it seemed to require all my attention each day just to take care of her. This left me little energy or desire to play with David and even less energy for my husband.

A couple of months before Rebekah's birth, we had broken ground on what would become our new home. Work had been mostly completed on a separate structure, which would be a detached office space. We were now living in this office as the builder started work on the main house.

One day I laid Rebekah on the master bed then lay down beside her. A few minutes later little David walked in with his toy logging truck, wanting to play. This had become one of his favorite toys as he played make-believe doing what his father supervised for a living. He loved making the plastic logs roll off the bed of the truck into a heap. Picking up one of the small logs, he did what many young children might have done and he hit Rebekah with it. The startled baby began to wail. In an instant I was off the bed grabbing David by the arm and proceeded to slap

his legs. I was completely out of control. Thankfully, Dave was home and stepped into the room, rescuing our son.

I knew at that moment that I wasn't normal but was too scared to admit it. The moment David struck Rebekah, an emotional response was triggered deep within me. In my tormented mind, I was finally fighting back for all the attacks that had been heaped upon me as a child. I was going to protect this little girl in a way no one had protected me. I was sick.

Within days, Dave hired a nanny to come to our home and assist us five days a week while he was at the office—as much for my health as for David's protection. From then on, with the majority of responsibility for David and the baby on someone else, all I did was nurse Rebekah and rest.

Logically, I should have been able to quickly regain my strength and begin to shoulder some of the responsibilities of the home. But while physically I had less responsibility, my mind was working overtime as it pulled up past memories, mixing them into future scenarios.

Searching for anything that might snap me out of this downward spiral, Dave suggested a family drive to the country. It was a beautiful Saturday. The autumn air was crisp and the leaves just beginning to turn. Dave buckled the children into their car seats and we headed out to enjoy some fresh air. I was shocked as we pulled up to Joe's and Sue's small wood house on my parents' farm, and I began to shake.

"Why are we here?" I questioned as a wave of nausea swept over me at the sight of the home of the man who haunted my dreams.

"I'm so sorry, honey," Dave apologized. "Your sister made something special for the baby and I thought you might enjoy seeing her. I wasn't thinking about Joe."

Reluctantly I emerged from the car, every nerve on edge. Dave carried Rebekah, while I held David's hand and the diaper bag. At the door I stood slightly behind Dave, hoping that he could

shield me from what was inside. I realized I had been holding my breath as Sue opened the door. I hadn't seen my sister in quite a while and recognized that I had really missed her.

As we walked into the living room, my eyes darted to the chair where Joe usually sat. I cringed as he turned toward us and willed myself not to run.

"Jenny, it's so good to see you," Sue said as she gave me a hug. "David is getting so big! And little Rebekah is just beautiful!"

In any other setting I would have relished her compliments, but in the presence of my abuser I sensed only anger and fear.

Dave patted my hand as Sue ushered us to the sofa in the dimly lit den before excusing herself to retrieve the gift she had made with her own hands. I kept my eyes on Rebekah and little David, busying myself with their needs to avoid conversation with Joe. I felt like a mother bear monitoring a dangerous animal that might at any moment attack my most precious possessions on earth—my babies.

Within minutes Sue returned with her soft bundle. The quilt was made out of the prettiest colors of blue, green, and pink. I could tell by the intricate design and hand stitches that Sue had spent months on this project of love. It was beautiful. As I reached over to give her a hug, I glanced at Joe. I caught him staring at Rebekah in an eerie way that left me disgusted.

"We have to leave now," I said to Dave, grabbing the quilt, diaper bag, and David's hand all in one quick motion. I headed out the door as Dave apologized to Sue and said good-bye. By the time he joined us in the car, I was crying uncontrollably.

"He will never hurt her! He will never touch my baby!" I repeated over and over.

As we backed out of the gravel driveway, it seemed that the joy of motherhood was being sucked out of me. Dave had hoped that the afternoon drive would help snap me out of my depressed

mental state, but it only pushed me further down to a place I felt I couldn't escape.

Women who have been through abuse just want to forget. Sometimes they delude themselves into believing it never happened. Having a baby girl brought it all back home for me. At times, even changing Rebekah's diaper would cause my mind to be overwhelmed with the memories of my own abuse.

"I would die before I let anyone hurt you like that, darling," I remember whispering.

Little did I know that as my mental state continued to deteriorate, I would feel compelled to take action on those words to protect my children from their fiercest defender—me.

I'm sure psychologists would say I was experiencing postpartum depression, and I don't discount that this is a very real issue. But in my case, the depression and fear had begun years before when I learned to use alcohol to numb the thoughts and get me through the day. The root went far deeper than any of us imagined.

As I grew worse, Dave tried to compensate in every area he could. He hired a housekeeper in addition to the nanny and tried to be home as much as possible when they weren't there to help me with the children. But nothing could still the unrelenting anguish.

Minor offenses would send me into a rage, and I was sleeping less and less. The nightmares increased and my mental and physical stability all but vanished.

Rebekah was about six months old when the builders completed our new home. We were excited to be able to move out of the smaller confines of the office space, allowing David his own room plus plenty of space for his and Rebekah's accumulating toys.

Dave worked hard to make our home one that would bring me peace. We ordered new furniture for the entire house. In addition, some of the most respected designers in the city had helped turn our home into something you might find in the pages of *Southern Living*. The upscale wallpaper, curtains, and furniture

complimented each other exquisitely. But they couldn't stem the turmoil of unhealed wounds that stalked my mind every night when I went to sleep.

"Please help me!" I begged one night, slapping Dave across the chest and waking him from a sound sleep. It was not uncommon for me to rouse him three to four times a night as I battled an enemy he couldn't see and didn't know how to defeat.

"Baby, I love you," he responded again and again, trying to calm my beating heart and wild eyes. "It's going to be all right."

Dave was the epitome of patience. Few men would have been willing to endure all the craziness that had become our lives. As he held me and stroked my hair, I eventually fell back to sleep, but neither Dave nor I realized just how sick my mind had become from the unhealed poison of the past.

Even during the daytime hours it was becoming increasingly difficult for me to function. I had to give up reading the parenting books as my mind could no longer focus on the words on the pages in front of me. One day I was grocery shopping with the children when a kind gentleman walked up to the cart and patted David on the head.

"How much would it cost to buy those children from you?" he said with a smile, complimenting David and Rebekah.

But to my crazed mind, his simple comment was a threat. As he walked away, I raced out of the store for the car, my heart beating at lightning speed. Abandoning the cart in the middle of the parking lot, I sped home, the unrealistic pulsating fear driving me on. I was spiraling out of control and didn't know how to stop it.

*Chapter 22*

# END OF MY ROPE

*A*s my mental state continued to erode, I became more reclusive, eventually avoiding trips to the store and other scenarios that could create panic. Yet the more secluded I became, the more restless little David became as he searched for the comfort of his mother and a playmate.

David was a very bright and typical two-year-old; however, his innocent but constant motion would eventually ignite my rage.

"Mommy come and play with me," he begged throughout the day.

I could never seem to find the energy to join my son and would watch guilt-ridden as he walked away with shoulders slumped.

Those days were a living hell. The anger inside me had become a volcano that erupted without warning, often spewing its wrath on my son. Afterwards I would beg his forgiveness for losing my temper, but I had become the thing I so despised—an abuser.

That realization finally pushed me to the edge to cry out for help.

When I married Dave, I believed that I could create a world in which all the abuse would disappear. I thought that marriage would magically transform my wounded soul into that of a wonderful wife and mother. My dream was now crumbling quicker than I could even imagine. I could no longer pretend.

Because of the constant state of emotional stress and lack of sleep, my body began slowly shutting down. My speech became slurred and my capacity to reason was completely gone. All I could think about was putting an end to the tormenting images that constantly flashed through my mind. Dave watched

helplessly as my condition worsened. My knight couldn't save me this time and he knew it.

It is very important to realize that if abuse is not dealt with, it will resurrect in some form in the life of the victim. The result is not pretty. One of the hardest things I have ever had to do is to forgive myself. Although I never sexually abused David, the verbal and physical blows he experienced at my hand were certainly damaging in their own right.

I had to come to the realization that I was not a good mother in those early years. I thank God that during those months when I rejected my own son, I had a husband who worked hard to compensate for what little David did not receive from me. Every evening after work, Dave played with him and held him close. He provided him with the security and comfort that I was unable and didn't know how to give. Dave never criticized me to the children but instead reaffirmed to them that Mommy was going to be all right—although by all outward appearances that seemed impossible.

Now that I am finally healed, I can praise God that the one good thing that came out of that terribly dark time was that it made me wake up and know that I couldn't handle it anymore. Even though Dave had put me in Christian counseling, I was still quite the actress. And while my counselor did help me, I was too afraid to reveal the depth of fear and rage I was experiencing when at home.

Over the years, as I have shared my story, many people have asked me if I took medication to control the depression and panic attacks. The answer is no. To be honest, I was too far gone to even recognize that I needed it.

When I did search for help through the religious system of my parents, I was encouraged to "pull myself up by my bootstraps"

and recognize what a wonderful husband, children, and home I possessed. Their best advice was to "just get over it." No one pointed me to the Word of God. No one told me that Jesus could heal me. With no hope in sight, I was desperate to end the pain once and for all.

On most mornings, my housekeeper, Laura, arrived by 10:00 a.m., affording me a few hours to rest while she watched the children. Rebekah was now eight months old and becoming quite mobile. She and David were beginning to interact. It was a time in childhood that most mother's relish, yet for me it only stirred my fear.

On one particular day, an hour before Laura was scheduled to leave, I already felt completely overwhelmed with every part of my life. This had become commonplace. I was terrified that when she left I would act out the mental images that were constantly flooding my mind—that I would harm my children.

Sweat beaded on my forehead as I paged Dave repeatedly, but the messages were not getting through. I had absolutely reached my limit emotionally and knew I could no longer go on this way.

As I made my way to the children's playroom, the events of the last few weeks replayed again in my mind. Scenes flashed before me of all my offenses and shortcomings with my husband and children, the worst happening just a few days before when David accidentally dropped Rebekah on her head in an attempt to carry her across the room.

*"What are you doing?"* I demanded as I grabbed him and beat his legs until they were red with welts. After calling 911 to make sure that Rebekah was okay, I rushed to put pants on David to cover his legs so that the medical personnel could not see what I had done.

"Mommy, I forgive you," he managed through tears as he crawled onto my lap. I didn't deserve the love of this sweet child.

As I reached the toy room, David and Rebekah's playful voices pulled me back into the present. I shook my head as if to dispel the awful hallucinations of harming my children—vivid images of abuse much worse than the out-of-control swats I had already inflicted on my son. The images were growing in intensity, and I had reached the end of my rope.

So now you understand what brought me to that fateful day in which I settled my children in their nursery. At that moment, all I wanted was relief as I wandered through the house in disoriented fashion. It was then that I walked into the living room where the gilt-framed portrait of the children and me seemed to mock me from its perch.

"It's a lie!" I screamed as I crumpled onto the floor, unable to stand beneath the weight of the pain filling every part of my being.

Sometime later, my husband walked into the house greeted by my sobs as I lay still on the floor.

"What is it, honey?" he demanded, rushing to my side.

According to him, my next words shook his world to the core.

"Dave, you have two options. Either give me the .357 and I'll go into the marsh and end it all, or admit me to an institution. I need help!" I managed, completely spent.

Dave had already paid a small fortune on counseling and tried his very best to give me everything I could desire from a material perspective. But none of his efforts could free me from my tormented mind.

"God, have mercy on my wife!" Dave cried out to a God he hardly knew…and was answered immediately by the God who knew all.

I remember Dave's tears falling onto my face as instantly peace settled over both of us. His desperate cry for help was answered.

A calmness I had never experienced washed over me as Dave continued to hold me in his arms. Something had changed. Although initially we didn't understand what it was, heavenly intervention was undeniable. That night, for the first time in months, I was able to sleep peacefully through the night. My long journey to a sound mind and a healed heart had finally begun. But there was still a long way to go.

## Chapter 23

# DELIVERED FROM THE PAST

*J*esus healed my sister and He can heal you," were the first words out of our housekeeper's mouth when I talked to her the next morning. Laura was in her early thirties with shoulder-length brown hair and a constantly cheerful disposition. We had actually hired her to help with the housecleaning, but when Dave had needed to let the previous nanny go a few weeks before, we had been unable to find an appropriate replacement. With my precarious mental state, we both recognized the importance of an outside figure assisting with the children. So even though she had been hired to clean, when she arrived for her weekly appointment, Laura would take over with the kids while I would start cleaning the house.

Laura also agreed to watch the children when I went to my weekly counseling sessions. My mother and sisters were unwilling to assist in this area since our church didn't believe in outside counseling. But God had sent us an angel in the form of this sweet woman.

The mother of three, Laura often talked about her children, their horses, some of their normal activities, and the joys of motherhood. I longed for the type of life she described, but it still seemed beyond my reach.

That morning I made the decision to call a national toll-free number with Focus on the Family to receive prayer. I had heard its founder James Dobson a few times on the radio and sensed it was a resource where I could find help. I didn't know where else to turn, but God already had a plan.

"My sister was sexually abused too," Laura informed me as I hesitantly addressed the issue of the upcoming phone call. I knew she would overhear the conversation and felt I needed to explain.

I was shocked as her words registered in my brain. I had gone to high school with her younger sister and never suspected that she or anyone else might have experienced the same horrific abuse that I endured.

"Jesus healed her and He can heal you," she explained with a certainty that held my attention.

Those were the words I had waited to hear all my life. As she said them, I knew the Jesus she was referring to was different than the individual from my parents' religion. Laura didn't tell me a bunch of things I had to do before He would heal me. Instead she made it sound so simple.

"Would you like to talk with Sarah?" she asked. "I am sure she would be happy to discuss this with you."

I nodded my willingness immediately, accepting this small lifeline for help. Once on the phone, I poured out my story to Laura's sister. It was as if I couldn't stop the flow now that the cork had been released.

"I've been there," Sarah said comfortingly. "You need divine intervention in order to receive healing from abuse of this magnitude."

"What do you mean?" I responded skeptically.

"Are you available to meet a friend of mine? She has prayed with many women who have experienced abuse and understands the importance of the kind of prayer that is needed. She knows what it takes to minister to these kinds of deep wounds."

Although I really didn't understand what she meant, I knew instinctively that this was an important step for me to take.

"I'm desperate," I replied. "When can I come?"

We arranged for me to make the two-hour drive the next morning to meet her friend Florence. After hanging up the phone,

a peace similar to that from the night before settled over me, easing my apprehension and confirming in my heart that I had made the right decision. Now I just had to convince Dave. At that moment I felt like a woman who had been trapped inside a pitch-black cave and finally someone had lit a match. This small flicker of light began to illuminate the prevailing darkness so that for once I had hope that I could begin to see my way out.

Arriving home that evening, I met Dave at the door with the news.

"I believe I can be healed," I began as I described the conversation from earlier that morning. "*Please* let me go tomorrow," I entreated. "I need to meet this woman who can pray with me."

Understandably, Dave was very skeptical. He had seen the religious fanaticism of my parents' church and was reluctant to let me walk into a situation of unknowns. Although raised Catholic, Dave had faithfully attended my parents' church with me since we had started dating. He admitted later that he found the church very odd and the people depressing. Yet he was scared to say too much for fear that I would choose the church system over him. By this time my brother had already been installed as the preacher, and to reject the church was equal to rejecting my family.

I watched as Dave considered the options before us. There was no denying that something had occurred in my life, and we both wanted to see that work completed.

"Okay," he finally said, nodding. Although he was hesitant in making the decision, we didn't know where else to turn.

The next morning, I awoke with an air of expectancy.

"Jennifer, are you sure?" Dave questioned one last time as I climbed into the car. Concern for my mental state as well as my physical well-being was etched into the look on his face. He remained silent as he glanced at the sky, noting the forming clouds. A tornado watch had been issued for our area.

"Honey, if this God can heal me, He can sure handle the weather. Please let me go," I said firmly as I kissed him and little David good-bye.

"Mommy's going to be all right," I told my son as I gave him a last squeeze. Even as I said it, my heart confirmed my words. I *was* going to be all right.

On the highway and finally alone with my thoughts, I began to emotionally prepare myself for what I might encounter during this time of ministry, certain I would have to face the past that I had worked so hard to ignore. Most of the time I contemplated what it would be like to actually live a normal, carefree life. Was it possible that I could be finally free from the ties of the past? That one thought became my consuming passion, propelling me forward.

A little over two hours later, I pulled into the driveway of a beautiful white two-story home in the suburbs of Raleigh. Even before I could get out of the vehicle, Sarah had walked out to meet me. The joy that radiated from her smile was contagious as she reached over to give me a hug.

"Wow, Sarah, it's so good to see you!" I exclaimed, returning her embrace. I let go of her arms and took a step back to get a good look at her. The most striking feature about my high-school friend was her eyes. They seemed to dance with joy, showing no hint of the sadness that I recognized in my own eyes each time I saw my reflection. Looking at her it was difficult to believe she had come through the same experiences as I. But indeed, she had been molested for many years at the hands of an uncle. The transformation that had taken place in her had to be supernatural.

As we walked into Sarah's home, I noticed that although smaller than mine, it held a beauty mine didn't possess. Sarah was quite the decorator and her interior looked like something from *Country Living*. But there was something more than just beauty in this house. It was a sense of warmth and peace that permeated within, making it truly feel like a home.

We visited a very short time before Sarah suggested we head to Florence's house. Although I enjoyed getting caught up on what had transpired since we had both graduated from high school more than ten years before, Sarah sensed my need for ministry. Only a short drive to her friend's home, I began to tense. I was both excited and scared. I hadn't informed my parents or any other family members where I was going. Instinctively I knew that they would not be pleased with the course I was pursuing. Seeking help outside the "system" was contrary to everything I had ever been taught, yet to stay in the system and continue as I had meant death—if not physically, at least inwardly.

As we walked up the steps to Florence's home, a voice inside began to warn me, *If you walk in that door, you won't be healed. You are going to lose your mind.* My breathing became rapid as additional thoughts began to pelt my brain. I didn't know what to do.

"Jennifer, you are going to be fine," Sarah encouraged. "You are getting healed of your past today."

I thought to myself, *If she only knew the millions of thoughts that are racing through my mind!* I wanted to run, but desperation drove me to stay.

Once in the house, I noticed that both Florence and her friend who had come to assist her were in their fifties. One had grayish white hair, the other dark brown hair and a deep olive complexion. Immediately the religious thoughts of my upbringing fought for control as I noted their short hairstyles. Both were also wearing pants... *How can they offer me any spiritual insights?* I wondered.

Sarah steered me to the kitchen table to join the women. As I sat down, I noted their Bibles but remained silent. I had no idea what to do next.

"The Lord said you have fasted for this moment, and He will honor your fast to be healed," Florence began.

My mouth dropped open. How could she have known that I had made the decision that morning to fast breakfast and lunch in preparation for the day ahead? They immediately had my attention. For the next six to eight hours, the two women walked with me through the painful memories of my past, allowing the Holy Spirit to peel back the layers of abuse, one by one, in every area. They seemed to understand my pain at a level that I now recognize was the compassion of Christ flowing through His servants, but at that time it was something I had never before experienced.

Matthew 18:20 says, "Where two or three are gathered together in My name, I am there in the midst of them" (NKJV). I couldn't help but trust the three women before me as I sensed the presence of God fill that kitchen where we prayed. It was as if Jesus himself were performing surgery on my wounded soul to remove the unresolved hurts that had been stuffed deep into the crevices of my life. Even though these women spoke of the Trinity and referred to a real hell—both of which I had been taught against as a child—and even though they looked very much like the type of women I had always been instructed couldn't know the Lord, I could not ignore the power of God that was so evident.

During our prayer, I cried out to Jesus and He revealed himself to me as a loving Savior—one who would never hurt me. For the first time in my life, I saw Him as the Son of a loving God, a God who loved me enough to send His only Son to die for my healing. I no longer felt rejected. On the contrary, I felt accepted and recognized that despite my abuser's words, I had not caused the abuse. Through the work of the Holy Spirit, it became clear to me that the enemy—the devil—had desired to destroy my life and had almost succeeded.

Over the next several hours these women lovingly helped me recognize the destructive patterns, thoughts, and strategies operating in my life, exposing them through the stark light of God's Word. At the end of our prayer, I made the decision to receive

Jesus Christ as my Lord and Savior. For the first time I understood that He truly was the Son of God!

A quiet joy surrounded us as we sat at the table and I felt the weight I had carried for so many years fall from my shoulders. In my heart I envisioned myself now totally liberated, running across a grassy meadow in a white dress shouting with joy, *"I'm finally free!"*

I have never known such love and peace as filled me at that moment. I didn't want to leave for fear that it was all a dream.

Before we stood to go, one of the women spoke prophetically to me: "You are going to be a part of a move of God that will see women healed from the abuse of their past," she stated.

I remained silent as I considered her words. It hardly seemed possible, but already that day, I had experienced the impossible as God restored my life.

I could hardly wait to get back to Sarah's home, so I could call Dave. Now in an upstairs bedroom, so I could have some privacy, I waited with anticipation as the phone rang.

"I'm healed!" I practically shouted into the receiver. "I can't wait to see you! How is David? Tell him Mommy loves him and I can't wait to see him," I gushed into the phone without giving Dave a chance to speak. I could hear the relief in his voice as he asked me questions about the day.

"I'm about to leave and will be home soon," I told him. "I'll tell you everything then."

As I turned back onto the highway to head home, I had no fear of the depression or mental illness returning. It was as if the scales dropped from my eyes and for once everything seemed clear and bright. I wanted to share this incredible joy and peace with everyone and immediately thought of my brother—now the

pastor of our home church. I would practically pass his house, just off the interstate, on the trip home. I had been basking in my newfound healing for a mere hour and fifteen minutes as I pulled into his driveway. Little did I know that in sharing my news, it would set off a chain reaction that would cause me to lose my entire biological family.

*Chapter 24*

# CONFRONTATION

*J*esus set me free!" I repeated over and over as I sat in the living room with my brother and his wife, sharing with them some of the highlights of my incredible day. I had expected them to rejoice in my news. Instead I was met with a reaction that I should have expected.

"What kind of doctrine do these people believe?" Scott questioned with obvious concern.

"I don't know what kind of church they attend, but they believe in the Bible. I'm free now. Isn't that enough evidence?" I asked, slightly hurt by his question.

I was like a caged animal that had suddenly experienced freedom. I knew what I had experienced and was unwilling for my brother's skepticism to force me back into captivity. I looked from Scott to my sister-in-law, Tammy, as I spoke. I could tell from their faces that they weren't rejoicing with me.

Much later I learned that Tammy immediately sensed the difference in me and was happy for me in her own way. But over the years in our family, she had learned what boundaries not to cross and was reluctant to give voice to her thoughts.

Although slightly daunted by Scott's and Tammy's reaction, I was determined that it would not diminish the truth of what had transpired. I had another forty-five-minute drive ahead of me before reaching home, and it couldn't pass quickly enough.

I pulled into the drive of our beautiful home—that had once been my prison—and raced into the house. Dave and little David

were waiting for me. As I looked into Dave's eyes, I saw the question and the hope. *Could it really be true?*

"I will never be the same, Dave. Jesus has healed me," I exclaimed, walking into his arms. Next, I turned my attention to little David who stood like a soldier at attention at his daddy's side. My heart ached over the past I couldn't change. Never again would he have to worry about how I might respond. I scooped him up in my arms and danced across the living-room floor with him.

"I love you so much, baby. Mommy's finally back!"

Dave stood transfixed with tears in his eyes as he watched us parade across the room. His silent prayers had been answered. I was a miracle in the making and no one could tell us any different. That night it was as if I were seeing everything in our home for the first time. *Wow, the decorators did a great job,* I remember thinking later as I walked through the living room, finally able to appreciate the details of their work. It may sound cliché, but now with Jesus in our home, everything seemed better and brighter than before.

First thing the next morning, I dialed my parents' number to share with Mom about my miraculous encounter.

"Your brother already called me, Jennifer. I have to tell you, we are all a little concerned," was her only comment. The disappointment in her voice ripped at my heart. How could they be worried when the change in my life was so obvious?

"Sweetheart, your family is different—your church is different," Dave said later, selecting his words carefully. "You probably shouldn't share with them everything you have experienced," Dave wisely suggested.

Submission, however, was never my forte; and in my zeal, I openly repeated my entire story with every member of the family.

To be honest, I couldn't keep quiet about what had happened to me. Remaining silent was no more possible than restraining the carbonated liquid inside a soda can after it has been shaken and opened. It is going to come out and so was my testimony.

Each night after Dave and the children went to bed, I would stay up for hours at a time, reading the Bible and feeding my hungry spirit. One day after discovering John 3:16, I began to weep.

*For God so loved the world that he gave his one and only Son, that whoever believes in him shall not perish but have eternal life.*

The Gospel was so simple! How could I have missed such a beautiful verse and the foundation of Christian belief for so many years?

Within six months of my conversion, Dave and I knew we could no longer remain part of the family church. The more I talked with my parents and siblings about what I believed to be deceptive doctrine, the more nervous they became in my presence.

"Baby, I don't know how much they can take," Dave warned as I expressed my ongoing need to speak with them about the truth. It was obvious to everyone that something had to give.

After thirty-one years, I could finally admit the bondage of the religious system in which we had been raised. Surely once I talked with my family members, they would be able to recognize this truth as well. I never stopped to consider the enormous impact my revelation would have upon the structure that dominated their lives.

By now, the leadership of the church was comprised almost entirely of family members. My brother was now the pastor and my father had stepped into the role of Sunday school superintendent and deacon. My mother played the piano and acted as

treasurer while my sister Kathy was a Sunday school teacher. In the last couple of years, I had taken on the role of youth leader.

As my knowledge of the Bible increased, I began to teach the newfound concepts to the youth, encouraging them that they could possess a deeper relationship and freedom in Christ. As you might imagine, this teaching didn't mix well with the theology of the church. It did not mix well with my brother either as we neared the inevitable confrontation that had been building since my transformation.

The sun was streaming through the windshield as Dave, the children, and I drove to church that morning in February. I was basking in the beauty of the moment and the peace that filled my heart. Today was the day we were finally breaking free from the church in which I had been raised. I felt no sorrow, only relief.

As I continued to enjoy the beautiful landscape during the drive, I heard the Father's voice speak to my heart, *I'm with you.*

*I know You are with me, Father,* I responded silently. I wondered at His comment, little realizing that within the next three hours, I would need His presence more than ever before.

"We've cancelled the youth Sunday school this morning, Jennifer," Scott informed me as soon as Dave and I entered the church auditorium.

Although our youth group was very small, it had become my mission field. I had already determined in my heart that since today would be my last time to teach them, I was going to completely share the Gospel and provide them with the opportunity to be born again. I sighed at the sudden turn of events as Dave and I turned to find our seats, my plan thwarted. Inwardly I prayed that the truths I had already revealed to the youth over

the last few weeks would be seed enough to dispel the erroneous teaching to which they had been subjected.

Dave squeezed my hand as we listened to Scott's sermon. Maybe it was my imagination, but every word seemed directed at me. In the past, I had been one of Scott's biggest cheerleaders in the service, often shouting amen or waving my hands. With my transformation, that had all changed. Today I sat quietly, in my mind rehearsing the conversation that would take place after the service when we would inform him that we would be leaving for good.

After the sermon ended, Dave and I waited as Scott talked with various members of the congregation.

"This is my brother, Dave. Please let me handle this," I whispered as Scott approached us.

We followed him into the fellowship hall where we could sit and hopefully share our news without incident. Our intent was not to cause offense, so I chose my words carefully.

"Scott, Dave and I wanted to let you know that this will be our last Sunday. We've decided to attend the Baptist church in our own community. The children are getting old enough now that they really need to be making friends nearby," I explained, referring to the thirty-five minute drive between our home and the church.

While the excuse was valid, Scott recognized it for what it was. Immediately he lashed out against us, certain our decision would have precarious consequences for our family if we dared to leave the system.

"How can you leave your family heritage? You know that Baptists believe in the Trinity," Scott almost shouted in response. "Jennifer, you will be raising David and Rebekah in false teaching!" he finished, now on his feet.

Although we had hoped to avoid confrontation, now that we were in it, I was not going to back down as I stood to look Scott

in the eyes. Our voices rose in anger as we argued. Finally I admitted the bitter truth.

"Scott, we are unwilling to raise our children in this doctrine of deception any longer."

As I said the words, I could see the anger flare in Scott's eyes. Wisely Dave stepped between us.

"You need to calm down," Dave spoke softly but firmly.

"Get away from her," Scott demanded, still trying to exercise a position of spiritual authority over us. In my heart, I believe there was genuine concern for us personally, but there was also something practical at stake. With Dave's lucrative business, we had contributed significant finances to the church—serious money that I am sure Scott did not want to lose. But nothing he said could reverse our decision.

"Scott, look what this church has done to our family. You have been a puppet at the hands of religion your entire life. You walked away from your dreams to fulfill *their* vision. There's no hope here, only rules," I continued.

For years I had watched as the religious leaders manipulated Scott with their dreams and needs. To become the pastor of this church had not been his vision but theirs. At one time he had had a bright future and was on his way to becoming a gifted attorney. But as our father aged, the pressure on Scott to continue our family heritage had increased until he eventually left law school to fill Dad's shoes.

As I finished, Scott took a step in my direction. Reaching out his arms, he laid his hands on my forehead and began to push, adopting a stance very familiar to me from my grandfather's services when he had tried to cast out demons.

"I take dominion over you and command you to come out!" he shouted as he continued to push me backwards.

Instead of toppling under his pressure, however, I sensed a strong hand bracing my back, reinforcing my stance and allowing me to stand my ground.

"Dear brother, if you'll notice, I'm still standing," I replied in a firm voice.

At that, Scott dropped his arms to his side as I saw the shock register on his face. Sinking back into his chair, he placed his head in his hands and began to weep uncontrollably.

Still sensing the firm presence behind me, I turned around to Dave. It was then that I realized *he* had not been behind me but was to the side observing. Then I remembered the words from that morning, *I will be with you.*

I looked at my brother with pity as we turned to walk out of the church for the last time. As I was growing up, my brother had been elevated to the status of hero in our home, our parents proudly proclaiming that he was the one who would carry on the proud heritage of our church. Whether willingly or under compulsion, Scott had given up his own dream and accepted the pastorate of this small church that ultimately was going nowhere. I wondered if he wished that he, too, could walk away as we were doing now.

As we drove home that day, I prayed for my family that they could know the truth and that God would heal our relationships. However, once my brother and other family members finally realized that we were resolute in our new decision, they made a decision of their own—one I should have seen coming but never believed would happen to me.

*Chapter 25*

# DISOWNED

*T*hroughout my childhood, our extended family followed an unspoken tradition of having lunch together each Sunday. Even after my brother, sisters, and I became adults and had families of our own, following church we all would head to Mom's and Dad's house on the farm. Once there we would change clothes and head to the kitchen to help Mom with the food. My mother was the best southern cook around, and the table for our Sunday meals was always loaded with her specialties. Following lunch most of us would nap, and then we would all head back to church for the evening service. But this all changed once Dave and I began pulling away. By the time we made the decision to leave the church, we had already stopped attending the luncheons and evening services, distancing ourselves from such constant interaction.

It had been almost a month since Scott and I had argued in the church, and I noticed that the entire family was treating us very differently. I loved my family and even if we didn't attend their church, I wanted to be in relationship with them. But now the change was affecting everyone.

"Mommy, how come we never see Granddaddy and Grandma anymore?" little David asked frequently. After our Sunday luncheons, Dad had often taken David on a walk around the farm to see the animals. Other times he would take him to the drugstore for a soft drink. As a child, David had no way to understand the tension in the family relationships. I considered his request; perhaps it was time to try to repair the breech.

"Hi, Mom. I wanted to let you know that Dave, the kids, and I will be coming for lunch tomorrow after church," I said, happy to hear her voice. We chatted briefly before hanging up. Immediately I called Kathy, to give her a head's up as well.

Little David wasn't the only one excited as we made the long drive to my parents' home. But even in my excitement to see everyone, I was apprehensive on how the family would respond to our visit. My fears were confirmed as we pulled into the drive. My heart sank as I saw the garage door down—a certain signal that no one was home.

"They can't be gone!" I said to Dave as I opened the door to get out. I walked up to the garage and peeked through the windows, looking for their car. The garage was empty.

My mind was racing with thoughts as I ran to the back door. Perhaps they had run to the grocery store for something…but that wouldn't explain why my brother's and sisters' cars weren't there. I tried the doorknob of the back door. Finding it locked, I then ran to the front. It was locked as well. As the truth of their intent dawned in my heart, I fell into Dave's arms and wept. *I had been disowned!* I knew my parents had been upset but figured that in time, they would be able to accept our decision to attend another church. I never dreamed they would shun me as I had been trained to shun others who had left our system.

"They knew we were coming and left," I cried to Dave as I climbed back into the car. I couldn't believe what was happening.

How a parent can disown his or her own flesh and blood proves, in my opinion, the dangerous power of brainwashing within religious cults. It is unnatural. In my case, it took approximately six months for the disowning to take full effect. In my heart, I believed that my family was simply trying to make a statement—a reprimand that would ease with time. But as weeks turned to months, I realized that their decision was permanent.

Looking at David and Rebekah in the backseat, my heart ached for them…especially little David who was old enough to truly miss his grandparents.

"Let's go eat somewhere fun," I suggested, trying to mask the pain of rejection.

"But I want to see Grandma and Granddaddy," David began to whine. I had no answers for my little boy.

I had known that my decision to break with the family church was going to have a high cost, I just hadn't realized how high.

*Chapter 26*

# MY NEW FAMILY

*T*he walk of a Christian isn't always easy," Roy and Velma Belon had told us students repeatedly during the days when they had sponsored the college gathering in their home. Obviously, this was one of those times. While I never doubted God's love or Dave's during those difficult months, I longed for my parents' love and to be reunited with my family.

On several occasions after the Sunday afternoon incident, I tried to make contact with them. I actually talked with Mom on the phone a couple of times, but it always ended the same as the topic of the church was approached and she would hang up. Dave and I just couldn't go back to that life, yet the pain of their rejection seemed to overwhelm me. Thank God He already had a plan in motion to restore that which had been lost.

Not long after the painful realization dawned that we had been disowned, I received a phone call from a dear friend. "Jennifer, I have a verse that I want to share. I think it is just for you." He then began to read, "Although my father and my mother have forsaken me, yet the Lord will take me up [adopt me as His child]" (Psalm 27:10 AMP).

Many times, the Holy Spirit will use men and women of God to encourage us along the way. This friend called not with worldly counsel, but with words of wisdom as he read the scripture to me. It was a beginning, but the pain was still very real and each additional contact I had with my family ripped open the slowly healing wound.

"Dave, please. I want to try one more time to see them," I begged on the phone like a little child. I knew my husband understood my desire, but he was more concerned with my mental and emotional stability in the face of the ongoing rejection.

"Honey, I really wish you wouldn't," he countered from an onsite project. "It will only cause you more pain."

"You're not here right now listening to David beg to see his grandma and granddaddy," I replied. "What can I say to him to make him understand? Besides, I want to see them too," I finished in a small voice. Finally, sensing my great need, Dave agreed to pray as I attempted to see my parents once again.

I held my breath as the phone rang once, twice, and then I heard her voice.

"Hey, Mom. How are you doing?" I said cautiously, explaining that David, Rebekah, and I would like to see her and my dad. To my surprise, she agreed. I was jubilant. I knew that if I could just see them, we could work this out.

"Mommy, I want to stay the night with them like I used to," little David pleaded as we gathered our things and prepared to get into the car. I stopped and looked closely at David, almost four. The anticipation on his upturned face and the hope in his innocent eyes was evident. He had no idea the complications behind his request. He just missed his grandparents.

"Oh, honey, I'm not sure," I hedged, not knowing what to say. It was one thing to allow us to drop by for a short visit, but having David spend the night was quite another.

"How about if I just pack your bag and we'll see, okay?" I responded as I watched a smile spread across his face.

I prayed the entire trip, my anticipation mounting despite Dave's caution.

"Honey, don't get your hopes up," he reminded me as I called to let him know we were on the road. "I'll be praying," he

promised as we disconnected. But from the moment we walked in their door, the conversation went sour.

"Hi, Mom!" I said as I gave her a hug. "We've really missed you! In fact, David was saying he has really missed spending the night with you and Dad," I said, trying to let her know how much we loved them.

"Oh, your dad and I made the decision that grandkids can't spend the night anymore," she responded immediately.

In an instant the wound was reopened.

"You're a liar!" I said quietly but with conviction. "I know for a fact that Kathy's kids have been spending the night here with you."

Mom didn't flinch but continued to stare at me with hardened eyes. *Why had she even allowed us to come?* I wondered.

I grabbed David's hand and turned to go. There was no use staying in a home in which we were so unwelcome.

The trip back was spent with David and me both crying. Thankfully Rebekah was too young to understand the dynamics of the difficult exchange.

"Lord, please heal my heart and our relationship," I begged through my tears.

After arriving home, I continued to pray, still too hurt to move past the morning's incident. Suddenly the ringing of the phone broke through my consciousness, startling me. I was caught completely off guard, so consumed with self-pity. As it turned out, it was a "God call."

"Jennifer! What are you doing?" said the familiar voice.

"Velma? Is that you?" I asked, stunned.

Since leaving college, I had had very little contact with the Belons, the sweet couple who had taken me under their wings after my difficult breakup with Jake. They had attended my wedding and had come to see me after David was born, but living in different cities and with our busy schedules, the relationship had since grown distant. It had been almost four years since I had

seen them. And now once again, at one of my greatest times of need, God was bringing them back into my life.

"Velma, you will never believe what I have been through," I said as the tears began again.

"Honey, we're here in Wilmington right now," she said. "The Lord told us to come and find you."

I could not believe my ears as I gave her my address. Within a matter of minutes their gray Volvo pulled into our driveway. God had heard my prayer. In that day He not only brought me much-needed comfort and a listening ear, but He also provided me a very special gift in the form of this precious couple. As our relationship reconnected, they would eventually step into the void left by my natural parents' actions and "adopt" me as their own.

Mom and Dad Belon immediately bonded with my children. It was their first time to meet Rebekah and their first time to see David since his birth. While we sat in the living room and caught up on the events of the previous years, they oohed and aahed over the children as if they were their own. My heart warmed again to this special couple whom God knew I needed.

Roy and Velma stayed for dinner, and I poured out my heart to them over the recent dealings with my family and how I had been disowned.

"God has done such a work in Jennifer over the past several months," Dave injected as we sat around the table after dinner, "but this has been really hard for her."

All of the abuse, molestation, and rape I had experienced in my childhood couldn't compare with hearing the words that finally came out of my parents' own mouths: "Don't ever come home again." But despite these challenges with my family, my passion and desire for the Word of God had not waned. I found that the only real antidote to my broken heart had been reading the scriptures of comfort and healing over and over each day.

As the months progressed, I continued to hope and pray that somehow God would heal the estranged relationship, but there was no further contact for quite some time. When the holidays rolled around, however, we received an unexpected invitation. It had been almost two years since the fateful day we had left the church. Now my sister Kathy was calling to invite us to join the family for Thanksgiving. The fact that we had to be invited only emphasized the state of our relationship; nevertheless, I was thrilled. I thought they were finally going to welcome us back. Instead it would be the very last Thanksgiving my extended biological family would ever spend together.

*Chapter 27*

# CARVING IT UP

*I* straightened Rebekah's pantsuit, adjusting the decorative pink pom-poms, and smoothed her hair for the umpteenth time before turning my attention to David. I wanted everything to be perfect and had dressed up the children for the occasion.

As we pulled into the drive at the farm, I noted that this time all the vehicles I expected were present. I couldn't wait to see Granny Jean, Kathy and her kids, Scott and his family, and—of course—my parents. The only ones missing were Sue and Joe. As had become typical for the last few years, he had kept her isolated from the family. While I would have liked to have seen my sister, I breathed a sigh of relief that Joe wouldn't be at the gathering.

The meal was to be served at five o'clock, so daylight was almost spent by the time we arrived. My eyes darted across the room as we walked in the door, trying to gauge the family's reaction to our entrance. I immediately walked up to my sister and gave her a hug, making sure I went to each member of the family in turn. Dad, Mom, and Kathy all seemed warm in their reception; but as I walked into the dining room to see Scott, it was clear that the passing of time had done little to erase the words that had passed between us two years before.

"Hi, Scott. How are you doing?" I asked, trying to break down the enormous wall that stood between us.

Rather than responding, he just looked at me, which said more than any words could convey. Nothing had changed between us. I knew, at least in his eyes, I was not welcome. Shaking off his rude response, I walked out of the room to join the others.

*If he wants to have an attitude, that's his problem*, I said to myself, unwilling to let his sour disposition ruin the day.

I walked over to Dave for moral support after the encounter. He looked at me knowingly and gave me a squeeze. Before and since, he has always been my pillar of strength.

"What should I do?" I whispered, referring to the situation with Scott.

"Just be a Christian," he commented. It was what he always said to me when referring to my family. What he really meant by the statement that day was, "Jennifer, lay low, get through the meal, and we'll leave without incident." I nodded and returned my focus to the others, determined that there would be no outburst.

The meal went well, although I don't remember much about it. What transpired afterward, however, will be forever etched in my mind.

After we had finished eating, I went into one of the back rooms to sing to the track of a new song for my nephew James (the son of Sue and Joe) and his wife. In spite of what his father had done, James and I had always been close. Even after the rest of the family had disowned me, he had continued to have contact with me, much to their dismay.

As the music ended, the sound of raised voices reached the back room where we sat. I quickly ran to the den where I found Dave and Scott in a heated exchange.

"What's going on?" I asked.

As Scott heard my voice, he spun around to face me, ready to unleash his arsenal of words at their true target. The source of the disagreement was a letter I had sent to each member of the family, sharing the foundation of our current beliefs. Because of my deep concern for them, I had hoped to expose the error of the church system.

As his verbal tirade continued, Scott took a step forward and pushed me back.

"Get your hands off her," Dave said as he stepped between us. In that moment I quickly took in the dynamics of the room. If I had hoped for assistance from my family, other than Dave, I would have been sadly disappointed. Dad was sitting in his easy chair, his eyes fixed on the television, although it was off. Mom was seated on the hearth holding Rebekah, her lips pursed in a smirk that seemed to suggest that she was actually enjoying the encounter. Rather than stepping in to diffuse the escalating episode, the patriarch and matriarch of our clan simply sat as spectators.

Then, to everyone's surprise, Granny Jean spoke up. "Scott, please! Even your grandfather wouldn't want her treated like this."

"You stay out of this," Scott yelled, momentarily turning his anger from me. In her late seventies, Granny Jean was the second wife of Grandfather Black who had started the church system now causing so much dissension in our family. You could see the look of shock on her face as tears welled up in her eyes from Scott's disrespectful retort.

"Back off, Scott. We're leaving," Dave said firmly, taking me by the arm and guiding me toward the door. James was already outside with David and Rebekah, having ushered them away from the conflict. As I reached out to take Rebekah from his arms, we heard the front door and turned to see Granny Jean. Asked to leave for speaking out in defense of me, her frail frame was shaking uncontrollably, overcome by the exchange. I looked back, but nobody else followed to see if we were okay or to offer comfort.

"Can you drive, Granny Jean?" Dave asked, concerned for her well-being. "Why don't you come home with us?" he suggested.

Just as we got in the car and were about to leave, we heard a loud howl, which I can only liken to the sound of a coyote, coming from inside the garage. It was an eerie, inhuman sound that sent shivers down my spine. It was Scott.

## Chapter 28

# DISCOVERING THE TRUTH—
# I GREW UP IN A CULT

*A*fter the ugly encounter, not one family member called to check on us or Granny Jean. A disconcerting discovery offered an explanation as to their lack of concern.

It was 9:30 a.m. on a Monday morning. Standing at the kitchen sink, I had my sleeves rolled up ready to tackle the dirty dishes from breakfast when I heard the Lord speak to my heart, *Are you ready for the truth about your family?*

"Yes, Lord," I responded obediently. But even as I mentally assented, I had a funny feeling in the pit of my stomach. The day had taken a very serious turn.

With the children away at school, I had already entered my normal morning routine, listening to the radio as I began cleaning the kitchen. About that time the program *Truths that Transform* with Dr. D. James Kennedy began to air. The topic of discussion that morning was religious cults.

Over the next hour, Dr. Kennedy gave a detailed description of the signs of a religious cult. I listened with horror as for the first time I understood that he was describing the system I had been raised in. I had known there was doctrinal error, but a cult...that reality hit hard. At the conclusion of the program, I dialed the toll-free number to speak to a counselor, absolutely shaken by what had just been revealed to me.

"Ma'am, you are a miracle," the counselor responded as I told him briefly about my childhood and the religion in which I had

been raised. "You definitely were in a cult," he explained. Any group that the rejects the reality of the Trinity is classified as one, I learned.

"Sir, I need to tell my parents!" I replied in response.

"If you do, you will have lost them forever," he shared with compassion. "From experience I can tell you that if you tell a cult member that they are part of a cult, it usually shuts down any further communication."

"Well, I've got nothing to lose then, because I think they've already done that," I told him.

At the conclusion of the conversation, the counselor prayed with me and offered to send me some books on the topic. I knew that my next step would be to research religious cults for myself.

As I poured over the material that arrived from the ministry a few days later, it only confirmed the truth. The organization started by my great grandfather four generations before was indeed a cult. It was a scary feeling but at the same time freeing. This newfound knowledge helped me to understand that my family's rejection of me was due more to brainwashing rather than something I had done.

The first phase of healing in my life had enabled me to understand that the sexual abuse I endured throughout my childhood was not my fault. This second phase was equally liberating as I realized that I did not cause my family to reject me. The pain of abuse and rejection that had covered my life was slowly being stripped away by the Holy Spirit.

I now had a Father in heaven who had adopted me and could handle any situation I would ever encounter. I love the words in John 8:32: "You will know the truth, and the truth will set you free." I posted this verse on a card in our house as a reminder of that important truth. Jesus is truth, and I knew He would never walk me down a road unless there was healing at the end of it. I found the Great I AM to be the "I AM, Jennifer, everything you

need." He revealed himself to be the provider of my mama, my daddy, my sister, and my brother as the words in Mark 10:29–30 became a reality in my life:

> *"I tell you the truth," Jesus replied, "no one who has left home or brothers or sisters or mother or father or children or fields for me and the gospel will fail to receive a hundred times as much in this present age (homes, brothers, sisters, mothers, children and fields—and with them, persecutions) and in the age to come, eternal life."*

When I gave up my biological family because of my love for Jesus, all of heaven came to attention. Even as those tormenting thoughts would still occasionally try to tell me that I would lose my mind, I knew now that they were simply empty threats that held no power. I had been blessed with a new mom and dad in the Belons. As for siblings, I now had Christian brothers and sisters all over the world. Most importantly I was learning that in every situation I could trust that He was going to see me through.

Although I desperately wanted to see my family set free from the cult, I knew that the task was far beyond my ability. All Dave and I could do was pray that God would open a door for us to talk with them. Surprisingly, we didn't contact them, but they contacted us.

## Chapter 29

# ONE MORE TIME

*J*ennifer?" came the familiar yet strange voice emanating from our voice-mail recorder.

I had waited nine years to hear from my family again, but now that my mother had called, I didn't know how to respond. With shaking fingers I dialed her back to find out her intent.

"We were cleaning out the closets and found your gown from the Miss North Carolina Fourth of July pageant. We'd like to bring it to you, if that is okay," she offered once we connected.

I had run into my parents on a couple of occasions in public settings during those years. The unexpected encounters were always uncomfortable, leaving me to deal with a backlash of emotions for several days.

"I'd love to see you," I choked out, my voice breaking with emotion. After inviting them to join us for dinner the next evening, she and I disconnected and my mind began to whirl.

I still received occasional updates on the family from my nephew James but otherwise had no idea how they were doing. One thing I did know, however, was that my family had continued to splinter.

Approximately six years before, Tammy—the wife of my brother Scott—had shown up on our doorstep around Christmastime. With gifts in hand, she asked to come in and shared the news of her own transformation and acceptance of Christ. Like me, she eventually came to a place in her life in which she felt she couldn't go on. Severe depression had overtaken her as a result of never feeling that she could live up to the strict standards of the religious system. In an effort to find relief, she had sought counseling. It was the Christian counselor who had led her to the Lord.

Of course we were thrilled but later discovered that the family blamed me for her decision and subsequent divorce from Scott. Truth be known, Dave and I had actually prayed for their marriage to be restored. As Tammy returned to the union after a separation, however, Scott became increasingly verbally abusive over her decision to leave the religious system. Eventually she made the decision to end the marriage. I thought of this as I dialed Roy and Velma for moral support.

"You'll always be my parents in the Lord," I said to Velma as I shared with her the startling news. "But I could really use your prayers about my parents' upcoming visit."

"We've been praying for this day and for reconciliation for years," Velma spoke reassuringly through the receiver. "We'll keep praying. Don't you worry," she reassured.

I plumped the pillows, checked my hair and makeup, and then started through the routine again as we waited for 6:00 p.m. to arrive.

"Honey, you're making me nervous," Dave half-heartedly complained with a laugh at my need for constant motion. As the time of their expected arrival came and went, I became even more uptight.

"What if they don't come?" I lamented.

"It'll be fine!" Dave insisted in an effort to keep me calm. But his words could not ease the nagging fear that was growing within me. Finally, I caught sight of their car as it pulled into the drive. Even though I had been up and down looking out the window for them for the past hour, I now refused to answer the door, instead insisting that Dave be the first to greet them.

Although slightly grayer than before, my parents hadn't changed much. As they stepped into the foyer, we stood awkwardly facing

each other, none of us quite knowing what to do. I wanted to run up and throw my arms around them, yet still uncertain as to their intent, I could not bring myself to take that initial step to reconciliation. Instead Dave and I invited them into the living room where we made small talk about the weather and other trivia until it was time to go to the restaurant.

During the meal, the kids helped deflect attention away from the unspoken "elephant" that occupied the room. Returning to the house after dinner, my anger began to build as I realized my parents were not even going to address the issue of our separation for the past nine years. My blood began to boil. Dave, sensing my body language, took my hand to stem the flow of words, but I couldn't stop myself.

"Before you leave I have to know why you are here," I stated in what I hoped was a calm, not accusing voice.

"Jennifer, when your father and I were cleaning out the closet the other day, I finally said to him, 'Enough is enough! We have to see her!'"

That was all I wanted to hear, assuring me that there was no ulterior motive.

"I'm glad you're here," I responded as I belatedly reached out to give them both a hug.

"How are things at your church," Dad asked next, quickly moving into the forbidden topic of religion. Instantly, Dave shot me a look not to respond, but that would have been like demanding "Old Faithful" at Yellowstone Park not to erupt. Dad had asked and I was going to answer.

I pointed to the Bible that lay on the table in the foyer. "The Word of God is specific and I believe it," I said without hesitation, referring to our differing belief in the Trinity and the saving power of Jesus Christ.

Of course, Dad couldn't back down either as we entered a religious debate. Fortunately, before it could get too out of control,

Dave and my mother stepped in to ask us both to quit—which surprisingly we both did. As they said good night, I kissed and hugged them both.

"Let's end our evening on a nice note," I said with a smile. Dave walked them out to their car as I collapsed on the floor completely drained. What an evening it had been.

A few days later, the number on the caller ID revealed my parents' phone number again. Pleasantly surprised at the continued contact, Dave picked up the phone.

"Let me talk with Jennifer about it. We'll try our best to come," Dave replied as he hung up. It was nearing my parents' fiftieth wedding anniversary, and my father had just invited us to attend the celebration.

"It's so odd having them back in our lives," I commented to Dave later that evening. I was happy and had wanted the relationship to be restored for so long but was still uncertain how to proceed. When we told the kids about the event, they were less than enthusiastic about attending a family function with people they no longer knew, much preferring to spend the day with their own friends.

"Mom, I already have grandparents," David reminded me, referring to his relationships with Grandpa Roy and Grandma Velma, Grandpappy Kostyal, and Grandma Mimi. My son had spoken with wisdom far beyond his years.

"Honey, what if your parents restate their vows in the church in which you were raised? Will you be able to handle that?" Dave asked wisely. In my naïveté, I was somehow still hoping for a "Father Knows Best," storybook kind of family. All I could think about now was what I would wear; how I would dress the kids; and seeing my siblings, aunts, and uncles again.

"Honey, if they do, I'll be able to handle it. We'll just be in there a short while anyway," I said, responding to his question

about the location for the event. Little did I know that it was about to become a non-issue.

Two days later there was a message on my answering machine for me to call my father. "It's very important," he said, urgency in his voice.

I dialed the number from my childhood by memory. Dad picked up almost immediately.

"Jenny, I have a favor I need you to do for me," he began. I thought he was going to ask me to say a prayer somewhere in the ceremony.

"I'll be happy to do whatever you need," I replied without hesitation.

"I want you to make sure that you and your family *do not* come to our anniversary gathering. Can you do that for me?" he asked.

My breath caught in my throat as I replayed the words in my mind. Did I hear what I thought I heard? There was silence on the phone for a few seconds as I regained my composure and said, "I'll be glad to do that for you. God bless you, Dad. I love you," I responded calmly and then hung up the phone. Immediately my composure disintegrated as I sat on the bed and wept.

Then, from deep within I addressed the real culprit behind the phone call. "You tormenting spirits, get away from me in Jesus' name. I will not allow you to steal from me any longer!" Even in the pain of the moment, I recognized that this was just one more attempt from Satan to derail my life.

As I allowed the peace of God to fill my heart once again, the weeping stopped and I walked to tell my husband, who was in his office next door.

"What's wrong, Jennifer?" Dave asked immediately sensing something amiss.

"You're never going to believe this, Dave," I answered. "I've been disowned...again."

## Chapter 30

# "WHY DID YOU LET IT HAPPEN?"

*A*lthough the reopened wound of rejection was painful, God remained faithful. Years before, this same incident would have sent me into a well of depression. Instead, by His grace, it was simply a bump in the road that He helped me over.

By this time, I was several years into my healing journey and had been actively reaching out to other women who had been hurt and abused. However, one significant instance early in my ministry revealed God's ultimate plan for my life.

Nervous excitement bubbled inside me as I contemplated what I would say that night at the women's prison. Although it had not been long since I had begun to heal from the scars of my own past, I had been invited to share my testimony with the local inmates. This was a new experience, which I didn't take lightly. As I walked the perimeter of our backyard praying for wisdom on what to say, righteous anger flooded over me for the loss of my innocence.

I do not have many pleasant memories from my childhood due to the abuse. Instead, pain-filled images dominate my recollections. I am sure there were many good times, I just can't remember them. Entire chunks of my life are simply missing from my consciousness. I am told that this is very typical of men and women who have lived through abuse such as I was subjected to.

As I mulled over my past and continued praying in preparation for the ministry opportunity, the irony of where I was standing dawned on me. I stood transfixed at the edge of the yard, looking across the marsh—the very area where I had thought about taking my life a few years before.

"Lord, why did You let it happen?" I asked, reflecting on the road I had been forced to travel.

A hush seemed to come over me as I sensed His gentle answer. *You had no covering. You were wide open for the enemy to come in and molest you.*

Although I did not fully understand the meaning of those words at that time, I did realize that my parents had not provided a protective covering over me. I have since learned that just as parents are responsible to physically protect their children, they are to also provide a spiritual covering through prayer. In my case, I had neither due to my parents' lack of knowledge and their belief system. Instead, there had been other principles at work.

To understand this, one must first realize that everything God created has been established on a *legal basis*. In short, when we obey His Word, we have a legal right to all of His blessings, including His divine protection. This was the life Adam and Eve enjoyed in the Garden of Eden. However, when they chose to disobey God's command, they gave up their legal right to those blessings and came under the devil's curse. They stepped out from under God's protection and were then under the control of Satan, open to all his destructive devices. Mankind has been suffering under that curse ever since.

But there is good news. Jesus Christ legally paid the penalty for all sin through the shedding of His blood. When we receive Him as Lord and Savior and come into covenant with Him, the power of the curse is broken over our lives and we can once again legally enjoy the blessings and protection of God.

Unfortunately, in the case of my family, my parents and grandparents chose a religion of their own making rather than receiving salvation by grace and submitting to the lordship of Jesus. This opened the door to demonic forces, and sin had free reign in our family, being passed down through several generations. The Bible describes it this way:

*I, the LORD your God, am a jealous God who will not tolerate your affection for any other gods. I lay the sins of the parents upon their children; the entire family is affected—even children in the third and fourth generations of those who reject me.*

DEUTERONOMY 5:9 NLT

Until I became a Christian, I was a fourth-generation religious cult member with no spiritual covering. Because of my family's choices, God had no legal right to step in and protect me. However, it is obvious from my story that He did maneuver people, situations, and circumstances to bring me to Him so that the cycle of abuse could be broken.

Make no mistake—the perversion of mankind was never part of God's plan. Instead it has transpired as people have made choices—of their own free will—to submit to evil desires influenced by Satan's dominion in the world. Jesus acknowledged the nature of His ruthless adversary when He said: "The thief comes only to steal and kill and destroy" (John 10:10). In the same verse, however, He offered hope: "I have come that they may have life, and have it to the full."

Once as I was reading the Bible, the Lord revealed to me how He feels about people who hurt little children. Jesus can heal and save anyone; however, if a perpetrator does not repent and abandon the abusive behavior, Jesus offered the following words of warning:

*Whoever causes one of these little ones who believe in Me to stumble, it would be better for him to have a heavy millstone hung around his neck, and to be drowned in the depth of the sea. Woe to the world because of its stumbling blocks! For it is inevitable that stumbling blocks come; but woe to that man through whom the stumbling block comes!*

MATTHEW 18:6–7 NASB

"Jesus loves the little children," as the song says, and He does not want them to be harmed. Abuse in any form is inexcusable to Him, and perpetrators will suffer the consequences unless they truly repent.

As I have come to understand these things, I now understand that it is not only for my own well-being that I am to live a life of prayer and obedience to God. The lives of my children are also at stake. As explained above, the consequences of sin are passed down several generations. On the other hand, when we live by God's principles, tremendous blessing is passed down. In God's own words:

> *I lavish unfailing love for a thousand generations on those who love me and obey my commands.*
>
> DEUTERONOMY 5:10 NLT

Think of it. God will lavish His love on a *thousand generations!* What I do today will affect the lives of my children and their posterity for a very long time.

I do not blame my parents that they did not provide this type of protective prayer covering for me. They simply did not know about it. And while I did pay a tremendous price for this lack of knowledge, God has, nonetheless, delivered me and healed me.

Sexual abuse may not destroy the physical body through death, but in reality it does kill a part of its victims. These wounds are so deep that only through the resurrection power of Christ can they be healed. That was the message I wanted to share with the women in the local prison.

Inner strength rose within me as I continued looking out over the marsh, reflecting on God's incredible mercy.

"Satan, you may have stolen my childhood and almost taken my motherhood, but I am going to deliver a devastating blow to your kingdom tonight when I tell these women that Jesus can

heal them like He healed me," I declared out loud. I was ready for battle.

That night, when I walked into the prison, I noticed that the majority of the women were African-American. I smiled. They didn't know it, but while I was Caucasian on the outside, inside I was actually their sister. They didn't know it, but my true parents—the Belons—shared their natural heritage. They didn't know it, but my past included a little African-American church where the sounds of the drums and the organ were the only things that could put my soul to rest during my torment-filled college years. I had more in common with the women than they realized.

When I stood to minister that evening, I felt the presence of God as I had never before. I understood what it was like to be locked up. The only difference was that my prison had not been visible to the naked eye.

That night I explained to the women that the only real key to freedom was by accepting Jesus Christ as Savior. I encouraged them that not only would He heal their broken hearts, He would give them entirely new lives as He had done for me. By the end of the service, there were women on the floor crying out for the same restoration that I had experienced. And God did not disappoint them as His presence manifested so strongly in that place. The service went well over the allotted time, but no one stopped us. I held weeping women in my arms as the power of God surged through them. Over and over again, I heard these dear women admit that they, too, had been sexually abused; and I realized the magnitude of perversion that has permeated mankind.

I hugged the women as we prepared to leave that night and laughed openly when one of them stopped me to share the skepticism that had been present earlier in the evening. She was the one who had whispered to the woman sitting next to her, "What does Farrah Fawcett have to say to us?"

She then went on to tell me, "We couldn't imagine what a white girl like you could possibly have to say to a group like us," she confessed. "But we had never heard any white woman preach like you," she said with a laugh.

As I left the prison that night, I knew I had walked into my destiny. God had not caused the abuse, but He could now use it to help bring healing to others who had experienced the same torment.

Over the years, I have often thought of Ann Graham Lotz's words, "Just give me Jesus," and have to smile, realizing it truly is that simple. We do not have a God who refuses to heal hearts and minds. He desires to minister to and set free those who have suffered at the hands of sociopaths and pedophiles. Those perverse individuals may have taken precious little children, used them up, and tossed them to the side; but God will raise the abused from the ash heap and set them on high.

When we truly grasp that Jesus is the Son of God and comprehend the depth of His love and redemption, then the journey to healing can begin. It is not an overnight experience, but when we allow the Word of God to guide us and direct us as He has promised, then we will see the chains begin to fall off one by one as we are freed from the past. We are never alone in this journey. The heavenly Father walks with us every step of the way. Isaiah 41:13 states it this way:

> For I am the LORD, your God, who takes hold of your right
> hand and says to you, Do not fear; I will help you.

No matter what difficulties life has thrown your way, whether you have been a victim of abuse or other significant challenges, you can be healed from the pain and memories of the past. I pray that my story will encourage you to take the Father's hand and allow Him to walk with you through the healing process. As you do you need to understand that there remains one more significant truth that you need in order to walk in total victory.

*Chapter 31*

# BREAKING THE CYCLE

*T*hrough my years of ministry since 1996, I have never met a woman or man who has been sexually abused who didn't have other instances of that abuse in their family history. When we go to a physician, the first thing typically required is that we provide a family medical history. Doctors want to know about our backgrounds medically because they understand that what has happened in our families in the past can have a direct effect on our present and future. While many people would not argue that diseases run in families, they ignore the fact that generational curses also run in families manifesting as strongholds of rage, alcoholism, drug addiction, sexual abuse, divorce, etc. (Please refer to the appendix for the scriptural foundation.) The good news is the cycle can be broken.

Since becoming aware of this significant truth, I have encountered generational curses rearing their ugly heads numerous times. One instance occurred in—of all places—my children's school.

It was a cold winter morning as I walked Rebekah and David into the building. Because of a meeting scheduled immediately afterwards, I was dressed nicer than usual, wearing my favorite full-length, black leather coat.

"I love you! Have a blessed day," I called out as David and Rebekah walked to their respective classes.

It is such a joy to take my children to school. It is my chance, first thing every morning, to instill in them how special they are to God and to me, to remind them that they have a destiny and what the Word of God says about them. (See Deuteronomy 28:1–14.)

That particular morning I was thinking what an honor it was to be a mom. I knew how close I had come to losing everything I had, and now each day was special. Walking back down the hall toward the parking lot, the peace of the morning was shattered as I heard a cry coming from the restroom, followed by the voice of an angry mother. The tone was eerily familiar. At that moment, the meeting I had scheduled took a back seat to the divine appointment I heard calling out of that public school restroom.

Making the quick detour, I entered. At first it appeared empty, but then I heard voices in one of the stalls. Immediately I recognized the rage that was coming from the mother and the whimpering from the child. I wasn't going to leave.

"Ma'am, is everything all right?" I asked, tapping on the bathroom stall—knowing full well that it wasn't.

"Everything is fine," she answered abruptly. Despite my pending appointment, the Holy Spirit wouldn't let me leave.

"Please let me help you," I pressed on. "I understand what you are doing. Jesus loves you." All of a sudden the door opened. Standing before me was the tear-stained face of a mother and a child with blood running down his face. The little boy ran into my arms.

"It's going to be all right," I said as I knelt on the filthy bathroom floor. As I looked up at the mother, I could see myself standing there years before. I recognized the abuse.

"You may see me all dressed up in these fine clothes," I told her, "but I was once in your shoes and was on the verge of doing the same thing to my children. Please let me help you."

That was all it took as she broke down and told me of her own life as a victim of abuse. Abuse always follows abuse.

The woman described her own history with a dad who had been a crack addict, abandoning her and her family when she was very young. This had set into motion a cycle of abuse, rejection, abandonment, and fear, typical of such trauma.

I dampened a paper towel and began to wipe the blood from the little boy's face. He was a tiny little thing with dirty blond hair, a worn winter coat, and old dingy shoes. He looked tired and his stomach growled several times during the cleanup.

"Let's get him cleaned up so that he can get into the cafeteria and get some breakfast," I stated.

Although at first glance it appeared much worse, the wound was small where the mother had accidentally broken her son's lip—which was already chapped from the cold.

After dropping her son off with his teacher, I turned back to the mother, "You need help and I know where you can find it," I began. "Let me tell you my story."

As I walked with her to her old car sitting in the front of the school, I noticed a little girl around the age of two buckled in a car seat, holding a stuffed animal. Although many children at that age would have been terrified to be alone in the car, she sat there perfectly contented, obviously used to the lack of supervision. I sensed the Holy Spirit speak to my heart that the woman needed gas for her vehicle and food for the child.

"Please follow me to the gas station and we'll get your car filled up," I suggested.

Obediently following, she pulled in behind me at the station. As she pumped the gas, I went inside and purchased food for her little girl. God had opened a door to meet the woman's immediate physical needs so that I could share with her on a deeper level about her spiritual needs. Although I am not a psychologist or a medical professional, I do know the Healer and I was able to minister to this hurting mother.

Later as I talked with a school administrator, I learned that the faculty was aware of the tense situation between the mother and her son. What I can tell you is that the woman did get the help and healing she desperately needed. A few months later she came into my office. I hardly recognized her.

No longer controlled by her anger, she was a beautiful woman with well-kept hair and a sweet smile. When I recognized her, I gave her a big hug and asked her to sit down and share what had transpired. The joy radiating from her countenance was extraordinary as she shared about the church she was now attending, her new car, and how Jesus had heard our prayers that day.

"I'm no longer losing my temper with my son," she explained. "For years my grandmother prayed for me and told me life was good, but I just couldn't see it. Everything is so different now. Life really is good."

The curse had been broken. It was a fresh start.

Yes, generational curses can be stopped, but not by ordinary human means. We cannot will them to stop, and they certainly will not "go away" on their own. Because their roots are spiritual in nature, spiritual weapons are required to destroy them.

After Jesus was crucified on the cross, He descended into hell to face the devil on his own turf. Colossians 2:15 states:

> *Having disarmed the powers and authorities, he made a public spectacle of them, triumphing over them by the cross.*[1]

Not only did Jesus defeat Satan and disarm all the powers of darkness, He then paraded them through the streets of the spirit world and made a public exhibition of them in their humiliated state! Now when the devil tries to bluff me into believing he has the upper hand, I simply remind him of that day in hell. No longer can he lord it over me and make me feel like a victim. I know the truth—that he is a defeated, powerless foe whose ultimate destination is eternal damnation. His bark is definitely worse than his bite.

---

1   See also Luke 10:18–20.

Not only was Satan totally defeated, Jesus has given *us* authority over him according to Matthew 16:19:

> *I will give you the keys of the kingdom of heaven; whatever you bind on earth will be bound in heaven, and whatever you loose on earth will be loosed in heaven.*

The first thing I did when the Lord revealed the reality of generational curses to me was to list those that had been a part of my family of origin—abuse, fear, rejection, promiscuity, and pride. I then asked Dave to tell me the ones he knew were on his side of the family. Together, through prayer, we then used the authority given to us by Jesus and bound all generational curses from operating in our immediate family. What a relief it was to finally have the confidence that my daughter, Rebekah, would never be molested as many girls in my family line have been due to having no spiritual covering!

It is important to understand that this is not a one-time prayer event. The devil is stubborn. Even after generational curses have been broken, his imps will try to come back in those same areas. Because of this, we must continually cover our families in prayer and give him absolutely no place in our lives. (For more information on breaking the cycle of abuse, please refer to the appendix where you will find scriptures and a prayer to stop generational curses from operating in your life.)

Let me share with you a situation that happened in my own ministry not long ago.

I received a phone call from a couple frantic to meet with me immediately. I knew them from a neighboring church but had no idea what difficulty they might be facing that would be so imminent. Yet the fear in the woman's voice was undeniable.

"Dave, can you watch the children, so I can meet this couple later this evening?" I asked him, holding my hand over the receiver.

Hours later I prayed as I headed over to the office, uneasy in my spirit.

"Lord, please anoint me to handle whatever situation might arise tonight," I prayed.

I knew that personally, in my own strength, I could not minister to anyone. The fact was, just ten years before, I had been a woman on the verge of losing her mind due to the years of abuse, and I had learned from experience that knowledge alone isn't enough to bring complete healing. I had studied numerous books on the topic of abuse and parenting to win the numerous battles in my own mind; and while the information was helpful, knowledge and worldly wisdom alone were not enough to set me free. It took the Word of God and His power poured into the deep wounds to truly heal me. It was for this type of anointing that I prayed as I pulled my jacket around me and made the short walk up the sidewalk to my office.

That evening would turn out very different from what I had expected. Once inside I waited, peering out the office window, watching for the couple. When they arrived I was surprised to note that their three-year-old daughter was with them.

"It's going to be all right. Jesus can handle anything," I commented as I opened the door, allowing them to enter.

"This is really bad, Jennifer," the mother responded. Looking directly into her eyes, I could see the distress etched on her face. My heart went out to her as her composure dissolved into tears.

I had just pulled a children's video from the bookshelf and was about to turn it on for their daughter to watch when they both stopped me.

"No, Jennifer, she has to come with us," they both commented. I saw the look of pain in their eyes and knew immediately that we were dealing with a case of abuse. Thank God for the Holy Spirit's guidance. As I had done many times, I claimed God's

promise from 1 John 4:4, "Greater is he that is in [me], than he that is in the world" (KJV).

As we sat down, I looked intently at the little girl for the first time, her head hung low. It was easy to recognize the shame that had characterized my own childhood. Taking her gently by the hand, I coaxed her to me.

"Come to Miss Jennifer," I said. "Let's talk and find out what has been happening. After we talk you can watch a show." I'm thankful for the tremendous favor I have with children and know it is the love of Jesus within me.

Her parents quickly informed me of the molestation their precious daughter had recently experienced. I prayed, searching my heart for the words God would have me to share. What could I do to help? As I lifted the child onto my lap, I asked her to tell me what had happened and cringed as she described a man performing vile acts on her little body.

Relieved and thankful for the presence of God filling the room, I looked into the child's eyes and told her how proud I was of her that she had told her mommy and daddy what had been done to her. Next I explained that she wasn't the one who caused the man to do these deplorable things. I let her know that she had done nothing wrong and that the fault was completely his.

After we talked awhile, the couple and I prayed over their daughter that God would heal her. My prayers with children are short and full of confirmation of the Lord's love for them, and this precious child responded to that as she lay against my chest and rested in my arms. Finally, I hugged and kissed her and gave her a little toy as she scampered off to watch a Christian children's program. Now it was time to minister to her parents.

"You are good parents," I assured them, battling against the devastation that threatened their family. "You also have a strong relationship with your daughter; otherwise she would not have even come to tell you what happened. If the enemy ever tells you her life is ruined," I continued, "you tell him that the blood of Jesus is more powerful than his plans to destroy your child."

I sensed God's presence remaining strong in the room as I continued, "If Satan tells you that your baby's life is ruined, remember me. I did not tell anyone of the abuse I experienced throughout my childhood. For years I lived with it and that led to a life of destruction. But Jesus touched me and healed me, and today I am whole through His blood. Go now and love your child as never before, and ask the Holy Spirit what you should do next to aid her healing."

With tears flowing down their cheeks, we prayed for complete restoration for their daughter and their family. I learned later that the man who had sexually assaulted the little girl had been arrested. Thankfully one more abuser was off the streets and this precious child was doing well.

What I shared with this family is the same thing I want to share with every little girl and boy and every man and woman reading this book who has been a victim of abuse. God has a plan for your life. He did not cause the abuse; but He can heal, restore, and make you whole from the inside out, giving you an entirely new life. There is no pain that Jesus cannot heal. This good news was prophesied in Isaiah 53:4, which says, "Surely He [Jesus] has borne our griefs and carried our sorrows" (NKJV). Not only did Jesus bear your sins on the cross, He also bore every emotional trauma and pain. Reach out to Him and allow Him to help you start your life over. Then watch Him make your dreams of wholeness come true.

That night as I left my office, I thanked Jesus again for healing me of all the devastation I had experienced. I cannot thank Him enough for giving me my life back. As I returned to the house, I looked up into the sky, touched with the knowledge that the same One who placed the stars there holds my hand every day. I never had to be afraid again.

*Chapter 32*

# BECOMING FINALLY FREE

$\mathcal{N}$ow, many years since starting my own journey of healing, I can tell you that healing from abuse is a process. Abuse deposits layers of scars on its victim, which manifest themselves in fear, rejection, a critical heart, low self-esteem, and more. Unless these scars are removed, the result will be a life in which the abused becomes the abuser as the cycle of violence continues. Our prisons will attest to this fact. Our schools, churches, and workplaces are filled with individuals who are covered in these layers, which are stealing their lives. The good news is that they can be free!

If you have been a victim of abuse, the first step is to allow the Healer into your life. I assure you, you can trust Him with your heart. He will be your protector. You can do that now with the following prayer:

*Dear God,*

*I am beginning to see that You can heal me and make me whole. I ask You to continue to reveal Yourself to me in a deeper way. To be honest, I have never really been able to trust anyone, and I need help in trusting You.*

*I acknowledge that I cannot deliver myself. I need a Savior, and I believe that Savior is Jesus. I believe He is the Son of God and that He died for my sins as well as for my healing from years of abuse. I ask You to make the shattered parts of me whole and to put back the things that were ripped out of me when I was abused. I believe Jesus arose from the grave, redeeming mankind, so I know*

*You can handle the pain, wounds, and loneliness that abuse has caused in my life.*

*Father, I ask You to lead me on my journey of healing. Guide me to a Bible-believing church and surround me with the right people to help me in my new walk with You. I ask You to give me a passion for Your Word and for it to illumine my heart and mind as I read it. Finally, I ask You to grant me peaceful sleep tonight as I rest in Your arms for the first time in my life.*

*Lord Jesus, I end this prayer, acknowledging that You paid the full price to free me from Satan's grip. You redeemed my life through Your blood and You purchased my healing by the stripes laid upon your back. Thank You for becoming my Lord and Savior. I love You.*

*Amen.*

If you are serious about becoming free from the layers of abuse, I invite you now to take the next step and make a seven-week commitment to work through the study book, the *Finally Free Bible Study: 7 Weeks to Freedom from Your Past*. Whether you work through this book in a group or individually, it will lead you through the necessary steps to become free of each and every robe of pain that has been laid upon your life. It will also lead you through the important steps of how to forgive your abuser as well as yourself.

You have a destiny to fulfill. You, my dear brother and sister, came from the heart of God and have much to do on Earth, now that you have become a citizen in the kingdom of light. You were created with special gifts and talents to do something only you can do, to reach people only you can reach. It is time to take back that which was stolen. It is time to fulfill your destiny. Freedom is what Jesus died for and freedom is what we have as His children. Come. Take that step and become *Finally Free*.

*Appendix*

# SCRIPTURAL TOOLS FOR YOUR BREAKTHROUGH

*T*o give you tools with which you can fight when the battle is raging, I want to share pertinent scriptures and prayers that you can turn to again and again for meditation and support.

## BREAKING THE CYCLE OF ABUSE

*You shall not bow down to them [false gods] nor serve them. For I, the LORD your God, am a jealous God, visiting the iniquity of the fathers upon the children to the third and fourth generations of those who hate Me, but showing mercy to thousands, to those who love Me and keep My commandments.*

EXODUS 20:5–6 NKJV

Note: See also Deuteronomy 5:8–10. Generational curses are passed down three to four generations, yet when the curses are broken and people turn to love and serve God, He showers His mercy upon them and a thousand generations to come.

*Choose for yourselves this day whom you will serve, whether the gods your forefathers served beyond the River, or the gods of the Amorites, in whose land you are living. But as for me and my household, we will serve the LORD.*

JOSHUA 24:15

Note: The first step to breaking generational curses is to make the choice to serve the Lord and to submit to the lordship of Jesus Christ.

> *I call heaven and earth as witnesses today against you, that I have set before you life and death, blessing and cursing; therefore choose life, that both you and your descendants may live.*
>
> DEUTERONOMY 30:19 NKJV

Note: We are not doomed to live under a curse. God has given us the right to choose a life of blessing!

> *Christ redeemed us from the curse of the law by becoming a curse for us, for it is written: "Cursed is everyone who is hung on a tree."*
>
> GALATIANS 3:13

Note: Jesus not only broke the power of the curse, He actually *became* a curse for us so that we might be free.

> *[Jesus said,] I will give you the keys of the kingdom of heaven; whatever you bind on earth will be bound in heaven, and whatever you loose on earth will be loosed in heaven.*
>
> MATTHEW 16:19

Note: Jesus has given believers the authority to bind evil spirits and generational curses.

> *Though we live in the world, we do not wage war as the world does. The weapons we fight with are not the weapons of the world. On the contrary, they have divine power to demolish strongholds.*
>
> 2 CORINTHIANS 10:3–4

*When the L*ORD *goes through the land to strike down the Egyptians, he will see the blood on the top and sides of the doorframe and will pass over that doorway, and he will not permit the destroyer to enter your houses and strike you down.*

EXODUS 12:23

Note: When we apply the blood of Jesus to our lives as well as to those of our family, the devil and generational curses are prevented from entering.

*[Jesus said,] If you abide in My word, you are My disciples indeed. And you shall know the truth, and the truth shall make you free.*

JOHN 8:31–32 NKJV

*They [the former tyrant masters] are dead, they shall not live and reappear; they are powerless ghosts, they shall not rise and come back. Therefore You have visited and made an end of them and caused every memory of them [every trace of their supremacy] to perish.*

ISAIAH 26:14 AMP

## A PRAYER FOR YOU

*Heavenly Father,*

*I declare that Jesus is Lord over my family and me, and I thank You for His precious blood that covers and protects us now. As Your children, we have a new heritage…a new blood line. We command all generational sins of our family to be broken now, in the mighty name of Jesus. I declare that my children and our family line is set free from the operation of [specify each reoccurring stronghold in your family]. I uproot these sins and their dominion over our family and clothe us with the full armor of God.*

*We shod our feet with the preparation of the gospel of peace and our steps are ordered and directed by You. We gird our loins with truth; and we speak the truth, operate in truth, and are discerners of truth. We put on the breast-plate of righteousness, and it covers our hearts and frees us from condemnation. We stand firm in Christ and nothing can shake us from our commitment to You. We put on the helmet of salvation, which protects our minds and thoughts. We cast down every imagination and every thought that would try to raise itself above You. We take the shield of faith to quench every fiery dart of the wicked one, for we walk by faith and not by sight. Finally, we take the sword of the Spirit, which is the Word of God. We speak Your Word as a weapon to declare Your blessings and protection over our lives and family, canceling the sins of the past through the blood of Jesus. Thank You that we are new creations created in Christ Jesus. The old has gone and the new has come.*

*In Jesus' name. Amen.*[1]

## DELIVERANCE FROM ABUSIVE RELATIONSHIPS

*I will call upon the Lord to save me—and he will. I will pray morning, noon, and night, pleading aloud with God; and he will hear and answer. Though the tide of battle runs strongly against me, for so many are fighting me, yet he will rescue me.*

PSALM 55:16–18 TLB

---

1 See these additional verses regarding the scriptural basis for this prayer: 2 Corinthians 10:5; Ephesians 6:10–18; Psalm 37:23; Proverbs 8:7; Ephesians 4:25; Romans 8:1; 1 John 1:9; and 2 Corinthians 5:17.

*Reach down from heaven and rescue me; deliver me from deep waters, from the power of my enemies. Their mouths are filled with lies; they swear to the truth of what is false.*

PSALM 144:7–8 TLB

*Through knowledge the righteous escape.*

PROVERBS 11:9

*Whether you turn to the right or to the left, your ears will hear a voice behind you, saying, "This is the way; walk in it."*

ISAIAH 30:21

*Do not be afraid—I am with you!*
*I am your God—let nothing terrify you!*
*I will make you strong and help you;*
*I will protect you and save you.*

ISAIAH 41:10 GNT

## A PRAYER FOR YOU

*Heavenly Father,*

*I need Your help. I feel trapped and cannot see my way out of this abusive relationship. When I think of leaving, fear grips my heart and paralyzes me from taking action. Not only am I afraid of what my abuser might do, I am also afraid of what lies ahead. You are my only hope.*

*I ask You to give me Your wisdom to know what to do and when to do it. Open my eyes to see the way of escape, then fill me with courage to take the first step. I know that You love me, Father, and want the best for me. I trust You with my life.*

*In Jesus' name. Amen.*

## Forgiving Those Who Have Hurt Me

Forgiving those who have harmed us is an essential step to walking in freedom. In fact, for us to be forgiven by God for our shortcomings, we must forgive those who sin against us. Holding bitterness and unforgiveness against an abuser is like drinking poison in hopes of it harming the other individual. The reality is that it only causes further damage to the victim. Forgiving an abuser does not in any way mean condoning or excusing the acts of treachery. It certainly does not give the abuser permission to continue abusing us. It is simply letting the person off the hook from an emotional and spiritual standpoint. This is not to say that taking legal action against a predator is wrong. In order to protect others, this is often necessary. In fact, most states require that any knowledge of child abuse be reported to the proper authorities.

> *[Jesus said,] In prayer there is a connection between what God does and what you do. You can't get forgiveness from God, for instance, without also forgiving others.*
> MATTHEW 6:14 MSG

> *[Jesus said,] Whenever you stand praying, if you have any-thing against anyone, forgive him, that your Father in heaven may also forgive you your trespasses. But if you do not forgive, neither will your Father in heaven forgive your trespasses.*
> MARK 11:25–26 NKJV

> *Bear with each other and forgive whatever grievances you may have against one another. Forgive as the Lord forgave you.*
> COLOSSIANS 3:13

> *[Jesus said,] Do not judge, and you will not be judged. Do not condemn, and you will not be condemned. Forgive, and you will be forgiven.*
> LUKE 6:37

*See to it that no one comes short of the grace of God; that no root of bitterness springing up causes trouble, and by it many be defiled.*

HEBREWS 12:15 NASB

## A PRAYER FOR YOU

*Heavenly Father,*

*Forgiving my abuser is probably the hardest thing You could have asked me to do, but I am willing to do it because Your Word says to do so. I understand that this is essential if I am to be forgiven for my failings. It is a spiritual principle.*

*I realize that the abuse was not my fault, that I did not cause it, and that the responsibility lies solely with the perpetrator. I also understand that in forgiving I am not saying that the abuse was okay. It was not. Forgiving does not mean that I deny what happened to me or that I am saying that the abuse did not have a devastating effect on me. It did take place and it has tried to destroy me.*

*Forgiveness is not a feeling but a choice, and today I make the decision to forgive the person who abused me as well as anyone who should have protected me. By faith I let go of the hurt, the anger, the bitterness, and the resentment. In its place I receive Your love, Your peace, and Your healing anointing. I extend Your love to the person who abused me and to those who let me down. I ask You to do a mighty work in their lives.*

*In Jesus' name. Amen.*

## HEALING FOR DAMAGED EMOTIONS

The first step to receiving emotional healing is to simply acknowledge the abuse and the pain it has caused. Denial, instead of making the pain disappear, will eventually poison everything you touch. Yes, it hurts and it can be terrifying to acknowledge, but it is absolutely essential if the wounds are to be eradicated and you are to experience true healing. While the Father will walk with you every step of the way, it may be wise to enlist the help of a qualified Christian counselor. I encourage you right now to ask Jesus to help awaken within you the emotions that were damaged and even shut down through abuse so that He can bring restoration to your heart and mind.

> *He is despised and rejected of men; a man of sorrows, and acquainted with grief.*
>
> ISAIAH 53:3 KJV

Note: Jesus is no stranger to emotional pain.

> *Surely he hath borne our griefs, and carried our sorrows… He was wounded for our transgressions, he was bruised for our iniquities: the chastisement of our peace was upon him; and with his stripes we are healed.*
>
> ISAIAH 53:4–5 KJV

Note: Not only did Jesus bear our sins on the cross, He also bore any emotional pain we could ever suffer. He wants to carry away your sorrow and heal your heart and mind.

> *[Jesus said,] The Spirit of the Lord is upon me, because he hath anointed me to preach the gospel to the poor; he hath sent me to heal the brokenhearted, to preach deliverance to the captives, and recovering of sight to the blind, to set at liberty them that are bruised.*
>
> LUKE 4:18 KJV

*The Lord will comfort Zion; He will comfort all her waste places. And He will make her wilderness like Eden, and her desert like the garden of the Lord. Joy and gladness will be found in her, thanksgiving and the voice of song or instrument of praise.*

ISAIAH 51:3 AMP

Note: You may feel like a parched desert emotionally, but days of joy and gladness are just around the corner.

*He [God] Himself has said, I will not in any way fail you nor give you up nor leave you without support. [I will] not, [I will] not, [I will] not in any degree leave you helpless nor forsake nor let [you] down (relax My hold on you)! [Assuredly not!]*

HEBREW 13:5 AMP

Note: Good news! You are *never* alone. God will walk with you on your healing journey every step of the way.

## A PRAYER FOR YOU

*Heavenly Father,*

*It is time to deal with my emotions that were damaged as a result of the abuse I have endured. I have felt numb for so long, I can hardly remember what it is like to feel. I don't want to experience the pain, but I now realize that running from it, denying it, or trying to dull it has only allowed poison to fester deep down inside me. The only road to freedom is to let these negative emotions out so that You can remove them and replace them with Your love.*

*This is one of the scariest things I have ever had to do, but if You will take me by the hand and hold me close, I am ready to begin. I can barely even talk as I feel emotions coming to the surface. Father, You know there is much I do* not remember and much I have chosen to forget because of the pain. I am asking You in faith to reach down and heal my wounded and shattered emotions. I apply Your blood now to my mind, will, and emotions and ask You to heal me and make me whole. I accept and receive Your healing in regard to every wrong committed against me.

In Jesus' name. Amen.

## PEACEFUL SLEEP

*God has not given us a spirit of fear, but of power and of love and of a sound mind.*

2 TIMOTHY 1:7 NKJV

*He who dwells in the shelter of the Most High
    will rest in the shadow of the Almighty.*

*I will say of the LORD, "He is my refuge and my fortress,
    my God, in whom I trust."*

*You will not fear the terror of night.*

PSALM 91:1–2, 5

*I lay down and slept in peace and woke up safely, for the Lord was watching over me.*

PSALM 3:5 TLB

*I will lie down and sleep in peace,
    for you alone, O LORD,
    make me dwell in safety.*

PSALM 4:8

*He will never let me stumble, slip or fall. For he is always watching, never sleeping.*

PSALM 121:3–4 TLB

*He gives His beloved sleep.*

PSALM 127:2 NKJV

*Let them not depart from your eyes—*
*Keep sound wisdom and discretion.*
*When you lie down, you will not be afraid;*
*Yes, you will lie down and your sleep will be sweet.*

PROVERBS 3:21, 24 NKJV

## A PRAYER FOR YOU

*Heavenly Father,*
*I ask You to give me sweet sleep and peaceful dreams.*
*Help me wake up healthy, happy, and rested for You have*
*not given me a spirit of fear, but of power and love and*
*a sound mind. I know that You are a good Daddy who*
*hears my prayers and that You watch over me even as I*
*sleep. I thank You that nightmares are a thing of the past*
*and not a part of my present or future.*
*In Jesus' name. Amen.*

## SEXUAL INTIMACY IN MARRIAGE

*Honor marriage, and guard the sacredness of sexual inti-*
*macy between wife and husband.*

HEBREWS 13:4 MSG

Note: Sexual intimacy is a sacred thing, designed by God for
the mutual satisfaction and enjoyment of both husband and wife.

*Marriage is honorable among all, and the bed undefiled.*

HEBREWS 13:4 NKJV

Note: When a person becomes born again, the blood of Jesus cleanses that person of all sin and uncleanness. In Christ, the marriage bed is pure and holy, free of defilement.

> *Christ himself has brought us peace by making Jews and Gentiles one people. With his own body he broke down the wall that separated them.*
>
> EPHESIANS 2:14 GNT

Note: Although this verse is specifically dealing with Jews and non-Jews, a wall that is just as real can be erected in the area of marital intimacy as a result of sexual abuse. Jesus came to break down that wall and to heal the wounds that caused the wall to be erected in the first place, making it possible for a husband and wife to truly become one—spirit, soul, and body.

> *What is clearest to me is the way Christ treats the church. And this provides a good picture of how each husband is to treat his wife, loving himself in loving her, and how each wife is to honor her husband.*
>
> EPHESIANS 5:32–33 MSG

Note: Those who have been abused need much, much godly love. This type of love is commanded in marriage, especially in how husbands are to relate to their wives.

> *Love bears up under anything and everything that comes, is ever ready to believe the best of every person, its hopes are fadeless under all circumstances, and it endures everything [without weakening]. Love never fails [never fades out or becomes obsolete or comes to an end].*
>
> 1 CORINTHIANS 13:7–8 AMP

Note: The God kind of love works miracles in the lives of those who have been abused.

*There is no fear in love. But perfect love drives out fear.*

1 JOHN 4:18

Note: God's love creates a safe environment where fear is stopped in its tracks.

*Submit to one another out of reverence for Christ.*

EPHESIANS 5:21

Note: When a husband and wife reverence Christ and conduct themselves in a manner that honors Him—being patient, loving, and kind, for example—submission comes more easily.

## A PRAYER FOR YOU

*Heavenly Father,*

*It is obvious from Your Word that sexual intimacy was designed by You to be mutually enjoyed by husband and wife. In my case, however, this gift has been perverted by the abuse I was subjected to.*

*I love my mate and want offer myself freely, but I need Your help. Transform my thinking as I meditate upon Your Word, and enable me to see sex the way that You do. During the times of intimacy with my spouse, help me to focus my mind on the present rather than being tormented by images of the past. Help me to feel secure both in Your love and in that of my mate, for there is no fear in love. As I grow in feeling safe, enable me to relax my body and enjoy this wonderful gift to the fullest. Thank You for perfecting everything that concerns me.*

*In Jesus' name. Amen.[1]*

---

1 See these additional verses regarding the scriptural basis for this prayer: Romans 12:2; Proverbs 5:18–19; Song of Solomon; and Psalm 138:8 NKJV.

# A Note from the Author

*I*f you have been a victim of abuse and would like prayer, please write to me. I know from experience the isolation that threatens to destroy the minds and lives of its victims. You don't have to be alone with your devastating secret any longer. You can be free.

Also, if this book has ministered to you, drop me a note or e-mail me at the address below.

Jennifer Kostyal
P.O. Box 10141
Wilmington, NC 28404
jennifer@jenniferkostyal.org

To find out more about Jennifer Kostyal and her ministry Transformed by the Word go to:

www.jenniferkostyal.org
Facebook: Jennifer Kostyal
Twitter: JenniferKostyal

*About the Authors*

*J*ennifer Kostyal is a dynamic speaker, teacher, author, and the founder and director of Jennifer Kostyal Ministries. She has been featured on *The Coral Ridge Hour*, Daystar Television's *The Celebration Show*, The Word Network, *Babbie's House*, CBN.com and more.

She is a popular speaker in churches and at women's conferences. In addition, she has a passion to reach women in the prisons, the largest majority of whom have experienced some form of physical, verbal, emotional, or sexual abuse. In 2009, she received the Volunteer of the Year award from the North Carolina Correctional Institute for Women. As she stood to receive the award the senior prison official stated:

> There is no doubt this individual was chosen before the foundation of the world to be called to minister to women in prison.... The response of our inmates to her is amazing. She represents hope to our inmates because she has lived their pain and abuse.

Jennifer graduated from the University of North Carolina at Wilmington with a Bachelor of Arts degree in Education. Through her personal testimony and teaching of the Word of God, she shares her belief in the power of Jesus to heal and make whole. As she shares of her healing from years of subjection to a

religious cult, sexual abuse, and mental torment, it gives people hope to believe again.

Jennifer and her husband, Dave, "one of the best presents Jesus has ever given [her]" make their home in Wilmington, North Carolina, along with their two children, David and Rebekah who are both active in the ministry.

*K*aren Hardin is a wife, busy mom, major multitasker, and writer on a mission to make a difference. The author of *Seasons of Life for Women* and *Seasons of Love,* she has a passion for helping others achieve their God-given dreams and reach their highest potential.

Karen and her husband, Kevin, also have a strong desire to minister to the unreached, which they have done in Asia for the past twenty years, residing there for seven of them. In addition to homeschooling their three amazing children—Michael, Holly, and Joshua—she is also the founder and director of her own publicity firm, PriorityPR Group & Literacy Agency. You may contact Karen at info@prioritypr.org or go to her website at prioritypr.org.

Additional copies of this title are available
wherever fine books are sold.

Also available by Jennifer Kostyal
*Finally Free Bible Study: 7 Weeks to Freedom from Your Past*

Has this book made an impact on your life? Or, do you have an area in which I can pray for you in your process of becoming finally free?

Please contact me at:

mail@jenniferkostyal.org
www.jenniferkostyal.org

*Jennifer* **Kostyal**
John 8:32 **Ministries**

P.O. Box 10141
Wilmington, NC 28404

Blessings,

*Jennifer*

*I*f you are serious about your desire to be free from your past, then I invite you to continue the journey with me.

I have identified six bondages that prevent people from living in the present because they are still bound to their past. If you are ready to take that step to be finally free, then join me in a seven-week study that will reveal each of these strongholds and how to break them off your life permanently.

You can order your copy of *Finally Free Bible Study: 7 Weeks to Freedom from Your Past* at www.jenniferkostyal.org.

Or write me at:

      Jennifer Kostyal
      Jennifer Kostyal Ministries
      P.O. Box 10141
      Wilmington, NC 28404

                    Blessings,

                    *Jennifer*